D0460975

Frances Ferguson originally trained as a nurse, but gave it up to get married and produce three children in quick succession. She started writing as a way of earning without leaving her infants; now that they are all grown up she is still writing, but for her own benefit.

Her grandfather was a judge in India who eventually retired to New Zealand, and most of her parental relatives still live there or in Australia. However, she herself has been settled in East Kent for the past twenty years, and says it is a good place to put down roots. When not writing, she is training as a Shiatsu practitioner.

# NO FIXED ABODE

A weekend break in the Kent countryside for Detective-Sergeant Jane Perry and her new boyfriend, Adrian, is disrupted when a nearby disused aircraft hangar goes up in flames. Once the inferno has died down, the charred remains of a well-known local vagrant, Old Mary, are revealed. The death is written off as an accident but Jane's instincts tell her that something has been overlooked. She delves deeper and soon stumbles upon another corpse. Further investigation throws up traces of blackmail, illegal drug dealing and theft and no one seems free from suspicion — not even Adrian . . .

*Books by Frances Ferguson*
*Published by The House of Ulverscroft:*

MISSING PERSON
IDENTITY UNKNOWN
WITH INTENT TO KILL

FRANCES FERGUSON

# NO FIXED ABODE

*Complete and Unabridged*

ULVERSCROFT
*Leicester*

First published in Great Britain in 1994

First Large Print Edition
published 1999

The right of Frances Ferguson to be identified as
the author of this work has been asserted by her
in accordance with the
Copyright, Designs and Patents Act, 1988

British Library CIP Data

Ferguson, Frances
No fixed abode.—Large print ed.—
Ulverscroft large print series: mystery
1. Detective and mystery stories
2. Large type books
I. Title
823.9′14 [F]

ISBN 0–7089–4100–1

Published by
F. A. Thorpe (Publishing) Ltd.
Anstey, Leicestershire
Set by Words & Graphics Ltd.
Anstey, Leicestershire
Printed and bound in Great Britain by
T. J. International Ltd., Padstow, Cornwall

This book is printed on acid-free paper

For Jon, Jenny, Julie, Alex,
and all the children

# Acknowledgements

With grateful thanks for their help to Clare Going, my editor, Shirley Russell, my agent, and Lesley Watson-Walker for proofreading to catch any local errors.

# Prologue

The body could have been a heap of old clothing.

A closer inspection would have shown a booted foot protruding from one end of the bundle of drab, grubby tweed. Or eyes peering curiously in from outside might have traced the hump of a hip, a drawn-up leg; might even have moved on to catch the outline of a shoulder. Not the dirty grey hair, since the head would be invisible from the window, hidden by the corner of a desk; the outflung hand would be invisible too where it lay palm down to the floor, almost as if reaching for the old felt hat which had fallen just beyond the fingertips. But in any case the single tightly closed window was of frosted glass and would permit no prying gaze. And it was unlikely, in this deserted spot, that anyone would come; no hand would push at the firmly locked door, break the window glass, force the lock. The shabbiness outside, the carefully unused look of the place, lacked invitation.

There was no whisper of sound. Rigor had stiffened the limbs, then departed to leave them flaccid. An earlier anger might have hung in the air — noise, raised voices, hands dragging at a discovered intruder. Then the almost casual, lethal chop of a hand, in a blow expertly delivered. All had receded into the shadows with the completion of the task, and departure.

The shape which had once been a person simply lay there, empty and untenanted, a testament to violence, but unseen and mute.

And awaiting a convenient time for disposal.

# 1

Jane Perry, sitting in a garden chair, stretched out her legs in lazy contentment. Her sunlit surroundings were decoratively autumnal. A tall beech hedge, all dry curling bronze, shimmered gently in the early-evening air, while here and there a yellow scatter of leaves patterned the rough semi-tended patch of lawn. A splash of vivid crimson foliage, not yet fallen, graced the top of a small, narrowly elegant tree. Beyond the garden, but visible only from the cottage's upper windows, there would be a view which widened over open fields, distantly fenced, an occasional oak or poplar spiking the horizon.

There was certainly something to be said for a country weekend, particularly one in which most of the afternoon had been spent in bed. She turned her head to call in the direction of the dark rectangle of the cottage's open back door, no more than a yard away.

'Adrian? Want me to do anything?'

He appeared in answer, a blue and white butcher-boy apron tied round his waist. 'No thanks. Half an hour in the oven and it'll be done. You just sit there and look . . . '

'Idle?'

'Mellow.' A small grin touched the habitual seriousness of his face; satisfaction was there too.

'I'll bring you out a drink in a minute.'

'Just as well you can cook, seeing I can't! Still, I did warn you, didn't I?'

'It's not obligatory for a lady cop.'

Jane smiled at his mild teasing. He showed an amiable acceptance of her profession. For a moment, the sheer unlikeliness of it caught her again: that she, who had always seen herself as urban by temperament, should have fallen into a relationship with a vet. And not one who dealt solely with domestic pets, either. He and his partner might run a small animal clinic in the city, but the main bulk of their work lay with farm livestock. Well, she was learning, she thought with amusement, and learning things in quite marked contrast to her usual concerns: that there were such places as goat-farms, for instance, and that cattle had to be injected against some fairly esoteric diseases. It all went to show how her life had changed since she'd moved out of London.

And for the better. Recently, certainly. She stretched again, and gave Adrian an affectionate grin.

'I'm being thoroughly lazy, aren't I? You were right, it's nice out here. What did you say that red tree is?'

'Sumach. The previous owners must have planted it, I'd guess, since it's native to Japan. I don't think we'll eat outside,' he added, glancing up at the sky, 'the wind's getting up, we may even be due for a gale . . . ' He looked down at her again and caught her mischievous expression. 'What?'

'Country lore?'

'Just ordinary weather sense.' A rustling shiver in the beech hedge confirmed his matter-of-fact statement, but he didn't elaborate on it, merely adding, 'I'm glad you like the cottage. It makes a good bolt-hole, doesn't it? Or it will when I've finished doing it up.'

He disappeared back into the kitchen without waiting for her reply. Jane was left to sit and pursue her own thoughts. It was, she realised, amazingly peaceful here. Although no more than half an hour's drive from the city, you would scarcely have known that it was so close, out here among the Kent farmlands and with the nearest village a good couple of miles away. Even the lane outside the cottage seemed to carry very little passing traffic, with only the occasional car or the chug of a tractor going by. It was, she decided — her thoughts echoed by the sweet torpor of a burst of birdsong — definitely a place to draw breath and relax.

That was certainly something she had had little time for lately. The city's autumn Arts Festival had brought a flood of visitors to attend this finale to the main tourist season. There had been street fairs and other open air entertainments to be kept in proper check; exhibitions to be guarded; a foreign dance company panicked by the non-arrival and, temporarily, apparent theft of half its costumes and scenery . . . All that, plus what seemed to be an extra crop of burglaries, car break-ins, minor assaults and bouts of disorderly conduct meant that it had been a question of double shifts for everyone over the last couple of weeks. And definitely no peace for a busy detective sergeant.

It was a cause of some thankfulness to discover she still had a private life when she surfaced from the latest bout of activity. A mere two months into the relationship, Adrian might so easily have shrugged and lost interest. Particularly since she had had to put off, more than once, the suggestion that she should come out and see the country cottage he was renovating. To be fair, it wasn't always *her* hours which got in the way: he worked highly variable shifts himself, with call-outs and emergencies.

It was only chance that they had met in the first place. If Jane had not been looking for somewhere to live . . . One of the rental properties on her list had been in the same street as his city small animal clinic. As it was, she had cast a doubtful eye on the presence of a veterinary practice, deciding it might make the street a less than restful place to live. A stream of dog and cat owners (and guinea-pig and pet lizard owners, for all she knew) would probably be driving in and out all the time and taking up all the parking spaces. She had certainly never guessed that the neat, dark-eyed man who fielded her dropped papers and stopped them blowing away could be one of the vets; those, imagination suggested, would be large rugged-looking individuals in overalls and gumboots. It was only after she had moved into a different house to rent in the next street, and they had met and given each other smiles of recognition in the local newsagent's on a Sunday morning, and then got talking, that she had discovered who he was: Adrian Reston, one of the two names brass-plated on the veterinary clinic's door. He also lived, on his own, in the flat above it. That made them near neighbours. And, somehow, things had moved on quickly from there.

Aside from variable hours, their working lives had little in common. That, however, seemed to provide no bar — perhaps even an extra curiosity about each other. Anyway, Jane had known straight away that physically he was her type. A tidy, serious-minded man, not much taller than she was herself, dark-haired, brown-eyed, and rather conventional in appearance. Somehow it had been no surprise either to find that the conventional appearance hid a passionate lover. Two months on, an initial attraction was turning into a deepening appreciation. For both of them, it seemed . . .

A sudden chill against her arm made her realise that the October sun had slipped behind the house to leave her in a patch of shadow. At the same time the promised wind rustled the hedge again more strongly, and lifted her blonde hair away from her forehead. Time to join him indoors, perhaps, instead of lounging out here. She stretched, trying to decide whether she was really cold enough to move. A flight of birds sent up an abrupt chattering somewhere nearby, then rose to hover, a cloud of flapping wings. Watching them as the whole flock suddenly wheeled as one to arrow off across the pale sky, Jane felt the comforting warmth of her cardigan being dropped across her shoulders, and turned her head to look up at Adrian gratefully.

'Thanks. I was just wondering whether I had

the energy to move and fetch it, or whether to come in altogether. You shouldn't wait on me so thoroughly, I might get used to it!' He was balancing two glasses of wine in one hand, and put them down on the wrought-iron garden table with a faint clink, but her eyes had gone back to the birds as they wheeled again in another sharply coordinated movement. 'How on earth do they do that — all of them turning at exactly the same moment? Telepathy?'

'Follow-my-leader. One initiates it, the others pick it up. It just happens too fast for you to see.'

'Sounds like those slow-motion films they used to show us on crowd control. No, I will *not* start letting things remind me of work! Stop me if I do it again, okay? I shall stick to birds, not humans! Do seagulls ever come this far inland?'

'Sometimes. It's not that far from the coast — only, say, twenty miles, that way?' Adrian hooked a thumb in the air, then reversed it to add, 'Not much further that way either, come to that.'

'Mm — I'm still getting used to the idea that you'll hit the sea in almost any direction, in this part of Kent! And — oh damn, something's just bitten me! Look at that, it's a positive cloud of mosquitoes!'

'Coming out for evening. Sorry, I can't light up a noisome pipe to drive them away — I don't smoke. D'you want to go in?'

'It seems a pity, but — oh, well, it's getting chillier by the minute anyway! And since I've got

8

a skirt on rather than jeans, and I suspect they're going to like my bare legs . . . '

He cast an appreciative glance at the offending limbs as she whisked them back under cover of her cotton skirt and began to get up. Soon, he was efficiently lighting a fire in the grate of the cottage's small sitting room, and piling logs on it; not long after that they were eating their meal in front of its dancing light. An evening of comfort, talk, touch, with some music they both liked on the radio . . . There was a growing ease in being together. Still so much of each other to explore; interests to share; differences to discover.

And, for once, actually time to do it in: the luxury of a whole weekend from Friday night to Sunday evening, instead of the snatched moments which was all they had had recently. And all of Saturday night and Sunday still ahead of them.

Much later, upstairs in the crooked bedroom under the eaves, Jane lay with her cheek comfortably against his bare shoulder. The wind had got up, as he had said it would, threatening to turn into one of this part of the country's characteristic autumn gales. It was curling audibly round the house, but she was drifting into a pleasurable drowsiness against the sound when she was suddenly jolted awake. A car tore by; then another, with an accompanying burst of loud music from an open window to vie with the engine sound. All at once there seemed to be a stream of them, driven fast and noisily with a scream of tyres and a heavy revving of engines. Headlights flashed and danced across the bedroom ceiling, filling the room with a flickering reflected light.

'What on earth . . . Christ, it's like waking up to find yourself in the middle of a race-track!'

'God knows where they think they're going. This lane doesn't even lead anywhere, except round through Dasset.' Adrian disentangled himself from her and scrambled out from under the duvet, a flickering white shape in the brightness of the intrusive lights as he made for the window. Peering out, he exclaimed with annoyance, 'There's a whole lot more of them coming, too. And what's that, over there?'

'Over where?'

'Across the fields. There's a hell of a lot of light, and they seem to be making for — now what?'

'Now what' was a sudden cacophony starting up, audible even behind the car engines. A thumping drumbeat shook the countryside, deafening even from a distance. A raucous wail above it made an upper threnody of sound and suggested there might be a tune somewhere in there as it carried in noisy gusts on the wind. Or possibly not, though it certainly seemed to be something answering to the description of music. Jane wrapped the duvet round her and stumbled to join him at the window.

There were lights in different colours flashing into the sky from across the fields now, like whirling searchlights. The cars seemed to be making in that direction, their headlights winding like a broken thread of beads as they wove their way along invisible lanes.

'Is there a house over there?' Jane asked.

'No. Only the old airfield.' Adrian's voice sounded tight with annoyance. 'What the hell can they be doing there? It's midnight, for heaven's sake! And that's private land.'

'An airfield?'

'An old one, I said — disused. There's nothing there but an empty hangar. There used to be a flying operation there offering quick flips across the Channel, but it closed down for lack of business. They *can't* be — '

'Yes, they can. It'll be a rave.' Jane was thoroughly awake now. The signs were all too clear, the conclusion inevitable. 'Someone's either rented the place legally, or — '

'They won't have rented it. No one even knows whose it is any more, though since it isn't decent grazing land I don't think any of the local farmers care much.'

'Then it's being used illegally. There's a hangar there, you said? Just the place someone might spot for a rave. Oh hell — hell and damn! I suppose I'd better do something.'

'No,' he said at once. 'Why should you? You're off duty!'

'Even so. That's obviously a rave — just listen to it! — so I'll have to phone it in at least. And since I'm on the spot . . . '

'A rave's just some kind of teenage party, isn't it? Leave it, let someone else deal with it.'

'How can I?' Resigned, Jane was beginning to unwind herself from the duvet. 'After all, I'm here.' Even as she said the words, the thought gave her pause. Here on the spot and, as the station gossips would no doubt rapidly discover, with a boyfriend . . . If she got dressed and went down to her car and called it in, she would undoubtedly be told to hang around for the night shift to join her, and someone would ask how she happened to be there, and — that would blow it, her private life becoming public knowledge. She was suddenly aware that Adrian was speaking again, a restraining hand on her arm, his voice more than insistent.

'You don't have to get involved. And you told me to remind you not to think about work. Well, I'm reminding you! It's just a bunch of kids whooping it up — and, okay, it's a frightful din and a flaming nuisance, but it doesn't have to be your affair. In fact, the best thing *we* can do is go back to bed and put our heads under the bedclothes!'

'I can't really — '

'Yes, you can. Someone else is bound to ring in and report it. Just listen to the noise. Most of Dasset and all the nearer farms will have been woken up by now!' He picked up the duvet she had dropped and began to wind it persuasively round her. 'Come on, Jane. This weekend's supposed to be for us.'

'I suppose you're right, someone else *will* report it. In fact they probably already have . . . ' She couldn't imagine any local farmer letting this much noise in the middle of the night go by without complaint. Adrian was pulling her back determinedly towards the bed, and she let herself be led. Even though she was still in two minds. A rave wasn't as simple as he made out, since there would almost certainly be drugs involved. Particularly 'E',

Ecstasy, and there had been a good deal too much of that circulating locally recently . . . On the other hand she wasn't in the Drugs Unit, that was John Clay's area of work, and he would have his DCs over here as soon as the first call came in. That had almost certainly already been done, so she wasn't really obliged to go and join in breaking up an all-night party, when that was a uniform job rather than one for general CID.

And she *was* off duty.

'I could ring it in myself, since I brought my mobile phone in when I arrived last night. But I suggest we don't. Forget you're a cop for once.'

'Ouch, you're cold!' Jane complained as he pulled her back into bed and wound his feet round hers. 'You're freezing all over.'

'Want to bet we can find some way of warming ourselves up — and distract ourselves from the din, as well?'

'Since we're not exactly going to get much sleep with all that going on?' She added on a laugh. 'You've got more energy than any two men have a right to, you! Must be your healthy outdoor life.'

'You don't feel as if you're objecting. I can't think of a better way to stop you wanting to rush off and be a dutiful public servant, anyway — can you?'

'I suppose you do know that raves usually go on for twelve hours at a stretch? No, Adrian, pax, that wasn't meant to be a challenge!'

But to hell with law and order, when the pillows could be pulled down under the bedclothes to help to muffle the insistent pounding drum-beat floating across the fields; to hell with everything else when

13

bodies could merge in delight. This was definitely a better occupation than sending herself back on duty. It would have been an unnecessary gesture anyway: someone else obviously had put in a complaint, since it was not long before the excitable wail of more than one police siren sounded a high ululation somewhere in the distance. Involuntarily, her mind noted that the force had managed quite a good response-time. Then that piece of official jargon sent her into a fit of the giggles, because just at the moment, for her, the words had quite a different application.

It was some time later when she realised that the distant heavy beat of music had stopped. Probably a while ago. The raucous sound of sirens was still blowing across on the wind, however: they seemed to be coming and going, and another one came wailing deafeningly past the cottage at that moment, on a vehicle heavy enough to make the room shake. It was on its way to join the others at the rave, apparently, since it echoed off in the same direction the original cars had gone. A paddy-wagon? No, it sounded bigger . . .

'It sounds as if they're pulling out all the stops,' she murmured, sleepy and relaxed. Adrian yawned against her hair, and shifted to snuggle even closer against her.

'Who cares? I told you someone else would deal with it.'

'They seem to have got a lot of extra light on the scene,' Jane commented, peering towards the window. 'It looks almost like . . . . It can't be dawn yet, can it?'

'Not nearly. Do settle down, honey. What are you getting up for? Oh, hell, how many more sirens?'

'I won't be a minute. I just want to see — Oh my god!'

'What?'

'It's a fire. A big one, too, it looks as if the whole place must have gone up! Christ, I hope they got everyone out!'

'You can't do anything about it even if they didn't,' he said from the bed, sounding rather more awake. 'A fire? I wonder what caught?'

'Everything, the way it looks from here. The last two we heard go by must have been fire engines. I hope — '

'Come back to bed, you'll only get cold again. You're not going to suggest you ought to go now? They must have got all the emergency services over there, and then some!'

'Yes, all right, sorry . . . You're right, anyway. There'd be no point in — '

'None at all. There'll be hundreds of people there sorting it all out, so what could you do? Whatever's happened has certainly been dealt with by now.' His voice caught on another yawn, and he repeated, 'Come back to bed!'

'I wonder what made it go up?'

'Maybe one of the farmers had been storing hay in the back.' He curled against her as she slipped back in beside him, his body soft in relaxation. He lay still for a moment, then sighed, and she could almost feel him sliding into sleep.

He certainly had a right to be tired. As she

15

did . . . All the same her mind buzzed for a moment or two. Fire. Hopefully, all the young dancers would have got out in time. In an aircraft hangar, the wide doors would surely allow everyone to flee into the open air fast?

It was no use worrying about it when there must be fire engines and ambulances aplenty at the scene. She slept at last, in spite of the noise of traffic grinding by to wander in and out of her dreams. When she woke, it was to a blissful sense of quiet, and a distant awareness that silence had come back some time ago. Pale sunlight was slanting in through the window; she was alone; there was a definite smell of frying bacon floating up from below.

The bathroom and shower were downstairs, and Jane blew Adrian an appreciative kiss as she crossed the kitchen, where he was presiding over a sizzling pan, looking tidy and cheerful, with no trace of the disturbances of the night in his face. He said merely, 'Sleep well?' as she passed him.

'Like a baby, in the end. What's the time?'

'Nine.'

Early by her reckoning when she was having a relaxing weekend. And there was he looking as bright and bouncy as if it was mid-morning. As she went into the shower she spared an amused thought for the fact that they obviously operated on different body-clocks. Was that another thing to which they would both adjust — that he was a dawn lover and she was a late-night person? Well, she supposed they could always do all their communicating in the middle of the day . . .

16

When she emerged rubbing newly washed hair, Adrian had his mobile phone in his hand, and was just sliding its aerial back in place. She must have missed the squawk of its summons against the hiss and spatter of the shower, unless he had been telephoning out. She raised an eyebrow at him, but before she could say anything there was a loud electronic bleep and he frowned, and returned the instrument to his ear.

'Yes, it is . . . What? And you can't raise him? All right, you'd better give me the details, then.' He listened, concentrating for several moments. 'All right then. Yes, okay, I'll have to take it. About half an hour from here, I suppose. Will you let them know I'm on my way?'

'Trouble?' Jane asked.

'Yes. The answering service can't raise Quentin, so I'm afraid I'm going to have to take off. A cow in trouble calving. Blast Quentin, he's supposed to be taking the calls this weekend!'

'You've got to go *now*?'

'Afraid so. Emergencies don't pick their moments, do they? It's a first-time delivery, and it sounds as if they might lose her and the calf if we can't — Damn Quentin! He's really going to owe me one! Look, I'm really sorry, but this could take hours, so there's no guarantee I'll get back. You stay here and have a quiet day anyway. I'll give you the keys so you can lock up. I'd better get my stuff from upstairs, I've got everything else I need out in the car.'

He was already halfway up the stairs. It was on the tip of Jane's tongue to mention that *she* had not been allowed to let work take precedence

17

over their weekend. Sweet reason had to counter disappointment. So, she was being abandoned for a cow. But if it might otherwise die . . . By the time he reappeared, she could offer a resigned, even sympathetic, expression.

'Aren't you going to have time for any of that breakfast you've been cooking?'

'Slap me a couple of pieces of bacon between some bread, would you? I'll eat it on the way. Look, honey, I really am sorry about this, but — '

'Think nothing of it. If a man's gotta go . . . You really don't think you'll get back?'

'I certainly can't count on it. But stay on, there's no need to spoil your day too. I expect you can find everything you want, can't you?'

He accepted the roughly made sandwich she was holding out to him, gave her a quick kiss which was rapid enough to show his mind was already elsewhere, and was gone.

So that was it. *Damn*.

Jane pulled a face to herself and sat down glumly to a congealing breakfast.

So much for their nice, quiet, escapist weekend. As if it hadn't already been disturbed enough . . . Well, not too much, in fact. But it was just as well they had brought both cars out here, and that she had come by her own transport because he had had some appointment out this way already.

She decided abruptly that if she had to spend Sunday on her own after all, she might as well do so on her own territory. There was plenty she could be doing in her own small house — if only making some attempt to clear up its usual untidiness, and catching up with necessary chores.

Once she had breakfasted and dressed she tidied up rapidly, made sure all the cottage windows were shut and the doors locked, and backed her car out into the lane. Then she pulled in again and backed out so that she was facing in the other direction. Since she was here, it might be interesting to drive round the other way and see where the side-track was which led to the airfield, the site of last night's rave. She could look and see how bad that fire had actually been.

It was certainly no problem to identify the right turning: a swathe of broken hedging and a verge marked with deep tyre indentations showed where heavier traffic than usual had passed this way. Negotiating another twisting length of lane, Jane rounded a corner to see, ahead, a wide gap in the hedge with a gate pushed back to hang drunkenly on one hinge. And on the rutted track beyond that, a white police car displayed its familiar yellow stripe, with the light blue Kent Police logo stamped across the middle of it.

The clearing up had not yet finished, then, and there was still an official presence here.

A uniformed figure straightened up from behind the car as she bumped up to it, and turned into a constable recognisable from her own station. At the sight of her he hastily dropped the cigarette he was holding, and stamped it out quickly against the ground with a would-be surreptitious size eleven boot.

'Hallo, Sarge. CID's over by the remains of the hangar, and the fire people said to tell you all not to put your hands on anything metal, one or two of the struts may still be hot. And the body's still inside where it was found — they didn't spot it until half an hour ago, but they haven't moved anything.'

'Body? Just the one?'

'Yes. No one else got trapped, and the only other injuries were from smoke inhalation and a bit of singeing.' He added grimly, 'A lot of people were lucky.'

But one person had not been, apparently.

It was worth going on to see what had actually happened.

# 2

There was still a fire engine there when Jane came over the crest of land which had blocked her view, its scarlet rectangle standing out against the blackened ground. Several cars were parked well clear of the working area and various figures were tramping about, some in the white helmets and heavy gear of the fire service, some not. A dark, twisted skeleton of struts showed how little was left of what must once have been an aircraft hangar, but now looked more like the tangled outline of some mad modern sculpture. Here and there, insubstantial wisps of smoky ash were lifted on the light breeze to blow grittily for a yard or two before sinking down again.

Puddles of water reflected the clear sky to make gleams of bright contrasting silver, and there were muddy ruts between which the odd tussock of grimed grass tried to suggest that this had once been a field. Further off, a wide strip of concrete — the old runway, presumably — stopped short at a crumbling edge, but otherwise looked surprisingly solid aside from the occasional crack.

At the back of the fallen and twisted girders but visible through them, Jane saw the familiar chunky outline of DC Kenny Barnes. He was standing beside a tumbled heap of flattened metal and torn-edged, scorched-looking material leaning at several sharp angles, deep in conversation with someone in fireman's uniform. He looked up as she picked her way across to him, and greeted her with a cheerful lift of his eyebrows.

'Hallo, Sarge, I thought it was your weekend off. This is Fire Chief Evans.'

'Yes, we've met before. Hallo, Chief Evans. Detective Sergeant Perry,' Jane added in case her name eluded him. 'This does look a mess!'

'It could have been worse,' the fire chief assured her, out of a weary and unshaven face which showed he must have been here all night. 'If the underground fuel tank had gone up, you'd have been looking at something like a bomb crater. And likely had a lot of fatalities, too,' he added grimly.

'There's still fuel here? Christ, that could have been really nasty!'

'There shouldn't really be any left. The outfit which used to run from here closed down all of

21

two years ago. Maybe what we can smell is just the remaining gas trapped in the tank — but it could have been a bad one even so.' Chief Evans pulled a face. 'Luckily we managed to cool the ground that side enough to stop it blowing. We're still keeping an eye on it even now, though it should be safe enough: there's no sign that it's doing anything. But if the fire had started that side instead of round here . . . Idiots, some people! Using an airfield? And it's not surprising the place went up like a torch, when the hangar was an old wooden-walled one!'

'But you did get everyone out, I gather? Apart from one?'

'By the time we got here they were all out in the open already, and running all over the place. With last night's wind, everything went up fast — and the fire didn't start near the doors, thank God. At least we can be thankful for that, and that they could get out.' Chief Evans cast a weary look at the surrounding wreckage, his expression acknowledging how much worse it could have been. 'No, all the kids were lucky — this time. But no thanks to the irresponsible idiots who did the organising! Your lot have nabbed a couple of them, I'm glad to say. Maybe they'll be able to tell you who it might be under there.' A jerk of the elbow indicated the heap of wreckage beside them. 'Whoever it was, they'd locked themselves in, which was pretty bloody stupid, considering . . . ' He glanced round quickly as someone called to him, and began to move. 'If you'll excuse me, I'll let your colleague tell you the rest. All right, Sub, I'll just take a final look at the tank before we stand down the pumps . . . '

He stamped away. Jane looked enquiringly at Kenny — and at DC Gary Peters who arrived quickly to join them at that moment, apparently from somewhere among the wreckage, his face and hands smudged with ash.

'So, what's the scene? We've got a body under there and no one's sure who it is?'

'They thought everyone was out until they started examining that bit,' Kenny told her. 'They were looking for where the fire started — point of origin, as they call it — and moved some stuff and found the body. They seem pretty sure the fire started there.'

'Was it where the electrical equipment was? The disco stuff?'

'No.' Kenny shook his head. 'That was all in the main hangar, down the side. The firemen had a poke round there first. This part was some sort of office tacked on to the back of the hangar. Maybe someone was in there counting the takings. All those kids,' he added suddenly, as if it had to break out of him, 'hundreds of them all squashed together — they can count themselves lucky the thing hadn't been going on long and they hadn't had time to get so high they didn't know what direction to run in! If I thought my lot would ever get mixed up in the rave scene . . . ' He broke off, his expression somewhere between fierce and sick, his mind obviously fraught with imagining his own young teenagers caught in a similar situation. Then he remembered himself and cast Jane a look of apology. 'Sorry, Sarge.'

'It's okay. But you were saying?'

'Yeah. This — ' he waved a hand at the debris beside them ' — must have been an office, like I was saying. Or some kind of small separate room, anyway. It seems to have been a bit more solid than the rest — or three sides of it were — because you can still see parts of the walls where they've fallen in . . . The roof came down on whoever was in there, they can't have had a hope of getting out. And it's where the fire started. It spread from there through the back wall of the hangar, because that was wood, like the Chief said.'

'What does he think — wiring? A cigarette thrown away in the wrong place?'

'He hasn't been definite, but I get the impression they think it was set.'

'*Set?* A deliberate fire — in these circumstances? Is he sure?'

'Not really, they'll need to get their assessors in to take a proper look. Could have been just someone fooling about. This person, whoever it was, had locked themself in there — apparently they can tell because they've found the locks. Or what's left of them. There isn't exactly a lot. We've given the pathologist a call, should be here soon.'

'Good. You've had a look? Whereabouts is it?'

'Over there, under that bit they've propped up.'

'I think I know who it is, Sarge.'

It was Gary Peters who spoke up abruptly after standing quietly by. As Jane looked at him, surprised, he went on: 'It's the clothes. They aren't completely burned away, and there's enough to see — I think it's Old Mary.'

24

'What, Old Mary the tramp?' asked Jane, startled.

Gary nodded. 'She always wears the same gear, and layers and layers of it. And last time she was pulled in for being drunk and disorderly I was there, and she kept kicking her legs up and insisting on showing us some scarlet satin petticoat she was wearing. She was very proud of it for some reason. I remember it particularly,' he added ruefully, 'because I got dragged in to try and help calm her down, and she bit me.'

'Yes, I've heard she can do that when she's been on the bottle. You think it's Old Mary under there — the corpse? But what on earth would she be doing right out here? She's one of those who always stays around the city, isn't she?'

'Yes, Sarge. But I think it's her, just the same. Maybe she'd just suddenly decided to go on the wander . . . or maybe she knew someone out this way? I don't think we've had her in for a while, so that *could* mean she'd moved.'

With Old Mary, it certainly could: she normally turned up at the station (under the restraining arm of a constable) with monotonous regularity. 'I'd better have a look and see if I agree with you,' Jane said, deciding, if unwillingly, that confirmation was due. She added, 'If you're right, it could be the explanation of how the fire started. If she was sheltering here, and she'd been on the booze as usual, she was quite crazy enough to have lit up some sticks in the middle of the floor to try and boil a billy. Maybe that's our answer.'

She edged her way in under the propped-up, blackened piece of debris the men indicated. As

25

she crouched down beside the uncovered form she had to control an instinct to gag. Shrivelled, blackened skin seemed moulded on to the shrunken shape, making it look more monkey than human . . . Across the midsection, a falling piece of roof or other debris must have protected the body from the most searing flames, since there was enough uncharred clothing there to see that there might have been several old tweed skirts worn one on top of the other. And a flash of scarlet was visible between two scorched edges. Part of an old leather boot could be seen, too, near what must once have been a foot. Yes, Old Mary had worn boots like that.

'Gary's right,' Kenny said quietly, looking over Jane's shoulder. 'I didn't notice before, what with — but yes, that does look like Old Mary's gear.'

'Yes.' Jane straightened up from her crouch and was grateful to be able to look away from the huddled figure — from the horrible inhumanity of its hairlessness, from the outlines of bone beneath that shrivelled skin. She was glad the face was turned towards the floor: the burned remains of that could have been even worse. 'Maybe she woke up suddenly with the noise and tried to light something and knocked it over. That disco music must have been terrifyingly loud from this close.' She pulled herself up quickly before she had admitted to knowing just how loud the music had been. Even from half a mile distant, let alone from right next to it. 'I suppose we'll be able to get a proper identification from her teeth or something. If she ever went to the dentist. But it does look as if you're right, Gary.' All three of them backed off, carefully avoiding tripping over any debris, and as they reached the open air again Jane added, 'I'd better go and put it to Chief Evans that we think it was one of our known tramps: may as well set his mind at rest that if it was arson, it was very unlikely to have been with intent. At least, Old Mary wasn't known for fire-raising, was she?'

'No. Just for boozing, swearing, muttering to herself, and biting coppers,' Kenny said drily. 'Social Services tried to settle her in a home more than once, that I do know. But she wouldn't co-operate. Poor old cow — she's been living rough on the streets for all those years, four or five since she turned up in the city anyway, and she comes to this. Pneumonia or a pickled liver would have been a lot more likely.' He turned his head and added, 'Oh, here's Dr Ledyard coming. Poor girl, it always seems to be her shout if we have to put a call out at the weekend!'

Jane exchanged a smile and a few words with Ruth Ledyard as the pathologist arrived to join them, wearing jeans and with her hair in a pigtail down her back but here to inspect yet another dead body with her usual calm. She would provide one of her studiously meticulous reports in due time but it did seem as if things were simple after all: one crazy old woman, caught in a disaster of her own making, but without real intent. It was lucky no one else had been seriously hurt . . .

Jane moved off to pass on her observations to Fire Chief Evans. Then she decided she had been here long enough, considering she was actually supposed to be on a free weekend. She wondered whether the Drugs Unit had managed any useful arrests — the 'E' supplier they had been hunting for, perhaps? — but no doubt she would hear about it after the weekend. And Kenny could be left to handle the removal of the body. She caught up with him to say, 'I'm going — I *am* actually off duty, I only looked in!' Then she left them to it, and went home.

Just an accidental death, and one which would cause few ripples: nothing vital to keep her here.

* * *

Monday morning was DCI Morland's most favoured time for holding CID planning meetings. Jane made sure she was on time, and noted that as usual the DCI gave as little acknowledgement of her presence as he could manage. She sat with dutifully blank face as he opened with a pep-talk about Targets for the Month, and the Importance of Detection as a Consumer Resource. His habit of sounding as if he was talking in capital-lettered headings seemed to be intensifying daily.

There appeared to have been no more than the usual amount of call-outs to burglaries over the weekend. It would be up to Dan Crowe, the DI, to assign follow-ups. The other Detective Sergeant, Peter Pettigrew, gave a careful report on the investigations he had been carrying out into some hard-porn videos that had been turning up in the city from somewhere: no leads yet about where they were coming from. Car crime was mentioned as being on the increase. Finally the subject of the rave came up.

'It's not really a local CID matter, since the organisers come from well outside our district and so did almost all the people attending,' the DCI pronounced, after Kenny Barnes had given his report. 'Sergeant Clay and his unit will be looking into the question of drugs being brought into our area, of course: he's already taking that up. However, one minor matter does fall to us. Confirmation of the identity of the local vagrant who seems to have been an accidental victim of the fire.' He glanced round at the assembled company and let his eyes light on Jane as if only just discovering her presence. 'One for Sergeant Perry to follow up, I think. I'm sure you can be spared from whatever else you're doing. Very well, that seems to cover everything for this morning.'

He made no attempt to wait for the DI's agreement that his senior sergeant was the one best able to be spared from other duties. Jane carefully avoided the guv'nor's eye, but knew he would be looking irritable as the DCI left them all to get on with their morning. It was like skirmishes in a very small war, the way Morland expended a lot of energy on doing his best to sideline her into tasks he considered the most lowly, and therefore suitable for a female detective. He had been worse if anything since she had got an official commendation for her last big case; but although the knowledge that she had the approval of his superiors must be anathema to him, there was little he could do about his prejudices. Except mark anything minor, routine, or mundane very firmly with Jane's name. She gave Kenny Barnes a grin and reached out her hand for the file he was holding.

'Mine, then. Another one for the bits-and-pieces pile on my desk. Will the fire service send us a report, or will I have to go and ask for it?'

'They'll probably send something in to the collator once their assessors have finished looking. And — yes, Guv?' Kenny asked as Dan Crowe loomed over them, looking crotchety.

'I want you on that rash of car break-ins on the Fairlie Estate. And never mind all that stuff about making up a profile on who might be doing it — we already know it's got Billy Tarrant's MO written all over it, so go and shake a few trees and see if you can't find a witness or two!'

'Yes, Guv,' Kenny said obediently, while Jane bit back a smile at the DI's blatant scorn for the guidelines they were all supposed to be following these days. Although only in his forties, Dan Crowe was an old-style copper when it came to methods of detection. She could almost swear she had heard him muffle a snort on hearing the police described as a 'consumer resource'. That might well be a contributory factor in his decision to leave and emigrate to Australia with his family; a fact she knew, since he had shared it with her confidentially, though it was still on the secret list so far as the rest of the department was concerned.

But he would be going. And Jane would be after his job. That was one very good reason for her to be seen doing everything which was thrown at her now with absolutely faultless efficiency.

'What do you want me to start on, Guv?' she asked him, giving him a cheerful look as he beetled his brows at her. 'I've got the Herne Bay burglaries from last week, a couple of Victim Support visits, that child abuse follow-up to do . . . '

'What about the armed robbery from last month, has anything further come up on that?'

'Nothing so far. If the blagger was local he's certainly keeping his head down.'

'Take the rest in any order you like, then. *If you can spare the time from that load of extras any plod could do!*'

He stumped away to sort out what everyone else should be doing. Jane allowed herself the flicker of a grin at his sour comment, and put the Old Mary file down on her desk. He would be on her side when his resignation went in and the search for his replacement began — and so, she hoped, would Superintendent Annerley. The mere prospect would drive the DCI mad, but with luck and some efficient work from her in the meantime, she might yet find herself in a winning position.

That was for the future. For now, she had plenty to get on with, and flicked through her list to see what could be considered the most urgent.

★ ★ ★

Dr Ledyard managed to produce her autopsy report on the fire-blackened body with commendable speed. Jane found it had arrived just before the end of her Monday shift. She decided to take it

31

home with her to read, since the old vagrant's death might be a minor matter but had to be fitted somewhere into her general workload. She would have to try to track down anyone who had known Old Mary well enough to know if she had any relatives anywhere to be informed of her death. The card in the collator's office had already shown her that they had not even got a record of the old woman's surname. That was a nuisance.

It was some time later when she picked up the typed pages to read, as a chore to be got through with her after dinner coffee. She ran through them quickly. The body presumably was Old Mary's — the remains of the clothing made that clear enough to allow the assumption. The report merely said 'Female, Caucasian'. How did they tell, with so much skin burned away? 'Age probably early-fifties.' Goodness, really? The old vagrant had looked a lot older than that to Jane, but perhaps that could be put down to living rough. And to drink. She skipped through the signs of ageing in the bones, and the section on contents of stomach and viscera, all of it couched with caution due to the effects of the fire. That apparently also made it impossible to state a time of death. It could be assumed as Saturday night, however, even if the autopsy report was careful not to say so. After all, that was when the fire had been started. And presumably — from the Fire Chief's comments as relayed by Kenny — by the old woman herself. Jane reached the next section, and paused, frowning.

Cause of death . . . no, that didn't fit.

It was one thing to note with surprise that what was left of the stomach showed no recent intake of alcohol. If the old woman had not been drunk for once, she could still have been confused. But Dr Ledyard's assessment of the lungs had been a surprise too, and now this?

A knock on her front door made her look up and stir herself to answer it. Finding Adrian on the doorstep, Jane gave him a slightly absent grin, then roused herself to greet him properly.

'Hi — come in! Did you find the cottage keys? I put them through your letter-box. I'm just having coffee, do you want some?'

'That would be nice.' He followed her through into the sitting-room, with its floor-length window on to a microscopic garden and its open-plan arch through to a small kitchenette. 'Did you manage to have a good day after I left you? And find plenty to eat, if only the leftovers in the fridge?'

'I didn't stay. Oh, damn, I forgot about what was in the fridge, too. Are you going out there again soon? I did put everything else away, but . . . ' She pulled a face at him and added on a chuckle. 'Yes, I did, honestly, so you can stop giving me that deadpan look. I've told you before, I'm only untidy on my own property, and that's purely voluntary!'

'I'm learning to live with it,' he told her tranquilly, and avoided stepping on three books and a newspaper on the floor as he moved to take the mug of coffee she was holding out to him. Well, she *had* explained to him, in a fit of early defensiveness, that her untidiness at home was the other side of the coin to her need to be highly

33

organised at work. And a reaction against it. He moved her briefcase and a blouse she had put out to iron off an armchair to give himself room to sit down. As he did so, he went on conversationally, 'How was the cow, Adrian? The cow is fine, thank you, and I managed to deliver healthy twins in the end, which turned out to have been the cause of the trouble.'

'Sorry, I should have asked. You saved several lives, then? Good for you.' Curling herself up on the sofa opposite Jane gave him a smile. She added a rueful apology. 'I might have remembered, only my head's still tied up in a path report. Someone died in that fire at the airfield — the rave, Saturday night.'

'Really? It was that bad?'

'And could have been worse because there's still some aviation fuel stored over there. Or it might be left-over gas, I think the Chief said. You did say the airfield wasn't used any more, didn't you?'

'Not as far as I know.'

'Mm. Well, apparently they were lucky the tank didn't blow up. The hangar's a complete write-off.' Jane reached out for the pathologist's report which was still on her mind. 'There weren't any fatalities besides this one. A few of the kids did land up in hospital, but mainly due to shock. Only one person bought it, and that was a tramp — trampess? — who's been known around the station for years. She seems to have been out there for some reason and sheltering in a smaller building at the back of the hangar. And since the fire people say that's where the blaze started, we've been assuming she must have caused it. But see how this grabs you. She didn't die of smoke inhalation, which would be usual: this autopsy report says there was no smoke in her lungs. And cause of death is down here as a broken neck. That seems a bit puzzling, doesn't it?'

'Not really. She was woken up by all the noise, and then when the fire started she tried to get out, but fell. Was she old? She could have had brittle bones.'

'No sign of that here. But I suppose . . . Maybe if she'd climbed in there somehow in the first place, and had to climb to get out, she could have fallen awkwardly. Caught her head against something . . . I suppose that could be it. It's odd, that's all. With no smoke in her lungs, that means she definitely has to have died elsewhere . . . '

'Sounds as if you're making rather a lot out of nothing. Anyway, could we talk about something more cheerful? I've just had a long day. And after losing yesterday, as well,' Adrian said wryly, with a sigh, and moved abruptly to join her on the sofa. 'You don't really have to pore over an autopsy report at nine o'clock at night, do you? I came round to see how you'd survived yesterday without me, not to hear about someone else's fatal accident! Oh, and there's a Rohmer film on at the university cinema tomorrow night, that one we've neither of us seen. Shall we go?'

Jane let him remove the pathologist's report firmly from her fingers and lay it back down on the coffee table. It was rare for him to show impatience with her work — in fact he was usually good at listening with interest — but as she glanced at him with a touch of surprise, she saw it was probably true he had had a long day. His face showed it. There were moments when she ought to remind herself that a relationship went two ways, and that she should not resent it if someone else wanted to distract her from after-hours concentration on her career.

All the same, as she set herself to being sympathetic and companionable, the thought of Old Mary lingered like a faint question mark in the back of her mind.

The answer had seemed simple. An old woman who lived rough, a known drunk — it was easy to imagine her hazily lighting matches under some twigs she had brought in with her. She could even have flung some methylated spirit on to try and get the thing going. And then . . .

But it was impossible for Old Mary to have started the fire, because if she had died trying to get away from it, there would be smoke in her lungs.

Somehow, while sheltering there, she had managed to break her neck. And *before* the fire.

That was puzzling, at the very least.

# 3

Going in to work next morning, Jane found the cause of death given in the autopsy still lurking at the back of her mind. A small thing, but puzzling: why should Old Mary have died not by fire or from smoke asphyxiation, but from a broken neck? And what on earth had she been doing out at Dasset anyway? Let alone in a locked office on an airfield, during a rave. There was something there which failed to make sense.

Other things distracted her as soon as she reached the CID room. As always, first thing in the morning, reports of overnight crime were coming in, requiring attention. The DI was out somewhere so it was up to Jane to allocate investigations, and she sent Mike Lockley off to a car lot which had just discovered several broken car-locks and the disappearance of at least two car radios; then Gary Peters to follow up a report of power-tools and a gas-bottle missing from a house garage — one of a rush of thefts from garages, which seemed to be the fashion at the moment. Peter Pettigrew was working on a school break-in, one which Jane had passed over to him from yesterday, and they discussed whether the caretaker could really have slept through the arrival and departure of a van big enough to hold half a dozen computers. Then a buzz on her internal phone offered the information that something had arrived at the collator's office which might be of interest to her, and she got up to go and see what it was Ellen Rushman had for her.

She ran into John Clay on her way there, and paused to give the drugs unit sergeant a smile.

'Did you manage to get any joy out of Saturday's rave? I heard you nabbed a couple of the organisers. I suppose you didn't manage to catch your 'E' supplier red-handed as well?'

'No such luck. Probably wasn't even there, though my DCs say it was too chaotic to tell.' Sergeant Clay told her sourly. 'The two organisers we got swear blind that there weren't any drugs involved at all, of course, but then they would! However, the fact is this lot were all outsiders. The rave was only held here as a last-minute switch — they were going to hold it at some place in Bedfordshire, but that got shopped, so they changed the venue at a few hours' notice. One of these boys had a cousin in Dasset and knew about the airfield, so they moved the whole shebang there.'

'So no local involvement at all?'

'That's how it looks. We've pulled the Dasset cousin in, of course, but it doesn't look as if we're going to find any useful leads.'

'Bad luck,' Jane said sympathetically. She knew he was urgently seeking the source of the Ecstasy which had been circulating among the city's teenagers in the last few months. Far too many of the small white tablets had been turning up for it to be chance, with more than one case of children as young as twelve being rushed to hospital in convulsions. It looked as if some new supplier had started operating on their patch — and after last year's big customs bust, when quantities of 'E' were found inside three-piece suites being imported from the Netherlands, very thorough searches were being made of all ferry freight, making it unlikely that the stuff could be coming in that way. 'Do you still think someone's making the 'E' locally?' she asked.

'If they are, we haven't managed to catch them

at it. My DCs haven't heard so much as a whisper.' The Drugs Unit, made up of Sergeant Clay and two detective constables, was a special group run separately from main CID, with its own office. 'It could be coming from anywhere for all we've heard,' John Clay said gloomily, but then perked up to give her one of his more usual smiles. 'So how are things in your neck of the woods? Any more Met experts been down to ask for help?'

There was a certain amount of mischief in the question: it always seemed to set off a small frisson of triumph if the Metropolitan police started asking for assistance from the provinces in something they had not been able to solve themselves. Jane grinned back, though she shook her head at the same time.

'The antiques thing? No, we haven't been able to put any kind of wrap on that. If there really is some big thieving ring sending small but valuable items out of the country this way, we've had no sniff of it.' A Met DCI had been down to give a lecture on what should be looked out for: very valuable stuff, apparently, though small in size — snuffboxes, miniatures, jewellery — with most of it stolen from country-house locations. Jane had, in fact, been arbitrarily sidelined from that investigation by DCI Morland, perhaps on the grounds that it might turn out to be important; it had landed in Kenny Barnes' lap instead. 'You should hear our DI on the subject of having enough on our own crime-sheets without being loaded with other people's dead ends . . . '

'Yes, I have. Oh, by the way — I was up in London myself last week, and ran into Steve Ryan.

Got invited to supper with him and Dr Ingle, too. I suppose you must be the only person around the station who wouldn't be surprised by that one?'

Jane was amused by the gleam of curiosity in Sergeant Clay's eyes, and his air of wanting to settle down to a good gossip. Matty Ingle, her beautiful friend and former flatmate, had made a sudden but decisive flit to work in London shortly after the departure of Sergeant Steve Ryan from his attachment here. The fact that the two were now living together was old news so far as Jane was concerned, even if the station grapevine appeared to have only just caught up with it. 'I do hear from them now and again,' she told John Clay sweetly, 'and I gather Matty's finding quite a lot of locum work around the hospitals! Oh, just to go back to another subject, I'm landed with the paperwork about that body found after the fire at the rave. So if your DCs were there and happen to have seen anything about the start of the fire, could they let me know?'

'I'll give Cooper and Bettley the nod.'

'Thanks. Well, I must go, I'm on my way to the collator's office, and Ellen will be wondering where I've got to if I don't turn up soon!'

As she gave him a smile and walked away, Jane was aware of his slight disappointment that she was not going to chew the fat over Matty and Steve. There was a tendency around police stations to know too much about other people's business. Perhaps it was inevitable, almost a definition of police work. It provided one very good reason for keeping her own private life under wraps, though.

Arriving at the collator's office, she paused in the doorway to give Ellen Rushman a smile.

'You've got something for me?'

'Oh, yes — it probably isn't terribly important, but Dr Ledyard sent something round by hand with a note. It was supposed to be included with the autopsy report but she said she was sorry, it must have got put down somewhere. It's your investigation, isn't it — Old Mary?'

'Yes. If it actually *is* her. I've still got to fit in a tour round our park-sleepers to check that she really is missing, and we haven't made a mistaken ID.' Jane came further into the tidy room with its plethora of maps, filing cabinets, index-card boxes and computer equipment: the heart of the station's information system, as the notice on the door marked 'Local Information Officer' suggested. 'I don't think we are wrong, but it's as well to be sure. Particularly in view of where she was found. You can tell me — I am right, aren't I — Old Mary was usually more or less a fixture on the city streets. She didn't usually wander far?'

'She certainly wasn't known for it. Do you want me to get her card out again and see if there's anything we missed last time?'

'No, thanks. It didn't really say much, anyway, did it? Except the usual! Drunk, Drunk and Disorderly, Drunk and Causing an Obstruction . . .' Jane pulled a wry face. 'Though not for a month or so, as I remember — which I suppose *could* mean she'd changed her patch.'

'No, I think she's still been around. I'm sure I've caught sight of her on the streets once or twice

41

during the day. She just hasn't been causing any trouble for once.' Ellen gave a look which mirrored Jane's. 'Yes, it would be a surprise if she'd actually reformed! Still, she's gone now, poor old thing. Here's what the doc sent over for you — I haven't opened the envelope, it only came in just before I buzzed you and I've been looking up something for someone else.'

She indicated a package on her desk, no more than a flat brown envelope with a very small bulge in the middle of it. 'Something extra for dental records, maybe?' Jane suggested, picking it up. 'If Old Mary ever patronised a dentist, though I can't imagine one who'd want her in his waiting room!'

'Heavens no, the smell would put all his other patients off! Anyway it can't be a tooth. The note said what's in the envelope was taped inside one of the boots.'

'Mm.' Jane tore across the end of the envelope, and something tipped out of the folded paper into the palm of her hand. 'I wonder what . . . '

'Something valuable?'

'Not to anyone else, I shouldn't think.' Jane looked at the pile of small beads in her hand. A thin wire was threaded through them, and the little heap looked darkened from what might once have been bright colours, a crack showing here and there in the glassy sparkle, perhaps from the intense heat of the fire passing over their hiding place. 'They just look like ordinary beads . . . '

She lifted a fastening pin in the middle of the wire as she spoke, and the small beads dangled. 'I think it might be a brooch. It hangs in a zig-zag — no, it could be meant to be an M!'

'M for Mary?'

'Could be. And I suppose you could call it another piece of confirmation, if so.' Jane turned the small brooch over in her hand. 'It can't be worth more than a few pence. I wonder where she got it from? She seems to have liked it enough to hide it in a special place.' Perhaps because it was the initial letter of her name, a hazy confirmation of identity. Who could tell? 'She wasn't ever one to go in for adorning herself, as I recall,' Jane commented, frowning a little as she tried to conjure up a vision of the old vagrant's usual appearance. 'Not like that other one — what was her name, Sophie?'

'Sofia, the young one with all the hair? I remember her because I was still on the cars when she was found OD'd in an alley. Must be two or three months ago now . . . She was like a magpie for what she called her 'jewellery', poor kid — even if half of it was only made out of silver paper. She'd do anything in exchange for something bright and shiny. And probably did, in a few dark doorways.' Ellen's voice was grim, and she added drily, 'Until the night when someone must have offered her a needle instead and shown her how to use it.'

'Yes. Still, at least she didn't last long enough to add addiction to her troubles. Well, I suppose I'd better take this round with me and see if I can find someone who remembers seeing Old Mary wear it. One of that bunch she used to drink with might, and I've got to see them, anyway, as I said.'

'Poor old girl, it's not much to leave behind you, is it? I suppose she had all her possessions with her in bags, as usual, and they've all been reduced to ash.'

'There certainly wasn't much left of anything.' Jane slipped the bead brooch back into its envelope and gave Ellen a smile. 'Can you let me know when the Fire Assessors' report comes in? Thanks. And I suppose I'd better give Social Services a ring, just to see if they've got anything else we haven't a note of. They're not likely to have a surname, though, or they'd have told us.'

Just one nameless vagrant. There really was no reason to let the small anomalies in the case nag her; all she was supposed to do was tidy up the details of the death, find some relatives if possible, make a brief report. It was not as if she hadn't enough else to do . . . Leaving Ellen to her neat surroundings, Jane took herself back to the CID room, but was barely there before another call came in; this time a report that the Salvation Army had found their band room had been broken into, and since the thief or thieves had not found any cash, they had apparently filched several trumpets instead.

She answered that one herself, and took the chance while she was there to ask whether the Salvation Army's charitable side had had any dealings with Old Mary, just in case they could provide a proper name for her. However, they could give her nothing new. Social Services had little to offer either, when Jane eventually found time to ring them, though it did come up that Old Mary had been seen by a doctor a couple of years back and was diagnosed as suffering from schizophrenia.

'Although the doctor listed her as paranoid schizophrenic, it wasn't considered severe enough for a Place of Safety Order,' the social worker said, sounding somewhere between harassed and defensive. 'She was given medication, but I don't suppose she ever took it, and we can't check up on everyone! We couldn't find a hostel which would take her — they won't, with the drinkers — and I don't suppose she would have stayed, anyway. It's really hard to settle the ones who actually choose to live rough.'

'Yes, it must be. What did she live on — Social Security?'

'More a question of hand-outs from the soup kitchen and what she could beg, I think. If they won't give a name they can't sign on. We certainly haven't got a note that she was registered anywhere. I'm sorry not to be more help. There'll be a small statutory grant for burial, if you can't find any relatives to take the cost over . . .'

A pauper's grave, with no one to mourn. 'Thanks,' Jane answered, 'that'll come in handy if I don't find any relatives. And it seems doubtful I will, from where I am so far. Thanks for your time, 'bye.'

No fixed abode, no money, mentally ill, frequently drunk. Basically, no loss to society. No loss to anybody at all, Old Mary. No matter how she had died . . . It seemed a sad reflection

45

on a life. Jane made a note on the file in front of her, and decided it was not really worth trying to question the soup kitchen volunteers. All they did was offer a hot meal to anyone who turned up at the late-night venue in one of the city's arcades.

She had to go through the rest of the motions, however: it was a death, after all. To make a final confirmation that the body found in the fire really was Old Mary, she would need to speak to the other members of the city's small but known vagrant population — not the young homeless who increasingly appeared on the streets of this relatively prosperous city, but the true bottom of the heap, the ones who lived their lives out of carrier bags and slept on whatever bench or patch of dry ground they could find, year-round, winter and summer. And late in the afternoon, she went in search of them.

They were likely to be moved on if they hung about too long in any of the more public places in their worn overcoats tied round the middle with string, their cracked boots and frayed leg-wrappings; particularly likely to be moved on if one weathered and dirt-grimed hand was clutching a suspiciously bottle-shaped paper bag. Jane knew where she was likely to find the ones she was looking for, since now that the tourist season proper was over (and barring actual public complaints) an official blind eye was likely to be turned in some of the gardens attached to historic buildings, or in the green spaces along the riverside Pilgrims Walk. Sure enough, after a patient tour round, she found a group of three vagrants occupying a bench in one corner of the Greyfriars Garden — an irregularly shaped small field surrounded by trees and tall hedges, a secluded patch of green which seemed almost too countrified to be where it actually was, in the middle of a city. A small stream meandered along one side and disappeared beneath a tiny medieval river chapel, behind its repaired flint wall; butterflies hovered here and there in the afternoon sun; the soft buzzing of bees sounded around the late-flowering hedges.

The three who had taken over the corner of the otherwise empty garden struck Jane for one fanciful moment as something out of a time-slip, three medieval peasants taking their momentary ease. The city's twelfth-century poor would have been no cleaner, and would have been bundled up in the same drab colours. Would probably have carried the same stale foetid smell when you came close to them, too. She pushed fantasy firmly aside as she walked over to them. Two out of the three lounging figures were ones she recognised, though the third was a stranger. The grey-bearded one was known as Jacko, and the small, bandy-legged, baggy-suited one with the bloodshot eyes was Irish and therefore always called Paddy by everyone.

They knew her, too, familiar as they were with a police presence. Jacko was already looking at her squinny-eyed. 'It's all right, calm down,' she told him. 'I'm not after you — unless you've got something special to feel guilty about? Never mind if you have, I'm not asking this afternoon! Can any of you tell me if you've seen Old Mary recently?'

'No, we an't. She don't mix much, that one, anyway.'

'Doesn't she? I've seen you drinking with her more than once, though.'

'On'y in the same place, not with 'er. Do she, Paddy? Not with us, not 'er. Kick you if you want wot she got anyway, don't she, Paddy?'

'She's no great one for sharing,' Paddy agreed, shrinking into himself as he answered in his Irish-tinged accent. He always tried to make himself smaller, almost as if he hoped to be seen as a little boy, with a hand held out for largesse. He slanted a glance up at Jane now. There were creases in his weather-browned face, dirt visible in the network of lines. 'Would it be worth anything, what you want to know?' he coaxed.

'It'd be worth my not telling you to go and find yourself a proper place to sleep for the night — and if I did that I'd send someone round to check up on you, and to move you on from wherever else you'd settled!' With that threat made, she softened it with a milder offer. 'It might turn out to be worth the price of a cup of tea, as long as you really spend it on tea and not rough cider. So, when *did* you last see Old Mary?'

'Must be a fortnight. At least that. Is it, Jacko? I didn't see her sooner than that, did you?' Paddy was doing his eager-to-please bit now. 'She hasn't been at the soup kitchen lately, not that I've seen her.' He glanced at the silent third to include him. 'Bill didn't see her either, did you, Bill?'

'I don't believe I know the lady,' this one said, with surprisingly rounded vowels. A heavily veined

48

strawberry nose suggested a long acquaintance with the drinking fraternity, and a stubbled face and threadbare clothes put him on a par with the others, though his voice suggested he had definitely come down in the world. A gentleman of the road, with the accent on gentleman, even if his one noticeable concession to it was remarkably shiny shoes. 'Old Mary? Is she, so to speak, one of us? And you, dear lady — do I gather from your words that you are the fuzz?'

'I'm Detective Sergeant Perry. You're new with us, are you? Just passing through, I hope?' She gave him a level stare to discourage him from feeling the local police might be a soft touch, and turned back to the other two. 'So you've neither of you seen Old Mary lately, right? And certainly not since the weekend?'

Jacko shook his head as did Paddy, both of them looking quite definite. 'Seen her in the distance the other day, but not since the weekend,' Jacko said, sounding as unwilling as if the words were being wrung out of him. 'Thursday morning, maybe. Could've been Wednesday. Not to speak to — just down the street.'

'All right. Paddy hasn't seen her for a fortnight and you haven't seen her since last week.' Paddy's grasp of time was unreliable anyway, but she would take Jacko's word. 'Right, next question. Do either of you know if Old Mary had another name? A surname? Did you ever see one written down anywhere, or hear one mentioned?'

They both of them shook their heads even more definitely. 'The social would know,' Paddy began

on a whine, but Jacko let out a snort which made
the little Irishman glance at him and then add,
'Mebbe not, with her fair ready to kill anyone
who asked questions . . . I'd not have cared to
do any spying on her myself!'

It was plainly true from his expression. Jane
fished in her pocket and brought out the little bead
brooch, holding it out so that both of them could
see it. 'Have either of you ever seen Old Mary wear
this?' she enquired, but received further shakes of
the head from two of them. Jacko, however, leaned
forward to look at it more closely, something in his
face making Jane wait, studying him with care.

'Jacko? You've seen this before?'

'Not on her I an't. It's just — no, I an't. She
did have a ring once. On'y thing she wore. Silla.
Took it off arter I noticed it, though. Didn' like
anyone asking about anything, she. Got the crazies
if'n she even saw you looking at her.'

'She was crazy anyway, lately. Ever since — '

'Shut up, Paddy! Wot you want Old Mary
for, any road?' Jacko asked, giving Jane another
of his squinny-eyed looks. 'She done something,
have she?'

'No. I'm not looking for her because she's in
trouble. Are you going to tell me where you saw
these beads before?' She looked at Jacko, then
reached in her pocket again for a fifty-pence piece
and held it out where he could see it. 'This help?
It's all I'm offering!'

'Didn't say I saw those beads . . . Orright, then.
It's like — not just like that, but them kind of
beads, only newer-looking mind, not dirty like

50

those — the hippies been selling them round the streets, weaving 'em into people's hair, that's all. And I did hear . . . '

'What?'

'Old Mary, she went with them. The hippies. That's why she an't been sleeping on the streets awhile, on'y walking around in the day. She got the crazies worse than usual, like Paddy says, started saying it were dangerous in the city, nights. Muttering about it like she do. And I reckon she went off to sleep at the hippy place where they live. That's worth more than one cuppa tea, innit?' he added, looking at the fifty pence with a mixture of cupidity and hope.

'All right — if you can tell me where these hippies live. Though I may know anyway. Out Dasset way?'

She had expected him to look disappointed by her knowledge: instead he looked surprised. 'No, not that side, and nowhere near so far! They're at — ' He stopped as Paddy nudged him, to Jane's annoyance, and looked sly. 'Lessee if I can remember . . . it might come to me . . . '

'You want to come back to the station with me and see if it does?'

'Lymans Oak,' he told her unwillingly, naming a place not far from the city's edge and giving her a very sulky look. Made all the sulkier by Bill murmuring fruitily, 'Oh, bad luck, old boy!' from the sidelines. Jane gave him a quelling glance, but returned her attention to Jacko as the man went on, his voice developing a querulous note. 'I didn' say she was there, so if she an't, it's not up to me!

Just, she took up with 'em, and they got a farm or something they're living in there, so I reckon that's where she bin staying nights this last few weeks. But if I'm wrong you don't come down on me!'

'No, all right, I won't. And here.' She pulled out a small handful of change, checked there was only one pound coin in amongst it, added it to the fifty pence, then passed it over to Jacko. She was probably unwise at that considering how he was likely to spend it, but he had given her something, so deserved at least a small return. To Paddy she said, 'You can get him to share it with you, it's all I've got! As to Old Mary, you may as well know why I'm asking about her. We found a body after an accidental fire, and it seems more than probable that she lit it to warm herself and then got caught in the blaze. So, just remember that and be careful if you're sheltering anywhere. And if you do remember anything more about her, come down to the station and ask for me. All right?'

She noted cynically before she walked away that Paddy had immediately put on an air of respectful mourning. By tomorrow he would undoubtedly be stopping passers-by on the streets with an air of fake misery and a whine, 'Me old friend's just died and I can't even afford a wreath for her grave, can you spare just a little to help me out?' With a dip of his curly head, even a tear or two squeezed out. He was too well known among the locals for many people to fall for it, but someone might.

Jacko, on the other hand, had suddenly gone very still, hunched into himself. From the way one hand had abruptly gripped his knee, almost

52

convulsively, one might almost think her words had frightened him.

Scared? By the news of Old Mary's death? Why — simply because it was a reminder of his own mortality?

She filed the impression away in her mind as she left them, wondering whether it meant anything.

# 4

It was only a short distance to Lymans Oak, but a glance at her watch made Jane decide not to try to fit it in this evening. She would need to ask around the station first to see if anyone had heard of hippies living there. She made the drive first thing next morning instead, with the wry feeling that Old Mary was taking up an unconscionable amount of her time, but at least she would be able to provide the DCI with a report showing meticulous thoroughness.

Her route took her through a less than decorative part of the city, a long road of industrial buildings, car lots, cash-and-carry wholesalers and large shed-like DIY stores, all opening themselves up for morning. Sweeping through them, Jane crossed an unmanned level crossing, then climbed through a brief area of thickly hedged arable land to find herself rapidly into Lyman Oak's one street. It was made up of a few neat gardened detached houses, then a row of cheaper-looking pebble-dashed semis.

These last meant she had come too far: one of the uniformed sergeants had been able to tell her that if there *were* hippies out this way, the only farm buildings they could be renting lay down a lane just before the semis started. She backtracked, and found the sharp turn he had described. After a short way it turned into a steep downward hill which was little more than a track, but as she bumped down it she saw a flash of red brick among the trees below. And then a tacked-up notice, hand-scrawled and weather-worn and attached to a tilted post beside the track where it widened out into a rough yard, announcing 'Lymans Farm'.

Lyman who had once also been the owner of an oak, presumably, and given his name to the area. Unless 'Lyman' meant something else in Old English.

The farm was just a house surrounded by trees now, with a few outbuildings behind it. Someone had turned a small square of spare land into what looked like an attempt at a vegetable garden. Behind that two lines of rope had been strung up to hold washing, with some children's clothes pegged up and hanging limply. The house was a medium-sized slab of unimaginative Victorian architecture in a liverish red brick under a gabled slate roof, and the windows had a narrow meanness. A wisp of smoke rose from a chimney topped by a red pot. As Jane drew up on the rutted half-circle of earth which lay in front of the house, she saw a battered transit van parked around the corner. The van had been painted lilac, with the addition of large multi-coloured flowers. Its appearance suggested she had found the right place.

A door on this side of the house — the front door, presumably, though it had no additional importance — stood half open. As Jane came up to it a small child appeared within, to gaze at her round-eyed with a thumb in its mouth, then disappear back inside. Jane located a small white bell-push on the door jamb, and pressed it. She half expected it not to work, but a clear buzz came from somewhere inside the house. A moment later a girl who might have been in her twenties appeared in the passageway.

She had fairish hair hanging loose past her shoulders, and wore a long patchwork skirt which brushed the ground, with a man's shirt hanging over the top of it. Light brown eyes regarded Jane questioningly.

'Good morning.' Jane gave the girl a pleasant smile. 'I wonder if you can help me? I'm Detective Sergeant Perry, City Police.'

'We're here legally. We've got a rent book,' the girl said at once. Her voice was soft and polite, but there was an immediate if faint stiffening of her shoulders. 'If someone's told you we're squatting, it's not true!'

'No, they haven't, it isn't about that.' The reaction was predictable, Jane supposed. 'I'm just making some enquiries. About — '

'What do you want?' The new arrival appearing abruptly behind the girl from some door on to the passage was definitely more aggressive: a tall young man with long, tangled, curly black hair, wearing nothing but faded jeans, which he was buttoning as if he had just pulled them on. His feet were large and bare, and he came round the girl protectively, standing foursquare as if to block any threat of entry. 'And if you're a cop, I'll see your warrant card!'

'She did already show it to me, Rocky — '

'Here.' Jane held it out again, offering it to the young man pleasantly. 'I'm sorry to disturb you,' she said to his scowl, her voice deliberately mild. 'I've come to ask if you happen to know an old woman called Old Mary?'

'Why should we?'

'*Rocky!*' the girl said, a definite reproach in her soft voice. She looked at Jane apologetically. 'I'm sorry, it's just that we . . . '

'You're apologising? After the number of times they've moved us on for nothing? Sometimes you're an idiot, Mel! All right, what do you want, Detective Sergeant?' He invested the title with scornful hostility and added, 'We're here legally, like Mel said. All of us. Ask the DSS, they're giving us housing allowance! And our children are well cared for, and they're all too young to be at school yet.'

'Rocky,' Mel said again, this time more firmly, 'do shut up, she hasn't come to ask about the children. She wants to know about Old Mary, she just said so! Yes, we do know her,' she added, turning back to Jane with a frank, clear-eyed gaze. 'We've been letting her sleep in our barn. She's homeless, after all, and there's no reason why we shouldn't give her shelter.'

'No reason at all,' Jane agreed, putting it in

56

quickly before Rocky could start up again. 'But she isn't here now?'

'No, she isn't.'

The words came in a different voice. A third person had arrived. This one was male again, but smaller and weedier, a thin young man with mousy hair pulled back into a pony-tail on his neck, a small straggly beard decorating his chin, and round metal-framed glasses from behind which peered a pair of large grey eyes. He insinuated his way between Mel and Rocky like a bony eel. He looked at Jane, frowning, his eyes blinking rapidly. 'Old Mary isn't here. Why?' he asked flatly.

'I'm trying to trace her. At least, I'm trying to trace her recent movements. She — '

'What made you come here?' the newcomer interrupted her, with the same brusqueness.

'Someone suggested she might have been sleeping here. One of the other vagrants — homeless people,' Jane said, keeping her expression pleasant and unthreatening. 'Because of this.' She reached into her pocket to hold the bead brooch out, as she had to Jacko and Paddy. 'We found it on — a body, I'm afraid. After a fire. The remains of the clothes suggest the body is Old Mary's. I'm simply trying to make a final identification.'

The weedy young man had turned an almost greenish-white and Mel had put a hand to her mouth; even Rocky seemed to have lost some of his aggression. It was Mel who spoke, her voice distressed.

'Oh, poor old thing! Yes, it must be her — that's

the brooch you made for her, Kieron. Oh, I'm sorry, that's awful!'

She turned to put her arms round the weedy young man, wrapping herself round him in a sympathetic embrace. 'Kieron loved her,' she said over her shoulder in Jane's direction, 'they were friends. And she was such a harmless old thing. She died in a fire? Oh, poor Mary!'

'Where was it?' Rocky asked, giving Jane a look which was marginally less hostile. 'She hasn't been here for days, has she, K? Not since before the weekend. You were wondering where she'd got to.'

'When?' Kieron asked on a gulp. He had pulled himself together and was addressing Jane again. 'Can you tell us when? And where? And — and how? What sort of fire? How did it start? What was she doing? I shouldn't have let her — Sorry. Sorry, it's just that she — '

'Kieron had sort of adopted her. She was like his granny.' That was Mel joining in again, full of sympathy, and giving him another hug. 'Oh, *dear*. We'll have a ceremony for her, K. Won't that help? We'll get the children to pick a whole lot of flowers and branches and we'll do it all properly. Sergeant, would you like to come in and have a cup of tea? I mean, if you've got some more things you want to ask? No, Rocky, don't be silly, if she's only come to tell us about Mary, why shouldn't she come in?'

'Thank you, I'd like to come in for a cup of tea, if I may?' Ignoring Rocky's scowl — though he did at least step back for her, unwillingly — Jane came across the threshold in response

58

to the invitation, and followed Mel and Kieron along the passage. She was aware that Rocky did an abrupt disappearing act behind her, a door closing behind him with a sharp click. He probably had a stash of pot, she thought drily, and intended to make sure it was well concealed just in case. In any event he obviously had no desire to fraternise with any representative of the police. Kieron seemed to be the one who might have the answers to her questions, anyway. Kieron who had adopted Old Mary, and to whom she was 'like his granny'. A charitable young man, apparently (or did Mel mean he actually had a grandmother like that?), though they all seemed to feel shock and grief at the news of the old vagrant's death.

The room Jane was led into at the back of the house was obviously the kitchen. A battered Aga gave off minimal heat in one corner, and there was a sink and a draining-board piled with recent washing-up. A back door led out from another corner, and a scrubbed table occupied most of the centre of the room, and held a packet of corn-flakes and a used cereal bowl. Kieron flopped down on one of the mismatched chairs which stood around the table, and put his head in his hands. Jane took another chair which Mel politely indicated.

'How many of you live here?' she asked amiably as the girl busied herself with an electric kettle.

'Five. Well, eight, with the children. The others aren't up yet. But the rent book is in my name, and it's all perfectly legal.'

'I believe you. I really didn't come to find out if you were squatting. Have you been here long?'

'Six months,' Kieron said, lifting his head. She saw his adam's apple jump in his thin throat. 'Are you going to tell me when and where Old Mary died?' he demanded.

'Saturday night. There was a fire over near Dasset — do you know where that is? On the other side of the city from here, quite a way out,' Jane told him as he shook his head. 'The fire seems to have been accidental. There was a rave going on, something happened and the building went up. It was thought everyone had got out, but then Old Mary's body was found in a small adjoining building. We think she must have been sheltering there. You're frowning?'

'No, I'm — ' He broke off as Mel put two mugs of tea down on the table, and since he seemed to have decided not to go on, Jane gave him a prompt.

'You were going to say?'

'I wasn't.'

'I did wonder what she was doing out there. It seems a long way off her usual beat.' So was this, in a sense: perhaps her experience of sleeping here had given Old Mary a taste for the country? 'Would you have any idea why she should have wanted to go over to Dasset?'

'She liked wandering, I think,' Mel put in before Kieron could answer. 'Perhaps if she had a bit of money she just got on a bus to see where it went. Oh dear, poor old thing. She didn't like being with people very much, you know. She just wanted a place to shelter so we let her sleep in the barn. Yes, Bethan love, do you want something?'

The child Jane had seen before had appeared in the doorway, thumb in mouth, the other hand pulling at its trousers. 'All right, love, I'll take you,' Mel said quickly, obviously translating the gesture. 'Good girl! Excuse me . . . '

She moved quickly to the child and took her hand, the two of them disappearing through the doorway. She had barely gone when Kieron gave Jane an accusing glare, his adam's apple jumping again as he burst out, 'I suppose you won't care much, when she was just a nobody misfit in your terms? I mean, the fact that she was a human being wouldn't matter to *you*, would it? Even if somebody killed her! Are you sure the fire was an accident?'

'You're suggesting it wasn't? Why?'

'I don't know. It's just that I can't bear the thought of her dying like that.' Abruptly, his head was buried in his hands again. Then he looked up to ask, with a gulp and an obvious effort, 'Do you — must I — do you want somebody to identify the body?'

'I don't think there's much chance that you could do that,' Jane told him with careful gentleness. 'One of our detectives recognised what was left of her clothes. There isn't much else to know her by, I'm afraid. Now that you've identified the brooch, I think we can be certain it's her. You're absolutely sure this was the one you made for her? Do you want to take a closer look?'

'I don't need to. It's the only time I ever tried an initial and I just made it for fun, once, as something to give her. Was she actually wearing it? I — I

61

didn't think she would, though she seemed quite pleased to have it.'

'I expect she was. She had it hidden in one of her boots, and I expect she valued it since it was a present. Kieron, did she ever tell you her surname?'

'No. I didn't ask her. I don't go round asking people things they don't want to tell, and if she just wanted to be Mary, that was her privilege, wasn't it?'

'Sure. There's no need to scowl about it. It's just that I've got to try to find out who she was, in case she had any relatives. She didn't tell you that either, I suppose, or ever mention anyone?'

'No, we didn't talk about anything like that.'

'Would any of the others know, do you think?'

'No. She didn't talk to them. Only to me.' He swallowed hard, his eyes fixed on his hands; then he looked up at Jane. 'We just knew her as Mary, that was all she ever called herself. 'Old Mary' sometimes, or just 'Mary'.'

'That's a pity. I do need to try and find out who she actually was if I can. In case there's anyone who should be informed. It looks as if all her possessions must have burned too, since she usually carried everything with her, and the fire was quite a bad one . . . Yes, what?'

'She didn't take everything with her. Her stuff's still out in the barn. That's why I was — wondering why she hadn't come back.'

'Really? Will you show me?'

He got up silently and made for the back door. Jane followed him, since he appeared to intend her to. Out in the open air, the barn was visible as a structure fifty yards from the house: three walls and a tin roof, with a small rickety shed leaning against one side of it, and the tumbledown brick shape of what might once have been a pigsty next to that. Their route took them past the parked transit van which bore a definitely out-of-date tax disc on its windscreen. Jane decided not to notice it. Moving in Kieron's wake, she saw that the barn had a couple of bales of old hay in its entrance, faintly mouldering, and a pile of logs. A path between them led into the interior.

At the back, in a dim corner under a dirty and cobwebbed window with cracked panes, a pile of blankets made a nest. A faded piece of Indian print fabric had been tacked up on the wall as if to add a touch of homely decoration. A few more mouldy hay bales made a rudimentary surrounding wall — with a jamjar containing a dead-looking branch perched on one of them.

Old Mary seemed to have made herself a home for once. Temporarily, at least.

'This is her place,' Kieron said gruffly after a silence. 'She liked to keep it private — the children know not to come in here. I promised we'd none of us bother her. She let me, sometimes, but — ' His voice was jerky. 'See, I told you, her stuff is here!'

Plastic carrier bags, bulging, their sheen catching the light. Two of them. Old Mary seemed to have got her life down to the contents of two supermarket bags, she never carried more — though the small canvas sack she usually wore slung across her back was not present. That she had apparently taken with her. It was unusual enough that she had not taken everything, for an old woman who always guarded her small store of possessions so jealously that she would bite and scratch rather than part with them, even when she was being put in a police cell.

'I'd better take those bags with me,' Jane said. She caught defensiveness in the stance of the young man beside her, and added, 'Kieron, I have to look! I do know she never liked anyone picking around in her possessions, but she's not going to mind now, is she?' The bags usually held nothing but old clothes and rags — together with odd bits of stale and festering food — and going through them was unlikely to be a pleasant job: it had always been an unpopular one when the old woman was brought into the station. There could be fleas among the clothing, or lice. Once, Jane remembered hearing, there had been a dead pigeon, a bundle of limp and bedraggled feathers, their colours dulled, the small corpse beginning to smell. 'I can look through the bags here, if you'd rather,' she told the young man patiently.

'No, you can take them . . . '

'Thank you.' She bent down to shake out the bedding in case there was anything there, but nothing showed itself. 'Did you give her the blankets?'

'We had some spare ones. Your lot didn't give a damn about her.'

'I think several people tried, so you needn't fire up at me. She just turned up here, did she?'

'I bought her a cup of tea once and we got talking. I said she could come if she — I don't see that it matters!'

'It doesn't.' She felt like telling him the old woman had been lucky to find someone she would allow to care for her, but left it for fear of being accused of sounding patronising. 'When was the last time you actually saw her?'

'Friday.'

'Morning? Afternoon? When?'

'Morning.'

'And she didn't tell you where she was going?'

'She didn't have to report in and out,' he said sarcastically, then added more flatly, 'no, she didn't tell me where she was going. Or *anything*. She just went off. She was here at eight, and then she wasn't at ten.'

'All right, thank you. Please thank Mel for the tea, as well, will you? There's no reason for me to come back into the house, so I'll just take these things and go. If any of you think of anything else which might be useful, perhaps you'd ring me at this number.' She scribbled it on a card and handed it to him. 'Ask for me — Detective Sergeant Perry.'

He let her pick up the bags, but left her and disappeared towards the house as soon as they came out of the barn. Jane picked her way round the house and back to her car, thinking drily that the hippy creed of love towards everyone might include tramps but stopped short when it reached the police. Except perhaps for Mel, who seemed to have retained a degree of politeness from what was

65

probably a conventional middle-class upbringing. Since this bunch seemed to have settled respectably for the moment instead of the usual travelling, they might also have dropped their defensiveness. But obviously had not.

She stowed Old Mary's bags in the boot of her car — with the brief hope that if there were fleas, they would forbear to emerge and spread themselves — and paused after she had got into the driving seat, contemplating whether to go on to Herne Bay since she was part-way there and had a different enquiry to follow up in that direction, or whether to head straight back. Best to call in and check that nothing more urgent had come up, before she decided on Herne Bay . . . Then she found her radio-communication set was on the blink again, annoyingly, only offering a crackling of static. After wasting time on several tries she decided it might be the surrounding trees (though it might just as easily be a loose wire, since the set had been erratic lately) and gave up and started the engine. She had just backed round to face the way she had come when the skinny figure of Kieron abruptly appeared directly in her path, making her brake sharply. He had something in his hand which looked like an old tin tea-caddy. As she wound down her window, he thrust it at her. He was blinking hard again behind his glasses.

'Old Mary gave me this to keep safe for her. You'd better have it. Just because we don't choose to join in with your society, it doesn't mean we're thieves,' he added pointedly. 'It's money, but since it was hers you'd better take it.'

'Thank you.' Jane accepted the tin without investigating its contents, and gave him a look to show she had no intention of being drawn into an argument. The tin rattled slightly as she put it down: a few coins was probably the limit of its contents, but she could see Kieron meant to stand on his principles. He gave her a look which was suddenly more amiable, and asked with a surprising access of helpfulness, 'Is your radio on the blink? I saw you from the window. I can probably mend it for you, if you like?'

'Thanks, but I'll have it looked at when I get back to the station. Do you do that as a job — mending radios and so on?'

'No, I do it as a favour,' he retorted — back to defensiveness again, she realised resignedly. He probably assumed she was asking to see if he was cheating on Social Security. 'I don't sell my skills. *You* may think that's the only way people should function — '

'This is turning into a pointless conversation. Thank you for the offer, and thank you for giving me this. Now . . . '

'If Old Mary knew something about somebody, would you investigate it?'

The question was blurted abruptly. 'Yes, certainly, if I had due cause,' Jane told him. 'But you'd have to tell me what, and give me details. So — what? Is there something you feel I ought to know?'

She was reaching to switch off her engine as she spoke, but he had already let go of her car window, looking defeated. 'It doesn't matter,' he said bitterly. 'I don't *know* any details. Just that she — anyway you'd rather think it was an accident, wouldn't you? No wonder she wouldn't trust anyone. You wouldn't listen to someone like her anyway.' And he turned on his heel, a thin figure hurrying rapidly into the house.

Dramatics? Or maybe simply the shock of hearing of the old woman's death when he had been fond of her, for whatever odd and unlikely reasons? He was an odd young man altogether. It sounded very much as if he had been taken in by Old Mary's paranoia, the delusions which had made the old vagrant so savagely suspicious of the world around her.

There was still the puzzle of the broken neck . . .

It would be better to wait and see what the Fire Assessors' report said: there might be some simple explanation in it for that oddity, since their reports were always detailed and thorough. It would certainly be no use going in pursuit of Kieron now to try to find out what, if anything, he was talking about. Jane slid her car into gear and drove back up the steep track to the top of the hill.

She paused to try her radio again when she got out of the belt of trees, but it still gave no more than an exasperating crackle. Irritated, she felt that that decided things: she had better leave Herne Bay for later, go back and get the set fixed, and see if anything pressing had come up in CID. In the unlikely event that nothing had, she could take time out to chase up that fire service report.

Her return to the station offered an immediate distraction. A hold-up at a sub post office had just been called in, with CID's presence urgently required. No one else was available, so Jane thrust the bulging carrier bags into one corner of the office, pushed the unopened tin into the bottom drawer of her desk, and went to deal with it.

Old Mary would have to wait.

★ ★ ★

It was another twenty-four hours before she had time to sort through the bags, and then she took them out to the yard — after a protest from the other occupants of the CID room — and tipped them out, to go through the contents with reluctant fingers. Clothing — if you could call it that — stained and grimy; a thick cardigan full of holes and unravelling at the bottom; rags, a bundle of newspapers. A few crusts and a mouldy meat pie came out from under those, and a smeared sheet of paper which had nothing on it except the word 'No' scrawled over and over, line after line. A leather glove; what seemed to be the sole off a shoe; a cracked and broken mirror. One almost new-looking silk scarf. A hard lump of something which looked as if it might once have been cheese. An old, empty perfume bottle of fancy design, and another woollen garment which was too shapeless to see what it might have been. There was nothing here to tell her much about Old Mary — except a reflection of what her life had been.

'What on earth are you doing?'

'Ragpicking,' Jane said drily, as Ellen Rushman paused beside her. 'And I wouldn't come too close! This is — guess what? — Old Mary's stuff.'

'You found it, then? I thought you said it was all burned up with her?'

'Not all. She used to carry a canvas sack thing, too, didn't she, slung round her? Well, it seems that was all she had with her last Saturday night, since I haven't found that. But this lot she'd left behind her for once. Jacko — you know Jacko, the old vagrant with the beard? — actually seems to have known something about the old bird, because he tipped me off that she'd gone off to shelter with some hippies at Lymans Oak. And sure enough he was right. I found a bunch of them at Lymans Farm, and Old Mary had been sleeping there. They even seem to have been quite fond of her . . . '

'Goodness, really? She must have changed!'

'Or there's no accounting for tastes. No, let's be fair, they were just being more charitable than the rest of us. New Agers aren't always the way *we* see them, I suppose; they do have a philosophy of life aside from confrontations with the police.'

'You mean funny haircuts and endless dogs on bits of string? And living on Giros instead of working?' Ellen sounded less than sympathetic. 'What are this lot doing — camping on someone else's land?'

'No, I think they're renting the house legally. And they've been here some time and we haven't heard about them, so they must be keeping themselves out of trouble.' Jane wasn't sure why she was defending Mel and Kieron's group, since she held no brief for New Agers herself. 'One of them had made that bead brooch for Old Mary, so I guess that finalises the identification anyway. I wonder what

I'm going to do with all this stuff now? Bundle it all up again, I suppose, and leave it out here for now. It certainly doesn't give me anything!'

'I'd have a good wash to make sure it doesn't,' Ellen advised with a grin, and went on her way. Jane followed her into the station a few moments later, to make for the Ladies and give her arms and hands a thorough scrub. She had already thought of that one before Ellen mentioned it; she hadn't actually seen any fleas but . . .

There was still the tin tea-caddy Kieron had given her, she remembered: might as well investigate that, too, while she had it in mind. Where had she put it — in her drawer? Back at her desk she found it, and lifted the tin out, flipping the lid open.

Its contents made her stare. A large folded wad of banknotes.

She upended the tin to tip the contents out on to the top of her desk. Two one-pound coins came out of the bottom — and a silver ring, rolling away across the desktop until Jane put a hand on it to stop it.

'She had a ring once — silla — the only thing she wore.' Jacko had said that. Jane let the ring rest on her palm. It was solid and heavy, old-looking, a little rubbed at its edges. There was a design of leaves and flowers round it, chased elegantly into the metal. And in the middle, making a centrepiece to the design — yes, those were initials! Engraved in elaborate style, but they started with an M. And then what looked like a J. And finally a B.

M.J.B. The old woman's initials? She must have had a very different life once, if this ring was hers.

And whatever her last name was, it had begun with a B.

There was nothing else in the tin. The wad of banknotes, however, looked a remarkably thick one.

Jane set herself to count them. Then she sat back in disbelief.

One thousand six hundred and ninety-five pounds.

One thousand six hundred and ninety-five pounds in used banknotes. Plus the two coins. Old Mary had been the owner of sixteen hundred and ninety-seven pounds.

Almost two thousand pounds, when she lived rough with no visible means of support? It made no sense. No sense at all.

# 5

She was allowed no time to think about it. Almost inevitably, the phone rang. Another house break-in. Since Jane was officially in charge of what was now called the Domestic Burglaries Team (in a reorganisation which would have made more sense if CID had had enough personnel to be put into separate teams, and of which Dan Crowe made a point of taking little notice, allocating everything to everybody), she had to respond. Jane thrust the money back into the tin, scribbled a rapid note to say how much there was, sealed the whole thing with sellotape, and took it to the custody sergeant to put in the safe; that much money needed to be logged in rather than left floating about. Then she made for her car.

Daytime break-ins seemed to be as common as those at night, now; in fact the night-time crop were usually into off-licences and cars in private car-parks — done over with monotonous regularity — or offices. Anything might go, from word-processors and faxes to pens and pocket calculators: if it could be turned for a fiver it would be lifted. Petty theft on the whole, but taking up a lot of police time. Jane spared a grateful thought for the fact that non-domestic break-ins didn't officially come into her remit, and that it was Peter Pettigrew's job to collect up the reports of those and provide the subsequent reams of paperwork. There was enough on the domestic side to keep her busy and use up several trees-worth of paper.

She went to soothe an angry householder, apparently as enraged by the fact that he now had a broken window and a forced door, as by the fact that his fax, video, and some spare cash left lying around had been taken. 'I was only out for half an hour! Why don't the police patrol the streets nowadays?'

'We do, sir, but we can't be in every street all the time. We'll make a check to see if your neighbours saw anything.' It was a Neighbourhood Watch area, as were most of the more well-heeled streets; not that that usually meant much besides a window-sticker intended to deter the criminally inclined. 'You've got a burglar alarm, but you say it was switched off?'

'We only put it on at night, or if we're away. I work from home so I'm usually here. If you had bobbies on the beat instead of putting them all in cars, this wouldn't happen!'

It was such a common complaint that Jane was tired of answering it, but did, patiently. 'We have to rationalise our numbers, and we can make a quicker response in different parts of the city if our constables are mobile. I'm afraid I have to say, if you want more police, please write to the County Council. We'd be only too delighted if they'd give us a bigger budget. Now, if you could confirm for me that you've told us everything that's missing . . .'

He was one of those who actually had written his postcode in ultra-violet on the back of his fax and video, which was at least something. Jane finished her notetaking, offered some more sympathy, promised that everything possible would be done, and escaped. Outside, she raised an eyebrow at the uniformed car-patrol which had taken the first call to the scene.

'Nobody either side or opposite saw anything, I suppose?'

'No, Sarge. They're either out or weren't looking out of the window.'

'That's about par for the course. I didn't like to tell him it's not even worth the bother of sending a SOCO in, we're not going to get much out of a quick in-and-out job. I'll just put him down for a Victim Support visit, that's about all we can do . . . though whoever goes will probably get an ear-bashing!'

'At least the house wasn't trashed,' one of the constables put in.

'No. I was tempted to point out that he was lucky it was a casual light-fingered perp rather than a yobbo. He'd only have gone on at me even more about bobbies on the beat if I had.' She shared an expressive grin with the constables, and added drily, 'Good thing there were two of you for once. No doubt he'd have beefed even more if the usual single-manned car had turned up!'

'And we got here within the ten-minute response-time for the call.'

One of the constables' radio crackled at that moment and he lifted it off its clip on his shoulder to answer it. A mugging had just happened in the hospital grounds half a mile away. This patrol was the nearest. 'I'll follow you on,' Jane said rapidly as they leapt into action. 'May as well, since I'm here!'

The nurse who had been knocked down and had her purse snatched on her way on duty wasn't badly hurt, luckily, and was at least in the right place to have the graze on her head quickly seen to. A male, IC 1, had been seen running away, but no one had been near enough to stop him. Or had been inclined to. Jane took down the necessary description to offer Ellen for a possible match on the files, which was about all she could do. She was barely back at the station before the next thing came up and she was on her way to Whitstable to cover another domestic break-in there. At least it gave her a breath of sea air, and she spared a brief moment's light-hearted envy for those who lived in houses right on the shore and could look out across the shingle at a wide expanse of water and bobbing boats. Though when winter closed in, it probably meant battering winds and the danger of having your roof blown off.

She was still getting used to having the sea so close, after her years of working in London. 'The seaside' still held a fascination, an urge to linger and watch the small working harbour with its piles of timber awaiting transportation, and the little fishing vessels moored with their orange and green nets spread to dry, beside the shellfish factory which sent a strong whiff into the air.

She pulled her mind away from the sense of holiday it gave her — no use feeling like that, she had far too much work to do! — and called in at the police sub-station to pass on something she had forgotten to say while the uniformed sergeant in charge there was still with her. Then she was on the road back to the city. Lowering clouds were promising rain, and she met a sweeping silver curtain of it before she had finished her six-mile journey. Fair enough, she supposed, since at least they had had a very good summer and autumn up to now. And with luck she would not have to go out in it again, but could catch up with all the additional paperwork she now had to write up. Eventually she might even be able to get back to the puzzle of Old Mary.

No such luck, however, since her damp arrival in the CID room brought her a message that a fraud case she had been working on several months ago now had a court date: would she please check and make sure the CPS had *all* the relevant papers? She muffled a groan as Kenny Barnes passed that one on, and then had to try to look willing as the DI joined in to beetle at her and growl bracingly, 'Well, it was your case, get to it!'

* * *

'No, sorry, I can't, there's no way I can be sure of getting off on time on Saturday. It's not that I wouldn't like to come to someone's barbecue, honestly — it's just that I've been chasing my tail for two days solid, and there's no guarantee that things are going to let up. And since it'll be my weekend on . . . '

'I thought you said you were on some kind of overtime ban, because of budgets?' Adrian's voice said in her ear down the phone.

'We are, officially, after all the extra work we did when the festival was on. But since they're also on at us about 'keeping to targets', ' Jane said, giving the words their full inverted commas, and a degree of sarcasm, 'all it actually means is, 'If you put in the hours don't expect to claim for them!' '

'Sounds out of order to me.'

'To me, too, but the force is supposed to run like any other business nowadays. With accountants calling the shots. So we get fewer police for more criminals, and they describe it as skills management! What we call it is bloody stupid, and that's the polite phraseology! Sorry. I won't go on about it, it's not your beef.'

'You do sound blue. Shall I come round and cheer you up?'

'No, don't, I'm flaked. I'd be lousy company. I've just spent a day and a half doing endless paper-checking just to make quite sure a clever slag doesn't get away with his fiddling, and that I didn't leave a loophole he could slip through . . . and that's on top of everything else I've had to do! Sorry, love, I'm just going to crawl into bed and *sleep*.'

Hanging up the phone a moment or two later, Jane wondered whether the small pause before he had said 'Okay' meant that he was offended. Surely not, when he usually understood the pressures of her work? And he was the one who had had to disrupt their weekend, not so long ago. She felt far from sociable tonight, though — even with him. No, it was all right, he had sounded as calm as ever when they finally said goodnight. And she had said she would see him very soon.

The barbecue he had wanted her to go to might be rained off anyway: it was still showery on and off, clouds hanging heavy then sweeping off to be followed by more, dark grey and threatening.

A night's sleep seemed to have cleared the muzziness in her head caused by having to check almost endless papers to make sure the CPS had them all — and against constant interruptions — so that Jane made her way to work next morning feeling almost sanguine about the rest of the paperwork which had, inevitably, heaped itself up on her desk. She could even admire the highpiled sky, lighter today, as she walked through a drift of leaves blown into the station yard from the chestnut trees outside. Autumn had thoroughly set in. She slid her entry-card into the electronic lock at the back of the station, and caught up with Kenny who must have come in just ahead of her.

'Morning. Hey, you look as if you've had a night of it!' she commented, taking in a weariness in his movements and the dark shadow on a chin not recently shaven. 'We haven't got any night surveillances on at the moment, so what went down?'

'The Drugs Unit's dawn raid. We've only just got back.' He took in the lift of her eyebrows and added, 'You didn't know about it? I thought someone said the info came from you. Must have been wrong. The Lymans Farm place?'

'*What?*'

'Lymans Farm. Out at Lymans Oak. A bunch of New Agers,' Kenny said patiently. 'No one had caught up with the fact that they were there, apparently, but when it came to light, the Drugs Unit lot decided that could be just the place for this 'E' factory they've been hunting. It was a chance, I suppose,' he added on a sigh, 'there *could* have been some clever-clogs young idiot among them with a chemistry degree and the ability to manufacture the stuff! So they got a warrant and we made a swoop and fairly tore the place apart. And got zilch. Well, two cannabis plants growing in pots on a windowsill, and a lump of resin which certainly wasn't enough to allow for a charge of dealing. But — '

'But?' Jane prompted as he paused.

'Oh, it was a mess, really. Yeah, all right, I suppose we had to try it — John Clay's lot certainly seemed to think so — but chopping holes in partition walls, and getting little kids dragged out of their beds, when there was nothing at the end of it . . . Well. If they didn't like us to start with, and they didn't, they certainly won't now!' He looked at Jane with an air of puzzlement. '*Wasn't* it you who set the whole thing in train? Something about Old Mary having a lot of money and it might have been for carrying drugs for this lot? Sounded a bit unlikely to me that anyone would have risked using her as a courier, but that seems to have been the idea that was flying about!'

Jane's jaw dropped. It might have been a reason for the old woman's unexpected wealth, she supposed. 'I hadn't got round to drawing any conclusions,' she said, 'and I certainly didn't pass the word.' She had mentioned to the custody sergeant that the money was Old Mary's, and a mystery, when she logged it in. Other than that who had she talked to about the connection between Old Mary and Lymans Farm? Ellen. And after that Jane had been too busy to pursue matters any further for the moment. 'Oh, damn,' she said half under her breath, 'damn and damn! It never occurred to me — I wish someone had thought to come and ask me!'

'And no one did? I think they set the raid up in a hurry, on the idea that bunch might have been tipped off. But, anyway, it was a no show.' Kenny gave her a wry look. 'And like I said, if the police weren't popular before, we certainly aren't now! They pulled one lad in for the cannabis, and for giving us a lot of aggro — tall kid with long black hair — but I doubt if it'll even come to a charge. Anything else you want to know, Sarge? Because if not, I'm off for a cup of strong black coffee!'

Jane let him go. It sounded as if it must be Rocky in custody. Lymans Farm as the site of the 'E' factory could have been a possibility, she supposed; she hadn't exactly seen all round it. But if there really had been a connection between Old Mary's money, her presence out at the rave and the farm, then surely Kieron wouldn't have handed the cash over to Jane and talked about 'Old Mary knowing something about somebody'. And she had had it in mind to ask him more about that, after she had discovered just how much of a stash Old Mary had had. She had made that much of a connection.

Not a hope of getting any co-operation out of Kieron now, after the raid Kenny had described. The Drugs Unit's eager leap to conclusions had certainly put the kybosh on that.

And it was annoying that no one had consulted her. Jane moved quickly towards the collator's office, to see if Ellen could tell her how that had all happened.

Ellen was alone, her usual neat and tidy self, sorting through one of her innumerable filing cabinets. 'Oh, hallo. Anything I can do for you? I won't be a moment, I've just got to find something for Traffic . . . No, we haven't got it, anyway.'

'I'm just wondering how somebody managed to

add two and two and make five? This drugs raid I've just heard about?'

'The one on the farm you told me about? Yes, it's a pity it didn't come up with anything after all, isn't it? Tom Cooper seemed quite keen on it.'

DC Cooper? If he was someone Ellen had a fancy for, as the slight blush on her cheek suggested, then she had no taste. Though there was no accounting for preferences, if she really went for black leather jackets decorated with a snarling animal's head on the back, and an air of ultra-macho conceit. 'You passed on what I said about Old Mary and the hippies out at the farm to him, did you?' Jane asked.

'He came in looking for the fire report, though it hasn't come in yet, and we were chatting about that and how you were doing with Old Mary. Yes, of course I passed it on to him about the New Age Travellers — I'm surprised you didn't, it's bound to be the Drugs Unit's business!'

'And then they set up a raid on the farm? It's just that I wish they'd asked me — never mind.' It was done now, and maybe Sergeant Clay had tried to get in touch with her to get the information at first hand, at a time when she was unavailable. 'I was a bit surprised to hear it had gone down, that's all,' Jane told her.

'I think they set it up in a hurry once they'd decided. And you know how often that happens. I'm always getting landed in the middle of it: why hasn't somebody told somebody this, why didn't uniform tell CID they'd already brought that person in!' Ellen made a moue. 'I think they're a bit annoyed up in Drugs that you've been told to deal with Old Mary, actually. They feel anything to do with the rave ought to have been left to them. Particularly with the New Age connection, once that had come up. Still — they've been and had a look at these hippies now, and even if it didn't come to anything this time, they'll have had a warning, won't they?'

Guilt by association. It was a common enough view: one which Jane sometimes felt inclined to share, too, since police experience showed it was often justified. 'If not this time, a warning against next time.' She knew very well what Kieron would make of that; had already heard him on the subject. And now could certainly write him off as a source of further information.

'I'm sorry if the Drugs Unit don't like it that I've got Old Mary on my plate,' she told Ellen. 'It was the DCI's choice, and they can have her with my blessing if they want her! I'd better have a word with John Clay about it, I suppose.'

She did, later. She would have gone up to the Drugs Unit's office on the first floor to do so, but caught him in the canteen instead. His DCs were there too, Tom Cooper and Neil Bettley — the latter a shy-looking young man, wearing a jumper which looked as if it had been hand-knitted for him by his mother. He and his partner could scarcely be more of a contrast, since Neil Bettley was gangly and spotty-faced while Tom Cooper had a smooth hard-edged air and a compactly muscled frame. They were sitting at a different table from their sergeant who was brooding over what looked like the remains of a late breakfast, and in conversation with a duty-sergeant from uniform who was a mate of his. Jane crossed to stand over them.

'John, mind if I join you for a minute? I just wanted a word.'

'I'm off,' Sergeant Morris said amiably, pulling out his chair. 'Have this one, I've kept it warm for you! John, bad luck again about this morning, but don't let it get you down. It might have let you put the 'E' business to sleep, so it was worth a try.'

'You've heard we drew a blank?' John Clay asked, giving Jane a look as his colleague moved away. 'It's all right, I'm not blaming you. I meant to send you down a thanks for the information when Ellen passed it on, if I'd got round to it. A bunch of New Agers keeping themselves suspiciously quiet on our patch — it had to be worth a look.'

'I didn't exactly . . . Look, something else Ellen passed on, but in the other direction this time. She mentioned this morning that you were a bit cheesed off with my being given Old Mary to sort out. That she ought to be yours. If you feel like that, by all means — '

'No skin off my nose,' he said, in prompt disclaimer. 'Why? Oh, because she was there, you mean, and a tie-up with the hippy bunch? She's got no more connection to drugs than you or I, to my mind: the idea that she might have been carrying the stuff for them was just a floater someone came up with. Something to do with her having money. I'd guess she pinched it. Anyway, the farm's in the clear now. It's a maddening one, that,' he added wistfully, 'it could have answered a whole lot of questions. They'd have had room to be making 'E' out there, they could have got the pill-making equipment. Even if they were only processing the stuff we could have squeezed them until they coughed a few names . . . Oh, well, no use thinking of that now, there wasn't a sign of anything, hidden or open!'

'And you had a thorough search, I gather? But about Old Mary . . . '

'No interest. Not now. I'd imagine the poor old bat must have thought she was hearing voices again when the rave started up, but since there's no proof of a drugs connection what happened to her after that isn't my bag.' He pushed back his chair and began to get up. 'Just shuffle a few papers and get her put in the ground is my advice. I don't know about you, but I'm a lot too busy to worry overmuch about a drunk schizophrenic who happens to fry herself to a crisp!'

The words were more practical than harsh: an accidental death, a body, so what? As he walked away, Jane knew that he was certainly in no mood to listen to any new theories she might produce. Which were still, in any case, half-baked . . . even if they might eventually connect Old Mary to the drug world. 'Knowing something about somebody.' And a stash of money. Possible blackmail? Something the old woman had seen on the streets which might let her put the bite on someone? And a drug dealer was the most obvious candidate.

No, certainly no use putting that to John Clay at the moment; he had just had one failure due to information he thought had come directly from her. If she wanted to put anything else to him, it would have to be a lot more than vague. And 'knowing something about somebody' *could* be just a question of hearing imaginary voices — that would be his first, and scornful, reaction, Jane was well aware. And, in any case, the information that Old Mary had had some secret knowledge came from Kieron.

As did the idea that her death might not be accidental. That somebody had killed her. That would fit with Jane's blackmail theory — if someone had wanted the old woman out of the way, for what she knew. It would fit all too neatly with the autopsy report, too; a broken neck, death before the fire started, someone else starting it to conceal murder . . .

Damn the fact that she could expect no further co-operation from Kieron now. He had been bitter enough already. After the tearing apart of his home — on what he would probably assume was her say-so — she could scarcely see him offering any help to the police at all.

She got up in her turn, and as she crossed the canteen to the door was aware of Tom Cooper's eyes raking her over. That assessing look, as if he was judging her like livestock, was typical of his type: macho man, feeling entitled to judge tits and bum and ankles on any female who passed him by. Jane walked on coolly, ignoring him. There were always one or two around any station; luckily for him she didn't have to work with him, or he would soon grow out of looking at her with that barely concealed leer. She forgot him as she moved into the corridor, her mind returning to its current concerns.

It was frustrating to know that she could merely be building castles in the air. Without more information it was just one death, and of a vagrant at that. Maybe it was all as simple as it had seemed in the first place.

Why kill Old Mary anyway? As Kieron had said, she wasn't the sort of person to whom anyone would listen. So why would it be necessary to get her out of the way?

# 6

'No, sir, I'm sorry, I haven't quite finished with it yet. I'm still waiting for the final details from the Fire Assessors, and I haven't tracked down a surname yet either. There are still one or two things I might try, to find out her proper identity.'

'You really should have managed that by now. There must be a record of her somewhere,' the DCI snapped, and gave Jane a minatory look. 'You must keep up with the things you're asked to do, Sergeant Perry!' Having satisfied himself with that open reprimand — doubly unfair, since he was perfectly well aware that he had had several other meticulous reports from Jane this morning — he turned his head to congratulate Peter Pettigrew for having been observant enough to link a caretaker with a school theft, with a resultant rapid clear-up of the crime. The deadpan faces round the room showed that everyone was aware he was playing favourites again. It really got him nowhere, Jane thought grimly, and perhaps she was lucky in that. It was an irritation, just the same, to be the butt of his endless undermining tactics.

'You're off tomorrow in lieu of the weekend, aren't you, Sarge? I'm planning to make another round of the antiques dealers then. Want me to take that ring with me and see if anyone recognises it?' That was Kenny Barnes, after the DCI's departure, offering her some amiable back-up.

'Thanks, that might be a help. I don't know if it'll get you anywhere. I doubt if Old Mary came from round here originally, so I don't suppose the initials will mean much — a family crest might have been more help. You must be getting quite knowledgeable about the trade,' she told Kenny with a grin, knowing that he had been footslogging it round the antiques fairs as a regular occupation, and between all his other tasks, to keep an ongoing presence felt and his ear to the ground in response to the Met's request. 'Are you going to be able to tell us all what to invest in to make a profit?'

'The prices they ask, we'd need more than a pay-rise to invest in anything! Do you know, you can get stung for a tenner for one old cigarette card nowadays? And they're even calling gasmasks, like my granny used to have left over from the war, 'antiques' now.'

'I suppose they are. Maybe you'd better go through your attic and see if you can make a fortune!'

'Chance'd be a fine thing! You couldn't offload broken rollerskates and Scalextric stuff with most of the parts missing even at a boot fair. And the sort of jewellery Val's got certainly wouldn't interest this thieving ring they think's moving the stuff across to the continent! That last list they sent me a couple of weeks ago doesn't half show that some people lead a different life. 'Miniature surrounded by emeralds, estimated price £100,000' — 'Snuffbox with ruby' — 'Antique diamond brooch, value £17,000' — if you leave that lot on display, you're asking for someone to break into your country mansion with nicking in mind!'

'And the stuff's too recognisable to turn up in open view, so that makes your constant trekking a bit of a bummer.' Jane pulled a sympathetic face at him, knowing the general feeling was that they were just going through the motions: whatever was being whisked out of the country, it would be doing so in a concealed fashion. 'I suppose they were bound to ask us, being near the coast and all. And our traders do a lot of perfectly legal exporting. You could hide that stuff inside all sorts of other things and try and get it through on the nod.' She gave him another grin for his shrug of acknowledgement, both of them well aware that Dan Crowe had done his share of fulminating over the waste of his manpower's time, with the view that since they had not a hint of a result, the whole thing was really a Customs problem. 'Okay, then, I'll let you have that ring before I go off tonight — just in case it might bring me something! And thanks.'

It seemed a vain hope. Old Mary couldn't take

up any more of her time today, anyway, whatever the DCI's views: there had been several more break-ins and other various crimes over the weekend for her to continue to process. Even taking Tuesday off, her due after a weekend's working, would set her behind . . . It would give her a lazy day, though, to prepare for going out to dinner in the evening and in a non-work mood. Quentin Hurst, Adrian's partner, had issued an invitation for them to spend an evening at his house. It was timed for her day off, Adrian had said with an air of determination, so he had already accepted for both of them.

'Okay, fine.' She had not met Quentin so far. 'He knows about you and me then, does he?'

'It came up, the way things do. It's not going to be a problem, is it? You did say Tuesday was the next time you were free.'

'No problem at all, so you needn't make it sound as if I'm deliberately unsociable,' Jane said lightly. 'Tell me again, he's got a wife called Marilyn and they live in Fordwich? Mm, that's one of the prettier villages, isn't it?'

'They like it. I'll pick you up about seven-forty-five, then, the invitation's for eight.'

His car, a Range Rover suitable for country fields, was still comfortable enough for riding on ordinary roads. Being Adrian's, it was also clean enough not to give Jane any worries about the dress she had chosen to wear, with its knee-length floaty skirt in bright floral colours. Since she had forgotten to ask whether the evening was a party or a casual dinner invitation, she had picked something semi-formal which would do for either. She was out of the swim of local social mores. Their arrival, at a house set back from the road at the edge of the village, showed a pleasantly elegant building in mellow old brick, with gable-ends suggesting antiquity. It stood behind a wall pierced with wrought-iron gates, a sweep of gravel drive edged with lawn leading up to the front door. No other cars were parked there, so either they were first or the evening was intended as a foursome.

'Nice house,' Jane commented.

'Yes, isn't it? They bought it last year.'

'Dinkies? Dual Income No Kids,' she translated to Adrian's raised eyebrows. 'Sorry, it's probably out of date slang by now, even if I only heard it the other day!'

'Quentin's got two children from his previous marriage, but they live with his ex-wife.' They were out of the car by now. 'Marilyn's — oh, hi, Quentin. We've arrived, as you see!'

This was addressed to the man who had appeared welcomingly in the doorway, the door opened before they could reach it. Quentin, Jane thought instantly and with amusement, *was* what she would have expected in a vet: tall, fair, weatherbeaten, bluff of figure and of manner, and with a wide and hearty smile.

He gave her a piercing look along with his welcoming smile. 'Glad you could come! So you're this Jane Adrian's always on about? Sorry, sorry . . . ' He gave Adrian a clap on the shoulder in laughing apology. 'Come on in! It's just us. I thought you wouldn't mind if we didn't drag in all sorts of other people. Anyway we want to get

91

to know you, Jane. Coat? Right, I'll put it on this hanger here. Do you want to freshen yourself? You don't look as if you need it!'

The smile he gave her reached his light blue eyes, and seemed to be appreciative — but with a degree of assessment there too behind it, she thought. From his previous words, there was a touch of 'Let's see what my partner's getting himself into'. She smiled back, shook her head at the offer of the cloakroom, and let herself be ushered in through a pleasantly panelled hall into a charming room, wide and comfortable, a picture window stretching across its width to give a view of the garden behind the house. It should have been duskily invisible, but was lit by a couple of lamps to show a patio, then lawn receding into trees and flowerbeds beyond. And Marilyn — it must be she — appeared from a door which apparently led through to a kitchen, a little breathless but echoing her husband's welcoming smile.

She must be twenty-five to her husband's — what? — forty, with a certain nervousness in her manner indicated by a plethora of gestures and a habit of smoothing her dark hair away from her face. She was slender but well endowed, gold jewellery cascading down her neck into her cleavage, and her eager, bright-eyed greeting of Jane had the air of someone who wanted very much to be liked. 'Oh, hal*lo* — I'm so glad you could come!' she said, seizing Jane's hand to give it a formal shake, then letting it go again with a laugh. 'Adrian, how lovely to see you, you don't come and see us often enough!'

'That's because he sees me far too often at work,' Quentin put in with one of his hearty laughs. 'Come on, people, sit down. What can I offer you to drink? I think we've got most things. Sherry? Whisky? Gin? Campari? Or I believe there's some vodka somewhere, if anyone fancies that?'

'What a lovely house,' Jane said, offering the polite preliminaries as she was settled into an armchair with a glass of sherry.

'Yes, isn't it? We absolutely fell in love with it. It's terribly expensive here, of course, being a conservation area and everything, but it was just the sort of house you dream about. It's lovely having this much garden, too. In the summer we always have our drinks outside. As long as it isn't as wet as it's been recently! Thank you, darling,' Marilyn said as Quentin handed her a sherry, darker and sweeter than Jane's. 'I'll probably have to take it with me in a minute while I flit in and out of the kitchen . . . You're not a vegetarian or anything, are you?' she asked Jane with sudden anxiety.

'No, I eat anything, thanks. And with gratitude when I haven't had to cook it,' Jane added, with a grin and a sidelong look at Adrian.

'You don't like cooking? Goodness, I love it! If you'll excuse me, I really had better just go and see . . . You did tell them it was only us, didn't you, Quentin? I would have asked Helen and Andrew, some neighbours of ours, to make up the numbers, but they're away,' Marilyn said apologetically to Jane, as if she might be accused of falling down on a hostess's duties. 'It's really a shame because I know you would have liked them — everybody does!'

93

She flitted away without waiting for an answer. Quentin cast an affectionate and tolerant look after her. 'Marilyn really does like to cook,' he told Jane, 'we'd be having non-stop dinner parties if it was up to her! How are you getting on with that sherry — ready for some more? And how long have you lived in this area? We don't seem to have run into each other before.'

'I've just realised that we have,' Jane answered him. 'I know we haven't actually met, but I had the feeling I'd seen you before, and it's just come to me where. The sports club? The one off St Stephens?'

'I play squash there. Good heavens, don't say you're a member too, and I haven't noticed you?'

'No reason why you should have. I don't play squash, I exercise in the gym.' With fitness a requisite for the job, she had found it practical to join a proper sports club with a suitable range of machines for working out her muscles. 'Since the place opened it's been a plus for the city, hasn't it? It seems to be able to provide everything that opens and shuts!'

'Yes, they're quite well equipped. I don't know about you, though, but I could do without that PA system of theirs.'

'You don't go for music piped into every room? They haven't gone so far as to put speakers in the squash courts, surely?'

'No, they haven't been that foolish — rather too much risk of getting them knocked off the walls! — but there's a couple in the gallery, and when they stop the music to give out an announcement, it can be quite a distraction. You can imagine it — there you are concentrating like mad, and there's a sudden bleep and a voice demanding that so and so call at the desk, and the ball whistles by your head while you're still taking it in.' Quentin gave a hearty laugh. 'Or that's my excuse, anyway!'

'Sounds like a good way to get a point replayed,' Jane said, grinning at him. 'I must say, it hasn't bothered me much. It's all so much aural wallpaper when I'm pedalling away on one of their infernal machines.'

'I must look out for you. Are you often there keeping yourself in shape?' His eyes suggested an approval of that shape. He added with a teasing smile and a glance at his partner: 'You should get Adrian to take part too, I've never even managed to get the lazy so-and-so to come and join me in a game!'

'I'm ball-blind,' Adrian retorted amiably.

'So you say, though I'm not sure if I believe it! Nor your claim that hauling sheep around is enough exercise for anybody. Do you keep fit by choice, Jane?' Quentin asked, returning his attention to her. 'Or is it something they expect of you in your job? Adrian tells me you're one of our noble police.'

'I am in the force, yes, and they do expect us to keep in shape. Do you know that you and Adrian are the first pair of vets I've met? I don't know why I've had that gap in my life up to now! Particularly when my father's actually got a share in a sheep-farm — though he didn't take it up until he retired from the army.'

That moved the conversation nicely away from a

chat about the police which she had hoped to avoid tonight, knowing from experience that it either made outsiders feel awkward or intrigued them so much that they started asking endless questions about the cases she had to handle. By the time she had finished explaining that her parents were actually in New Zealand, though she had not been born or grown up there, Marilyn was back, and after some more general chatter they were ushered through into a very decorative dining room. This was panelled again in light wood, though only halfway up the walls this time and with a pale silky wallpaper above it. Someone with good taste (and plenty of money) had obviously set their touch on the house.

Even with only the four of them, the meal was distinctly formal and produced with a lot of care: melon cut into shapes and decorated; veal with an excellent sauce, potatoes done in a special way and vegetables clearly chosen for their colour combination; an elaborate pudding . . . Marilyn had obviously done it all herself, but managed to produce everything at the right moment with only the barest flurry, an enviable skill. If that was the kind of skill you wanted. Jane wondered if that was how Marilyn spent all her time. There was certainly no mention during a wide-ranging conversation of her having any other job.

It was all very pleasant, and she did manage to steer the chat away from police work, even though Quentin seemed inclined to try to return to it. Marilyn conscientiously produced a regular stream of other topics of interest, like who had seen what at the theatre, and whether the festival had been a good one this year, and what everyone thought of the latest political scandals. At the end of the leisurely meal she whisked Jane off upstairs, offering a small, sweet scolding to the men with, 'And don't you two dare start talking shop again, I'll expect the coffee to be ready by the time we come down! Quentin darling, you'll see to that, won't you?'

'All right, sweetie, I know it's my job!'

'Are you hoping they might do the washing up as well?' Jane asked, on the stairs. 'I was going to ask if we shouldn't lend a hand with it.'

'Oh, *goodness*, no, it'll all go in the machine!' Marilyn looked quite horrified at the prospect of guests weighing in with offers of help, but disguised it with a little laugh. 'Quentin only makes the coffee because he's so good at it — Kenyan Blue with a touch of South American. Getting the mix exactly right is an art, he says.'

Jane accepted a visit to the guest bathroom — very well equipped with fluffy towels — and gave Marilyn a smile as she was summoned into the master bedroom for reapplication of lipstick. 'This really is a lovely house — did you buy it like this, or do it up yourselves?'

'Quentin gave me a free hand with the redecorating. Do you really like it? It took me months choosing the right colours and materials.' Marilyn looked round with a becoming air of deprecation, though Jane could certainly have found no fault with anything. 'I'd have quite liked to have trained in interior decoration, it's always interested me — keeping the character of a place, you know?'

'I wouldn't have thought you'd have needed any training, you've obviously got a talent for it already. Do you do something else — as a job, I mean?'

'No. I used to be a secretary before we were married, but — ' Marilyn blushed a little, ' — I'd like to start a family. It just hasn't happened yet, but I don't want to take on anything else if . . . Well, you know how it is.'

'Yes, I see. Don't you get bored doing nothing else in the meantime? Sorry, that wasn't supposed to be a rude question, and you've obviously had enough on your hands making the house so beautiful. I was only thinking . . . I know how busy Adrian is, Quentin must be the same,' Jane said, trying to be tactful rather than admitting she could not imagine sitting in a house — however beautiful — without a job of her own. 'You could — oh, cook professionally, to judge by tonight, and go in for gourmet freezer meals. *And* offer people advice on home decoration. And do it all round your family when you have one. If you wanted to, of course.'

'I don't think I'd want to. It might take up too much of my time.' Rather to Jane's surprise, there was a touch of shrewdness in the other girl's eyes for a moment, as if she knew her options but had already weighed all the considerations. It was gone again as Marilyn gave her wide, nervous smile and a flutter of her hands. 'I'd rather be here for Quentin when he *is* free . . . though I must say it does worry me when he goes off flying. It would be so awfully easy for him to crash, however good he is at it. Please don't tell him I said it bothered me,' she added in a quick appeal, 'it'll sound as if I'm grumbling about him having a hobby which takes him away as well as work, and I'm not.'

'Oh, does he fly? What sort of planes — those little light ones? I've always fancied going up in one of those!'

'Have you? I wish I did. He took me up once and it gave me vertigo. You're lucky Adrian hasn't got a passion like that. Quentin's been a pilot for years and he loves flying. My husband with his head in the clouds.' She pulled a face, half amused, half resigned. 'But I warn you, if you ask him to take you up, don't be surprised if you find yourself stuck at Manchester or somewhere because the weather's closed in — that's *just* the sort of thing which always seems to happen! So please don't encourage him by saying you want a trip. You won't, will you?'

There was something behind the light words, but Marilyn had whisked out of the room before Jane could pin it down. Following her back down the stairs, it was impossible not to wonder whether she did, in fact, resent the fact that her husband's hobby took him away from her a little too often, and would rather no one set him off on talking about a passion she did not share. Which made it a surprise when Marilyn swept into the sitting room saying brightly, 'I was just telling Jane about your plane, darling. She was frightfully interested, so you can tell her all about the flying club!'

'Oh, er — interested, are you, Jane? That's more than you could say for Adrian, but maybe that's because I *will* get stuck at points north and leave him holding the baby.'

'Like the other weekend, for instance,' Adrian said drily.

'I know, I know, I should never have been tempted to go up for a spin on the Friday, I've already had a telling off for my tardiness from my wife — haven't I, darling? Bloody instrument problem. It grounded me for two whole days at the other end of the country.' Quentin offered that with an air of repentance. 'I'm banned from talking about anything to do with the air for — how long, sweetie?' He gave Marilyn one of those looks which suggested a family quarrel with its echoes still resounding. 'Now then, coffee, everybody — and a snifter with it? Not for you, Jane? I know you won't, darling. Adrian?'

'Did you have to deal with that rave which happened at the airfield the other week?' Marilyn asked, coming back into the conversation and raising her eyebrows at Jane, with an air of being determined to show that she did after all tolerate the subject of flying, and by so doing would show the forgiveness of her nature. 'We read about it in the paper and Quentin was quite annoyed about it, weren't you, darling? Such wanton destruction, with the fire and everything.'

'At least it was an unused place,' her husband said, 'or, possibly, some of the instructors may have used that field for landing practices with their pupils, but it's probably too much of a mess for that now. If a rave turned up at one of the fields in use, they'd get short shrift — bloody cheek!

We've got security guards at our club when the place is empty.' He was busying himself handing out cups of coffee as he talked, and it did smell as nice as Marilyn had promised. 'Anyone would be annoyed, though — bunch of out-of-control kids mucking about on other people's property! I hope someone's suing their parents for every stick and stone of the damage! Is that police business, Jane? Seeing the malefactors get stung, as well as locking 'em up?'

'No, we don't even decide who gets prosecuted nowadays. We just catch them, and then the Crown Prosecution Service takes over. You'd better not start me on that,' Jane said lightly, with a grin at Adrian. 'It's one of the things I'm known to grumble about!'

'You grumble, and I listen. It's no worse than examining a cat with canker,' Adrian said — a bland retort which sent Quentin into guffaws, and Jane into a laughing threat to slap him.

'Isn't it rather an unpleasant life in the police?' Marilyn asked, looking somewhere between dubious and genuinely curious. 'After all, the kinds of people you're dealing with . . . That's not a silly question, it *can't* be very nice!'

'It isn't, some of the time. But it's a job somebody has to do.'

'By all means!' Quentin brought out heartily, at the same time as Adrian came back in with, 'And a job Jane's keen on. You've got a real career lady here, Marilyn, so it's no use thinking you'll get her to admit there are too many disadvantages to it! Still . . . you don't have to make a close study of the rear end of cows, I suppose she'd say, or come home with a tick attached to your ankle and having a good feed!'

'Adrian, please!' Marilyn reproached him with a shudder. '*Not* when we've just been eating. I know I married a vet, but my goodness, there's a time and a place!'

'Sorry,' he told her, with one of his nicer smiles. 'Go on, change the subject and I promise I'll behave. Oh, what's the latest on that planning permission argument for the houses at the back of here? Have you heard yet whether you've managed to scotch it?'

★ ★ ★

'That was a good evening,' Jane commented, much later, leaning back in the passenger seat as Adrian turned the Range Rover round expertly to take them out of the drive. Their host and hostess stood on the step waving them off, having apparently been so unwilling to let them go that it was now one a.m. 'And it was nice of Marilyn to say how glad she was to have met me finally.'

'I expect she meant it.'

'Really? What on earth can you have been saying about me?' She made it a light tease — while wishing he had let her drive, since she had stuck to coffee for the latter part of the evening and Adrian had not. Unfortunately her suggestion that she should take the wheel had met with a prompt no. 'Quentin's quite a charmer, too, isn't he?'

'He's the gregarious type.' Adrian made a turn

for the more countrified route back. Though that was probably on the grounds that they had met roadworks on the other route, Jane was relieved. Not that he wasn't driving skilfully, but here there was less likelihood of meeting a night patrol and being given a random pull over . . . He had to be over the limit after that last whisky, however little it showed. She made herself relax, and carried on the conversation. 'I don't think you'd ever told me Quentin was a pilot, had you? Oh — '

Her gulp was an involuntary response to Adrian's swerve round a rabbit which had frozen in the middle of the road, a gleam of terrified eyes showing a startling scarlet in the headlights. 'Sorry about that,' he said, 'but it's all right, I didn't hit the fool creature! Where were we? Oh, Quentin and his plane. Didn't I tell you? I suppose it just hasn't come up.'

'Like it just hadn't come up between you and him exactly where your cottage is? He seemed almost startled to hear it was out there. I'm surprised you haven't let Marilyn look at it.'

'I don't want it done up within an inch of its life, thanks!'

'Yeah, I see, though you have to admit she's done the house beautifully. Hey, didn't you think there were a few undercurrents floating around about Quentin's flying exploits? Does he do it that much, is that why she's fed up?'

'I think that's because she knows her own husband a little too well. He's — well, fond of women, so when he goes off overnight, she's apt to wonder if it's an excuse for a fling. 'Come with me in my plane' — and then somehow a good reason for having to stop overnight.'

'Oh, I see. Yes, that makes a bit of sense.' It brought the slightly too casual words upstairs into focus. As if Marilyn had not been too sure even of Jane. Poor girl. 'Does he actually go in for flings, or does she just suspect it?'

'I wouldn't know. I do know that when his last marriage broke up — which was over Marilyn — the impression given was that she was the last straw, and the last of a string.' Adrian glanced at Jane and added with unexpected pugnacity, 'He'd better keep his hands off you!'

'Hold up! I may have said he was a charmer, but all he was tonight was sociably flirtatious — not even that, really, just paying me attention as a guest. Anyway, it goes two ways. I do have a choice in the matter, and that doesn't include other people's husbands. Idiot!' she added, with plenty of scorn, but letting her shoulder lean against his briefly.

'Good . . . Are we going back to my place or yours? I suppose if I say mine, you'll insist on creeping home in the middle of the night, since it isn't a weekend and you're working tomorrow?'

'It's just that I'm more organised if I wake up in my own place. It's easier to get my head together. But I don't mind, mine or yours.'

'We could stop having 'my place or yours' discussions at all if we moved in together. There's plenty of room for both of us to live in my flat. It's got more space than your house. Or if you don't want to move, I could.'

'It's — a bit soon, isn't it?' Jane asked, thrown off balance. This was the wrong time, the wrong place. 'I mean, we've never got as far as discussing . . . Anyway, you know my untidiness would drive you mad!' she pointed out, changing tack to a lightly rallying tone. 'Hadn't you better wait and see if I can improve?'

'We could meet that one halfway. So what about it? We could try it out in the flat — or the house — to start with. Since we're only just round the corner from each other, it wouldn't take either of us much trouble to move. We could do it this week. Tomorrow, for that matter!'

He really was serious. Suddenly, Jane didn't want to point out to him that there were complications of which he was unaware. Such as, if they shared an address he would have to be cleared by the authorities. Standard police rules. It was something which hadn't come up between them, there had been no reason to mention it . . . She couldn't even give him a key to her house, unless his background had been examined to make sure he had no criminal connections. And making their relationship official would bring everything into the public domain, subject to beady-eyed scrutiny. She had not wanted that — she *didn't* want that just now — when she had the hope of promotion coming up. She knew all too well how these things worked; there would be an immediate assumption, somewhere up the line among the top brass, that if she had other things on her mind besides her career, she was less good promotion material. Her head buzzed with all of it — and along with that was the knowledge that if turning him down meant losing him, that was something she didn't want either. 'You're driving too fast, we've just passed the thirty limit,' she warned without thinking, and then bit her lip as he braked sharply with obvious annoyance. Out of a silence, she tried to pull herself together.

'Sorry — I know that wasn't an answer, but look, you can't just throw the idea of living together at me out of the blue, when we haven't even talked about it!'

'We're practically living together now, aren't we? Except in two different places. I love you — in that overworked word nobody ever mentions properly any more — but if you haven't had time to know whether you . . .'

'I wish you'd stop and change places and let me drive. All right, this is a bloody tactless moment to say so, but if you veer like you did just then . . . We're coming into town, and if we meet a patrol they really will pull you over for something like that! Particularly since it's the end of the month and anything's grist to the figures.'

His response was to put his foot down, quite deliberately, and shoot a yellow light. 'Adrian,' Jane said between her teeth, 'you know damn well you're over the limit, and for God's sake, I'm in the car with you! What good do you think that's going to do, if you're stopped and breathalysed?'

'Make them turn a blind eye? Even if they don't, at the moment you're a private citizen!'

No, she wasn't. And never mind the problem of living together, careers could founder on very little — if the police officer in question was a woman. There had been at least one case, very publicly reported, where promotion had been blocked on the excuse of 'being present at a drunken party'. And in a situation which would just have been laughed off, for a man. Gossip, innuendo, a few jokes, that was all it took; and the city's sub-division was a small station, with DCI Morland hovering like a spectre behind Jane's shoulder. She opened her mouth to try something which would sooth Adrian's temper, cursing herself for the tactless blurting she had managed so far — and in the middle of something important to both of them! — but although he had thankfully slowed to a more decorous pace, Adrian spoke first, with a bite in his voice.

'That's it, is it? I ask you to live with me, and all I get is a lecture on my driving, and how it might affect your job? Can't you ever forget you're a cop? Or is that the whole point — your career comes first and last and in the middle? The bit where you're a woman just gets sandwiched into the cracks, if there. What would it take to get your real attention — for me to be a police superintendent, so that you'd get a leg up as well as a leg over?'

'That's not fair! Let alone that I told you right at the start that I keep my private life and my working life separate — which is why I've hardly *had* a social life since I moved here — what you've just said is bloody insulting! If that's how you really feel, I'm glad I've found out now! And you can stop the car and let me out. I'll walk the rest of the way!'

'I'm sorry. Look, I'm sorry, I didn't mean it,

it was the drink talking. You're right, I'm a lot more pissed than I thought. Quentin does hand them out. Jane, I'm *sorry*. What on earth's going on up there?'

They were halfway through the city, on a piece of road which bordered the river one side, the row of houses which backed on to it giving way to trees which curved away with the river's meandering course. Just ahead, a car had pulled up with its door open, and a man's figure was dancing up and down in front of it, while a girl was apparently trying to restrain him.

'Stop,' Jane said quickly. 'No, stop, I mean it, it isn't anything to do with quarrelling!'

'She does look as if she could do with some help.' He was already pulling in to the side of the road as he spoke. 'You stay there, I'll — '

'No, I will. That's one of our WPCs. And since — as you say — I can't ever forget I'm a cop, *I'll* go. And on my own. We can manage perfectly well without you!'

She spat that at him, still too furiously enraged to be thoroughly sensible — and with a tiny frisson of guilt to add to her fury, though she wanted not to acknowledge that just now. But she was already off and running to the pair in the road, both of whom she could recognise as she came up to them, her anger under control, training taking over.

WPC Rachel Welsh greeted her arrival breathlessly though still with a calm air, one arm trying to restrain the dancing, writhing figure of Paddy the tramp. 'Oh, it's you, Sarge, thanks for stopping! I'm out on night obs, and I wouldn't normally have pulled over, just radioed in a report, but he practically threw himself under my wheels! He's not dangerous, it's just that I can't make out what he's saying.'

Jane had guessed the girl must be out on observation from the unmarked car and the lack of uniform. It was the job of an obs car simply to tour round and keep an unobtrusive eye on things, reporting anything worth police attention. Paddy at that moment dropped into a heap on the road, mouthing and sobbing and clinging to Rachel's ankles. 'I have called it in,' WPC Welsh said, 'there should be a car here in a moment. He seems to be in a panic. Just D and D, I suppose.'

'Paddy? Pull yourself together! You know me, Detective Sergeant Perry. Pull yourself together and stop holding on to the constable's legs, do you hear me?'

There was a sob by way of answer, though the sternness of her voice seemed to get through to him and he let go, huddling himself up small. There was the abrupt sound of a siren, still distant but coming their way. Jane glanced round, to see Adrian standing hesitantly nearby. She said quickly to Rachel, 'I'll stay,' and then walked over to Adrian, to speak quietly but stiffly.

'Go home. Now. I'll get a lift. There's a squad car coming, you can hear it, and since you *are* pissed, you'd better get lost!'

'Look — '

'No, *you* look. You're just a concerned citizen, as things stand, but if I can smell the whisky on your breath, so will other people. So unless you want to

109

find *me* arresting you, along with this other drunk, get in your wheels and go!'

He was probably going to find that unforgivable, along with the stinging undertone she delivered it in — but she turned on her heel and went back to where Rachel was bending over the tramp's shabby form. She heard Adrian start the Range Rover and drive away, and the siren coming closer. But the young WPC was turning back towards her, her voice cutting with a sudden sharpness across Paddy's babble.

'I think I've got what he's saying — there's someone in the river. Come on now, Paddy, again. What was it you saw? No, try and say it calmly, then I'll understand you!'

The seamed face was streaked with tears, glinting in the lamplight as he twisted to and fro, mumbling. It seemed to be the sight of Jane again which brought his words out with sudden clarity, through his frightened and drunken tongue-tangling.

'It's Jacko! He's dead, floating. We saw him, 'n Bill's gone off up there to follow — it's Jacko, he's in the river. Oh, Holy Mary, he's dead, he's dead!'

# 7

The arrival of the squad car brought torches to shine on the river as they followed its course along a footpath which led along the side of a large car park, and then past a school to come out at the Kingsmead road the other side. 'The River Walk', so called, had opened a couple of years ago with signposts put up for the tourists. In the darkness, there was an eerie quality to the winding path with its landscaping of trees, the dancing torchlight catching on sweeping branches dipping low into the river on the other side (a wooded island, unreachable and unused) and the dark gleam of the water chuckling high against the banks. After the recent rain, it was higher and more fast-flowing than usual. In summer, the river was a more torpid creature than this, winding a slow and decorative way through this piece of city greenness and gurgling across stony shallows in a gleam of rusty yellow, the russet of old thrown-away bricks showing here and there on its pebbled bottom. Tonight, it was a place of swirls and eddies curling from bank to bank, a muddy brown tide moving inexorably onwards.

Paddy stumbled ahead of them as they made their search. After a few moments there was a husky 'Yoohoo!' from somewhere up ahead, and the swaying figure of Bill — strawberry nose and all — appeared in the torchlight, waving an unsteady arm.

'Here — over here — 's' come into the bank, but I can't get close enough . . . '

'Here, let me, Sarge.' The burlier one of the two night patrol constables pushed past Jane quickly to make a scramble for the bushes where Bill was pointing, his partner following him. His voice came back with, 'Yeah, that's it all right. George, hang on to my arm and I'll try to heave him up before he floats away again . . . Hang on to something else as well, you nana, or we'll both go in! Here, you, give us a hand — yes, you can, get hold of that branch and then reach for the leg . . . All right, if you can't, take the torch and shine it down!'

Jane signed to Rachel to keep Paddy back, and moved to where she could see. A dark waterlogged shape near the bank, with a ballooning overcoat keeping it buoyant . . . Bill was holding a wavering beam on the scene, while the constables were linked together for stability and the burly one leaned down, struggling to get a proper grip. 'Anything I can do?' she called.

'Don't think so, Sarge, there isn't room and it'd be too many cooks. I think I've got him, if I can just — George, get an arm round my waist, will you? Then I can give a real pull and see if I can't roll him out!'

They were lucky the zigzagging current had brought the body close against this bank, not the other. The roots of a bush seemed to have held it there, for the moment at least. With a grunt, the constable gave a heave — and then he and his partner were suddenly tumbling backwards in a tangle of shadowy arms and legs, several muffled curses sounding clearly.

'Damn and fucking hell! No, it's all right, he did come half out before I let go! Quick, George — '

They had scrambled back and were tugging at the shape half in and half out of the water, their hands getting a better purchase now. Jane moved quickly to take the torch from Bill, aware of the reek of cheap spirits on his breath. She shooed him back gently out of the way so that she could shine the beam steadily on the constables' labours. They had done well to get the body out: it would have been a bad option if the floating thing had moved away again and one of them had had to plunge in to try and rescue it. No real rescue either from the look of things. The dead weight, and the way it had been floating face down, suggested Paddy had been right.

'No life,' one of the constables said, confirming it, his hands busy somewhere around the neck. 'No, he's definitely a goner. It's Jacko, isn't it? Bloody old fool. I suppose he just fell in!'

'Good work getting to him, anyway,' Jane told them. She could hear Paddy starting a muffled keening behind her. And Rachel Welsh's voice — with steady efficiency — making the necessary call on her personal radio that an ambulance was needed. 'Are you two all right? Apart from wet and muddy?'

'No problems, Sarge. We'll just heave him up on to the path . . . Good thing he was seen tonight. Would have been nasty for the little kids coming to school tomorrow morning if he'd still been here where they could see him.'

'Yes, a shock. He doesn't look as if he's been in the water long.' The body lay on its back now, in a wet sprawl of dripping arms and legs and tangled clothing. And Jacko's bony face turned up whitely in the torchlight; closed eyes, the gleam of a sharp nose, hair and beard a straggly darkness.

'It's probably the cleanest he's ever been, poor old sod,' the constable called George said, his voice showing how much the casual joke was probably reaction.

'Yeah. Upstream from here ... He probably went in off that path opposite the Miller's Arms, at a guess. There's no wall there to stop anyone. Can't have been higher up or he'd've been caught in the millrace. Unless he went in at the other arm, by the Causeway. Sarge, d'you want to leave it to us, now? I mean, you don't look — '

'No, I was coming back from an evening out and stopped when I saw something going on. If that's all right with you, I may as well take off. I'll put in my penn'orth for the report in the morning — this one's not going anywhere.' A second distant siren suggested that another squad car was coming, or it might be the ambulance. 'Well done again for getting him out,' she told the constables, giving them a smile as she handed the torch back, adding, 'and for not getting a ducking while you were doing it, too. That water's flowing a bit fast for comfort, let alone that it's probably mucky!'

As she moved away, another squad car was drawing up on the road; she saw too that Bill had staggered to a halt and was doubled over throwing up. Though thankfully not over WPC Welsh's shoes. It was rapidly established with the newcomers that they would take the two vagrants in. 'Give them a dry bed for the night, anyway, after we've got a statement out of them,' somebody said. 'If they're sober enough to give us statements before morning!' It was agreed too that Rachel Welsh should go on with her obs duties. The WPC hesitated, then looked at Jane.

'I could drive you home, Sarge, since I'm touring round.'

'Thanks, if you wouldn't mind?'

In the car, Jane glanced across at the girl at the wheel. 'Sure you don't want to go back to the station for a bit? You'd be entitled, after finding a body.'

'No, I'm fine, Sarge, honestly. I didn't do much except stand around, anyway.'

'Cool as a cucumber?' Jane asked with a smile. She had worked with Rachel Welsh from time to time, and had found her likeable as well as intelligent and efficient. She knew, too, that the young WPC had ambitions to get into CID eventually. 'Do you like night obs?'

'Yes. And it's a start for being non-uniform,' Rachel said with a grin.

'Still a glutton for that kind of punishment? We're getting more mixed up these days anyway, what with Victim Support visits being done out of uniform, and all this team business which goes across the demarcation lines.' Jane caught herself out in a sudden small shiver. The lateness of the hour. Jacko's body. 'We do seem to be losing our vagrants lately,' she said idly, 'that's two this month. It's just along here, Rachel, you can drop me at the corner — thanks.'

'No trouble, Sarge. I just thought, since your friend had gone home — I hope you had a good party before all this came up, anyway. Goodnight.'

The mention of Adrian was a reminder of their quarrel. The bitter, stinging words came back like an echo as Jane let herself in at her front door. If that was how he really felt . . . If that was how he really felt, perhaps she had given him cause. She would have preferred not to face that. Why did her job have to bring such added problems, ones which surely didn't affect other people's careers? Or perhaps they did. But surely not so much extra care, so many restrictions, such a hedging about of one's private life!

And Jacko. Poor old Jacko. It was only the other day that she had been talking to him about Old Mary.

She stopped suddenly in the middle of her bedroom, with her dress half off over her head. Then she pulled it right off, but slowly, her mind moving along new channels.

First Old Mary. Then Jacko. And what was that impression she had had — that Jacko had been afraid when he heard of Old Mary's death?

Maybe she was being imaginative. Maybe there was no connection. Unless there was something going on that more than one of the vagrants knew about . . . Something that made news of the death of one of them a warning of danger?

Had there been any others in the vagrant population who had died recently, in casual, easily explained accidents, which might not be accidental at all?

She was running ahead of herself too fast. She had no real grounds to assume there was a killer out there. Jacko's drowning had the simplest and most innocent scenario in the world: a drunken stumble on an unfenced path.

'Sarge? You're not going to believe this, but I've got a result for you! And it came up as casually as anything, before I'd even got the ring out to show the bloke!'

Kenny's beaming face was full of triumph. 'Old Mary,' he said, standing foursquare in front of Jane's desk and watching her face, 'real name, Marianna Troughton-Beck. And that's the initials, isn't it? That's a T in the middle, not a J. It just looked like a J because of the curlicues! And would you believe what the old bird was, once upon a time and a good few years ago, before she turned as batty as a coot and took to the road? Go on, have a guess!'

'I couldn't even begin to. That's brilliant, Kenny, you've actually come up with her name for me? Come on, tell me how you managed that amazing bit of detection. I've been following every avenue I could think of, and come up with sod all.'

'Well, it was like this, see. I was wandering round the antiques fair someone had fixed for Tuesday at the Red Cross Centre, having a shufti and asking my usual casual question or two, and I reach this old bloke. And as soon as I've said who I am, he comes out with, 'I read in the paper about Marianna, has there been a funeral yet? Because I knew her in the old days, and I'd quite like to pay my respects.' He thought we'd have found out by now who she was, before she took to the road and turned into Old Mary. He's a travelling bloke himself, one of those casuals who goes to fairs all round the country. So then, of course, when he found out we didn't know, he told me — name, history, the lot!'

'And she was . . . ? Go on, tell me. Little as I want to spoil your fun it's no use my going through a list. All right, a brain surgeon who once operated on him? A famous opera singer?'

'You're slipping, Sarge,' Kenny said smugly. 'She was, once upon a time, a very respectable, highly reputable, and thoroughly posh antiques dealer. She had a shop in London — Chelsea — in fact it's still there, and being run by her nephews. I've got the address for you!'

'Well, I'm hornswoggled. Gobsmacked! He actually knew, and for definite, that Old Mary and this Marianna Troughton-Beck were one and the same?'

'No doubt about it. He says he's seen her around when he's been down here, but he never liked to try speaking to her. Seeing as how she'd gone so far down in the world. Most people wouldn't have known who she was, he says, but he used to do the London beat a lot in the good old days, and about ten years back he had a bit of a run in with her — as she was then — over something he'd got at an auction and she'd wanted. She was just beginning to get what he called 'temperamental' then. It was a couple of years after that when she dropped out of the scene and the polite word was that she'd had a breakdown. And, Sarge, I'd say I've got the answer for you about that money, too. Apparently these nephews of hers who run the shop now, a pair of cousins who are just called Beck without the Troughton, don't actually own the place and she still does. That's according to this helpful old bloke of mine, Reg Plimpton. And he reckons that they were sending Marianna money regularly — to keep away.'

'Good God, you've solved all of it for me in one swoop! I suppose you gave Reg Plimpton a look at the ring, to make doubly sure?'

'Of course. Definitely hers, Marianna always wore it. He wrote me a signed note identifying it. He was off to another fair up in Norfolk, and I didn't want to lose him business by asking him to stick around and talk to you. There's enough in what he told me, yes?'

'Certainly is. I'll buy you a beer, lunchtime — or something stronger! I definitely do owe you for this!'

'It was just a piece of luck. And I nearly didn't take in that fair, since it was billed as being all furniture and that isn't what we're looking for. Just goes to show what a lucky chance can do for you. Here, this is the identification of the ring Reg Plimpton gave me, and here's the notes I made on what he told me, and the address of the shop in London.'

'Thanks,' Jane said with gratitude as Kenny handed the pieces of paper over. 'I'll have to ring up these nephews ... I wonder if they know yet that she's dead? No, probably not, it wouldn't interest anyone but the local press to report it.' And that had been no more than a small paragraph on an inside page, as an addendum to the story of the rave. 'It's a piece of luck Reg Plimpton reads local papers wherever he is!'

'Dealers often scan them to see if there's any house clearances — a lot of them make their living that way, seeing what they can pick up that might be worth something.'

'You didn't get anything for your own investigation?' Jane asked, to show that she cared, though it would have been all round the department by now if he had.

'Not a hope. The honest ones look concerned, and the bent ones look as blank as Harry and hope I won't guess what else they might be doing. The people the Met want have to be big fish, and I haven't met any of those. To know about,' Kenny corrected himself with a wry look, 'though I wouldn't know, would I? If the scam they've got going *is* coming through here, it's going to be through someone who's got their connections wrapped up too tight for me to spot.'

He accepted Jane's sympathetic grin and wandered away. To other waiting tasks, to judge from the pile of files in his in-tray. Jane looked at the two sheets of paper he had handed to her, knowing that she really did owe him a favour for this. If only that fire report would finally come in, she had everything she needed for her own report now . . . All the relevant facts, anyway. Even if no answer to any theories.

But one theory was shot down. If Old Mary, alias Marianna Troughton-Beck, had been receiving a regular allowance from her nephews, there was no need to imagine her stash of money came from blackmail. It was just as well Jane had not jumped the gun and put that one to Sergeant Clay. No drug-dealer having the bite put on him; just a couple of family members paying off an inconvenient relative to keep her away, and out of their hair. Still the legal owner of the business, but mad, drunk, dirty — and very bad for trade.

Jane reached for the phone. No, better to ring the Beck nephews after she had been able to check the Fire Assessors' report.

But while she was here, and with the phone in her hand, she might just put a call through to the pathology department, and see if they had dealt with Jacko's body yet, and could confirm that he actually had drowned. Just in case . . . It was probably untrue that there was some mad vigilante out there who had decided to clear the city of its riff-raff, but such things had been known to happen — a lethal lunatic preying on the weakest and most helpless. It was the sort of whisper which often reached the police far too late, after the street people had known it for some time amongst themselves.

She found herself put through to Dr Ledyard, on duty again. That was a help since Ruth Ledyard was easier and friendlier than her boss. 'Yes, I did that one first thing,' she answered Jane's query amiably. 'Death by drowning. There's some bruising, but it's consistent with a fall. I'd imagine he hit his head as he went into the water, on the bottom possibly if it wasn't deep where he went in. I'd guess that knocked him unconscious so that he couldn't help himself. He was malnourished and he'd had a skinful to drink. You've got some reason to question it?'

'Not really, I just wanted a confirmation. A bruise on his head, you said?'

'Temporal area, probably caused by something like the corner of a brick — that would fit if he went in head first and down to the bottom with his weight behind him. The injury didn't kill him, it was water ingestion into the lungs which did that.'

'It looks straightforward then. Thanks, that was all I wanted to know. Oh — while I'm on, you remember the burned fatality from ten days ago? I'm right, aren't I, the lack of any sign of smoke in her lungs does mean she must have been dead before the fire took hold?'

'Yes . . . I haven't got my notes to hand, and I did send you the full autopsy, didn't I? Fracture of the second cervical vertebra, with an immediate stop of the autonomic nervous system. That was it, wasn't it? Death would have been almost instantaneous. I was looking for asphyxiation from smoke, but when I found there was no chance of that, I looked again to see why. In simple terms, by the time there was fire, she'd already stopped breathing.'

'Thanks, that was the way I'd translated it, but I just wanted to be sure. And I'm sorry to keep quizzing you, but I don't think you said: was that injury consistent with a fall?'

'Difficult to say. You didn't give me much to work on with that one, so have a heart, don't ask me to say if she had bruises!' Dr Ledyard gave a pleasant chuckle. 'There was virtually nothing left in the way of tissue round the head and shoulders. It was only the fact that she was wrapped up so much that gave me any organs to look at, and with those being heat-affected as well, I couldn't be at all accurate as to when she actually died.'

'Yes, I remember,' Jane said quickly, reminding herself that pathologists were always unsqueamishly practical by reason of the job. 'I was just a bit surprised, in view of the condition of the body, that it wasn't the fire which killed her. That she seemed to have been dead first. If she fell, would it have to have been fairly awkwardly, would you say?'

'Mm. All right, at an angle, certainly. And with something in the way. There was an inward fragmentation of the bone, though that can be caused by a whiplash effect, the head being thrown violently backwards. It *could* also be consistent with a hard blow at exactly the right point. You could actually have it from a karate chop . . . Now I come to think of it, I have seen that type of fracture in a fall from a height on to some railings, and that one was fatal. Vertebral fragmentation ruptures the spinal nerve sheath and causes instant paralysis, including the diaphragm and intercostals when it's as high up as that. So the person simply stops breathing. Is this being a help, or am I leaving you behind on the technical details?'

'Somewhat. But thanks anyway. And for letting me take up your time.'

'No problem. Just don't quote me as saying anything I didn't put down in the report,' Ruth

123

Ledyard said on a laugh, 'or *I'll* get it in the neck! Anything else?'

'No thanks, and thanks for your help.'

'I should be able to let you have the one on the drowning later today, if our secretarial staff haven't got too much stacked up. We've still got your burned lady here, by the way; we can release her any time you like?'

'We've only just tracked down an identity and some relatives, so I'll have to let you know about that one. Thanks again, 'bye!'

Dr Ledyard had shown no particular curiosity at being asked for further information, but then pathologists rarely did: they merely handed down their findings. Her clarification had brought Jane no definite answer. This way, that way — you could still look at the deaths two ways. Though Jacko's did seem simple . . . No one in the uniformed branch, certainly, was taking it any other way, and it was their case, an accidental drowning called in by the night shift and requiring no further investigation. Paddy and Bill had been given a bed in the cells for the night, and had given their story. Such as it was. Jane had already heard it by making a casual enquiry when she handed over a brief report to say that she had been present at the finding of the body.

'You could scarcely squeeze a word out of either of them, they were so hung over,' Sergeant Morris said with a grin. 'No hair of the dog round a cop shop! It was all pretty straight up, anyway. They'd all agreed to meet up and sleep at Solly's Orchard, opposite the Miller's. Jacko went on ahead of the

124

other two to stake their claim in case anyone else had had the same idea. It's a nice piece of shelter, and I gather the three of them had practically put their mark on the place as theirs in the recent bad weather. Paddy and this Bill came staggering along later and Jacko wasn't there. Then they saw him in the pool below the wall — it's deepish, just there, even when the river isn't running. There was something about trying to reach him with a stick, but all that did was push him out of the corner and into the current. I reckon he either went in off the path the other side and got swept across into the corner, or he was stupid enough to stand up on the wall for a piss and then tumbled off. Anyway, the rest you know — they tried to follow the body downstream, both as drunk as lords and panicking all over the place, and Paddy jumped in front of the first car he saw for help, and it was our obs. He's a very subdued lad this morning, is Paddy.' Sergeant Morris added with a touch of sympathy, 'He depended on Jacko. For brains, since he hasn't got many of his own!'

'Perhaps he'll depend on Bill now.'

'I doubt it, I think that one's going to be off, sharpish. 'I want to be on the road,' he said in that fruity voice of his, and I think he meant it. One less to bother us, so that's something! It'd be nice if he took his recent little oppo with him, but Paddy's been a fixture round here for too many years — and besides, M'lord Bill didn't look too keen. He was trying to ignore Paddy trailing after him when we let the two of them go, anyway!'

The sergeant, on custody duty today, had turned

away just then in response to the racket one of their other overnighters was making in the cells; incensed at still being incarcerated, apparently, yelling that he didn't believe nobody had been able to get hold of his brief yet. Jane had walked away thoughtfully. Nothing surprising in Paddy's being subdued, of course. Nor in Bill's abrupt decision to leave the area. But it had kept that faint question mark there in her mind, as she went back to the CID room and to her desk — to be greeted by Kenny and his news a few minutes later.

Marianna Troughton-Beck. A much more respectable name than Old Mary. And a much more respectable life, once. She would be due a proper funeral now, presumably, and one with relatives who might not actually mourn her loss, but would probably feel it decent to pretend to do so. The Beck nephews would be glad to get her finally out of the way — which was an interesting thought, though probably not a relevant one. Unless one of them happened to be an expert in karate . . .

Jane buzzed through to Ellen to ask again if the fire report she wanted had arrived (it had not) and would have rung Chief Evans to enquire politely why, if Dan Crowe had not called her in on a conference at that moment about another hijack of a TIR: its cargo had been cigarettes again, and the MO tied in with a similar one last month. She worked steadily through the day, concentrating on the jobs in hand, and the ability to switch off from unwanted thoughts. At least, she persuaded herself so. Until she arrived home in the evening, to find a large bouquet propped up against her front door.

Red roses, long-stemmed, obviously hothouse — and in a position, she thought with exasperation, where anyone could have nicked them. Though nobody had. There was no card to be seen with them, but maybe that had been put through her door . . .

She let herself in. And heard a movement in the room beyond.

Before she could do more than stiffen, Kieron came into view, blinking at her defiantly through his glasses.

# 8

'What the hell are you doing in my house?'

'Your lot didn't think twice about coming into mine!'

'Yes, well, I had nothing to do with that. I don't care whether you believe me or not!'

She was watching him carefully, and had already let the flowers and her briefcase drop to the floor, as if casually. Never underestimate a possible assailant, however apparently weedy. Never assume a situation is not dangerous. 'If you're here on a pay-back, it's not really necessary, is it?' she asked him, her voice firm but calm. 'I'm not responsible for what the entire police department does, believe it or not. And actually I was sorry when I heard about it. Do you mind telling me how you knew where I lived?'

'I followed you home the other day.'

Had he indeed? She must be slipping not to have noticed. Particularly if he had been driving that brightly painted transit van from the farm. 'And today, how did you get in?' she asked levelly. 'I hope you're not being stupid. Breaking and entering carries a charge!'

'I didn't break anything. You didn't even have a deadlock or shoot the bolts on your front door — you ought to be more careful,' he told her, with reproof in his tone and an air of righteousness which in other circumstances would have made her show her annoyance. 'All it took was for me to walk up to your door with a bag of tools as if I was a workman you'd left a key with, and let myself in with a piece of wire. No one passing would have seen it wasn't a key — don't they teach you anything? I mean, if you don't have a deadlock, the least you could have done is put the bolts on the front and let yourself out round the back, which is rather better protected, and come out by your side entrance . . .'

'Kieron, grateful as I am for your lecture on security — ' which she would take in, instead of letting herself be careless again, she knew bitterly ' — don't you think we'd better get to the point of this? What are you here for? I can't believe you'd decide to trash my place because yours was trashed — you aren't the type. I'm prepared to forget the fact that you've broken in, if you'll tell me what you want.'

'I haven't damaged *anything*, and I wasn't planning to! I don't believe in violence.' He gave

her a scornful look with that. 'I . . . I just wanted to
. . . all right, so I was proving a point as well, but
I've only come to ask you what you're doing about
Mary? And I certainly wasn't going to come to the
station to do that!' he added, scorn still in his voice,
but a stubborn defiance in his expression. 'I don't
fancy mixing with a bunch of child-frighteners and
stupid animals! But you did at least seem as if you
might — you probably don't, so perhaps it wasn't
worth the bother!'

Worth the bother or not, he abruptly dropped
into the nearest armchair. And added, with a bitter
look, 'Go on, you're nearer the phone than I am
now, so go and call for reinforcements and have
me arrested!'

'Kieron, for goodness' sake, is that what you're
after? Considering you've already given me a
lecture on the art of burglary?' She offered him
that irritably, but as a friend might. Instinct was
telling her that he genuinely was not dangerous,
but training still kept her wary, and using a tone
of voice calculated to defuse any sudden change of
mood. 'You've behaved like an idiot doing it this
way, quite frankly, when if you wanted to talk to
me it would only have taken one phone call! But
all right, you're here, and I want to talk to you,
too. Fancy a cup of tea?'

'Only if you've got herbal. And *are* you doing
anything about Mary?'

'I've found out her real name. I've found out
that she's got some relatives, and I'll be in touch
with them in a few days. I haven't just swept her
under the carpet.'

129

'Have you tried to find out if somebody killed her?'

'That's what I want to talk to you about — why you think so?'

'Because . . . ' He looked up at her, his face a picture of frustration. 'I know she was sick. I know she drank — though she'd almost stopped that, and it wasn't easy for her. Sometimes she hurt all over — it's like coming off anything else, she *hurt*! But she had a reason for what she was doing, even though she wouldn't tell me what it was! And something or somebody made her afraid, though she was too stubborn to give in to it. And then suddenly she was gone, and you turned up and said she was dead. What would you think?'

'I'd wonder how sick she was, considering she was a diagnosed schizophrenic and could have been having paranoid fantasies. No, it's no use your looking at me like that, she was, that's simple fact. Suppose you tell me everything you know, and then I can work out how to go on from there? And whether there's any real basis for suspicion. You'll have to trust me. And I promise, I *will* follow through anything you tell me. For instance,' she said quickly, aware of the doubtful look on his face, 'did she ever say anything to you which implied that all the vagrants were in danger from someone? That someone might be — attacking them, even knocking them off?'

'No.' He looked genuinely surprised. 'All of them? Skinheads or something? No, it wasn't anything like that!'

'You're sure?'

'Yes. Why, have you . . . ?'

'No, it was just one line of enquiry I was following up. So, what, Kieron? What particularly about Old Mary? What had she been doing that you say she had a reason for?'

He looked at her with changing expressions flitting across his face, grey eyes wide and magnified behind his glasses. Then he seemed to come to a sudden decision and thrust a hand inside the denim jacket he was wearing. Though Jane stiffened instinctively, the hand came out holding nothing more than an exercise book in a torn and grimy plastic cover; it seemed to have a discoloured Mickey Mouse on part of the front of it, and looked like something a child might have thrown away.

'I found this. It was hers. She used to write in it.' The look he was giving Jane now was somewhere between guarded and defensive. 'You'll probably say it doesn't make any sense, but you're the detective, aren't you? I think it's a kind of diary. Where she'd hidden it was — well, that doesn't matter, but it was thoroughly hidden. Your lot didn't find it, and they certainly tore the place apart enough!' The last was a return to bitterness. And disgust. 'If they had, they'd probably have assumed it was a coded list of all the *drugs* we'd been selling,' he said with heavy scorn, 'being as how we have to be guilty of something, and probably that! You just can't tell the difference, can you? Between people like us and the Convoy, for instance! Two cannabis plants, and you're sure we're all dealing in smack and planning riots!'

'All right, Kieron, we've been there, and I've

131

said I didn't have anything to do with that. And if you'll give me Old Mary's diary, I promise I'll do everything I can to see if it leads me anywhere with her death.' She held out a hand for it, and he came to his feet abruptly and passed it over. And gave her a mocking look, as if he had sensed her instinctive reaction to his sudden move. He was certainly no fool. She went on speaking, quietly. 'Is there anything, anything else at all, that you can tell me about what you think she was doing? Since you're sure there was something. Anything she told you, anything that came up in conversation?'

'If I think of anything, I'll let you know,' he said coolly, and made an elaborate point of keeping plenty of space between them as he bent to pick up a bag from the floor — a workman's toolkit, which must be the one he had mentioned to her earlier. 'It's all right, I'm really not planning to hit you with this! But then of course you believe in a culture of violence, don't you?'

'Be fair! I walk into my house to find you here! Am I supposed not to assume you could be a nutter, or at least a very angry young man, when you're standing here having plainly broken in?'

'People judge others by themselves,' he retorted. 'You're always telling people to trust you, too. I suppose it never occurs to you that it might go both ways? I'm going now, unless you really do want to arrest me? I won't offer any resistance if you insist on doing that, even though I'd really rather you didn't.'

'I said I'd forget it. This time. If ever I find you inside my house again, that would be a different matter. I suppose,' Jane said drily, 'you're not actually a professional burglar by trade? Because, and please note, if you make a habit of going round letting yourself into people's houses, I've now got you firmly in my sights, and you'd be highly unwise to risk doing it again!'

'My profession, when I had it, was to be a sound engineer with a band,' he said, with lofty emphasis. 'And although I don't believe in property nowadays, I don't believe in theft either. Can I go?'

'I'll show you out. On your promise *not* to let yourself in again, ever.' Though she would remember the bolts, another time, and probably get round to fitting a second lock too. 'Thank you for bringing the diary, but if you want to get in touch with me again, phone!'

'Or I'll come to your door and knock. I'll even say I'm sorry if I scared you.' He seemed to feel that was necessary, from the heavy politeness with which it was delivered. 'You will do something about Mary, won't you? Really? She was a person. You can't just shrug your shoulders and say she was only a tramp so it doesn't matter.'

'I don't shrug my shoulders about anybody. *Anybody*. Have you got that, or do we need to have a philosophical discussion about it?'

He simply gave her a look, and stepped out through the front door as she opened it for him. Closing it firmly behind him, she found herself letting out a breath. She had addressed him almost as if he were a recalcitrant younger brother . . . Somehow, at that moment, in her exasperation, it had almost felt like that.

But he could have been something a lot more dangerous.

All her instincts told her that he was not, but the stretching her nerves had received made it a relief to get him out of the place.

As she walked back into the main room from the minuscule lobby, the first thing to catch her eye was the bunch of roses she had let drop to the floor.

Maybe she was wrong and Kieron had brought them and left them propped there, unlikely though that seemed. But she turned on her heel again rapidly with her eyes searching the floor inside the front door, and was immediately reaching down for the square white envelope which lay there. She had missed seeing it with Kieron's unexpected appearance. Nothing on the outside, but it did look as if it might have come with the flowers.

The message inside was in Adrian's handwriting. It said, 'Sorry', underlined three times, and went on, 'Can you forgive the unforgivable? I have to hope so. Adrian.'

This time she really would refuse to be a cop first. Old Mary's diary went down on the table unopened as she glanced at her watch and reached for the phone. And then decided that answering in person was better. If he had come round to put the bouquet on her step he couldn't be doing an evening clinic. Now she was hesitating as to whether to change first — and deciding that she would, because the neat suit she went to work in made her look too much like her police self.

Letting herself out fifteen minutes later, she

made a point of seeing the front door was bolted and going out via the back: the sliding patio windows which led into her small garden had special locks top and bottom, and were fiddly but extremely secure. As Kieron had pointed out to her. Presumably the previous owners had fitted them so carefully in deference to the fact that there was a small side alley with a gate into the garden. As she left the house that way, Jane had an annoying sense of taking care after the event. Knowledge too of how much worse it could have been, and how much of a fool she would have felt to be a burglary victim. Or worse. It was something to shrug off for now, but she knew how careless it could have looked if she had had confidential papers with her at home . . .

That, again, was something to put out of her head for now, and she walked with quick light steps to the corner, hurrying as she came round it. There was still a light in the surgery, but there were also lights visible in the flat above it, so Adrian must be home.

'I'm so sorry — Why, hallo! Detective-Sergeant Perry — what a pleasure to see you again! I didn't ram you with the corner of my cat-basket, did I? Marcus has just been in for an injection, so I'm afraid I was looking at him rather than where I was going!'

Oliver Devereux had met Jane during the Arts Festival, when he had been attending a talk, illustrated with taped music, on Italian Baroque composition, and she had been there too in an official capacity because there were some valuable old instruments on display. They had actually had quite a conversation, because one of the instruments had come from his shop: he dealt in what he called 'objets'.

'It was my fault, not yours. I hope I didn't shake — er — Marcus up!' The owner of the name was glaring visibly through the wire mesh at the end of his hooped wicker basket, with bright sapphire Siamese eyes. Somehow it was a surprise to think of Oliver Devereux as a cat-owner — though if he had one, Jane supposed it would be a Siamese, as sophisticated and elegant-looking as he was himself. Tall, fair, and narrow-boned, and with a straight and aristocratic nose, Oliver Devereux almost had a likeness to his pet, not least in the creamy bleached colouring both shared. 'What a very beautiful animal,' Jane said politely, disguising her amusement with an admiring smile.

'Yes, he's a blue-point, and very well connected. Are you fond of Siamese? If so, you'll know how thoroughly they can rule one's life!' Oliver Devereux made an amused and rueful face, as if sharing with her that he knew the remark was precious, a deliberate affectation of the slightly camp by someone who was not camp at all. 'Don't put your fingers near the cage. He's in a biting mood, and I intend to ignore him! So tell me, what brings you into this part of the city, to cause us to have this fortunate meeting? You're not still on duty this late, I trust?'

'No, I live round here, and I'm just on my way to meet a friend.' He might not have guessed, perhaps, that jeans were not her usual garb for work. And that she had taken some care with her appearance. 'You're simply here to come to the vet?' she asked, making conversation. 'I remember you said you live at the south end of the city.'

'Yes, I do. Though I imagine this is a very pleasant area to live. I could have been quite tempted by the mews development when it was built — so nicely in keeping with the area, in spite of being modern. But a little noisy, I decided. I have quite enough of street-noise in the shop.' He smiled at her again, looking annoyingly inclined to stay and chat indefinitely. 'I shouldn't grumble, should I, since a frontage on a street the tourists like to patronise does at least bring me customers!'

'I hope business has been going well?'

'Oh yes, indeed, we've had plenty of American visitors this year, and they always set a high value on history. I've managed to shed quite a few collectable pieces — china in particular, and some ivories I quite thought might not go, in view of the ban.'

'That's nice. Oh, I wonder . . . ' He was here, and the thought had popped into her head. 'Did you know by any chance that one of our city tramps, one who recently died and whom we knew as Old Mary, used to be an antiques dealer? A long time ago, of course, I'm not suggesting it was current! I've just discovered her name was really Marianna Troughton-Beck, and that she used to be quite well known. So I'm wondering now if I would have found out sooner if I'd asked the trade?'

'Good heavens! No, I hadn't the least idea.

Troughton-Beck? I don't think it's someone I've heard of. She can't have been in the same line.' He looked a fraction disconcerted, and Jane wondered abruptly whether the question had been tactless. One should hardly, perhaps, point out to a successful antiques dealer that someone in his trade had fallen to the level of becoming a vagrant. 'What an extraordinary thing to find out. Yes, Marcus, all right, I *am* about to take you home!' This in response to a yowl — more of a growl — from the basket in his hand, a scrabbling suggesting its tilt had become a cause of discomfort and the delay one of impatience. 'I'm so sorry, Jane — I hope you don't mind if I call you Jane? — but his lordship is beginning to disapprove of me rather thoroughly . . . '

'I didn't mean to keep you. Goodnight, Mr Devereux.'

'Oliver,' he supplied charmingly. 'And I do hope we shall meet up again. That Italian Baroque concert was a delight, wasn't it? How nice it would be if we had that kind of thing more often. Come along then, Marcus, I shall take you away and we'll let the lady go.'

He gave Jane another of his rueful looks and walked quickly away. His car must be parked somewhere round the corner. Jane waited for him to be gone before she made for the outside staircase which led up to the flat above the clinic, though he did not, in fact, look back. It had been a pleasant chance meeting, and she had found him as likeable as on their first acquaintance. It occurred to her that he might be a useful contact, if Kenny wanted someone in the upper end of the trade who might be knowledgeable about high-value goods. Then she put all that out of her head quickly, and ran lightly up the iron stairway, to raise her hand to the brass knocker on Adrian's door.

She had not completely worked out what she was going to say. Except to thank him for the flowers. As the door opened, she saw a hesitancy and a hope in his face which was probably mirrored in her own, and then they were both speaking at the same moment.

'It's forgivable as long as you didn't really mean it, and I was pretty lousy to you too — '

'You came. I was going to come round and beat on your door if you didn't — '

They both stopped. Then he was pulling her close against him in a fierce embrace, relief brightening the serious dark eyes, the door kicked shut behind both of them.

Falling into each other's arms was one answer.

For the moment, at least.

# 9

'It came in yesterday afternoon. I know you wanted it, but so did Drugs Unit, and I really did feel they took precedence over Old Mary and her accident. So I buzzed them first. After all, there may have been some evidence they could use in the debris.' There was a faint snappiness in Ellen's voice, and

139

the look she gave Jane suggested she was all ready to be aggrieved if Jane complained. However, the snap was explained another way as she went on, with clear annoyance, 'They sent Neil Bettley down for it straight away, and it hasn't been sent back down here, so presumably they've still got it.'

Neil Bettley, quiet and boring, arriving for the Fire Assessors' report when she had hoped for — expected — her favourite, Tom Cooper. That much was very easy to guess. Jane concealed her annoyance and gave the other girl a conciliatory smile.

'I'll just have to go up and ask John Clay if I can have a look, then, won't I? Oh — did you get the note I sent you to say that Old Mary's real name is Marianna Troughton-Beck?'

'Yes, I did, thanks, I've put it on the card. Though we're not likely to need info on her any more, are we, so I may as well tag her card for the DL file . . . Hallo, Jim, can I get you anything?'

Someone else had arrived in search of information, and Jane went on her way. Up the stairs, and the first door on the right: the Drugs Unit's office was almost directly above CID, though it was smaller and accommodated far fewer staff. Lighter, though, since being on the first floor it did not need the venetian blinds which were supposed to add privacy to the ground-floor offices. As Jane walked in, in response to the 'Come!' which answered her tap on the door, she saw that all three of the Drugs Unit's complement were present, and apparently in the middle of a conference.

Neil Bettley was sitting at his desk, and cast her a

shy look from under his thick eyebrows; John Clay was behind his own, larger, desk; and Tom Cooper was outlined against the window, his shoulders leaning against the frame. There was a calendar on the wall beside him which showed a scantily dressed model archly draped across the bonnet of a car, her rear end presented to view to show minimal lacy panties, and the rest of her twisted round towards the camera with a simpering pout, while her topless upper half bounced pneumatically. It was the kind of calendar which had been banned from most areas of the station and was now only to be found decorating the inside of the door of some lockers; its presence directly opposite the entry seemed designed to signal that this was an all-male working area. Jane, who had seen worse around various stations, cast it as bland a glance as if it had been a bunch of flowers, and waited for a break in the conversation.

'Sorry, Jane, won't be a minute. You were saying, Tom?'

'Only that it's obviously coming down from the smoke. They've only got to come down the M2 for the evening, haven't they? And that slag uniform pulled in with the tablets on him — he's not even properly local, comes from Gravesend originally, he's only got a room down here!'

'His story is that he was given the stuff here, though. And by someone he meets in the dark and conveniently doesn't see! I'd dearly like to know how he thinks we're going to swallow that one, but I haven't managed to shake him.'

'So they're big boys, and he's a small fish, and

he knows better than to offend them. Uniform had a bit of luck to pick him up, he's got no record. Could get away with probation, I guess, so we haven't got much to offer to break him. I reckon he's going to stay close-mouthed, and the only thing we can do is pass the word to the Met that one of their big suppliers seems to be working our patch.'

'Well, at least he's had to put his hand up to dealing on his own account. I suppose that's something. You're probably right about the rest.' Sergeant Clay gave a sigh, then turned his attention to Jane. 'Sorry about that, didn't mean to keep you waiting. It's just that we've had another flood of drugs turning up: it looks as if someone's just decided to let a new consignment loose on us. And a variety of uppers, this time, along with the 'E'. It's a well-organised job, this one, and it doesn't seem to have any weak links to give us a lead. I suppose that does indicate the big boys.' He sighed again, then came out of his abstraction to give her a smile. 'So, what can we do you for? If it's another bunch of hippies, I'm not sure if we want . . . '

'No, I'm just on the scrounge for a look at that fire report from the rave. You've got it up here, Ellen told me?'

'Have we? I can't see that it would give us any leads. We've already sent the organisers back where they came from, and that one's a dead duck. Let's see . . . ' He was riffling through the papers on his desk. 'Bloody paperwork. I don't seem to have it amongst this lot. Anybody got it?'

'You told me to check it, Sarge, remember?' Tom Cooper spoke without moving. 'Nothing to interest us, though. Not enough left to interest anybody, what with that mad old coot and her can of petrol!'

'Petrol?'

'Yeah, they found the burned-out can, love — she probably found it there and opened it up to try and drink the stuff, but spilt it instead! No use expecting sweet reason from somebody like that.'

Jane could have done without the casual 'love', and the faintly condescending tone. 'If you've finished with it, perhaps you won't mind if I take the report away with me?' she asked pleasantly, giving a glance towards Sergeant Clay. 'I do have to make some notes for my own report, and I'll need to put down exactly what happened.'

'Instant stir fry,' Tom Cooper said, with a grin to show he was appreciating his own joke. He added one of his raking glances, the look in his eyes suggesting Jane was supposed to realise he was mentally stripping her as he went on talking. 'No, I guess you ought to be sorry for the crazy old bat, since she ended up doing herself in. I suppose all the loud music frightened her or something, and she got some loopy idea about driving them away. But if you want to check out for yourself what this says, here!' One hand reached out to push the stapled papers across his desk in Jane's direction. 'It's all yours, girl. We only had it to make sure they hadn't found any charred remains of packets of pills chucked away!'

'Thank you.' First 'love' and then 'girl'; no, she

really did not like Tom Cooper. But if his own sergeant ignored his distinctly insolent manner, there was little she could do. 'All right if I take this, then, John?' she asked Sergeant Clay, keeping her eyes on him pleasantly.

'Oh, I don't know, what's it worth?' John Clay said, pretending doubt with a sudden heavy jollity. 'What's the going rate for a borrow of something that really belongs in our files? Hm . . . '

'You'd rather I read it here? Or, if you're back on the demarcation lines — '

'No, take it, and it can go back in the collator files when you've finished — only joking.' Sergeant Clay relaxed and leaned back amiably in his chair, but kept his eyes questioningly on Jane's face. 'Anything new downstairs in CID? There's been a murmur or two about staff changes coming up. Or is it just one of those rumours?'

So that was it. 'Nothing that's recently come to my ears,' she told him truthfully, but concealing a sudden sharpening of her attention. Had the news come out that Dan Crowe was vacating his DI's job? He had been playing his cards very close to his chest, but if he had finalised things, something might well have reached the grapevine and set John Clay off on trying to pump her. 'If you've got some gossip, you tell me!' she invited.

'Mm. Well, if it hasn't reached you, perhaps it isn't true. Though the way I heard it, there might be a bit of interesting news any time now.' A bleep from his phone set him reaching for it and cut off any further information as he started a conversation which was plainly full of complicated queries from

144

the other end. He gave Jane a wave as she picked up the report she had come for and mimed her thanks.

She left him to it and took herself back downstairs, wondering what he had heard. If it was a murmur that the DI was resigning, that meant Dan Crowe had got his emigration plans properly sorted out at last, and knew for sure that he would be going. And when. He would probably give the powers-that-be at least two months, maybe three, to find his replacement . . . She would have to keep her ears open. If he didn't tip her the wink that things were starting to move. He might or he might not. Although he had shared with her confidentially that he had plans to go, he might not want to look as if he was backing her as his replacement too openly.

The CID room was as quiet as when she had last left it, with only Gary Peters working silently at his desk, and Peter Pettigrew looking up something on the wall-chart. If the DI was about to drop his bombshell, the news plainly had not got this far. Jane forced herself to stop speculating, and made herself sit down to make a concentrated study of the bare two pages of the Fire Assessors' report. She had the excuse that the DCI had already reprimanded her for not having closed the Old Mary file yet, so that for once — until the next phone summons provided an interruption — she could bend her mind to seeing whether there actually was real cause for Kieron's suspicions. And her own vague and half-formulated doubts.

She had taken a quick glance this morning at the

diary Kieron had given her, but it had only been a very brief flick through the first few pages, over an apology for breakfast which she barely had time for after rushing in and hurrying to change. And with her mind still only half on the need to switch to her official self. She and Adrian had talked little . . . though she had managed to explain that living together would mean he had to be officially cleared. That had plainly disconcerted him, even if he tried to cover the fact. She had not mentioned anything about her hopes of promotion, leaving that too delicate a subject in the circumstances. Too like a confirmation of his angry words. It seemed that he would allow the question of moving in together to go into limbo for the moment, anyway.

There were more satisfying ways of making up than talking. Trying to detach her mind from the memory of that (if unwillingly), Jane remembered how she had opened the diary for a quick assessment of its likely contents, but had found only what appeared to be lines of nonsense, sometimes scrawled in zigzags across a page, sometimes in cramped tiny writing. It would need time, and probably a lot of care, to see if there actually was anything there of importance, and she had thrust it into her briefcase with the feeling that she would wade through it *only if*. If it looked as if there was need. If nothing else proved conclusive. That was what had taken her to Ellen to enquire after the fire report again.

It was in front of her now, laying out its findings clearly. The fire had definitely started in the small office attached to the hangar. Scientific tests showed evidence of petroleum spirit, in positions which implied it had been flung against the walls and across the floor. A burned-out can which had contained the same inflammable liquid had been found under the debris. The remains of some wax (with a careful description of its melted composition) had been scraped up, and suggested ignition had come from a lighted candle. Conclusion: arson, by persons unknown, though the body found at the scene could be the perpetrator, if ignition was caused accidentally before escape. Note: method of leaving a candle to burn down in a place previously rendered highly inflammable is common in insurance fraud. Check should be made on owner of property (name given) though this appears to be a defunct company with no current address.

It was thorough and conclusive — but it still left the question open.

Two possible scenarios.

Old Mary, crazed with anger by the disturbance of her peace, flinging petrol around with intent to set light to it and drive the interlopers away. But then falling, somehow, and breaking her neck; her fall knocking over the candle she had already lit, setting off the conflagration. That was the one Tom Cooper had described — the one everyone would be inclined to go with, Jane knew.

In the alternative scenario, someone else had set the fire. After Old Mary was dead. And had locked the door and walked away.

If the latter, the fire-raiser would have to have been entirely ruthless, to care so little for the danger to hundreds of teenagers partying just the other side of a wooden wall . . .

But why kill the old woman? Just because she was there? Because she had stumbled into some previously planned insurance fraud? The rave, after all, had been moved to that location at only a few hours' notice, and could have landed in the middle of someone's plans.

If this defunct company could be shown to have a suspiciously high insurance on the hangar buildings . . . That seemed unlikely, but perhaps ought to be followed up. But with no current address . . . and they would be hardly likely to put in a sudden claim, when they had had to leave a body there . . .

It would be much easier to go for scenario one, already taken for granted in most quarters. Simply leave it there. It was even tempting.

But she had promised Kieron she would look into the old woman's death thoroughly. So that meant the diary.

If any of it made any sense at all.

Jane reached into her briefcase to pull it out. As she opened the cover she saw there were several pages missing at the beginning, a torn edge left, perhaps where the previous owner had used part of the exercise book and then thrown it away. The size and shape of the pages brought a sudden reminder of the single grubby sheet Jane had found in the old woman's bags, the page which had simply held the word 'No' scrawled all over it.

The first written page was full of jumbled words with no deference to grammar. The word 'ache ache ache' appeared, written over and over. And 'nuisance, only nuisance, stupid, why care'. Something had been heavily scratched out, then, 'not deserve, not'. Then a sudden change into a surprising, almost poetic literacy, with 'Anger burns, anger cleanses, welcome it!' A turn of the page showed more of the same.

Halfway down the third page the handwriting abruptly went small, crabbed and tidy, and for a few lines there was a clarity which caught the attention. 'I am afraid. Afraid that I shall go back into the darkness again. The monsters are there and lie in wait for me. But out here, too, are monsters: which is worse? The real or the unreal? The real, also, are to be feared, and with reason.' And then she had written, in clear capital letters, 'BUT I WILL HAVE HIM!'

That could be interesting . . . Could it?

It would have been more so if the next bit, though still in the tidy writing, had not lapsed into an evocation of a fire-breathing dragon consuming the world, oddly vivid, weirdly lucid in the way it was written, yet making only its own sense. A space was left below it, then, underlined, 'Not the devil, one of his scavengers.' Another space, but after that the handwriting growing more ragged again, the grammar disintegrating into a strange litany of unconnected words.

It was dislocating even to read, like a glimpse into someone else's insanity. If it was all like this . . . Jane sighed, and flipped through the pages. She could try somewhere at random. Or start at the end and work backwards. The exercise book was not full; here were a set of blank pages.

Beyond them, inside the last page of the book, she found something completely different. Not handwriting, but a list — of hieroglyphics.

At least it looked like a list. It was set out in lines, and there were dates here and there. Against them were dashes, figures and squiggles.

The dates appeared to cover the last two months. The rest could have meant anything.

Some kind of code?

A vague echo nudged its way into Jane's mind as she ran her eyes along the top two lines again. Had she seen something like that before somewhere? Not exactly, but similar? She looked up quickly and addressed the room at large.

'Anybody seen Kenny today?'

'He's in court, Sarge,' Gary Peters told her. 'All day. Maybe tomorrow as well, if it drags on. That assault and battery from three months ago.'

'Oh. Damn . . . '

'Sarge, this list of thefts from garages, do you want them kept separate or put in with the house break-ins? They're all part of domestic, but do you want them in date-order with the others, or in a different file?'

'The ones we've had lately have all had a particular MO, haven't they? Let's give them their own file, then. That reminds me, I ought to do a follow-up on Sams Road today.' Jane glanced at her watch. 'I promised a return call at the sub post office, too, in case Mrs Singh spots anyone with one of the stolen benefit books. All right if I go on with that, Peter, since I saw her the first time?'

150

'Fine,' Peter Pettigrew told her, wrinkling his brow with his usual look of anxiety but obviously happy for her to continue with this part of non-domestic break-ins.

'I'll go now, then, before the next bunch of crises hits us.' It would be a relief to escape from Old Mary's nightmarish ravings. And until she could get hold of Kenny to check her theory, she might as well leave it: other things were certainly more urgent. She hesitated, then decided to photocopy the hieroglyph page on her way out, just in case it proved to be of interest. There was, surely, a possibility that she *had* seen something like that before.

Leaving the CID room, she did her detour, then signed out to carry on with the return visits which were all part of detective work. When, of course, they had time to make them, to reassure burglary victims that the police really were taking a proper interest in every case.

The Sams Road householder was out, a still-boarded front door showing where a thief had gained access by breaking its glass: that was the one, Jane remembered, where both the house's owner and his neighbours had been angrily sure the perpetrator came from 'that gipsy family in the flats' and had had to be told, patiently and several times, that if no one had actually seen the break-in, the police could hardly make an arrest on pure suspicion. She put a note through the letterbox to say she had called, and went on her way. The sub post office, tucked into one of the city's older streets, was an easy visit, since Mrs Singh was

151

pleased to see her and uncomplaining about the lack of arrest so far. No one had been foolish enough to turn up with an illicit benefit book, as yet, but the Singhs seemed to have recovered from the shock of the hold-up, and to be satisfied with the assurance that investigations were continuing. Walking back to where she had left the car, Jane glanced into the windows of the well-kept shops she was passing.

Most of them had the jut of medieval beams above, and a decorative air of antiquity to attract the tourist, though there was still a small butcher's in reminder of the time when this part of the city had been residential enough to need its own local supplier. And a fruiterer's, tucked in between a silversmith's and a leathergoods merchant. Otherwise, this was an antiques dealers' area, every other shop offering the polished shine of well-kept old furniture, a display of delicate porcelain, a warming-pan hung up to catch the light. Or old dolls artistically arranged in a group, with their white china faces, elaborate tresses, and slightly musty-looking clothes. Jane had just reached that shop when its proprietor leaned into the window to add a strangely knobbly vase to the other side of his display, adjusting its position with concentrated care. Creamily blond hair, narrow aristocratic nose, an elegant hand against a turned-back shirt cuff. Jane paused in recognition, then took three steps on and reached for the shop door.

Oliver Devereux. Well, she was passing, so why not make use of him?

'Good morning, can I — Oh, hallo!'

'Another chance meeting,' Jane said sunnily. 'I hope you don't mind, but I was just walking by, so I thought I'd stop for a moment.'

'But how delightful! Do tell me, did the dolls catch your attention? They're quite a fetching group, aren't they?'

'They're certainly eyecatching.' A trifle spooky to Jane's taste, with their pale faces and slightly too real artificial eyes, their flat gaze and yellowed clothing a little too redolent of ghost stories about Victorian children. 'I suppose they're valuable, too, are they? I mean, people collect them?'

'Indeed they do, particularly the high-quality Swiss and German dolls. Some of them are quite beautiful and I can scarcely bear to part with them.' He gave her a smile with that, and again there was that air of having knowingly sounded effete, playing it as a game when that was not really his line at all. He became brisk to add, 'And how do you like my shop? Is there anything particular I can interest you in? A Clarice Cliff jug which has just come my way? Or I've got some rather delightful Cheshire dogs — '

'I'm afraid I haven't come to buy. I'd make a very bad collector anyway, I wouldn't know where to start. I just wondered if you'd mind if I picked your brains?'

'Please do. And since it's you, I won't make any charge.' He smiled at her as if to make sure she knew that was merely a tease. 'What can I help you with, Jane?'

'I came across a sort of list.' She reached into her leather shoulder-bag and produced one of the

153

two photocopies she had made. 'It doesn't make any sense to me, but then I thought I remembered that dealers — your kind of dealers — used a code to mark their goods. I'm not wrong about that, am I? And could this be the same type of code?'

He took the paper she was holding out to him, and studied it. There was a moment when she thought he was going to give her instant confirmation; a kind of blank, concentrated attention which looked as if he was reading words, not squiggles. Then, disappointingly, he raised an eyebrow and gave a faint shrug.

'My dear, this *could* be somebody's notation, but it isn't one I've met! Some dealers do tend to be quite individual in the marks they use. Where did you find it?'

There seemed no harm in telling him. 'You remember I mentioned an old woman called Marianna Troughton-Beck who used to be in the antiques trade? It was in the back of a kind of diary I've been given of hers. So I thought there might be a connection. If she'd been going round making a note of things, perhaps, even out of habit.' That seemed a reasonable explanation, off the top of her head, without saying that Old Mary might just have been murdered, and that if so, anything she had written down might be highly relevant. 'You say it *could* be a dealer's code? It was just, you know, that I thought I might have seen the same sort of thing on labels attached to antiques.'

'Well, yes, but as I say, it depends on which area of the trade she was in. And as we do all

154

like to keep our secrets, one firm can use a very different code from another. But how intriguing — a diary. Does it say anything else in it, to give you a clue?'

'To be honest, it doesn't seem to be anything but nonsense. She spent the last years of her life as a schizophrenic, and what she's written is — well, fairly incomprehensible as a whole, and probably part of her illness. I haven't read all of it yet, but it doesn't look very sane. It was just the list, at the end — it made me curious.'

'And where did you think you might have seen marks like that on labels?'

'On . . . I don't know, jewellery? That's about the only thing I might have looked at, if ever I've been near an antique stall,' Jane admitted with a grin. 'You turn the label over for a price, and all you see is dots and squiggles!'

'Marianna Troughton-Beck . . . No, it still doesn't ring a bell. I'm sorry I can't be more help.'

'You have been. If you say different firms use different codes, I can ask her nephews. And maybe they can tell me exactly what she's written down, if anything. Thank you very much for letting me pick your brains. Oh, how's the cat? Has he recovered from yesterday?'

'Marcus? He's still sulking a little, but no doubt he'll be back to his usual self in a day or two!'

'I hope so. Well, I'll be off, and stop taking up your time — thanks again!'

He assured her charmingly (though a little absently, she thought, perhaps because a possible client was now lingering outside looking at his window) that she was always welcome to his time, and was still standing there watching her as she left. The photocopied list she had taken back from him tucked again into her bag, Jane thought that the idea of talking to him had been worth it: it appeared that Old Mary's list could be a dealer's code, even if one he did not recognise. Perhaps she should ask to make a trip to London and go and see the Beck nephews, rather than just telephoning them.

She whizzed into the CID room feeling a renewed energy — and found a change of personnel, with Mike Lockley sitting on the corner of Gary's desk in earnest conversation with him. The conversation was obviously intriguing to both of them, but broke off sharply as she came into the room.

'Oh, hi, Sarge.' Both the young men were looking at her with unexpected curiosity. As she raised her eyebrows queryingly, Mike went on, 'Have you seen the notice? Out on the board? The Super was just putting it up as I came in . . . '

'Really? What?'

' 'Applications are invited for the post of Detective Inspector, CID, City Sub-division',' Mike quoted, giving the words their official weight. 'The guv must have got DCI somewhere! He might have let on, to us at least! So we're up for a new guv'nor, and I suppose they'll be running an ad all round. Are you going to put in for it, Sarge?'

It was like Mike to be that direct. 'I'd better go and see what experience they're asking for,' Jane said, too coolly for anyone to know the way her heart skipped a beat. And hiding any indication of the fact that a roughed-out application was already there, waiting, in her drawer at home. 'So the guv's off? Well, well. That's going to be a farewell party and a half, when we get to it. We'd better start collecting now!'

She put the things she was carrying calmly down on her desk and turned on her heel to go back outside and inspect the notice-board. Well, hell's teeth, it would be an obvious pretence if she made a gesture out of not being immediately interested.

She had enough years as a sergeant behind her to have a chance. She *ought* to have a good chance to make DI — here or somewhere else — on her service record; and here was what she wanted . . . DCI Morland notwithstanding.

It was out in the open now, and she was certainly going to go for it.

# 10

'You want to make a trip to London, on this?' DCI Morland gave Jane a look which could only be described as pettish. 'That seems to me to be making a great deal out of nothing, Sergeant Perry. I should have thought you could have done everything necessary by telephone. Still, I suppose we can do without you for a day.' His expression indicated that a year would be even better. 'Very well, make an appointment

157

with Miss Troughton-Beck's nephews as soon as possible — but please don't put in for excessive expenses!'

'No, sir. It's just that I felt it might be advisable to see the Becks personally, to clear up the final details about their aunt's death.'

'I've said I'll allow it. So if that's all, Sergeant, some of us have real work to do.'

His sour snap suggested to Jane that he knew about her application for the DI job, carefully submitted on Monday after a weekend's working over it. When she could; when Adrian wasn't around. The DCI's clear discomfort also indicated that he had been unable to find a strong enough complaint against her to take to the Super as a counter against her being considered. Jane gave him one of her very obedient, butter-wouldn't-melt-in-mouth looks, and picked up her Old Mary file as he thrust it back at her across his desk.

She had raised none of her doubts in the report, merely putting down the available facts in a clear and official fashion. That seemed the safest way of dealing with it, since experience had taught her that circumventing the DCI, unless she had any hard facts to offer, was the best method of operation. She certainly planned to avoid inviting his criticism that she was letting her imagination run away with her. With the word 'female' clearly there, if unsaid, before imagination.

Safely out of his office, she contemplated the knowledge that he had looked more than ever as if her mere existence was nagging at him like a sore tooth. That could mean the Super had said something which indicated he found the idea of promoting her feasible . . . No, she emphatically must not start counting her chickens. She, as well as anybody, knew how much it would depend on the competition. But she ought, at least, to make the short list, and she knew she was good on interview.

She had better try not to allow herself to think about it at all. That was scarcely easy, with Dan Crowe's resignation the main topic of gossip around the station, along with the startling news that he was leaving the force altogether and emigrating. Whenever the topic of the DI job came up, Jane received speculative glances; though most of them good-natured, she thought. No, she really would resist dwelling on the subject, and fretting over whether she actually had put enough into her application to make herself sound thoroughly efficient and go ahead. Now, more than any time, was when she should be looking at her most calm and capable, and demonstrate to anyone who cared to see that she was simply getting on with her work.

Dan Crowe would probably grumble about her permission to disappear to London for a day when there were cases aplenty here. However, Old Mary had already had to go down the list for several days as other things arrived which, as usual, needed dealing with urgently. And the DI was at least in a thoroughly good mood, with his emigration plans definite at last, a firm offer in for the sale of his house (which was, apparently, what he had been waiting for), and the pleasure of having sprung a

159

surprise on the entire station, bar the few cronies whom he had sworn to secrecy. Among them Jane. She had kept that to herself, since he obviously wanted her to.

Back at her desk, she switched her mind determinedly over to the task in hand. She had managed to catch Kenny Barnes and ask him if the list out of Old Mary's diary looked like dealers' marks to him — as the department's current resident antiques expert — but he had said cheerfully that as far as he was concerned they could be Greek, and that the Met DCI had not covered that kind of thing when he provided a crash course on what they were supposed to look out for. Kenny pointed out that Old Mary's list seemed to have two sections, and they looked different to him, but Jane had already noticed that. Otherwise, he could offer no more constructive help than Oliver Devereux had. So that left the Becks. Just in case it was something relevant.

She punched up the number Kenny had given her courtesy of Reg Plimpton, and heard the ringing tone the other end. Then the pause and click which indicated an answering machine, and a light tenor voice came on the line.

'This is Laurence Beck. I'm sorry there's nobody available to take your call just now. I shall be in the shop again on Thursday morning, and we open at nine-thirty. Please do call if you would like to be shown what we have in stock. If you would like to leave a message, please be kind enough to do so after the tone.'

Perhaps he was away on a buying spree. But at

160

least he had told her when he would be available. Jane waited for the tone, then spoke.

'Mr Beck? My name is Jane Perry, and I'll call on you at ten am on Thursday in your shop. I'll look forward to meeting you then.'

It was unfortunate that he would probably hope she was a prospective customer, but if she had added her rank and the City Police number, it might have sounded threatening. Like trouble of some kind. Neither could she put the blunt message on the machine that his aunt was dead. Jane shrugged, and leaned forward to enter the appointment clearly in her desk diary, with a scribbled mark beside it to show that she still had to clear it with the guv. Still, the DCI had okayed the trip. Then she made a sudden, glad mental note that she could beg a bed from Matty for the night before, if she was going to London: it was a good excuse to catch up with her friend. And with Steve, now Matty's other half. She would ring them tonight.

She flipped the Old Mary file shut and reached for the next to study while the CID room was temporarily empty of everyone besides herself. Yet another domestic burglary. This time, someone appeared to have picked the lock. She devoutly hoped it wasn't Kieron.

★ ★ ★

'Oh, this is great! Come on in, and let's have a private gossip before Steve gets home!'

Matty's face was split by a wide, welcoming grin.

161

Her beautiful dusky skin glowed, and her eyes were clear and bright. The relationship with Steve was obviously working.

'You look as if nesting's suiting you,' Jane told her friend in a teasing voice, adding, 'I hope you haven't had to take time off from work to see me? I remember what it used to be like when we nominally shared a flat but hardly saw each other because you were working all the hours God sends!'

'Doing locum work doesn't tie me up so much. It's all good experience, though, and keeps my ear to the ground for any mega job which might be coming up.'

She hadn't changed that much, then. 'You seem to be well fixed here,' Jane said, glancing round the pleasantly homely flat, with Matty's medical books displayed along one wall, a collection of thrillers and motoring magazines which were obviously Steve's on another. She had found it, in a street which must be somewhere at the edge of Steve's East End patch, without difficulty. 'Handy shops within reach, various hospitals only a quick drive up the clearway, and Steve's cop-shop ditto? And I could even find somewhere to park!'

'But you still don't miss London. You said so on the phone. So come on, stop standing there like a polite visitor, and plump yourself down and tell me ALL!' Matty said on a chuckle. 'How's the DCI? How's your love-life? How's — '

'Help! All right, the DCI — awful as ever, but I'm fighting back. My love life . . . yes, I do have one again at last, his name's Adrian. And he's a

162

vet. No, don't start to laugh, it's no more surprising than you making off with an East End copper!'

Old friends as they were, it was easy to dive in and catch up, the months between vanishing as they always had, over the years, whenever they came together. By the time the sound of a key in the door heralded Steve's arrival, they had caught up a great deal, and were relaxed and easy, curled up in armchairs and talking nineteen to the dozen. He too, Jane thought, as he came in with his bouncy step, looked as if the relationship was working. There was a happy glow about him as he crossed the room to give Matty a kiss, then came over to offer Jane a smacker on the cheek as well, with just the faintest hint of his old flirtatious grin.

It was funny to remember that she had once found him uncomfortably attractive. Now, she could simply give him an affectionate grin at his teasing greeting.

'So how's the lady sergeant from the sticks? Still turning the place upside down and catching all the villains?'

'Don't know how it is around your place, but we've got the usual petty-crime-on-the-increase figures and we're lucky if we catch one in ten. Dan Crowe's leaving us, he's just put his resignation in . . . and yes, I am putting in for the job! No saying whether I'll get it, of course.'

'You *will*,' Matty said fiercely, as she already had before during their catching-up session. Steve raised an amused eyebrow.

'You'll give Humpty Dumpty conniptions, and that I'd really like to see!' Steve had coined that

163

name for DCI Morland when he worked in the city, and to hear it again made Jane chuckle. 'No, seriously, what's the competition? Or don't you know yet? We'll keep our fingers crossed for you, that's for sure!'

They went out to eat at the local Indian restaurant, and it was a pleasant and relaxed evening, some shoptalk, some general chatter. Coming back, Jane caught herself wondering how Adrian would have fitted in. Would he like her friends? It was impossible to know. Or how much it would matter to her whether he did or not. She had caught a keen-eyed look from Steve when it came up, in passing argument, that the job they did could make relationships difficult; but his statement that that was as true for a man as for a woman had led back along more general paths. Together with his usual accusation that she was too feminist, hers that he didn't know what he was talking about, and Matty holding the bridge between. But it was, even so, a good evening. And Matty would probably tell him about Adrian, later: there was a closeness between those two which bespoke a lack of secrets.

And an air of permanence. They should have been an ill-assorted couple, as a diplomat's daughter and a meat porter's son: different backgrounds, different skin colour, different professions and ambitions. But as Jane settled down on their sofa for the night, she thought that it certainly looked as if each had found exactly what they wanted from the other.

In the morning Steve was in a rush to get to work, Matty was not due at one of her hospitals until later, and Jane hunted through the A to Z for her best route to Chelsea. On parting from Matty, there was a hug and a promise to meet again soon — 'If it's possible!' — and then Jane was on her way, threading through the London traffic. Back to her work persona, and concentrating on what she would say to Mr Laurence Beck.

His voice on the answering machine had been a pleasant one; not that that was any guide. It would be interesting to see how he received the news of his aunt's death. With relief, possibly — though that need hardly mean he would turn out to be a karate expert who had happened to be in Kent on the night Old Mary died. At some point Jane would need to introduce a polite line of questioning on what the diary notations might mean. Old Mary could simply have been following old and dimly remembered habits, anyway, scuffling round antiques fairs marking notes on other people's goods and prices.

As Jane turned into the wide, respectable street which held Beck Antiques, her eye was immediately caught by a police car further up, blue lights still flashing, a small crowd of loiterers gathering to watch. Someone in an apparent state of extreme distress was being helped towards the car by a uniformed constable who was speaking rapidly into his shoulder-mike at the same time. Jane saw a space at a meter and nipped into it smartly, another car coming fast behind her giving a hoot of annoyance, then hastening on to screech to a halt double-parked behind the police car. Several figures leapt out of it. Plain-clothes police — definitely.

Something was going down, here. Jane locked her car thoughtfully, thrust a coin into the meter beside it, and glanced round for the numbers on the nearest houses. Whatever the local force was up to, there was no reason why it should affect her appointment at Beck Antiques. She was a fraction early but not enough to matter. The shop should be up in the direction of the police cars.

The shop was the destination of the police cars.

She saw the sign on its elegant black frontage as she approached through the crowd: it was one of only a handful of commercial properties set in amongst the Georgian elegance of this mainly residential street. In fact, her passage was abruptly blocked by a uniformed constable as she slipped her way through the curious loiterers and tried to get closer.

'I'm sorry, madam, please move along to the other side of the road, and if you'd all just keep this area clear for the moment . . . '

Jane caught the constable's attention by letting her weight resist the urging of his arm, and had her warrant card out and on display before he could voice a reproof. 'Do you mind if I come through? I was supposed to have an appointment with the owner of Beck Antiques. So what's up, have they had a robbery?'

'Oh — er — sorry, Sergeant. If you want to go on through, would you have a word with the guv'nor? He's the one in the brown raincoat, by the doorway there.'

A busy-looking man, the guv'nor: he was having an urgent discussion with another of the uniforms, but looked as if he might fly back inside at any moment. As Jane came up to them she received a piercing look, noticing a distinct air of annoyance in the pair of sharp grey eyes. However, the display of her warrant card again brought her official acknowledgement, and he interrupted his discussion to listen to what she had to say.

'You had an appointment with Laurence Beck? When did you say you made it? Oh, on the answerphone. Well, you're a bit late, I'm afraid, Sergeant Perry. DCI Carter by the way, Chelsea. We've got a body upstairs, and it's Laurence Beck's — probably. The cleaning woman who found him seems to think so, anyway, and it's his gaff. Harris, get those people cleared away. There'll be the SOCO and the pathologist and the ambulance soon, and they've all got to park somewhere!' He turned back to Jane after that aside, gave her a thoughtful look, and added, 'I'm going back up, you'd better come. Mind telling me on the way what you were seeing Laurence Beck about?'

She told him, briefly, as they took a flight of stairs which led up from just inside the doorway — not the shop's door, but one beside it, though apparently part of the same premises. An archway at the top took them a sharp left into what was obviously a flat, elegantly furnished and at the moment rather full of people. 'Breaking the news of an aunt's death?' DCI Carter said. 'You don't know him, then? Pity, I was hoping you could give us a second identification. We could do with one. The cleaning woman apparently didn't know if he'd got any family.'

'There's a cousin — '

'Is there? Any idea where?'

'Runs the shop with him, I was told. I don't have any other address.'

'Thanks for that, anyway, we're just looking for likely — Yes, Davidson? Found something useful in that address book by the phone?'

As he moved, Jane saw through the gap he had left, across to the far end of the room.

A body lay sprawled on the floor, the head mashed and flattened. Round it, dark stains and splashes; not fresh blood, but rusty. A lot of it, some splashed up on to the far wall, too. Even with the windows flung wide, there was a smell in the room of which she had already been all too aware: the strong, sweet odour of putrefaction.

If this was Laurence Beck, he had been some time dead.

'I shouldn't look unless you want to — it's not pretty. He's in his dressing-gown, so it looks as if he may have heard something and got up, and caught a blagger in the act. That was a savage beating.' DCI Carter was back, his voice laconic. 'Maybe someone couldn't get into the shop, and thought he might keep some stuff up here. Anybody found a safe?'

'How long — ?' Abruptly, Jane's words came to a halt, as she heard her own polite voice coming from the tape by the telephone. Someone was playing the answering machine back. 'Sorry, yes, that's me. How long do you think he's been dead?'

'Wouldn't like to guess, but since the weekend maybe? The cleaner told us she only comes in on

Thursdays. We'll have to wait for the pathologist to give us an accurate answer. It seems you've had a wasted visit, Sergeant, doesn't it? What do you want to do — stick around and see if we can find the cousin? Or just go back?'

It was nice of him to give her the choice, when most forces would be loth to welcome the presence of strays from another area into the thick of an investigation. Jane caught back a gag as the smell from the room hit her again, but managed to say steadily, 'Would you mind if I stick around? Since I'm here.'

# 11

Later, at the area police station, Jane ran into someone she knew, another sergeant she had worked with when she was still in the Met. That gave her an immediate in with the local crowd and her presence started to be taken for granted. They had found an Andrew Beck in Laurence's address book and rapidly managed to establish that this was the cousin. He arrived at the station some time later, a tall, black-haired man with lines of bad temper clearly graven around his mouth. He had already been taken to identify the body and had confirmed that it was his cousin Laurence. Now, in an interview which DCI Carter had given Jane the nod to attend, he was being asked politely to fill in some details.

'I'm nothing to do with the shop any more. We had a parting of the ways a couple of years ago, and I'm a property consultant now. No, Laurence and I didn't see each other. You may as well know — I'm sure somebody'll tell you! — that we didn't get on.'

That could be guessed, since his was definitely the voice on an answerphone message left at an earlier time than Jane's. As she remembered it, the sound had been a positive snarl, saying, 'Laurence? If you've gone off to an auction again without getting in touch with me, it simply isn't good enough — you've got to give me an answer about signing those papers! It's in your interest as well as mine, not that you'd care about mine!' DCI Carter gave him a politely considering look, and put a question.

'I've gathered from the neighbours that the shop hasn't been open since last week. Did your cousin often go away — to auctions, for instance?'

'Yes. There was one up north on Monday, he could have been expected to attend that. He was away when he had to be. When you deal in specialised goods people don't necessarily expect you to be there all the time.' There was a jerky note in Andrew Beck's voice as if the shock might be getting to him, but the brown eyes, so dark as to be almost black, held an impatient scorn rather than any sign of sorrow. Jane realised suddenly of whom the eyes reminded her — Old Mary. Definitely a family likeness. 'My cousin's been running the business on his own since we parted. He had good security precautions and a proper alarm system to the shop. You say it hadn't been broken into? Well, there you are, then. Someone must have got in through the flat door instead and hoped to go down the inside staircase from the flat. Have you looked at the stock to see if anything's missing?' he asked, an abrupt question containing what was all at once a much more genuine concern. 'Still, at least he won't have been fool enough to leave anything out on display!'

'There's no sign that anyone's tried to tamper with the safe downstairs. Or with anything else. Perhaps chummy was frightened off when he found himself faced with your cousin. And by what he'd done. Do you still have an interest in the business Mr Beck?'

'I still have a financial interest, yes.' That came after the barest beat of a pause. 'Laurence paid me a dividend. We didn't dissolve the partnership, we merely chose to do different things.'

'You're still an equal partner?'

'Yes.'

'So you'll have been half owner of the shop?'

'Yes. I don't know where this is leading, Chief Inspector, but if you're suggesting what I think you're suggesting — '

'I'm not suggesting anything, sir. How many people might have known if your cousin was planning to be away? If it was a speculative break-in, say, and our burglar thought the flat above the shop would be empty?'

'God knows. He'd probably cancelled the milk or something, and then changed his mind about leaving. I'm no expert on the workings of my cousin's mind, Chief Inspector. And I can't tell you what stock he was carrying, either, or whether he might have taken some up to the flat to look over. Antique jewellery's not my line; Laurence was the one who decided to carry on with that, not me.'

'That will have been a profitable business?'

'If you deal in good quality stuff, it's valuable. Worth a thief's time. And Beck's has a reputable name.'

'And the partnership now devolves on to you? As well as the ownership of the shop?'

'Look, if you're trying to suggest I went round and hit Laurence over the head . . . '

'I don't believe I suggested anything like that, Mr Beck. I wonder, what were the papers you wanted him to sign? We've come across a message you left him.'

'Yes, I did,' Andrew Beck snapped, without waiting for DCI Carter to continue his steady drip of questions, 'but that was merely a family matter, and nothing that needs interference from anyone outside! I couldn't get hold of him — as you must quite obviously have heard — and yes, we did disagree about most things. But that, Chief Inspector, was why we chose to avoid each other's company. I haven't seen Laurence for — oh, weeks, if not a couple of months. When we dealt with each other it was by telephone, or in writing, or through our lawyers. I'm not going to pretend we liked each other, just because he's dead. We didn't.'

'But you were still partners. And I've gathered Mr Laurence Beck was a bachelor. With no issue.

No brothers or sisters either. And the shop — you did say you owned that jointly? Now that's slightly surprising, as it happens, because I thought I had a note somewhere that Beck Antiques was actually the property of an elderly lady. Perhaps I'm wrong . . . Hearsay, was that, Sergeant Perry?'

His glance invited Jane, sitting quietly by, to comment. 'Yes, it was, sir,' she admitted. 'Marianna Troughton-Beck was merely *thought* to be still the owner.'

'Oh, my damned aunt! I don't know where you've got that from — Laurence's papers? She may have had a technical right, but I doubt if it would have held up in court. Anyway, I really can't see that this is relevant.'

Andrew Beck's air of impatience had intensified — but he had said 'have had', Jane had noted with interest. The past tense . . . He had known Old Mary was dead? Before she could dwell on it, the man was going on, bad temper snapping in his eyes, a note of deep sarcasm in his voice.

'How long is this going on, Chief Inspector? If it's going to be much longer, I shall ask for my solicitor to be present. My cousin's murdered in what's obviously an attempted robbery — or an actual one, for all I know — and you're quizzing me about the business, and who owns it, in such a way that I'm beginning to find the implications insulting! And for your interest, Laurence may have been a bachelor, but I have a wife. As we work together as well as live together, she can account for every moment of my time. *Should* she need to! Now, can we get this farce over or should I, in fact, ring my solicitor?'

'You're entirely welcome to if you wish, Mr Beck, but no accusations of any kind have been made. As the tape recording you gave your permission for us to make of this interview will show. I'm merely trying to establish all the details so that we don't need to go over them again. I'm sure you'll understand that we need to — since, after all, your cousin has been murdered, by persons unknown?'

'I intend to leave within the next five minutes. You have my address, so you know where to get hold of me.'

'Interview terminated,' DCI Carter said blandly into the tape recorder, giving time and date, and switching the machine off. 'Thank you very much, Mr Beck. Oh — ' it was as if he had sensed Jane's sudden restiveness, and he gave her a glance and then went on obligingly, ' — I wonder if you'd mind a moment or two more of your time, though? Since Sergeant Perry has come all the way up from Kent for an appointment with your cousin, and hasn't been able to keep it?'

'Yes, what?'

The look Andrew Beck gave Jane out of those dark eyes was suddenly watchful, in fact distinctly guarded. As if he knew there was to be a switch of subjects, and could guess to what. 'I'm terribly sorry to have to bother you at a time like this,' she said, offering it with a deliberately apologetic air of sympathy, 'but I'm here because I was given the name of you and your cousin as Marianna Troughton-Beck's next of kin. Unfortunately she died in an accident two weeks ago. It's taken us this much time to track down whether she had any relatives, I'm afraid.'

'Marianna's dead? You don't exactly surprise me. She was still living rough, I suppose? It's all right, there's no need to tell me tactfully that she was a tramp! And still as mad as a hatter, no doubt. All right, you've told me: what do you want me to do about it?'

It was a blank acceptance of the news, delivered with very little evidence of concern. It was impossible to tell what he was thinking; whether it was relief, foreknowledge, or sheer impatience again. 'We need somebody to claim the body and arrange a funeral,' Jane told him. 'I'm sorry, as I say, to — '

'There's no need to be tactful, I hadn't seen her for years. And when I did you could scarcely call it a friendly relationship. All right, give me an address to contact, and I'll deal with it — when I've got the time.'

'Your aunt left a large sum of money.'

'Laurence! Yes, I know, the fool would insist on sending her cash regularly to some Poste Restante address or other. Anything else?'

'I have some written notes she left, but I can't make any sense of them. I was going to ask your cousin whether they could relate to something in the antiques trade.' Jane produced her photocopied sheet and passed it across to him. He glanced at it briefly with raised eyebrows, and then handed it back to her.

'It wouldn't make any sense to me. And I can't imagine why she should have been doing anything to do with the trade any more. But you'd need Laurence for a translation. I never dealt with any of that. In fact, Marianna never saw me as more than a convenient body to send on errands — or as a shop-sweeper!' There was both a sneer and a distinct tinge of angry bitterness in that. However, he caught himself up quickly to add with throwaway casualness, 'I never thought period jewellery was much of a man's game anyway — much more something for a woman to pore over. Or someone like Laurence. She'd probably turn in her grave if she knew *I* was the one to end up burying her — too bad!'

He had got to his feet with the words, though he accepted the card Jane hastily handed him, with the contact number for the City Police. It was clear that he considered his visit to the station thoroughly over, and DCI Carter made a point of having him politely shown out. However, as soon as he had gone the DCI's voice became a brisk snap as he turned to his own sergeant who had been observing the interview.

'This one's not going to take us long, Phil! I reckon we've got our chief suspect. Good motive, since it sounds as if he gets the lot. Means, since we didn't see any signs of the door being forced — I'd say he just rang the doorbell and his cousin came down and let him in. Opportunity, he knew damn' well what his cousin's movements were and when it was safe that he wouldn't be missed for a few days. And he's a nasty piece of work to boot! The SOCO didn't find any fingerprints besides the deceased's, but there were a good few smudges and signs of things being wiped — to make it look as if it was a blagger whose prints are on file, no doubt! Mr Andrew Beck will have an alibi, of course: he started to offer us one without being asked, didn't he? Well, we'll just have to break it!'

'That message on the answering machine, Guv? From the guess which is all the pathologist would give, that was left after the TOD.'

'Trying to be clever. Like making no secret of the fact that there was no love lost. Time of death, until we get it accurately, is anything from Friday night onwards to Monday: just wait until we've got it pinpointed and we'll have more to work on. But it's money all the way, this one, with the sole heir right in the frame. I wonder how soon he'll ask to go and look in the shop safe, so he can gloat?'

'Pity we didn't have enough to hold him on straight off.'

'He won't do a flit. Too sure of himself. And there's the inheritance to think of. Ah — Sergeant Perry, sorry, I'd forgotten you for a minute. You got everything you wanted, did you?'

'Yes, sir, thanks, and thanks for letting me ask.'

'You're welcome. You may have to get someone else to bury the aunt, though. I'm hopeful of nailing clever Mr Beck!'

He was looking grimly happy about it, as if he could see a good result ahead. Jane herself was less sure, though as it was not her case, she knew better than to offer a comment. Andrew Beck struck her as simply bad-tempered rather than guilty of murder. There had been nothing but an impatient disbelief in his eyes when it became quite obvious where his interlocutor's questions were leading. Still, the DCI could be right, Laurence Beck's cousin could be a good actor playing a subtle game. Andrew Beck certainly had the most to gain from his cousin's death.

Particularly if he *had* already known that Old Mary was no longer alive to claim her property.

That gave her something to think about. If he had known, then how? And he had made no attempt to get in touch with her own police force to offer an identification of the old woman's body. If Andrew Beck was aware that Laurence was sending Marianna money, then he probably knew where . . . Was it possible that the man was a wholesale murderer, and was obliterating his relatives one by one?

She forbore to raise that point with DCI Carter, since it was speculative anyway. She was thoughtful as she set out to drive home, after a cheerful farewell from her former oppo and a civil one from DCI Carter, in between his checking of SOCO reports and chasing up information on Andrew Beck's financial standing. It was much later than Jane had originally planned to return, and the traffic, in the late rush hour, occupied her attention for some while. However, by the time she had queued her way across the Dartford bridge and emerged to take the correct motorway for the eastern side of Kent, she could join a steady stream of cars and lorries without any need to keep her eyes peeled for a turn-off for a good few miles.

Part of her journey had been wasted, since she had got no more information on Old Mary's list of hieroglyphics. Only Laurence, apparently, could have given her an answer. She did know now, though, that Beck Antiques specialised in period jewellery. So did that take her anywhere?

Could there be something which had caught Marianna's attention because of her specialised knowledge? Something she had discovered about items in her particular field being fenced?

Something Old Mary, the former Marianna Troughton-Beck, had known about somebody . . . somebody dangerous enough, or endangered enough by her knowledge, to need to get rid of her . . .

Jane found herself sitting straighter in her seat as an idea formed in her brain. Could there possibly be a connection with the scam Kenny had been investigating? Small, highly valuable stolen items being passed, and their export arranged out of the country. Some of the things on Kenny's list had certainly been jewellery.

Now that was something to set her mind racing round the possibilities. An expert on the scene, somebody who could drag out of the mists of her past the necessary knowledge to know the genuine article when she saw it . . . Where? That was less important for the moment than trying to work out if this was a tenable theory. Marianna had seen something, and it had aroused her suspicions enough for her to tell Kieron that there was something she knew. Or was trying to find out. She had started to keep a list . . .

But someone had spotted her. Or had learned that she had said something to somebody. So —

It was all unprovable. If only Jane had been able to talk to Laurence Beck, he might have been able to translate the list for her. It was more than a pity the man was dead. If he had not been, he might have been able to tell her whether the hieroglyphics described items known to be stolen. In his line of work, he would have had notification from the police on anything suspect which might be circulating. Think again if anything led in that direction, cast back . . . Old Mary had known what she was doing was dangerous. Kieron seemed to think so, her diary suggested it, and Jacko had said it outright: 'She got it into her head that it were dangerous in the city, nights.' That could be why she had taken the uncharacteristic move of begging a place to sleep at Lymans Farm, as a refuge during the hours of darkness when she would be at her most vulnerable . . .

A cold finger touched the back of Jane's neck. She could add Jacko in to the equation. Not a casually lethal tramp-killer. Instead, the disposal of anyone who might have shared Old Mary's knowledge; anyone to whom she might have talked. Hence Jacko, known to be her sometime companion. And then Laurence Beck, who kept his aunt supplied with money to live on, and might be someone in whom she had confided. As soon as it came out that the police had discovered who Old Mary was, her nephew, in the trade himself, became a risk . . .

Someone was being very careful to cover every track. Was it possible?

The person would have to be based in the city. No one from elsewhere would have known Jacko as well as Old Mary. But this person would also have to be able to pass a message up the line that Laurence Beck was a danger too, now. Perhaps, even, to Andrew Beck. If he was involved after all . . .

She could be building castles in the air. Three deaths, but purely coincidental. Two of them could even be accidents. But surely all three, and within a short space of time was too much coincidence!

It was all theory, guesswork, links which were possible but unproven. It gave her an intuitive sense of having caught hold of a pattern. Intuition . . . dear God, DCI Morland would really rake her over the coals for that! And just now — well, it would be useless even to offer such a suggestion.

She would have to go back to the diary. That there was something in it to give a defininte lead was her only hope. Surely there had been one thing there already which suggested Jane was thinking in the right direction: that declaration of intent in those capital-lettered words, 'BUT I WILL HAVE HIM!'

Someone about whom the old woman had been determined to find incontrovertible proof . . .

For a moment, Jane was almost inclined to pull over on to the hard shoulder, switch on her inside light, get the diary out of her briefcase, and start to read it here and now. She had brought it with her to show Laurence Beck the original as well as the photocopy. She knew, even before the idea had properly formed, that that would be a ridiculous thing to do. Let alone that it was highly illegal to use the hard shoulder as a convenient parking place for an hour or so while she tried to wade through something far better studied at leisure. She gave an exasperated grin at her own idiotic impulses (a fine time to get entangled with the Motorway Police, for a start!) and reached forward to switch on the radio for some mildly distracting music. If there was one thing her job ought to have taught her, it was not to get absorbed in her own train of thought when she was at the wheel of a car!

Taking the turn-off for the city when she reached it, she drove steadily and just within the speed limit down the swoop and curve of the dual carriageway, keeping a watchful eye on the TIR in front of her which seemed overinclined to change lanes. A French one: she was surprised it hadn't filtered off for the bypass and a straight route to Dover. She managed to get shot of it at last as she reached the roundabout which gave her a clear and sudden view of the cathedral's high towers, floodlit in the falling dark, the sign that she was home at last. It had been a long day . . .

There was no need to call at the station tonight, and she turned off to thread in a back route through the city streets in the direction of home. She might just dump everything and nip out again for a takeaway; it would be simpler than thinking about cooking and pleasanter than a probably stale sandwich. Then she could let her mind start to buzz again.

As she let herself in through her front door with what was now two keys, she was congratulating herself on the fact that she had actually got round to having a deadlock fitted, saving the fiddle of keeping on going round the back. Then, as she switched on the lights, she stopped dead in disbelief.

Books, papers and cushions strewing her living room floor, a chair overturned, the contents of her coffee-jar poured in a brown train across the debris, along with salt and sugar forming white paths, with the half-emptied sugar bag dumped on the top. Knives, forks and spoons catching the light where they lay scattered randomly, though the half-open kitchen cupboards showed unsmashed crockery . . . Every drawer of her desk had either been pulled right out or was hanging askew, what had been their contents a drift of paper underfoot.

She had seen enough burglaries to be glad there were no trails of spray-paint (or worse) decorating the walls. And her most immediate thought was a numb acknowledgement that now she knew, at first hand, the sense of sick violation she had seen so often in other faces.

Belatedly, she noticed that her hi-fi was missing, speakers and all. So were the rented television and video.

She could see how her visitor had got in. The safety locks on the sliding patio window had been neatly cut out, top and bottom, with a glass-cutter. When she rented the house, Jane had been assured that those windows were safety glass, the landlord even giving a demonstration of how a blow would bounce off them. Small use that had turned out to be, when someone had taken the clever and quiet option of cutting round the locks!

Before she could let her mind automatically start assessing whether that was a new MO or simply one she had not seen over the last few months — and before she had managed to force her feet towards the stairs, to see what mayhem might also lie above — the phone rang.

At least that was still there. It was even still on its usual wall-mounting. Jane detached the receiver, and heard Adrian's voice speaking her name.

'Hi, yes, I've just got back. This minute. And guess what? I've been burgled.'

'Darling, I'm sorry! I'll be right round!'

He rang off fast before she could say she had got to ring the station and get the whole, idiotic process of being a victim started. Actually, she decided that could wait. The perp was well gone, obviously some time ago: she could even see where rain had blown in through the cut-out holes and then dried. At least he had pulled the main windows shut again, or she would have had rain all over the floor as well as all the other mess. The break-in had probably happened last night.

Hell and *damn*! What an end to a day which had already faced her with a vicious murder. Wasn't that enough?

And what a nastily clever little perp, too, to have picked his time so well; to have chosen an occasion when she was safely away in London overnight.

# 12

'Bad luck, Sarge! Do you want us to put a call in for CID, or will you do that yourself?'

The patrol car which had come rapidly in answer to Jane's call had contained the same two constables who had fished Jacko out of the river. They stood looking large and uncomfortable in the middle of her chaotic living room, casting her awkwardly sympathetic glances. The mixture of victim and sergeant was obviously a difficult one to handle and they had not quite sorted out whether to suggest calming cups of tea, or crack the usual in-house jokes; were not sure either how much notice to take of the presence of Adrian, though Jane had offered them a frame of reference with a casual, 'This is a neighbour who's come in to give me some back up.' She made a deliberate effort to pull herself into briskness, and gave them a weary grin.

'No, there's no need to drag anyone else from CID out. I may as well wear both hats and make my own notes! It's not worth calling in a SOCO either — just one more of the usual jobs to add to the list!'

'Someone's done a neat job of getting in,' said George, stirring himself into official busyness and going over to peer at the window. 'Haven't seen one done like that before, have you, Dave? Though

I suppose we will, now someone's got the idea!'

'Yes, I know, they're getting cleverer all the time. If you two wouldn't mind, once you've had a look round to witness all this, you might go and give the houses each side a knock to see if anyone heard anything. Would you believe,' Jane said in exasperation, 'I'd just put an extra safety-lock on the front door? So chummy comes round the back with a bright new notion!'

'They're always going to get in if they want to, and you can't live in Fort Knox.' Dave, the burly one, offered that as if to prevent her from blaming herself. 'My dad was done the other day, and he'd followed most of the advice I gave him. Can you see what's immediately missing, Sarge? Other than the trashing?'

'Hi-fi, television and video from down here, and my electric typewriter; upstairs they've thrown everything around but the only things definitely gone are a gold locket and a ring. I didn't have much to make it worth their while.' The thought of fingers pawing through her clothing drawers was as nasty as people always said it was. 'I shan't know properly until I've tidied up, and I followed due procedure and left everything as it was. It feels odd, that,' she told the constables, trying for rueful humour, 'and I even had to remind myself not to start putting things back! One of you had better look upstairs so you can make your notes, okay? Otherwise it's only my word, isn't it?'

They moved around checking, then George, with a glance at her, found the kettle under a heap of books, and after testing it to see if it was still working, set it to boil. He rescued a packet of teabags from beneath something on the floor, and then began picking up cutlery, a thorough look round downstairs having been completed. Adrian, who had remained silently and protectively beside Jane, moved to join him. A moment later Dave reappeared from his trip upstairs.

'They may have turned the beds upside down but at least they haven't messed them,' he commented consolingly. 'Looks more like a search for what they could lift than spite. That's something! Even the stuff poured around down here isn't more than half-hearted. I'll go and check those houses — back in a moment.'

As he departed, Jane looked quickly at his partner. 'Look, it's all right, you needn't try to help tidy up. Nice of you, but it's . . . I'll have a go at it slowly.'

'That's okay, Sarge. You're bound to feel a bit shaken up — I would!' George gave her a shy look and then moved to make a cup of tea as the kettle began to steam. He had clearly made the decision that victim treatment was in order. He added over his shoulder, 'You'll need to make those patio doors secure for the night. If you've got a bit of wood and some nails, I could fix that for you.'

'I can do that,' Adrian put in. 'I think I've got some suitable bits of chipboard or something at my place.'

'Right, sir. You'll need to put something all the way across . . . '

They went into a huddle about the most suitable way to do it. Jane was aware of feeling extraordinarily helpless — was this how it usually took people? — and only too glad if someone else would make decisions. Her house . . . At least she had had no confidential papers from the station. And she could tell herself wryly that she might now find all sorts of things that she had thrust into desk drawers and forgotten. A pile of bank statements fanned themselves out at her feet to show how thoroughly everything had been emptied. Looking for money, probably; well, they had failed to score there, she never kept any around. That was probably why they — or just one perp, he? — had pulled all the books out of the bookcase, too.

Could it have been Kieron, coming back to prove a point after all?

No, that was too unlikely. This was just an ordinary thief, finding a way in to see what he could grab. Another MO to list (and to check if anyone had actually done the same in the past), but an MO which would probably bring an arrest eventually — since slags made a habit of repeating themselves.

She found someone had put a mug of tea into her hand, and looked up quickly from where she had taken refuge in a righted armchair. 'Thanks — make one for yourselves, too. Might as well, until you get your next call.' The constable had already reported back, his shoulder hunching his personal radio to his mouth in the characteristic gesture, and the message coming back clearly in a crackling version of the duty-sergeant's voice: 'Okay, I've logged that, and tell Sergeant Perry tough luck! You'll be there for a while? Let us know if you need any further assistance.'

Dave came back with the news that nobody had heard anything from the houses either side. Par for the course, and Jane barely knew her neighbours anyway. She tried for conversation as the four of them drank sweet tea (she didn't actually like it sweet but it was the thought that counted) and that was when something else came up, to startle her out of the torpor which seemed to keep taking her over.

'It's a bummer about DI Crowe, isn't it?' Dave remarked. 'There's a piece of bad luck, if you like!'

'What — leaving, you mean?'

'No, the accident. Oh, you said you were away all day so maybe you won't have heard? He turned his car right over this morning, and landed up in hospital.'

'Jesus! How bad?'

'Double fracture to the leg, a couple of broken ribs — he's going to be all right, though, just stuck in a hospital bed for a fair while! A gravel lorry had shed part of its load, the DI came round the corner right on to it, and went into a skid all over the grit. What's he got as well as the leg and ribs, George — concussion and abrasions, wasn't it? No worse than that, luckily. But it's a lousy time for it to happen, just when he was due for a whole round of farewell parties.'

'Christ, yes! But you're sure he's all right? They haven't got him in DIL or anything?'

'No, not that bad — the word came back that he's 'comfortable'. Which I don't suppose he is, poor . . . I mean I don't suppose lying there with a broken leg and concussion feels much like comfort,' the constable hastily corrected himself. 'Well, I guess we'd better move on, Sarge — if you'll be all right?'

He was showing a nice degree of fatherly concern, a reminder that the force always believed in offering a particular care for its own. 'I'm fine, thanks,' Jane told him, and added a deliberately cheerful joke to prove it. 'I'll be able to do my own Victim Support visit, won't I? If you'll put your report in, I'll add mine to it in the morning. Hope you have a reasonably quiet time for the rest of the night.'

'If the slags'll let us. Night, then, Sarge. Night, sir — and you'll get the temporary fixing on that window?'

'Yes, I will,' Adrian answered the polite enquiry. But as soon as the two constables had gone, he obviously felt that gathering Jane up into his arms was a greater priority. Grateful as she was for his comforting presence, she was hard put to stand still and let herself be hugged. Her mind was all at once less occupied with the shock of the burglary than with the news of Dan Crowe's accident.

'If the guv's landed up in hospital, I'm going to have to — '

'Think about that tomorrow! You were as white as a sheet when I arrived, and you don't look much better now. Can you leave all this? I think you — '

'I think I'm bloody hungry. I've suddenly realised I haven't had anything to eat since a rapid canteen sandwich at lunch.' She didn't want to tell him not to fuss when he was being nice: part of her might have been quite glad of the fuss anyway — if Dan Crowe's accident had not taken priority in her mind. 'Could you be a love, a real love, and go and get me some fish and chips? Yes, I know, scarcely the most elegant thing to want, but at least it's quick and nourishing!'

'Your own particular treatment for shock? All right, if it's what you fancy. And I'll get the wood for the windows at the same time. You'd better come and stay at my place tonight, though — yes, you had, you can't sleep here!'

'I can . . . I'm going to have to clear up the mess anyway. And it's only the kind of scene I see almost every day; it just happens to be my house this time.'

'You are so damn stubborn!'

'Yeah.' The look on his face made it necessary to be honest. 'Hey, I'm grateful that you're here. Really. And staying here rather than taking refuge in your flat is like getting back on a horse when it's thrown you, you know? What I'd actually be grateful for would be if — well, if you wouldn't mind — if you'd stay here too? Would you?'

'You'd be more comfortable at the flat. But if you put it that way . . . ' He smiled at her and shrugged, but she could see that her request had headed off an argument. And had pleased him. It had been an entirely genuine appeal, too. She had to clear up the mess; she had to stay here; but it would be a lot easier if he was with her.

And that was almost a surprise; that for once she really would rather let her guard down than pretend even to herself that she could handle on her own the shivery sense of having been invaded.

'All right, then. We'll both stay here — and we'll both get the place cleaned up. It shouldn't take all that long, with two of us,' Adrian pronounced, with a determined jut to his chin which made Jane decide that he was actually an angel in disguise. A very tidy angel. The present chaos would probably be changed to a state of neatness her house had never known. 'I'll be off to get you your fish and chips, then, and fetch the wood. You're sure you'll be all right?'

'I'm fine. Honestly. Look, I'm almost completely recovered — or I will be when I've had something to eat!'

She would have to be, she thought as he went away. It was a fact which would have passed him by, but if Dan Crowe was hospitalised, she was going to have a lot to do in CID. She hoped the guv was genuinely all right . . . It would leave her in charge, as the senior ranking sergeant; and unless the DCI stirred himself from his preferred administrative fastness and came back to work on the ground, she would have a lot of organising to cope with. No bad thing to be seen doing it just now, either. She would need to be thoroughly on the ball. Not a hope that she could allow herself to suffer from the trauma of a mere burglary; she would have to settle down and show just how smoothly and efficiently CID could run under her direction.

But first the dire job of clearing up here, and she might as well make a start. She reached absently for her briefcase to put it out of the way.

At least she had had Old Mary's diary with her, or that might be in pieces by now like last year's desk-diary, on the floor at her feet and displaying a ripped spine and torn pages. Someone had even bothered to pull that out of the back of a drawer and search through it — in case there was any money hidden between the leaves, presumably?

Picking it up to walk across and drop it in the bin, Jane thought that this morning seemed a long time ago. Her arrival to find Laurence Beck had been murdered. Andrew Beck's interview, and the Chelsea DCI's conviction that he was the killer. Her own theories . . . She was going to have little time to follow those up, with the guv in hospital.

Somehow she would have to make time.

As she looked round at the chaos of her home, a shiver abruptly came over her again, and she was glad Adrian was staying. Whoever had been here, going through her things, it left a nasty taste in the mouth. A feeling, not just of outrage, but of threat, her own space suddenly not her own, and unsafe.

Everyone who had had a break-in felt like that; she had seen it any number of times in faces, heard it in voices. And she had been through worse, so it was strange to find that something so minor should hit her as hard as it did. Dealing with burglaries was an everyday occurrence, and she knew from experience that facing a killer was far worse . . . Perhaps she was more accustomed than she realised to thinking of her own four walls as a safe space, quite separate from her working life.

It was better to counter this idiotic degree of shock with annoyance, the angry realisation that she had no chance even to put on some music to brighten the labour of clearing up. The thieving slag had taken her sounds system! He wouldn't get much out of it, anyway, since she had had it a good five years and wouldn't have considered it worth much even on a trade-in. It made a good focus for irritation, however, as she set about picking things up, while trying not to tread instant coffee even further into the green carpet.

★ ★ ★

For the next few days Jane felt as if she was chasing her tail. The DCI did decide to come down and run the department, which frequently caused more confusion rather than less since he had his own extremely picky methods of organisation and insisted on being asked about everything, however minor. The result was a lot of time wasted on 'meetings to report back' and a minute examination of every current case. (Not Old Mary's, however: that file was swept aside with an irritable, 'This one can surely be left alone by now, Sergeant, we must concentrate on the priorities!') When he reached the report of the break-in to Jane's own house, he received it with a sigh, and a barely concealed accusatory look as if she had added herself as a burglary statistic out of what must have been carelessness. And to ruin his month's percentages. No sympathy there, but then she would not have expected any. Jane kept up an air of deadpan obedience at all times, and acknowledged wryly that Dan Crowe had worked round the DCI, rather than to him, more than she had ever given him credit for. And with the DI as a buffer, the department had definitely run more smoothly — even if in his own individual way.

But this was all good practice.

A rapid collection had been made around the station to send flowers or fruit up to the hospital; someone had suggested whisky too, but the general consensus was that a nurse would only confiscate it. Jane managed a quick visit of her own, as one of a stream of people popping up to check on the DI in person.

She found him sporting a vivid black eye and a swollen bruise on the side of his mouth as well as his other injuries, and in a very bad temper. It did at least transpire that he had been told he would be healed in time not to have to change his emigration plans. But there was no chance that he would be coming back to work again; the rest of his time in the force would be taken up by sick leave. His wife, who was sitting beside his bed knitting throughout Jane's brief visit, gave him the quelling look of the long-married, and raised her eyebrows at Jane.

'He's like a bear with a sore head, but I keep telling him he's lucky it wasn't worse! And yes, Dan, I can get all the arrangements made, and the house packed up, without your having to lift a finger! I'd probably have had to anyway, wouldn't I? I've done everything enough over the years, while you've been chasing villains!' She probably had, too, as a police wife. 'I'll manage, and so will your sergeant here, so you can give up looking as if you want to snap her head off, and thank her for the flowers she's brought you.'

'There's no need. It's all right, Guv, I only looked in to tell you that we miss you already.' A daunting look from Mrs Crowe instructed her not to talk to him about work, and Jane gave him a grin. 'I won't stop, since I can see Inspector Grainger on his way up the ward to visit you. So I'll just say, from all of us in CID, get well soon!'

'Humph. There's a whole lot of stuff I was going to — '

'Stop trying to talk, Dan, or the swelling on your mouth will never go down! Here, I'll give you a drink . . .'

Jane left Mrs Crowe applying a straw to her husband's lips, and after giving him another sympathetic grin, took herself away. He was stuck where he was, and they were stuck with his absence. It was a pity . . . It looked as if she and DCI Morland were going to have to spend a couple of months head-to-head.

Or maybe the top brass would try to make an earlier appointment, in the circumstances. She might be in a position to know if that was on the cards if she was suddenly called to an interview board.

She had had no time at all to be sociable over the last few days, though Adrian had been patiently there. And thoroughly supportive. He had made time to be around for the glazier who came to mend her window; let her use his word processor to type out her insurance claim, as well as a letter to her landlord; was there again for the TV rental company to bring her another set, since they would only call during working hours. She had actually given him a key to the house, against the rules or not. He was the only person to whom she could let out her exasperated grumbles about the DCI, and he had listened patiently to those, too. She had not actually mentioned that it was all tied up with her promotion hopes, aware that this might still be a delicate subject. At the moment, the last thing she wanted was another quarrel flaring up.

At least he seemed to understand that she was forced to be exceptionally busy for the time being, in a state where work really did have to take precedence. It was bad enough that she had been carrying Old Mary's diary about with her without the least chance to look at it — but while she had the DCI on her back, there was frustratingly little hope of being allowed time to follow that up. There had been no word from Andrew Beck about arrangments to bury his aunt, but for all she knew, DCI Carter might have arrested him for murder by now.

Two days later, she arrived in the CID room from a long and abortive session at a domestic (to which Morland had insisted on sending her when it should have been someone from DVU, the Domestic Violence Unit) to be pulled up short by the sight of someone standing in the middle of the empty room, looking round consideringly. A tall man with the broad shoulders of a rugby player and a head of thick brown hair. And a face she knew from the past, too. She stepped forward, smiling, as he turned towards her.

'Well, blow me down, it's Chris Hollings, isn't it? In case you don't remember, we were on the Special Course together.' It was the one all graduate entrants did if they passed their probationary period on the beat, and part of the accelerated promotion scheme. She wondered what Chris Hollings had done since and how far he had risen: they must be much the same age, give or take a possible year's seniority on his part. 'What are you doing down here?' she asked. 'Visiting? Looking for information? Something we can do for you?'

'Hallo, Jane. I wondered if it might be you when I saw your name on the list.' He gave her a pleasant smile. 'I thought you'd gone on in the Met, but I've been out of the country for a while, and people move around. As for what you can do for me . . . sit down and give me a thorough orientation! I'm your new temporary DI.'

'*You* are?'

'No need to look so surprised. You're short of one, aren't you? And I've got the rank. I've just finished a spell with Europol as liaison, to see

198

if we really can get a European Police Force off the ground. Off with one job and not started the next, you might say. So here I am. Ready, willing and able!'

Able and ambitious, she remembered: apt to come out top of the class. As had she, once or twice. She was not surprised that he had reached Inspector's level already and he might well have Chief Inspector in his sights next, always supposing the Sheehy Report was not adopted and that rank abolished.

He had not exactly been a mate, but she had found him rational and unprejudiced and easy to work with, she remembered. Also capable of turning on the charm and being quite the diplomat. Quite high-powered, too, as he obviously still was if he had been sent to use his skills to liaise with Europol.

Waiting for his next posting, he had obviously been seen as a handy body while the applications for permanent DI here came in. She gave him a genuine smile.

'I can only say, welcome aboard! And, you're a blessing, in fact: we've been dead short-handed this past week, with the DCI having to cover both jobs!'

And little did he know, being a thorough pain in the neck. That was something he would soon find out.

Though if he was still the diplomat he used to be, he would handle that.

And he, of course, might have Morland eating out of his hand.

# 13

He did. The DCI went round looking like a dog with two tails, and telling anyone who would listen how lucky they were to have someone as efficient as DI Hollings to take over at short notice. His air of satisfaction was so plain that, used as she was to his dislike of her, Jane still could not help feeling a faint sting of resentment. His open inference that he had had to carry an enormously heavy load since Dan Crowe's accident because there had been no one in CID capable enough to share it was outrageously out of order. It was scarcely likely to give Chris Hollings a good impression of her, either; though as she remembered him, he was a fair-minded man and would make up his own mind.

His first move was to call everyone together for what he called 'an afternoon rap session', for which he perched informally on the edge of someone's desk.

'It's going to be a tough one taking over a strange department at a moment's notice — tough for you too, to be faced with a complete outsider, and one none of you know from Adam. Well, apart from Sergeant Perry, because she and I actually trained together — a bonus for me, that! What I'm going to do for the first few days is more or less lie low and let you carry on. I'll be having a look at everything during those days, and watching how you all work. But I must emphasise, that's not to look for things to criticise, merely to check out everyone's strengths. I know you can all think of a dozen other things you should be doing at this moment but this meeting isn't a waste of time, it's to start getting to know each other. We'll start with me. I'm Christopher Hollings, and I've been a DI for eighteen months. I started out in Birmingham, then I was in Surrey, then for just over a year I've been in Strasbourg. I'm married, no children as yet. So, who's going next with a potted biography?'

Definitely a believer in modern management methods, with a breezy, friendly openness with his staff and an air of wanting to do things by consensus. Everyone began to respond to his amiable manner, Jane could feel it. A different style from Dan Crowe's snap and growl, but he intended to get them pulling with him rather than against him, and it would probably work. He was good at asking for opinions, listening to them with apparent deference but not letting them run on too far. He wound things up after twenty minutes and told everyone cheerfully to go on with whatever they should have been doing, but summoned Jane to join him in the DI's small private office.

The door shut behind both of them, he gave her an amiable smile but wasted no time. 'I've noticed you've been giving me back-up with the troops. Thanks, that's a help.'

'An unsettled department is to no one's advantage. We've been at sixes and sevens enough lately.'

'I'd imagine you have, but it's a good sergeant's job to do what you've just been doing. I assume

201

you've put in for the permanent DI job? I wish you luck.' He gave her another of his smiles. 'I'm not going to ask you for a rundown on the DCs, because I'd rather form my own opinion. Your other sergeant hasn't been with you long, I gather, so I expect he's still finding his feet. Any sidelights you can give me on the way things have been run to date?'

'The DCI likes to have regular reports, and has a weekly planning meeting. The rest of the time he usually leaves day-to-day stuff to the DI, but he particularly likes the monthly figures in on time.'

'Yes, I've gathered he's an administrative type. He said he'd give me a free hand.' Had he? Chris Hollings didn't know how lucky he was! 'Thanks. Now, anything you want to ask me?'

'What do you want to be called — sir or guv?'

'Chris from you when we're alone, either of the others the rest of the time. We'll see what they decide to call me, shall we? So let's move on. What I want from you now, is all the files of all the current cases. I need to bone up on everything fast, so I'll get my head down and do that.'

He had set himself a major task. For those first few days, Jane found herself running the department with a great deal less hassle than she had had recently. After that, though, she discovered that their amiable temporary DI was not going to treat the job as a comfortable stop-gap, not at all. He called another department meeting and set about a brisk and thorough reorganisation.

'I'm going to make some changes to rationalise things. The special responsibility groups you've all been working in seem to have become rather blurred, don't they?' If they had, it was because Dan Crowe had taken little notice of them.

'You've got various skills between you, and we need to utilise them to our best advantage. Sergeant Pettigrew, you were in Traffic up in Rochester before you moved down here to CID, weren't you? So I'm going to put you in charge of all car crime: thefts from and damage to vehicles is one of our major problems, and I think it would be valuable to have you concentrating on that area. DC Lockley, you'll work to Sergeant Pettigrew on this.

'Now, Domestic Burglary: Inspector Grainger from the uniformed side is going to be i/c that as an overall matter, but from here I want DC Barnes to take over responsibility for that — you've been local to this district all your life, Kenny, so let's make use of your expertise on local villains. Sergeant Perry will take over responsibility for all burglaries from business premises — liaison with uniform again, of course, you'll know who your particular contact for that is. And DC Peters can work to Sergeant Perry. I think you'll make a good team.

'I'll be in charge of violent crime hold-ups, assaults and so on; as well as being in overall control, of course. Obviously things will come up which don't fall into a single specific category, but I'd like each of you to be particularly aware of your own area, and to have that at your fingertips. If you need extra personnel from uniform for any particular job, do try and find someone from the same responsibility unit — it's easier to grab the nearest available body, I know, but I've been talking things over with my opposite numbers, and we've agreed to try to rationalise that. Any questions?'

'We'll need to borrow between the groups if there's a big job on — '

'Yes, obviously, but that doesn't mean not being aware of your own area in general terms. Oh, by the way, another thing I've noticed. I'd like you all to make a lot more use of Collator Profiling. It's a useful tool and may throw up someone you haven't thought of. Yes, Kenny?'

'This antiques investigation for the Met which I've been on. It's not domestic burglary, or not from here, anyway — '

'I've already arranged to shut that one down. We're leaving it to Customs from now on. We can't be expected to cover their territory, and you've already done what the Met asked for, a check around. I gather it's something of an international matter but if anything else comes up on it — liaison cross-Channel, say — it can be done by either Sergeant Perry or myself, as the best linguists.' He either remembered, or had looked it up in her file, that Jane had various European languages to her credit.

'Let's look at other cases we can finish with. The tobacco hi-jack, I think. It doesn't seem to be going anywhere, and since it was done just off the motorway, the perps may not be anywhere near our area; so we'll leave it open but not spend time on it. This six-month-old stabbing — no point in imagining we're going to get anywhere with that one. The investigation into the tramp's death — there isn't really anything there to make it suspicious, unless Drugs want to go on following it up . . . '

'I'd like a word with you about that one, sir.'

'Really? All right, see me in a minute. Now, if nobody's got any more immediate queries, the next task has to be exchanging files and making sure you've all got the right ones for your unit.'

He had done a thorough job in changing everybody around; a brisk new broom, even if he was only a temporary one. There would be some grumbles, but the revised system would work its way in. Jane quashed the thought that he might have been a little less thorough — he had a right to have things done his way while he was here — and went to talk to him about Old Mary.

He listened to what she had to say with concentration. However, when she had finished, his decison was quick and final.

'No, you haven't got enough to draw conclusions. The other vagrant's death sounds like a perfectly ordinary accident, so let's leave that one out for a start. The nephew's murder — that's London's baby. You can give them a ring to see if they've charged the other one — Andrew, was it? — because we need to know whether he's going to come down and make funeral arrangements anyway. But I think you're making too much of a leap in connecting them. This list the old lady made could be anything, but since she was once a jewellery dealer, the best thing you can do with it is let Customs have a copy just in case it makes any sense to them and might contain something which turns up on their export list. If they want to circulate it, it's up to them.

This boy who set the whole thing off by saying the old lady had some secret knowledge: that's too tenuous, and with a schizophrenia case, she may have imagined she had all sorts of secrets, so he's being a bit credulous there. I think you've handled it well in trying to calm him down, but I can't see anything there to make us give time to following it further.'

'There's still the way she died.'

'You've said yourself that an accidental fall could be feasible. The fire report clearly suggests she could have been responsible for the arson, too. And I'm leaving that for the Drugs Unit to follow up, since the whole rave thing is their area. You can give them the diary if you think it might help them — an illustration of her state of mind? But as far as we're concerned, I'm not prepared to recommend we go any further, so we'll close it. All right?'

The last two words were merely a token. And, summed up his way, the decision to close was reasonable. If only there had not been something in Jane's bones to tell her it was not reasonable . . . If she wanted to think like that, she could only do it privately, with his decision firmly taken. 'Very well, sir,' she said — and saw him give her a quick thoughtful glance for the 'sir'; though it had been habit rather than an indication of disagreement masquerading as obedience. She probably would remember to address him as Chris in the normal way, as she had been instructed to do when they were alone in his office, as now. 'I'll call London about Andrew Beck, and then shut it down. It seemed worth putting to you, though.'

'Yes, why not? And, as I said, pass a copy of that list to Customs, on the offchance. Now, about the non-domestic break-ins I've put under your responsibility. I know you've been dealing with domestic, but as you've had one of those yourself recently it seemed better to change you over. Besides, what you've got now is going to include the more major stuff, like warehouse jobs, as well as all the petty business premises theft. I wanted someone senior on it, with an organised mind.'

At least he showed no inclination to shuffle her off into 'women's areas'. That made a nice change from Morland. And perhaps — since Morland had given him a free hand — she would no longer be landed with every minor job. As she left the DI's office with Old Mary's file in her hand, Jane could only feel that Chris Hollings' temporary tenure had its advantages. He was someone she had no qualms at all about working for, and if he was a little bit too prone to brisk reorganisation when the next occupant of that office might want to do things another way, he was entitled to do things his way for now . . . Some of his methods and skills might be worth learning from, too.

But she was still stubbornly convinced he was not right about Old Mary. And she would make no move to pass the diary on to the Drugs Unit. She had taken another couple of tries at studying it in the only time she could find, a few occasions in the evenings at home. It was not an easy read. Even where the writing was apparently rational, the old woman seemed to have a liking for elaborate metaphors and flowery language. The fire-breathing dragon had appeared again, in terms which looked as if it might be Marianna's vision of all the wickedness in the world; but then there was a scuttling golden rat as well. And an owl. And some creature just referred to as the scavenger. A sinister one, that last, giving the feeling of red eyes and tearing teeth and slinking evil in the dark. It was more as if she was weaving a story than giving anything on which Jane could take a clear hold. It was scarcely good late-night reading, either, more likely to induce nightmares than offer clues.

But there was an intelligence there which was more Marianna than Old Mary. If a sick mind, an intelligent sick mind . . . Jane knew that she would persist with it, just in case. Somewhere in there, there might yet be a lead to show whether she really had sensed a pattern of events, and one with wider implications than anyone else was prepared to envisage. A reason why all three deaths might be murder, for instance. Murder by someone who was involved in something big enough to make the least risk intolerable. Someone with a hidden face . . . No, the diary would stay in Jane's possession for now.

A copy of Marianna's list of hieroglyphics could certainly go to Customs, however. That was an idea which just might bring forth something. Jane typed a rapid note to enclose with it, and slid both into an envelope for mailing. Then, since she had been charged with officially closing the Old Mary file and might as well continue to make it her first job, she looked up the Chelsea police number and punched the digits out on her phone.

The sergeant who was an old colleague was the handiest person to ask for, rather than bothering DCI Carter. By a piece of luck he was on duty and available, and was happy to give her the information she wanted.

'No, they haven't been able to charge Andrew Beck. He was well and truly alibi'd for the TOD — the pathologist couldn't come up with more than Saturday night or Sunday for that, but Andrew Beck's wife says he was with her all weekend. The DCI still has his doubts, since nothing's missing from the premises, but they're treating it as either murder in pursuit of an attempted robbery, or a possible gay killing now. The latter's because they still reckon Laurence Beck could have let the killer in. He may have fancied a bit of rough and brought someone in with him.'

'No witnesses to that?'

'No, but it's a quiet street and if he brought someone back late at night, there's no reason why anyone should have seen him. There's a doubt on it because he wasn't known for that — kept himself to himself, more — but Andrew Beck's implied several times that cousin Laurence was gay. So that's where it is at the moment, with no result as yet. Though it still could have been a careful lock-picker, on the blag, and going in through the flat to avoid the shop alarms. There was some pretty valuable stuff in the shop safe, I heard, well worth somebody's time.'

'But nothing taken. You'd have thought having gone that far, someone would have grabbed the loot.'

'Maybe Laurence got the beating he did because he wouldn't give out the safe combination. It's a fairly sophisticated job. The DCI doesn't go with that one, he'd still like to see his first theory work out. But like I said, Andrew Beck's too well alibi'd. So they're having to look elsewhere.'

'Thanks. And if Andrew Beck's out free, I can expect to hear from him sometime, I suppose, about burying his aunt's body? That's really what I wanted to know. Thanks for bringing me up to date, and nice to talk to you again, anyway.'

Ringing off, she sat for a moment contemplating what she had heard, one finger to her mouth. She was only allowed a moment, though, before a summoning bleep had her lifting the receiver again, to hear a voice from the switchboard.

'There's a Mrs Singh on the line for you, Sergeant Perry, do you want to take it?'

'Yes, sure, put her through.'

Mrs Singh's lilting Indian voice told her that one of the sub post office's stolen benefit books had been presented for cashing — though as instructed she had not refused payment or tried to keep the book, merely taken a careful look at the customer. 'I can give you a very clear description, Sergeant, as you asked, and I have his signature as well. Will this help? He has gone now, but you did tell me not to try to keep him.'

'Yes, that's right, it's better not to take the risk. Thanks very much, Mrs Singh, I'll be down straight away.'

'If you could make it not for half an hour, I shall be closing the post office then for lunchtime so this

210

would be better. And if any more are offered for cashing during that time, I will do the same thing, and look at the face to describe.'

'I'll be there in half an hour then. Thanks again, Mrs Singh.'

A very sensible lady, and one who could be relied upon to offer a good description, too. Jane glanced at her watch, and decided she might as well go now and buy a sandwich on the way. A crusty one from a baker's would be more appetising than what the canteen could offer. She put her head round the door of the DI's office to tell Chris Hollings where she was off to; remembering, as she told him, that this one actually was her right job now, as it was a theft from business premises. Though it could also have been called violent crime, his own area, since it was a hold-up with a fake plastic gun. That particular demarcation line was not worth raising in the middle of an ongoing case, and she went to let herself out of the back of the station and get her car.

Sergeant Morris was in the yard organising a couple of constables on what seemed to be a rubbish-clearing detail. He looked round as Jane came towards him.

'We've got an edict from above on keeping the outside tidier,' he greeted her. 'Can you pass the word round your lot that if they've got bags to dump after shredding, they don't just put them down? Everything's got to go in the actual council bins, because anything else doesn't get taken away!'

'I'll put a reminder up on the board in large

letters. I'm as guilty as anyone, I left those there.' Her eye had suddenly caught two bulging supermarket bags as a constable unearthed them from behind a full black plastic sack. 'I meant either to put them for burning or just get them taken away with the rubbish. Sorry!'

'Looks as if there's some newspapers in one of them; don't bin those, Stevens, take them out and put them in that other pile. The Sea Scouts could do with them for their paper collection.'

'No, don't!' Jane began quickly, remembering what might be adhering to any newspaper out of one of Old Mary's bags. And as the bags had lain there for some time by now, who knew what insect life might have bred? She was opening her mouth to explain, and advise the hesitating constable to bin the lot without disturbing anything, when another thought abruptly occurred to her. Local papers. And advertised sales. She'd been ignorant of the connection at the time but suppose Old Mary had made a mark in the newspapers, against some saleroom or antiques fair. 'I need those myself, if you wouldn't mind,' she said. 'Sorry, could you just take them out and — give them a very thorough shake, and hand them over?'

'Still clearing up after your burglary, and need some extra newspaper to wrap breakages in?' Sergeant Morris said sympathetically as the constable did as he was asked. 'I know, the binmen still don't like too many sharp edges thrown in unwrapped, even though it's all mechanised nowadays. If you want any more, help yourself. The Sea Scouts can do without if you want to use it.'

'This'll be enough, thanks. And I'll remember to tell CID about the rubbish rules.'

She need not rescue Old Mary's bags in their entirety: she had gone through the rest of the contents quite thoroughly enough the first time. And it was only an offchance which had made her take the papers, still there after all when she would have assumed the bags she had dumped and forgotten to be long gone. Jane gave the crumpled pile of newspapers another thorough shake before she put them down on the front seat of her car — despite a dim memory that fleas liked warm-blooded company, so perhaps the sojourn outside would mean that there was no danger of finding any.

It was probably going to be a pointless job running through the printed columns for possible markings, anyway. The old woman had probably been saving them to wrap herself up in rather than for any other reason. And Old Mary would be an unlikely type to draw lines around anything which interested her.

But Marianna might.

Traffic turned out to be thin between the police station and Northgate, so that Jane arrived in a parking space a good twenty minutes before Mrs Singh would be free to see her. Even the purchase of an inviting crusty roll from the nearby sandwich bar only took a couple of minutes, and Jane decided to sit in her car and eat it now. She might as well start a riffle through the rescued papers at the same

213

time. There were not that many of them, and it was just a question of running a rapid eye down each page.

The crumpled state of some of the papers, and several unidentifiable smears, made the task less than inviting. And there was no indication that anyone had shown an undue interest in any advertised antiques sale or fair, anyway.

Jane flicked over another sheet — and stopped abruptly, her eyes instantly caught by the scored marking outlining something on the page. A photograph. Unfortunately, a photograph with a smear right across it, as if some piece of food had slipped down inside the paper just there; but the caption was readable. It said, 'Some of the many visitors enjoying the Mercury Air Show at Markham Field. There was a good attendance for this charity event and many people brought a picnic and made a day of it. More pictures, page 21.'

On this picture, if the reason for circling it had been the faces on show, the smear had rendered all the ones on one side invisible.

Jane turned to find page 21, her eyes noting as she searched that this local weekly's date was mid-September. Some three weeks before Old Mary's death. Why had this particular air show been interesting? It must surely be the old woman who had marked it because the lines round the picture were drawn in particuarly virulent purple biro. Some of the diary was written in that same ugly, identifiable, and not very common colour.

On page 21 there were several more photographs but only one had a similar outlining. This one was undamaged and showed a picture of a large and smiling man posing in front of a light aeroplane, a flying jacket round his shoulders, the white wings and struts of the small plane throwing the face into clear relief. And if Jane had not already recognised him, the caption told her without doubt: 'Quentin Hurst with his Beech aircraft, one of the many planes on show as part of the day's festivities.'

Why should Old Mary have been taking an interest in Adrian's partner? *Why?*

# 14

There was nothing else in any of the papers. Just those two photographs with their purple outlining. Turning back to the first, Jane peered at it again, trying to see if anyone else was recognisable. In the unsmeared side there was what appeared to be a family sitting on the grass: mother, father, two small children, picnic things laid out around them, all of them looking upwards towards the sky. On the smeared side, and further away from the camera, all that could be seen was two pairs of trouser-legs, as if two men had been standing talking together. The dark stain, which looked suspiciously like some kind of thick greasy gravy going up to the top of the page and right through it, obliterated the heads, shoulders, and upper torsos of the trousered figures. No, that was a shoulder, in some kind of jacket. It could just possibly be Quentin again, with the print making his flying jacket look darker than it had in the other photograph. This man was not so tall, though, surely: by trying to look through from the other side, Jane could just see an outline which suggested an inexact fit. Surely Quentin had broader shoulders, and was a bigger man altogether . . .

If the reason for marking the photograph was because it showed the faces of those two men, in conversation with each other, that point had been lost now. A careful scrape with her fingernail merely tore the paper. Jane was suddenly aware that it was possible she herself had been responsible for the blot across the picture during her search through the bags; she remembered finding she had plunged her hand into something extremely soggy, and using one of the newspapers to pick it out and drop it on the ground. Damn! If she had only looked at the papers first. But there had seemed no reason to do so. Most tramps collected newspaper to spread out and lie on for the night if necessary or to use as rudimentary coverings, for warmth. It had seemed something natural for Old Mary to be carrying about. Something expected and unimportant.

A good hiding place for a paper containing something Marianna *had* found important. For some reason of her own.

Photographs. Of three men at an air show.

Why had Marianna kept them? As a record of certain faces? As a proof that two people knew each other? That was an interesting possibility.

An unnoticed press photographer taking a casual picture . . .

There was one place where Jane could find the original picture: the newspaper office.

She remembered Mrs Singh, looked quickly at her watch, and knew she would have to follow the newspaper up later. It was time to do what she was actually supposed to be doing. A description and signature of the person cashing one of the stolen benefit books should provide the lead they wanted on that: if the cashee was not the thief himself he would undoubtedly be able to lead them in the right direction. She must deal with that first before she went back to her own private investigation on Old Mary.

Mrs Singh's description was as clear and helpful as anticipated, and another book had been offered for cashing during the half-hour, too. It was benefit day so the thief's associates, or people who had rashly bought the books cheap, were obviously chancing their arm. Jane made her notes, then radioed in to see if a surreptitious police presence could be arranged for the afternoon. Then she took off on her own personal detour on her way back to CID.

Half an hour later she was feeling an acute sense of frustration. *Cityscene*, as a small-scale free newspaper pushed through house doors and funded by its advertising, kept no back copies. She had made her enquiry as a private citizen, but the answer would clearly have been the same whoever she was.

'It wouldn't be worth our while, love, with our

kind of turnover. We just bung'em all out. And
if there's the odd bale left over, we sell it off for
recycling.'

'What about copies of the photographs you use?
You must keep those, surely?'

'Oh, yeah, we've got a library file of prints in case
there's some we might want to reuse. Ask Cathy,
over there.'

Cathy over there could find a small bundle of
prints on the Mercury Air Show. The one of
Quentin was present. The one Jane particularly
wanted was not. 'We got people to send in their
own snaps, as a promotion, since we weren't going
to cover it for a couple of weeks until all the charity
stuff was in. That one must be one of those, and
we didn't keep them afterwards, just the press ones.
No, sorry, we didn't keep any addresses for the
people who sent them. We weren't paying, just
running it as a 'see your own snaps in the paper'
thing.'

There was nothing among the retained prints
which showed a shot from the same angle, or
even of the same picnicking family. These were
all more official, composed of planes, pilots, the
presentation of a prize, a charity banner with
smiling faces beneath . . . Jane went through the
bare dozen she was offered, but could see nothing
relevant at all. It was a dead end.

Someone probably still had that particular copy
of *Cityscene* stuffed away with their other old
newspapers. But that was a frustrating thought
too, since Jane had no way of finding out who.
She had certainly not got it herself; she made a

habit of binning the free papers as soon as they came through the door.

The reason why Marianna had marked that particular picture was going to elude her. However, there was the one of Quentin.

Quentin at an air show.

There could be any one of a dozen reasons. Perhaps Old Mary had liked animals and had known someone whose dog he had treated. Perhaps he had given her money for a cup of tea once and she had remembered his face. Perhaps she had just *liked* his face, in the picture.

But it was a fact that Old Mary had died at an airfield. A disused one, but a place where planes could still land.

Jane drove back to the station deep in thought, but had to switch track on arrival because, as usual, there was too much else requiring her attention. Everyone was still juggling files and trying to catch up on the change of responsibility areas. Last night had brought two off-licence break-ins, yet another one at the Tourist Information Centre, and one to an office, all of which she now had to take over from Peter Pettigrew. Someone had tried to force the door of one of the antiques shops, too, though without success because it had set off an alarm which must have frightened the blagger off; but that was hers too with the dealer wanting attention paid. It brought a reminder of Oliver Devereux, and as Jane drove home at the end of the day, she wondered whether she could use the acquaintance to pick his brains again. What might Marianna have seen which would make her suspicious? And where? If jewellery had been her speciality, who in this area might particularly interest her?

As Jane parked her car and got out she saw Adrian on her doorstep. He looked as if he had just let himself out of her house. While half of her was pleased to see him, she was immediately and uncomfortably aware that the other half of her felt a distinct awkwardness.

He had seen her coming and stood waiting for her. 'Hallo — you're late back! I did knock, but then I thought you might be in the bath so I hopped in to see, before you had to get out dripping. Busy day?'

'Very. How about you?'

'Tolerable. It was my turn to do the evening clinic but we didn't have many so I finished in good time. Do you want to eat out?'

'Not really, thanks. I've got some stuff I want to catch up on . . . '

'I thought you might say that, so I put a couple of chops in your fridge. Don't worry, I'll cook them. Is that a problem?'

'No, of course not,' Jane said lightly, 'but you don't always have to feed me.' Since the burglary, they seemed to have slid into being together for all their free time. The question of living space might not actually have come up, but it was gradually happening, whether she was ready for it or not. And tonight, with so many things on her mind, she wasn't. 'I shan't be very good company,' she said over her shoulder as he followed her into the house, 'I told you how it is at work at the moment!'

'But this new DI must be improving things, isn't

he? Sit down and put your feet up if you're flaked. And there's some wine here if you want a glass.'

'I'll go upstairs and change first, thanks. Adrian — '

'Mm, what?'

'Nothing.' No, she couldn't exactly ask him politely if he didn't want to be on his own for the evening. Or request her key back. Why did everything have to be so damned complicated? 'I'll just go and change, then,' she told him, managing a smile, 'I'll be down again in a minute.'

'Oh, Quentin and Marilyn want us to go out there again for some party they're giving,' he told her retreating back, 'do you fancy it? I was thinking that we really ought to ask them out to a restaurant first, as a pay-back for last time.'

Her feet had paused on the stairs. Quentin . . . It was probably nothing at all, but she still couldn't. Not just now. 'Could we leave it for later?' she asked without looking round. 'And the party's not really on for me. Sorry, but I really don't know what hours I'll be working.'

She went on up the stairs without waiting for his answer. As she stripped off her clothes and went to turn on the shower, she heard him switch on the television. And the sounds of him moving about. It was utterly ungrateful of her to feel moved in on; that although they had a relationship, he was taking too much for granted . . . It was just today which was making her irritable. It had held too many complications. Her *life* held too many complications! All she wanted was the chance to draw breath, to think her own quiet thoughts.

Maybe thoughts about how much she could risk on a private initiative, following up a case she had been told to drop. Maybe too a contemplation of how the promotion stakes for the DI job might actually be going. She had heard on the grapevine that there had been several applications in by now. Would she hear soon about the short list?

She went downstairs again trying to look cheerful, ate the meal Adrian capably cooked, and sat down on the sofa with a cup of coffee and the day's paper folded to the crossword page. If he had not been there, she might have had another go at Old Mary's diary . . . Instead, she was giving polite general answers to the questions he was asking her about work, appreciating that he was deliberately trying to show an interest in it, but wishing he wouldn't. When there was a sudden rap on the front door, she jumped to her feet quickly and went to answer it.

Kieron stood on the doorstep, blinking at her.

She gave him no time to speak. 'Not now — this really isn't a convenient time. Come again some other time, or — yes, I really am thinking about it, and properly!'

'All right. I only came to make sure you were.'

'Fine. Be in touch later, okay? Goodnight, then.'

As she came back into the living room, Adrian raised an eyebrow. 'Who was that?'

'No one. Well, someone collecting for a charity — I told him to come back another time. Do you want some more coffee?'

'No thanks.' There was a thoughtful pause, and then he said, 'I think I might go home. You'd rather I did, wouldn't you?'

'Look, I'm sorry, but I did tell you I was unlikely to be good company.'

'But not that you were only going to answer me in monosyllables, or shoo away mysterious visitors.' He came to his feet. 'Do you want to say what's really up? Because something is!'

'No, this is just what I'm like some of the time. Everyone gets work on their back sometimes — you must!'

'I'll share my thoughts on spavined fetlocks with you if you want me to. Why do I get the feeling that you've spent half the evening wanting to ask for your key back, but not quite managing to say so?'

That was too close. 'I'd be ungrateful if I did, I suppose,' Jane said, too dry a retort. She was aware enough that there could be hurt behind a certain grimness in his eyes to rush on: 'Look, it's just that I'm used to having space, okay? And I told you about that business of having to be officially cleared. That's actually supposed to apply to keys too, and I can't help it! I . . . There's a lot going on just now, and I can't — All right. Look. Just now, just *for* now, because I'm being kind of assessed on my work, I can't think about anything else. But I can't talk to you about it either. If that makes me impossible to live with, that's just the way I sometimes *am* — impossible!'

'Yes, you are, sometimes. But I don't have to assume that the male voice at the door was actually a rival, and one you didn't want me to see?'

'Bloody hell, Adrian!' She stared at him with a mixture of outrage and disbelief. Without that, she would have felt a strong desire to burst out laughing. If he had been sitting where he could see the door and had caught sight of Kieron's entirely unprepossessing face and figure, he would never have come up with that one. 'Sometimes you can be — Oh, think what you like! And if that's the sort of conclusion you jump to, *go away!*'

'All right, it's just work, then, is it? As usual? You won't leave it behind when you come home; you won't allow anything else any kind of priority; you won't even talk about it. In fact you just want everything your way, don't you? So I'll just have to decide if I can live with it. If, of course, you ever decide you want me to live with it.' He was on the move, walking towards the door. But turned before he reached it, with a bitterly angry look on his face. 'You won't even tell me what's been obvious from the few things you have said — and from the comments of those constables who came when you were burgled. You're after a promotion in your department, aren't you? To Detective-Inspector? I'm not stupid. The one who's in hospital was just about to have a whole lot of farewell parties, and the one who's here now is temporary. But *you* couldn't tell me, could you?'

'Not after what you said last time about how different things would be if you were a police superintendent!'

She saw his flush and regretted the acid remark as soon as it was uttered. 'I did apologise for that,' he said between his teeth, 'and you *said* you'd accepted it!'

'There's still the feeling that you meant it,

though. And the fact that I *am* in the police but you don't seem to want to accept that — '

'If I minded your career I wouldn't have taken up with you in the first place, would I? What I do mind,' he told her with heavy sarcasm, 'is being shuffled off like an inconvenience whenever you think that being seen with a man might affect your career prospects. Being told continually that you 'don't want to make it official', with a whole lot of excuses — '

'They aren't excuses! I do have to report the fact if I'm living with someone, *and* get that someone checked up on! Do you think I like it any more than you do? It's just the way it is, that's all. And prejudice against women does exist in the force, too, so I have to be more careful than . . . oh, if you can't understand, there's no use in talking about it!'

'If you don't want to tell me the truth there's no use talking about anything, is there? How can I possibly tell if anything you say is a genuine reason . . . Or if it's just something about *me* that makes you refuse to commit yourself?' There was a whiteness around his mouth now, and the look he gave her was stone-hard. 'It's all right, I'm going. You can have your space back — and maybe you'd care to think about the whole bloody question, if you can be bothered! Oh, and here's your key!'

He threw it into the middle of the carpet. A second later the front door had banged behind him.

Oh, *hell*! Hell hell hell.

Adrian had the sort of temper you only found

in quiet men. He kept things to himself behind an amiable, placid exterior, but then exploded with them.

She did want the promotion to DI. She did want the chance to move her career a rung higher. She deserved it! And she did want a clear sheet, just now, and no opportunity for some biased top brass on an interview board to assume that because she was a woman, the man in her life must be her main priority. It would be too good an excuse to give them.

But she knew, as she pulled her knees up to her chest, instinctively curling up for comfort, that she also wanted Adrian. If she hadn't just lost him . . . With an intensity which felt almost like despair, she knew she wanted his warmth, his seriousness, his passion; the look in his brown eyes when something amused him; his practicality. Even his damned tidiness. She might even include his temper, since some of what he had said had certainly been deserved.

And then there was the way they used to be able to discuss things, anything and everything . . .

He was right, she did want things her way. All of it. The promotion prospects with no cloud over them, no complications — but also the man . . .

She wanted to be able to ignore that other thought, not let it obtrude. The one which said, You're a cop. Just as he's always complaining, you're a cop and you're not allowed to forget it. And you might have reason to suspect Quentin. Quentin, who is Adrian's friend and partner.

She straightened herself abruptly and reached for

her briefcase, and the contents which she seemed to have been carrying around with her endlessly.

Damn everything! But at least she could do something constructive. She would make another attempt at Old Mary's diary.

As she opened it dispiritedly, her fingers felt the thickening between two pages. She had half noticed that before, but it was an old exercise book and two pages might easily have got stuck together. It even looked as if it might have been done with glue. Yes, now she looked, it was almost neatly done, and she could feel that the thickening ran in a narrow line along the top, bottom and sides.

She stared at it with a frown. Then she jumped to her feet and moved quickly to the kettle. It was worth trying. If envelopes could be steamed open, maybe this kind of glue could be melted away with steam too. The fastening of the pages did look oddly purposeful.

She made herself work slowly and patiently, keeping the steam to the edges, trying not to let the rest of the page get too wet. After several moments she was able to peel the corners apart. Then the rest.

The opened pages, bumpy from the damp and warmth, showed one side blank but one side filled with Old Mary's small crabbed writing. It was done in pencil, but with a firm neatness, each line clear. When Old Mary — Marianna — wrote this, she had been having one of her good days.

It began with straightforward lucidity.

*When I knew that he had killed the girl, I decided to watch him.*

# 15

Jane read the page through quickly. Then she read it a second time. Then she sat and stared at it, her heart thumping.

It read with clarity. There was the occasional lapse into the usual flowery language, but aside from that, it could be taken as a reasoned, rational statement.

But Marianna had taken the trouble to conceal it, as if it was to act as a hidden promise.

It spoke of a girl who had been killed because she stole something out of a man's pocket. A piece of jewellery he had shown her with the promise that it should be hers, in exchange for her body to use roughly in the dark. Twenty-four hours later the girl had been dead — but in the meantime, and before it had been taken back from her, she had shown Old Mary the trinket she had filched.

The passage described the man as 'the devil's scavenger' and talked of the respectable face he wears, away from the dark underbelly of the world'.

There were no names — except for a brief reference to 'Laurence', in passing, and then only as 'perhaps the only person I have ever been fond of', written as an addendum to a denial that this girl had meant anything to the old woman. 'A stupid helpless little fool, a nuisance' — that was her verdict on the girl. And yet, something about her death had obviously jerked Old Mary out of her private, savagely escapist world, and back into being Marianna.

A dead girl . . . Raking through her mind rapidly, Jane remembered a conversation with Ellen about Sofia, the young vagrant who had been found a few months ago, dead of an overdose, in an alley. A girl who had dressed herself up with glittering scraps of silver paper and loved anything she could call 'jewellery'. Yes, it fitted. Sofia had been young and even quite pretty, in her grubby way, though mentally unstable.

Another murdered vagrant, then. The first, in fact; a death which had started off a train of events.

Sofia had been offered a piece of jewellery to tempt her, then had stolen it when it was not given. And it had been something valuable, recognisably valuable enough for Old Mary to delve into her past expertise and identify it for what it was. She had already known this 'scavenger', it was clear, and his habit of using Sofia . . . Perhaps all vagrants had known about him. Jacko, too.

This brought the whole thing together with a vengeance. And vengeance was also what it was about. Marianna had written, 'I shall watch him, see who he meets, find out what crooked game he is playing — for justice!' That was clear enough.

Was there enough here to take back to Chris Hollings? Jane reluctantly doubted it. DI Hollings had made too much of a point of Old Mary's mental state. A known schizophrenic who could be assumed to suffer from fantasies. No, there would have to be more before Jane could show clear cause to keep the case open. Even with Laurence's murder . . . Had Marianna, in fact, confided in him?

But two photographs, one halfblurred, and one piece of clear writing, was all Jane had; scarcely hard evidence.

And one of the photographs was of Quentin Hurst.

That was such a difficult one that she really did not want to contemplate it. Quentin, whom she had met pleasantly and socially; Quentin who was Adrian's partner. Quentin who, as a pilot, provided a connection between Old Mary's investigations and her place of death.

Or perhaps there was no connection at all. You could scarcely say incontrovertibly that there was a link on the strength of one outlined photograph!

The only thing to do was to go back to the diary and read it, all of it. Try to see if there was something in all those other pages which the hidden one made clearer. All that fantasy story about strange creatures: the scavenger, the owl, the rat . . . Perhaps it was not intended to be clear. Perhaps there was a kind of code in it. Maybe Marianna was keeping a record of her watching, but couching it in such a way that it was deliberately hidden, out of the same paranoia which had made her glue out of sight the only page which was straightforwardly comprehensible.

Jane read and re-read until her eyes were tired and the writing danced too much to be legible.

It was incredibly hard to read anyway, with the breaks and bad days of meaningless scribble. It was scarcely surprising that she woke in the morning feeling as if her temples had been stuffed with cotton wool, and with the definite impression that some mad tympanist was choosing to pound on the backs of her eyeballs. It was no help at all to see a grimly lowering sky as she let herself out of the house after a gulped cup of coffee, and she arrived for work in a bad temper. A mood not helped at all by the fact that she had had to drive to work past the veterinary practice windows and remember not to give her habitual glance up at Adrian's flat above.

Her temper was not improved, either, by the fact that Kenny Barnes seemed to be badgering her for further details about her own burglary the minute she got into the CID room. Though, being Kenny, at least he was asking her politely.

'No, I didn't get a SOCO in, there didn't seem much point. And yes, the holes did look as if they were cut out with a glass cutter. Why, have you had another one with the same MO?'

'Not so far. There was one done like that a year ago, but that slag's inside serving a sentence. Are you all right, Sarge? You look a bit as if someone's been painting panda-circles under your eyes!'

'I just sat up too late. Where's sir — not in yet?'

Sir, alias the DI, came sweeping in energetically at that moment, and Jane had to try her best to look as bright and enthusiastic as he did. Which was definitely not easy when her head was still

231

pounding. Half an hour later under the influence of three aspirins it seemed to have calmed down a bit; at least enough to be ignored.

If Dan Crowe had still been here he would probably have growled a caustic enquiry at her by now as to whether she was hung-over, and she would have grinned back at him and said she probably was. He was that sort of guv'nor. Had been.

Mid-morning brought a call which had to be hers to take, but which made her heart sink for the sheer irony of it. The veterinary practice in Broomfield Street had just reported signs of a forced entry at the back of their premises, and items missing from their surgery room: CID presence, please.

'Yours, Jane. Gary's still on the off-licences, isn't he? All right, check with someone from the business premises team on your way out, but I expect they've already sent a car.'

'Right, sir. I know those particular vets — '

'Do you? Oh, yes, that must be just round the corner from your own place. Maybe some perp's decided to do a regular case of that area. Get them to give you the usual list of what's missing, and radio back if you want the SOCOs in.'

For a brief moment she was uncharacteristically tempted to tell Chris Hollings not to teach his grandmother to suck eggs. She took herself off instead, with a heavy irritation at the tricks life could play. She had to face Adrian in her official capacity today of all days. But with luck he might not be there.

He was, and so was Quentin. Both of them looked

unfamiliarly medical, in white coats. Quentin was in the process of what was obviously a row with the receptionist, who was looking injured and was in the middle of a spirited spot of self-defence.

'Yes I did lock up! I must have, mustn't I? You saw the door was forced! And yes, of course I reported it, you made enough fuss last time about its being my fault when some syringes went missing — '

'Ah, Jane, good heavens, it's you!' Quentin exclaimed heartily, catching sight of her. 'They've already sent us a constable, she's out at the back looking at the damage with one of our technicians. We scarcely need to have bothered you, really, it's all extremely minor — someone forcing the door of our surgery room at the back. It looked like an easy door to jemmy, I suppose, and they must have hoped there was something in there worth stealing.'

'And is anything missing?'

'That's the ridiculous thing, nothing but a handful of vitamin ampoules out of a cupboard in there, and that won't get him anywhere. Except rather healthy!' The joke was forced and he cast another look at the receptionist which had a distinctly hard edge to it. 'This building's extremely well locked, and there's no sign that anyone's tried to get in here. We're rather wasting your time.'

'I'd like to have a look at where the break-in occurred please. And — um — Mr Reston, you live in the flat above, don't you? Did you hear anything?'

'No, I didn't.'

Adrian's voice was flat, and he had been standing there silently, not looking at Jane after one brief glance at her face when she arrived. That had been the reason for her formality. Quentin let out an uncomfortable laugh, and then tried for heartiness.

'Yes, this is official business, isn't it! Adrian, you'd better take her through to look at — '

'I've got to go out on that call, so I'll leave it to you. Excuse me.'

He turned away and leaned over the receptionist's desk to start a conversation which was audibly about veterinary business. Quentin, after a disconcerted second, began to usher Jane through to the back of the building. Whether his discomfiture came from Adrian's attitude, or simply from being faced with Jane in her official capacity, it was clearly there, and led him to keep up a stream of words.

'It's this way, if you'd like to follow me? Through here. We have a surgery room for operations at the back in a separate building. There was no reason to go out there this morning until after we'd done the clinic. That's over, as you can see by the fact that we've got no clients waiting. This is our back entrance and the surgery room is just opposite. Oh, perhaps you've had a tour round before?'

'Yes, I did, once. You don't keep anything in the way of dangerous drugs in the surgery building?'

'No, we don't. The anaesthetics and analgesics we carry are all firmly locked up in the main building. We're required to have a secure place, of course, and we do everything according to the law. This is the door which was forced . . . Ah,

234

here's your constable.'

It was Rachel Welsh, neat in her uniform today and discussing something with another young woman in a white coat who was standing beside her. The room, which looked like a long wooden shed on the outside, was spotless within with a plastic-tiled floor, the gleam of steel and chrome equipment, and a half-size operating table. WPC Welsh looked round at Jane's arrival and broke off her conversation with the technician.

'Hallo, Sarge. It looks as if the door's been jemmied with a tyre-iron, and I'd guess it was a casual after drugs. They aren't kept in here, but this cupboard on the wall had vitamin ampoules in it — he just seems to have snatched a handful and made off, since there were a few on the floor.'

'That's all that's missing?'

'Yes. The drawer where we keep the instruments, and the steriliser, haven't been touched,' the technician said. 'And everything else in here is pretty much screwed down!'

'Mm. It does look like a casual, doesn't it?' The splintered edge of the door, which Jane had inspected on her way in, looked like an amateur's work: someone with, as Rachel had said, a tyre-iron or something similar doing a quick leverage job. 'Has anything like this ever happened before?' she asked formally, glancing at both Quentin and the technician.

'No, nothing, we've been lucky enough to be left alone. And as you say, it must have been entirely speculative.' It was Quentin who answered. 'With so little missing, I really do think we shouldn't have wasted your time.'

'It's better to report it. Your receptionist said something earlier about syringes going missing, another time?'

'Oh, that turned out to be nothing — just a box mislaid. Put into the wrong cupboard. If you've seen all you want here . . . '

'It may be worth getting someone down to dust for prints. If it was an amateur breaking in he may not have bothered with gloves, and it could be someone we know. If you wouldn't mind keeping this room closed up until I can get someone down — '

'No, please, I don't find that necessary. Besides, I need this theatre for an operation this afternoon. And before that we need to get the room ready. Please, just list it as a minor burglary, or whatever you do, and leave it there. Vitamin ampoules are scarcely a great loss, and having my schedule disrupted would be a much greater one!'

Quentin's words held an impatience trying to conceal itself behind politeness. Had the technician cast him a slightly surprised look at his claim to need the theatre today? That was interesting. All the same, if he wanted to refuse to have the burglary followed up, Jane could only let him. She made her notes on what they had found, inspected the locks on the main building to make sure nobody had had a try at them, asked to take a look at where genuine drugs were actually kept — and then left, with the feeling that Quentin, behind an air of heartiness, was actually hustling her out of the place.

Perhaps only because seeing her this way made him uncomfortable. Or because he was busy.

She would have to pass the word to John Clay that this had probably been a drugs-related break-in, even though nothing of note had been taken. There was also the point that it could be tried again, if it had occurred to someone that veterinarians carried drugs and might be an easy source of supply. That took Jane up to the Drugs Unit office some time later, with a copy of the break-in report to hand over for the files up here.

Sergeant Clay was alone in the office today, his DCs out somewhere on their investigations. Jane explained what she had brought him, and he gave her an absent look.

'Thanks, we'll file it and take note. Vitamin ampoules, eh? Someone's going to be disappointed when they try injecting those! It's an addict working on his own, from the sound of things, if he just grabbed a handful — one of that bunch from the squat in Terry Road, I shouldn't wonder. We might take another look at them when we get the time, and see what they've got lying about.'

'Heroin still not your main problem? It's been better hasn't it, since you got that supplier a few months ago?'

'Yes, that dried that one up nicely. And from one or two attempted break-ins at chemists, they haven't found a new source yet. There's one of two trying injecting amphetamines instead, with more of that about.'

'Are you any further on with the 'E'?'

'Ah. Well, since it's you . . . but keep it strictly

under your hat! Customs has had a whisper in the last few days, from across the Channel. We're working with them, and the Dutch police got in touch with us again yesterday with some very interesting information. They reckon something's going in and out from their end by light plane. And coming this way, they think. They thought it might be crack, but 'E' is certainly a possibility, and amphetamine powder. It might be just the break we're looking for — someone bringing it in that way, in quick flips across.'

'A connection with the rave at the airfield?'

'We've thought of that, and the Dutch were certainly suggesting something may have been flown out that weekend. Still, with the rave only being moved there at the last minute — ' He gave a shrug to show how unlikely a connection would be. 'One thing's for sure, it's unlikely anyone would use that place for landing again, whether they have before or not. Too well known, after the fire. Anyway we can't do much until we get the next message from our Netherlands opposite numbers, because those small light planes can land more or less anywhere. But they've promised to give us the tip the minute they know anything, and *then* we may get a result!'

Jane opened her mouth to mention Quentin Hurst — and then shut it again. No, she could not finger him on the strength of what she had got. She probably ought to . . . But her head was buzzing again, the cotton-wool feeling inside it returning in full force. Through it, nothing seemed obvious. Only the fact that Quentin was a pilot, Quentin had a connection with Old Mary, Old Mary had known something. But about jewellery, not drugs . . . She managed to give John Clay a smile to indicate that she sympathised with his hopefulness, and that she wished him luck. Then she left him. If he could break his 'E' case, that really would be a boost.

But there were other people who owned and flew light planes besides Quentin; people to whom Jane had no connection at all. It might even be Dutch pilots who were doing the smuggling . . .

She could surely wait and see. There was no need to stick her neck out, and raise suspicions about a man who might have nothing to do with any of it at all.

The thought of sticking her neck out brought the knowledge that her neck was hurting as well as her head now, a sore throat beginning to rage. It was probably just acting in sympathy with the pain behind her eyes. She should never have spent so much time trying to read Old Mary's crabbed nonsense. She was suddenly caught by a wave of irritation, and part of it was the knowledge that depression was catching at her too, a depression she could all too clearly trace back to Adrian's manner towards her at the surgery. She ought to be able to detach herself from it. It ought not to be there interfering with her work. She never let anything interfere with her work!

And there was the gloomy thought that even when she went home tonight, she would have nothing to distract her, since that bloody slag who stole her sounds system had left her without radio or cassette player. Television was nowhere near the same as being able to put on some music as soon as she got home.

There was a cure for that. She had no real need to wait for the insurance when her credit card held a healthy lack of balance at the moment. The clock showed her it was lunchtime. Jane was instantly on her way out, determined to rectify one shortcoming in her life at least.

With a new and definitely superior hi-fi system loaded into the boot of her car, she drove back to the station telling herself that she felt better. She had bought some throat pastilles and a new bottle of aspirin, too.

Some time later, she was at her desk checking a statement form when she was suddenly aware that Chris Hollings was standing directly in front of her. She looked up, trying not to wince at the eye movement required, and heard him say firmly, 'Go home!'

'What? Sorry — '

'I said, go home! What have you got — a virus? 'Flu?' He reached forward and placed two fingers briefly on her forehead. 'Yes, I thought so, you've got a raging temperature. Go on, pack up, and go home to bed — and that's an order!'

'I'm perfectly al — '

'No, you most certainly are not. You probably shouldn't have come in this morning. You'll be no use to yourself or to anyone else here, and all you're doing is spreading germs. Don't tell me you're never ill, because you've obviously got 'flu or something like it. I hardly need to send for the FME to tell you that!'

'I do feel pretty awful . . . Is there 'flu going round? I didn't know.' She felt more than awful: all her symptoms seemed suddenly to have increased. 'Perhaps I'll just finish this and . . . '

'You won't finish anything, and I gave you an order. Go!'

'Yes, sir. Sorry. I'll probably be all right tomorrow.'

'You won't be back tomorrow. Are you fit to get yourself home?'

'Yes, sir.' She tried to stop her legs from wobbling as she got to her feet. 'I'm sorry about this. It'll leave you shorthanded. But I think you're right, I'd better . . . '

'We'll be decimated rather than shorthanded if you sit there giving it to the rest of us,' he said, sounding brisk rather than sympathetic. He gave her a smile, however, as he added, 'And don't worry, everyone has to fall by the wayside sometime! You're not the only one, either. Two more people have gone down with what's probably the same bug from uniform. There's nothing important enough here to require you to work at death's door, so come back when you're better, but not until!'

'Flu, not simply eye-ache and depression. She should have realised that was what it was, making her feel fit for nothing all morning. She had probably been succumbing last night too. Staggering into her house when she reached it (and wishing she had not felt forced to make the effort to unload her new sounds system from the car boot), Jane felt an ache in every bone, and a light-headedness which brought all sorts of unlikely things into her mind.

241

That revue sketch she had taken part in long ago at university, for instance; the one with the song whose words went, 'You feel all feverish and you're aching too. But how do you know if it's love or 'flu?' She ought to have thought of that earlier. She ought to have realised she was simply down with a virus. It was just that she was normally healthy and avoided catching things. But, oh God, her head really was throbbing: all she wanted to do was forget everything else, and lie down.

★ ★ ★

Three days later she was on her feet again: pale, and with a persistent cough, but her temperature was normal.

She was still forced to stay at home, however. She had called in, only to be told that there were no urgent messages for her, no work which could not be assigned to someone else for the moment, and a week was being considered the minimum recovery time for this particular virus. Unless she wanted longer. She was certainly not to come back before a week was up.

She had had too much time to think already. Through clouds of fever, some of the time, but also in calmer moments. During the fever, it had seemed far too clear that Quentin was involved. Must be. Perhaps that was the only reason he had invited her over to dinner and had asked so many questions about her work, always trying to find out what the police might know. And perhaps Adrian was involved as well. Maybe he had only taken up with her in the first place so that she would talk to him and act as a useful channel of information. There was the fact that his cottage was so close to that airfield . . .

And Adrian had already been there, in that area, on the Friday afternoon, before Jane joined him that night. Suppose the rave and the fire were merely chance . . . Suppose what had happened to Marianna on that airfield had taken place on Friday, not Saturday . . .

Marianna had not been seen since that Friday. She could well have died on that day. The autopsy had made a point of refusing to pinpoint a precise time of death, stating it could have taken place within a forty-eight hour period. The fire had made it impossible to be more specific. Suppose she had actually been dead not *just* before the fire, but a whole day before it?

And the fire had been necessary to conceal that fact?

Adrian could not have set the fire, anyway: Jane had been with him. But he could have been concerned in the old woman's death if that had happened a day earlier. Maybe the invitation to the cottage that weekend had merely been a nicely ironic cover.

In her saner moments she could see that particular nightmare stemmed from an attack of fevered paranoia. Her only excuse for that bitter suspicion was that a high temperature might make one consider anything. Not Adrian, no. Definitely not. She surely knew him too well. And if she needed reassurance, there was always the fact that

243

he would scarcely quarrel with her if he had merely been using her as a useful conduit to find out what the police might or might not know. She really could rule him out, and it had been ridiculous even to consider otherwise.

There were times when having a trained police mind was a disadvantage, and led into the murky waters of distrust and betrayal.

But Quentin . . .

He had an expensive lifestyle. An ex-wife and children whom he was presumably supporting. A new house in an expensive location, and a new wife given carte blanche to redecorate it as lavishly as she chose. Owning his own plane must be costly. To use that plane advantageously for a bit of drugs-smuggling might well be a temptation. He could possibly pass the drugs through his practice, somehow, using it as a place for storage and distribution without anyone but his criminal associates knowing. He had certainly been angry with his receptionist for calling the police in, to a chance and minor break-in; had not wanted it examined.

No, she could not dismiss Quentin.

He could be the one described as 'the owl' in Marianna's diary — since an owl would have wings. Perhaps the photographs she had outlined had even been intended to show all three of the people she described in her code-words. All of them at the air-show. And two out of the three of them in conversation with each other. Perhaps they had all been there for a meet, innocent-looking among the crowds.

Marianna had started watching someone because of a piece of jewellery. But jewellery could be smuggled out at the same time as drugs were being smuggled in, so the old woman had stumbled across an even more comprehensive operation.

And had died at an airfield. Her reason for being there? To watch — and get proof.

It was beginning to add up all too well. A group of people: the owl, the rat, and the scavenger. All of them part of an operation which involved the export of stolen jewellery, and the import of drugs. The theory was working; it was starting to hang together.

But Jane still had no proof, no hard facts!

Her enforced convalescence made her as restless as the thoughts which went round and round in her head. She mooched around her living room, and stared out at the wintry grey night closing down on her small garden, before she twitched the curtains closed impatiently. Another four days of this before she could go back to work! Not that she was actually feeling fit for much, and this was the first time she had got dressed for a whole day. She was sourly aware, as she looked round, that her living room was beginning to resume its accustomed untidiness.

One thing she could do was unpack and assemble her new hi-fi, still lying in its boxes. Then she could play some music again at last, or listen to the radio. She moved quickly to begin unwrapping everything. It was a pity she had fallen for a sales-pitch and bought something which was all in separate sections, needing sorting out and fitting up properly. It would give her a better quality sound, so she had been assured; unfortunately, it also seemed to have damnably complicated instructions.

When the knock sounded on her front door, she was in the middle of trying to work out which coloured wire went where. She stopped dead. If it was Adrian — oh, hell, she was in no state to make that kind of decision just now. Or in any state to quarrel with him. Or to know whether she wanted to make up. Or would be wise to make up. If Quentin truly was as involved as she thought he was, it made things not only awkward, but . . .

The knock came again. Her lights were on, so she could hardly pretend not to be here. She cast an exasperated look at the tangle of coloured wires on the floor beside her, pulled herself to her feet, and went to answer the door.

The figure on her step was not Adrian. It was Kieron.

# 16

'You told me to come back.'

'So I did. You'd better come in.'

'I did try phoning,' he said as he came across the threshold, sounding faintly martyred about it, 'but you weren't here. So I came. To see whether you — '

'I was here. I just unplugged the phone after the

first couple of cold callers wanting to sell me new windows. Then I forgot to plug it in again until this morning. I've been here nonstop because I've been ill in bed with a virus. It's all right, I'm over it, it won't still be catching!'

He seemed unworried about that, anyway. As Jane ushered him past her, she saw his eyes go at once to the collection of things on the floor. 'I was just trying to put that lot together,' she began, but he had already dropped to his knees to examine it.

'You've got that bit connected wrong. Not a bad set, though — but if you'd asked me, I could have told you where to get better speakers. Do you want me to set it up?'

'I'd forgotten you were an expert. Yes, please do, be my guest! And maybe you can tell me why they don't get someone to translate things from the Japanese more comprehensibly. Is it any use offering you tea or coffee? I still haven't got anything herbal.'

'I wouldn't mind some orange juice, if you've got any,' he told her, sounding unusually meek.

He was in luck, since she had discovered that Adrian had stocked her up with several cartons, tucked away in the back of the fridge. Jane poured him out a glass, and another one for herself, on the grounds that it was healthy. She could see, with slight exasperation but also fascination, that Kieron was connecting things up with ease and no need to consult the instructions at all. That was useful of him, at least. He seemed to be looking round judiciously to see the best places to position

247

things in, very much the professional sound man he had claimed he once was, and she suspected she was going to find her living room thoroughly rearranged.

'I noticed your old one was crap when I was here before, so I'm glad to see you got rid of it. You can't have been getting the best sound quality even from that, with the way you had the speakers set up.'

'I didn't get rid of it. I had it stolen. I suppose it wasn't you who cut out the locks on my windows and strewed everything around — as another piece of proving a point? No, it's all right,' she added drily as he stopped dead and stared at her, 'I assumed it wasn't, or I'd have been round to question you!'

'If it had been me, I'd have picked the front lock again. Including your new one,' he retorted, adding, with a sense of superiority, 'it's not bad, but once you know how . . . '

'Stop telling me things like that, unless you actually want me to put you on the police lists as a possible suspect for any time your kind of expertise comes up. Yes, you may well look anxious.'

'Not about that. You had a burglary? What else did they take? I mean, no one with any sense would want that crappy sound system you had. Did they take Old Mary's diary?'

'Kieron, that really is taking things too far . . . ' For a sudden and very uneasy moment the idea resonated with her. Maybe that was what someone had been after. The burglary had been a search, not just an ordinary break-in. No, that had to be impossible. Who could have known she had Old Mary's book — besides Kieron himself? 'I had the diary with me, as it happens,' she told him. 'And, yes, I am still looking into her death, though I have to tell you, everyone else considers the case closed. There are a few things I want to know from you, too. First, did you know that Old Mary's real name was Marianna Troughton-Beck, and that she used to be an antiques dealer?'

'I told you, I didn't know her name. And I didn't know she was a dealer, either.' He had turned away and started moving furniture about — without bothering to ask for her permission — and spoke over his shoulder. 'You'll need to put the second speaker somewhere over here . . . What else have you found out?'

'We'll leave that. You asked me for a police investigation and you're getting one. Did you look at the diary? And do you know anything about the list at the back of it?'

'No. I mean, yes, I looked, but only briefly. I saw she'd put something in code at the back. I don't know what it is.'

'You're not being a lot of help, are you? All right, did she — what are you looking for now?'

'A tape to play to see how the balance sounds. Preferably a decent quality one. This'll do, I suppose. Now, if you — '

'Listen to me! All right, listen to me while you're doing that. And I am grateful, you've got it set up in a fraction of the time it would have taken me. Did Old Mary ever — ever — mention any names to you, or show a particular interest in anyone, or . . . ? Yes, that sounds fine, but how about giving me an answer?'

'You're the detective, and I've already told you, she didn't tell me any names. This doesn't sound fine, they've set the treble too high, but I can fix that.' He took a small screwdriver out of the back pocket of his jeans and began dismantling something, his head bent, his face only half visible. 'It only means reversing a couple of things . . . You're beginning to believe that Mary was killed, aren't you?'

'It's possible. I don't know, though, and I need some help. One or two things have certainly come up, but you can't quote me on that — What did you say?'

'I said, I'd hardly quote you, would I? The rest of your pigs would probably lock me up for troublemaking, wouldn't they?'

The first statement had been in a sulky mutter; this was offered clearly with a look of defiance. Jane gave him look for look until his eyes dropped. Then she said drily, 'So am I a pig — in your terms. You should bear that in mind. And if you had even the briefest look at the diary, you'll know it isn't exactly easy to read. Or not most of it. But I've got another question for you. You said you didn't know why Marianna — Old Mary — should have gone out to Dasset. But when you and she were talking, did she ever show any interest in airfields? Or — not just airfields, but any place where a light plane might land?'

'I don't think so.' He bit his lip thoughtfully, looking up at her with those large grey eyes which looked so magnified behind his glasses. 'She did borrow some maps, though. That was after — she asked me if we'd got any maps, large-scale ones, and I found some for her. She didn't say what she was looking for.'

'That was after what?'

'Nothing,' he said, his eyes going back to the wires he had in his hand. She sensed evasion; also, from the stubborn set of his mouth, that she would get no further if she pursued it. 'I told you, she didn't talk to me. When she wanted me to do something, she didn't say why. But I know she was working on something, and that it was like a — I was fond of her. I know you think it isn't possible for anybody to have been, but I was!'

'I believe you. Those maps she borrowed from you: did she give them back? And have you still got them?'

'You think she might have marked something on them? I think I can probably find them. They were Ethan's, but I doubt if he took them with him when he left, since they were local ones and he and Sarah decided to go to Wales. I suppose you do realise,' he added, with a sudden return to scathing accusation, 'that because of your lot, some of our lot decided to move on! I might even have gone with them, if I hadn't wanted to make sure you were going to keep your promise about Mary!'

Jane was opening her mouth to reply, but another knock came on the door. She was suddenly to be beset by visitors, it seemed. As she got up to answer it she saw Kieron go back to readjusting the different parts of her sound system, and even by the time she had reached the door, the notes of a Vivaldi tape had started to fill the air again. With a more mellow sound than she had heard from it before, she had to admit as she drew the door open on the night outside.

This time, it was Adrian.

The light striking his face showed an expression both wary and stubborn, but he spoke before she could.

'That constable of yours came round again today, and she said you'd been away from work sick. With 'flu or a virus or something.'

'Yes, I have been.'

'Ill in bed and running a high temperature, she said. You could at least have — Can I come in? Or do I get the door shut in my face?'

'Come in.' She stood aside for him, aware of a confusion of feelings, and not least the one which said she felt totally unfit to sort them out. 'It was nice of you to come round and enquire,' she said with polite formality, 'but I'm a lot better. Oh, this is someone who's putting my sounds equipment together. I bought it just before I went down with this damned 'flu, and it's been sitting there. That sounds good, have you nearly finished?' she enquired in Kieron's direction, suddenly aware that he had stiffened and was regarding Adrian with a distinctly hostile look.

'Yes, it's done, though if you want it perfect I ought to do something to the bass as well. I told you, these aren't the best speakers you could have got. You can adjust the graphic equaliser when you're playing something less orchestral, but you'll hear an overload on bass if the music is something heavier than this.'

'Thanks, I'll remember. And thanks for doing it.'

'It's something I know about. Thank you for the orange juice,' he said, picking up the empty glass and handing it back to her with what appeared to be a slightly defiant flourish, and a sidelong glance at Adrian which did, definitely, appear to be hostile. 'I suppose you do know that you wouldn't get ill if you stuck to juice or herbs instead of all that stuff with caffeine in? Well, I'd better go. And I won't forget what you asked me, about the light planes and airfields!'

That was delivered like a parting shot, half casually, half as if trying to prove that he had a right to be here. He would be unaware that Jane was immediately cursing him for the reference. He made for the door, a skinnily unprepossessing figure with his straggly beard and scraped-back pony-tail, adding insouciantly, 'You needn't bother to let me out.' Then he was gone, leaving the smooth runs and cadences of Vivaldi filling the room with their peace and beauty.

'What on earth was all that about? And who is he?'

The questions were not quite casual, and registered uneasily with Jane. 'Weird, isn't he?' she said lightly. 'But he's some kind of expert on sound systems so I thought I might as well use him. The whole damned thing was a lot too complicated for me, but it sounds good, doesn't it?

And I wouldn't know personally whether the bass is out of true or not, would you? Have a listen and see what you think.'

'Jane, are we speaking or not?'

'We seem to be. I mean, I'm not intending to talk to myself. Last time I saw you I think I was already starting to run a temperature.'

'I thought about that. And I was going on at you about answering me in monosyllables! Can we forget it?'

'Maybe we should take it slowly.' Hell and damn! And bloody, bloody Quentin . . . 'I'm not trying to be unfair. It's up to you if you decide to chuck me. Just at the moment I'm not in any fit state to — I'm still recovering from this damned virus. Today's the first day I've been out of bed all day.'

'At least I know you better than to tell you not to drink caffeine.' She could see that was an attempt at a joke. 'I really only came round to see that you were all right. And to — yes, all right, I was unreasonable in what I said about your promotion, wasn't I?'

'I may not even get it.'

'But you've got every right to try. And not to have me pushing you for decisions. I'll admit I don't see why there has to be such an overlap into your private life, but if you say it's so, I suppose it is. I'd better learn not to sound so damned over-possessive, hadn't I?'

Why did he have to be so bloody reasonable? It was unfair. 'I meant what I said about needing space,' she said, uneasily aware that if other things had been equal, she could have met him closer to halfway than that. 'And you do come on sometimes as if you think I have a string of other men in the background. That would make me a complete liar, wouldn't it?'

That piece of defensive attack plainly disconcerted him with its switch of subject. But there was truth in it, even if she had only used it to keep him at arm's length.

'It's probably over-exposure to Quentin and his women. I've had to cover for him with Marilyn more than once when he's supposed to have gone home and then she's rung because she thinks he's still working. He does have rather — movable tastes. That's a strange look on your face. What is it?'

He would be totally unaware that his words had brought an immediate, involuntary thought: Quentin the scavenger? Not the coded owl, but something worse? Jane pushed that away rapidly, but it left a nasty aftertaste. 'Nothing. I mean, I was only thinking, Marilyn's got a lousy break if he's like that. Still, he's your partner, so I suppose you do have to cover for him. Adrian, will you tell me something?'

'Yes?'

'With honest truth, what's the most important thing to you in the world?'

'With honest truth?' She saw him take in the unexpected question, pause, and contemplate it seriously. 'All right then. To do my job as well as I can. It has to be that. I can see where this is leading!'

No, he couldn't. 'So the practice is important to you?'

'Very. Obviously. Was that some kind of test? To see if I'd say, nothing matters more than you?' He gave her a level look. 'Or was it what I thought it was, a way of saying, if my job's important as that to me, why shouldn't yours be to you? For God's sake, Jane, I've already conceded you that point! What more do you want — me in a crumpled heap on the carpet? Is that your version of equality? Because it isn't mine! And if the only result of my coming round here is going to be another quarrel about the same old subject, then I might as well not have bothered to care whether you were ill or not. And I may as well go now. Is that what you want?'

She made no answer. Part of her seemed to be standing aside coolly, watching him professionally, telling her that if he did go, then he really was innocent of involvement in a conspiracy. She could get rid of any last lurking doubt. Because if he had been part of something criminal, and she the patsy to be pumped for information, then she would be too valuable a contact to lose. It was a deeply distasteful thought, one she should have been shocked to find herself thinking . . . yet, against her will, the professional side of her was still thinking it.

Because doubt and cynicism came with the territory.

There was another part of her which was acknowledging that she was going to lose him anyway, if she had to hunt down his partner,

256

a man who was also his friend. If Quentin was guilty, then her job was going to come between her and this man watching her with questioning grimness, in ways which had not even been touched on yet.

There was another, very small, part of her which whispered that it was as well to let him go, if he was even an innocent associate of a criminal. Nothing was more guaranteed to put the kybosh on her career and any future hope of promotion. It was something they were all warned about, right from the beginning. But at the same time, there was some piece of her consciousness which — for once — cared nothing about her career prospects at all, but wanted only to rail against the sheer unfairness of it all. Why should she have to be faced with that kind of choice? Why did everything have to come down to her damned *job*?

He waited what must have been a full thirty seconds to see if she would give him a reply. Then, when she had still said nothing, he turned on his heel and walked out.

★ ★ ★

Jane went back to work at the end of her week off, trying to look brisk and determined rather than pale, and still with a cough. She supposed it was her appearance which made the duty-sergeant give her a curiously sympathetic look when she signed in, and tried for extreme cheeriness.

'It's all right, I won't still be catching! How

many more people went down with the najjer, after I did?'

'Your CID lot seems to have managed to miss it apart from you. We've had a few more from uniform. Nasty, is it?'

'Fairly murderous, but at least it didn't last long. All the same, I'd try and avoid it if I were you.'

In the CID room she got sympathetic looks again, particularly from Kenny Barnes who seemed to feel she rated being brought a cup of coffee instead of having to fetch it for herself. 'Nice to have you back, anyway, Sarge. We've managed without you, but there's the usual bunch of stuff needing your superior brain.'

'I'll have to work on making my brain superior then, won't I? Our DI not around yet?'

'Um — he won't be in the department until this afternoon, I reckon.'

'Okay, gives me time to start catching up. Oh, you've nabbed the sub post office blagger? How was that — tracking back who sold the benefit books?'

'Yes, it left a trail as straight as a die. We even got an identification for buying the plastic gun — said it was a present for her little brother. It was a her, by the way: the motor-cycle gear stopped anyone spotting that!'

'Mrs Singh did describe the perp as 'a slight young man'. Good, I'm glad that one's been put to bed. Any others?'

'A few likelies on my domestics, but we're still following up on them. Nothing on yours, though. Not that we've sussed so far. Someone'll come up with the glass-cutter trick again soon, though, I expect, and then we'll be able to try for a cough on it.'

If it had been an ordinary burglary. Yes, of course it had. She was simply catching Kieron's paranoia.

The others trailed in, and all seemed to think she rated special treatment. It seemed to be her day for everyone to be nice to her. With Chris Hollings absent, she worked steadily through to catch up on what had happened while she was out of the place. The usual . . . She worked until almost lunchtime with remarkably few interruptions. Call-outs seemed to have got themselves into a routine so that everyone knew without asking who should take them. The DI must have been exerting a lot of busy-bee organising ability. Well, learn from his methods, then. Jane had just got that far when something Mike Lockley was saying caught her attention.

'What was that, Mike? Something about the Drugs Unit?'

'Just that Sergeant Clay's hopping mad again, Sarge. They had a combined operation on with Customs, something about a drug consignment coming in by plane, but all a stake-out gave them was a no show. So then they tried a raid round all the light aircraft clubs and a grilling of all owners, but they got nowhere with that either. Sergeant Clay's sure there must have been a tip-off, in spite of the fact that he'd been keeping the whole thing carefully under wraps!'

'Oh. That was — bad luck.' She could barely

frame the comment. Hell and double, treble damnation — that question of hers to Kieron! And his repetition of it in front of Adrian!

A straight conduit to Quentin, if an innocent answer had been given to a casually phrased question.

'When was the raid?' she asked Mike, trying to sound merely interested.

'Day before yesterday. Half the day wasted on the first stake-out, because something was supposed to come in very early morning. Then the rest of the day going round the flying clubs. He said it looked like hard info, too, and the source had given them a whole day's notice. Must've been a leak somewhere.'

And there was time for the leak to have been hers.

She really ought to tell John Clay that. She ought to put it to him that she had doubts about a certain pilot, anyway. It might still be tenuous, but she really ought.

She had better go up and see him right now.

The Drugs Unit office was empty; only that simpering calendar on the wall. It would be better to see John Clay in person than to leave him a note. If it *was* possible that she had blown his stake-out . . . There could be any number of other reasons. A leak the Dutch end. A change of plan because of the weather. Oh hell, if only she knew!

The sound of the door opening made her turn round from John Clay's desk and she found herself face to face with Tom Cooper. He was on his own and gave her an immediate, narrow-eyed, leering grin.

'Well, hallo, love! Can't do without our company? Or are you looking for a transfer, to get away from your new boss?'

'I beg your pardon?'

'You didn't get an interview, did you? Well, they wouldn't want a woman, I reckon. Besides, I'd guess the other two were only token, wouldn't you? Considering they'd already managed to nab their top candidate as a stop-gap! They've just finished holding the interview board, anyway, and sure enough the one getting the congratulatory handshakes is DI Hollings. The other two fellas in suits have had their hang-around for nothing!'

He was enjoying this. Maybe he could even tell from her expression — try as she did to keep it merely interested — that she had not even known about the interview board. Everyone else had, Jane realised suddenly. That the interview board for the DI job was today. And that she had not even made the short list.

She bloody well ought to have done! They could at least have given her that.

Even if Chris Hollings' appointment was a fait accompli, they could have put her in for an interview, to show on her record that she was considered possible promotion material.

Tom Cooper was looking at her with all the satisfaction of a cat who had found the cream. She wasn't giving him a petty triumph to enjoy. She hid her fury behind a fit of coughing, then raised her eyebrows and gave him an enthusiastic smile.

'Sorry about that, I'm still hacking! DI Hollings has got the job? Oh, good — saves a lot of trouble, when we've just got used to him. He'll be good, too. Look, Constable — Cooper, isn't it? Sorry, some names just go out of my head! I was going to leave a note for Sergeant Clay, but it wasn't really important, just one of those marginal things which might or might not interest him. I'll probably run into him later, anyway.'

She escaped, trying to calm herself. Oh, yes, Chris Hollings would be good, no doubt about that. But what was that about his having already been the top candidate before he was nabbed as a stop-gap? If that was true . . . If that was true, what was all that about asking Jane if she was in for the job, and wishing her luck? Without saying he was in for it himself?

Rot him, then! He could at least have been honest.

# 17

She had to live with it. And with good grace. When he came into the department she looked up and said calmly, 'Congratulations. I heard you got the job.'

'Thanks. Come in and have a word, will you?'

When they got into his office she regarded him with politely raised eyebrows. 'Sit down,' he said, giving her one of his charming smiles. 'I was sorry to find they hadn't put you up to the board. I'd have said you deserved it. They only called three of us in the end. The other two were older, and pretty strong candidates. Wanting to make the appointment quickly must have come into it, and I expect they decided you'd got plenty of time. So next time for you, mm?'

'It must have been pretty well sewn up, with you already here. The word on the grapevine is that you were always a candidate — is that right?'

'Yes, I was. I was still lucky to get the appointment, though — against that competition. I think the fact that I was at school down here may have come into it, they felt it gave me a local edge. Kings,' he added, by way of explanation, while she was taking in that he had never mentioned that either. 'I wasn't an outstanding scholar; just one of the general hoi-poloi!'

Scarcely hoi-poloi, at the city's top public school, attached to the cathedral. 'It gives you a local edge, as you said,' she agreed.

'Yes. The reason I called you in was — well, we might as well get it straightened out, to avoid any crossed wires. Any resentment?'

'Why should there be? You were the best candidate for the job, and you got it. I probably could have done with knowing that you were actually in for it — '

'It seemed as well not to mention it. Would you have done? Anyway I might not have been appointed, so no point in starting hares.' He seemed to consider that a perfectly fair statement though Jane was sure he had actually been working on quite different reasons: smooth management, keep your sergeant on your side. And don't for a moment let her guess that you know perfectly well you're going to be slipped into the permanent job. He must have been aware how little chance anyone else stood, once he had been invited to fill the gap. He really need not have given her the false bonhomie of wishing her luck.

'I think experience has already shown that we can work together well,' he said briskly, obviously taking her politely blank face for agreement. 'I've got a few more ideas for the department, now everything's settled, and we must have a get-together on them some time. But for now, how are you after your 'flu? Feeling fit to get down to things again?'

'Perfectly, thanks. And I'm glad to see I don't seem to have infected anyone else — at least, the others all seem to be fit and well.'

'Yes, we've been lucky. Me particularly, since my wife's had it! I think you'll find we've managed to get the new organisation running well during the week you were away . . . ' He switched to current department business with his usual briskness, and to filling her in on what had gone down. A street-fight with a stabbing was one case which had occupied his own time, and he wanted Jane's thoughts on the way the evening rota was organised. Or was pretending to want her thoughts, since it was obvious he already had his own ideas.

She knew, as she went back to her desk to plunge herself back into work, that she must not — *would not* — let any small seed of resentment fester. He truly had been the best candidate for

264

the job. Though she had not missed the fact that all three who had been shortlisted had been men. Bloody Morland would have been dancing in his socks about that! But she was not going to let herself dwell on that one, either. Except for the usual tight-lipped but resigned acknowledgement that one fact was as true as ever: you had to be twice as good, if you were a woman, before you were even considered for promotion to the higher ranks, in this so-called equal opportunities force.

She had always known that, so there was no point in dwelling on it. And she had thought from the first that Chris Hollings was no bad person to be working for, hadn't she? Better than most. So she would just have to swallow her feelings and give him the efficient back-up it was her job to provide.

And wait for next time. There might well be a next time, even here. She couldn't see DI Hollings standing still in his career for more than a year or two . . . And no, she would not feel bitter about that one, either; the fact that she had really wanted the job, and he, in all likelihood, was only looking on it as a stepping-stone!

She trailed back home at the end of a day filled with deliberate efficiency and goodwill, and tried not to look sourly on the fact that the latest copy of *Cityscene* had been left stuffed halfway through her letter-box. It wasn't this issue she wanted! She had not gone back to John Clay, either, with the admission that she might have been responsible for his stake-out's failure, or with the doubt about Quentin. She felt deeply unwilling to do so. It might still be nothing. Surely it was better to let it rest?

She let herself into the house after a wrestle with the oversprung letter-box which resulted in a torn and mangled paper, making her feel unduly cross and also dispirited. She had probably quarrelled with Adrian about absolutely nothing. She had not even been shortlisted for promotion. There was still a sting in that, a sense that it had been less than fair treatment of her work and her record. The final choice a fait accompli or not, they might at least have given her that . . .

She was simply going to have to try not to think about it.

There was some post on her mat: that, at least, had been pushed properly through her door. She picked up a couple of brown envelopes which looked like nothing more interesting than promotional material, and an airmail from her parents which she put aside to read later. The last item was a fat packet in some re-used wrapping, with no stamp, and her name written on the outside in spidery writing.

She opened that one first, and found a badly folded Ordnance Survey map. There was also a note written on lined paper, in the same untidy handwriting:

This is one of the maps Mary borrowed. I can't find the other one. I don't think Ethan made the marks on this. I asked some of the other vagrants too to see if Mary had ever talked about airfields, but nobody knew anything. Are you back at work? I came but you weren't here. I'll come back sometime to see how the sounds are working.

The signature began with a large K, the rest a scribble, but it was plainly Kieron. The idiot — she had not meant him to go round asking all and sundry about airfields!

Maybe — if someone had their ear to the ground — that was how the word had got out. Not through Quentin at all. Though the leak was still down to Jane for having mentioned it.

The map was a bonus, however. She unfolded it and spread it out on the floor, the widest space. It was largescale, and covered quite a lot of the local area. An outlying part of the city showed at one edge, but the rest was fields, roads, minor lanes, villages, even farms.

It was the area which included Dasset. And nearby, the tiny logo of a plane against it, was the place where the rave must have been held.

It was marked in ink with an X.

A careful and thorough search brought up another X, several miles from the first. There was no plane logo this time: it appeared to be just a field.

And there was a third one, on a field again, nearer to where the mapped land ended in the curling edges of the coast, with pale blue beyond to indicate sea.

Places where planes coming across the Channel illicitly could land?

They certainly could be. Yes, very definitely could be! Where had Marianna got her information from? How could she have known about these places, if they were what Jane was supposing they were — landing grounds for smugglers? People who were moving goods illegally would hardly talk about it with someone in earshot, even if that person was merely a tramp.

Jane looked at the map again, then folded it carefully and put it in a desk drawer. Then she took it out again and put it into her briefcase. Just in case. No, surely Kieron could not be right that her burglary had actually been a search for Old Mary's diary! It must have been coincidental that she had had the diary with her, and had been safely out of the way for one night. All the same, she was going to carry the map and the diary with her all the time from now on.

It *was* a ridiculous suspicion, though. How could anyone have known? It seemed highly unlikely that Kieron would have talked about Old Mary's scribblings to someone else.

Jane had mentioned the diary to Adrian.

She was back in the same rat-trap. Suspicions and conclusions. The thought of questions asked with a casual heartiness, and answers innocently given. But innocently — definitely.

Any danger, any risk, was being meticulously dealt with. Jacko. Laurence Beck. So perhaps also Marianna's apparently incomprehensible diary . . . Incomprehensible except for that one concealed, but very clear, page. That might set the cat among the pigeons, if what it said was true.

It all came down to what Marianna knew. And about whom.

Jane jumped up restlessly, trying to decide what she ought to do about it. She could not face another session with the diary just now, trying to work out what it might or might not mean. And what she had, if more than before, was still not enough to take to the DI. Her new permanent DI, she thought drily. He had already dismissed her ideas too thoroughly. There was no way she was going to look as if she was out to prove something, deliberately crossing her new superior as a point of principle. If she went back to him with the Old Mary file as it stood, it could look like that. There was no way either she was going to lay herself open to being told not to use her imagination so much. Not just now. And, yes, maybe there was a touch of injured pride in that!

She decided abruptly that her head would be clearer when she had had something to eat. And as she had not laid in any groceries during her 'flu period, that gave her every excuse not to cook but to do the takeaway routine instead. Only, not the nearest chippie, or the nearest takeaway . . . . She picked up her briefcase — despite feeling foolish for doing so — and went back out to her car.

She took herself right to the other end of town, even though she knew that she really could not keep away from the streets around her house indefinitely, just so that she would avoid the risk of running into Adrian. For now, she told herself that the Indian takeaway in Northgate had the best reputation, and she was only going there for that reason. And because there was a good Chinese takeaway down there too, in case she changed her mind as to what she wanted. In fact, it was the Chinese which won out, mainly because she could park right in front of it. She made her choice, then stood in the small brightly lit shopfront waiting for her order, leaning against the counter and idly watching the television set high on the wall.

'Hallo, Jane!'

She had been too busy regarding some distant guerilla warfare on the screen to hear anyone else come in. It was Oliver Devereux who stood there smiling at her, as smooth and bland as ever, his eyebrows raised in surprise.

'I saw you as I was walking past. Do you often come down to the Lok Kwen, or is this just a lucky chance? I have to admit, I do get tempted by their crispy pork myself occasionally. I hope you've ordered it, it's one of their best!'

'I don't think I have.'

'Then you must add it at once.' He gave her a beaming smile and turned to the girl behind the counter to give the instruction. 'There — you'll see I'm right! Do you know, I think I'll follow your example and eat Chinese tonight. Since I'm still here, after an evening's stock-taking.' He began what was obviously an expert order, then stood back and looked at Jane again. 'You're not, I hope, working down this end, and finding yourself a takeaway while you're on watch?'

'No, just relaxing at the end of my day. How are the antique dolls, have you sold them yet?'

He began to tell her a story about a customer, making an amusing tale out of it. He seemed quite glad to stand and chat while they both waited for their orders. His charm was soothing, and a good distraction. As a way of responding, Jane made a story of her own out of the installation of her hi-fi, making Kieron out to be an expert from the shop where she had made her purchase and ruefully describing his apparent need to move all her furniture around to give her the best musical reception. And that led to a discussion on music generally . . . Oliver appeared to find her company entertaining, and it was somehow no surprise when he said with a smile, 'You know, I've been wishing I had your phone number — in case I hear of another Italian concert coming up — but yours is unlisted, I don't doubt, in your profession. Perhaps we could exchange numbers in case either of us hears news of any more musical treats due to happen?'

Well, why not? He was pleasant company. And could be useful, too. She was not going to raise the subject of Old Mary while they were standing in a takeaway, but she had already thought of him as someone whose brains she might pick again. She agreed to an exchange of telephone numbers, and wondered lightly whether she would actually hear from him. After all, she was as free as air. She could pick her company as she chose. There was nothing at all to stop her seeing Oliver Devereux, if he chose to seek her out.

Nothing at all: not work, and not any man who might previously have been in her life either.

It was a surprise all the same when he rang her up two evenings later, and asked her out to dinner.

She accepted. It had occurred to her that she had no actual knowledge as to whether or not he was married. He had never mentioned a wife, and said nothing about one now as he issued the invitation with charming hesitancy, saying apologetically that he knew it wasn't a concert, but he had enjoyed her company so much that he was sure they would find plenty to talk about. There was a restaurant he was convinced she would enjoy. It was a little bit tucked away and not everyone knew about it. She said yes, she would love to; and no, of course she would be happy to meet him there rather than having him come to pick her up.

It was merely a dinner invitation, and he was merely a friend. And she was thoroughly tired of watching her step and avoiding the least hint of gossip. Where had that got her, except into a mess of painful complications?

It had certainly not got her promoted, that was for sure.

She had seen nothing at all of Adrian since their last quarrel. Kieron had not turned up either, which was slightly surprising. She would have expected him to come back and pester her as to whether the map had been helpful. She had not managed to make any more sense out of the diary, try though she did; it was just the same old stuff, the rat, the owl, and the scavenger. She could see that it *could* be a kind of record of links between them, but her attempts to get inside Marianna's mind were both wearying and frustrating. She was, however, getting a clearer picture of the scavenger. He seemed to have some reason to be out at night. He could be expected to turn up in certain places . . . and was someone of whom Old Mary was deeply afraid.

He was bad. It came down to that. Bad, and corrupting; there was a shivery sense of deliberate cruelty about him, a delight in ways to hurt.

Dressing for her evening out with Oliver Devereux, Jane decided she might ask him what he thought about the idea of moving small antiques out by light plane. It could hardly matter mentioning the subject now, when John Clay's drug raid would already have alerted anyone who might have reason to be wary.

She took deliberate care over her appearance. There was a slight sense of defiance in choosing a dress which brought out the deep blue of her eyes, intensified anyway by a judicious touch of make-up; paying careful attention to the smooth blonde flick of her hair; sliding on the sapphire ring which had been her great-grandmother's, and which her burglar had luckily missed because it had been at a jeweller's having a loose stone fixed. Oliver was an elegant man himself, always well dressed and with never a hair out of place, so she might as well do him — and herself — justice. Sliding her feet into high heels, Jane decided her appearance was eminently satisfactory. And as she had recently bought a new winter coat which was both warm and smart, nothing need spoil the overall effect.

She went out to her car, picking up her briefcase on the way to lock in the boot. She had been doing that for the past week, whenever it was unsuitable to be carrying it or have it in the office beside her. It was probably a ridiculous habit and sometimes made her feel as if she had caught Old Mary's paranoia. All the same it had become a habit.

273

She had been wary of making copies on the station photocopier for fear of questions being asked — and the diary was certainly too long to photocopy without raising at least a casual query from a curious colleague — when it was a case she was supposed to have closed. And she had not got round to making a visit to any of the public copy shops . . . She should perhaps do that. After all, the diary, the map and the photographs were all she had to prove that she might have a valid theory, and was not just wasting her time.

The restaurant was as tucked away as Oliver had said it was, though Jane had in fact heard of it. And that it was very, very expensive. The kind of place where there would be no prices displayed on the menu, because if you needed to ask, you were not the sort of person to afford them. It was in a cul-de-sac off a narrow street and could almost have been a private house, save for one small and discreet notice with a lamp to light it. It had its own private parking round the back, with a rear entrance which could be used to save customers an extra walk. Oliver had told her how to find that, too, from an entrance in the next street. Parking in the shadowy area, surrounded by a high wall and trees, Jane saw that there were two other cars — both expensive. One, she hoped, probably Oliver's. Though he had given her apologies in advance, in case she was here first.

He was already there, she found as she made her way in through the rear entry — discreet again, merely a door which one might have supposed led somewhere private. A short passageway brought her out into a low, beamed room of great charm, with logs crackling in an inglenook fireplace, and a mere three tables, at one of which there was a party of four. The other two were empty but one was laid with napery, silverware and glinting crystal glasses. And Oliver was standing at a minute bar in the corner — no more than a beamed nook, though set about with bottles — talking to a darkly genial man with a seamed face.

'Here she is,' Oliver said welcomingly, stepping across to draw her into his group of two. 'Jane, this is our host, Henry. And since you said you haven't been here before, I'll explain that here, that does mean host. Henry will serve us whatever dishes he has decided to cook today, and choose our wines for us, and woe betide anybody who doesn't appreciate his choice! Though I think it would be impossible *not* to find the whole thing perfection . . . '

'He says that to make sure I don't decide to take offence and throw him out,' Henry said genially. He gave Jane an appreciative look, and reached out to shake her by the hand, his own firm and warm. 'Good, you look like a worthy guest, m'dear! Let me take your coat. Now then, you'll start with a dry sherry — though if you absolutely refuse to drink sherry, I suppose I'll allow a Madeira instead.'

Jane assured him that dry sherry would completely suit her, which earned her another look of approval. Soon he had drifted off to exchange banter with the group of four, then away into some inner fastness. Oliver raised an amused eyebrow at Jane.

'He really is capable of throwing people out if he dislikes the look of them. But how could he, with you? I thought you might find this place a nice surprise, and the food is a genuine delight!'

It was. Served at a leisurely pace — by Henry himself, popping in and out, sometimes adorned by a chef's hat — they worked their way through an elegant and delicious but unidentifiable starter, then small slivers of trout, then roast beef done entirely traditionally, but tasting better than roast beef ever did and melt-in-the-mouth tender. Different wines came and went. The third table remained unoccupied and there was ample room for privacy, yet a pleasant air of sociability. It was like being at a dinner party given by an eccentric host. Jane supposed there must be staff in the kitchen, but they never appeared in here. A pudding eventually appeared, after a long wait, a confection of cream and what appeared to be fresh summer fruit. Nobody, certainly, would have dared berate Henry for the long pauses between courses, which frequently seemed to happen because he had decided to join in somebody's conversation. It was all very easy, pleasant and relaxing. Oliver was a stimulating companion. She was learning one or two things about him as well.

One was that he, too, had been at Kings — The King's School, to give it its plain and proper title. 'Do you by any chance remember someone called Christopher Hollings?' she enquired.

'Yes, very well. He was a couple of years junior to me. You needn't tell me why you're asking. He's just moved back here, hasn't he? And he's in your own profession?'

'You still know him?'

'Quite well. My first wife and his wife happen to be step-sisters. And as a result of a meeting at the wedding, my uncle married his second-cousin's aunt — if that's not too confusing a relationship for you?'

'Possibly, but I'll bear with it as long as you don't go on to say that his first wife and your wife are also related!'

'I don't believe Christopher's got as far as a second, and my second has a great many relatives but none of them English. We live a fairly detached life — she's in Italy at the moment.' He gave her that answer lightly, but with a smoothly unspoken acknowledgement that he knew what she had been asking. 'I don't expect Christopher and I will socialise, except perhaps for a nod in passing to acknowledge the relationship. Have you ever been married, Jane?'

'Not so far.'

'I don't think I'd entirely recommend it. Life is rather more peaceful with a cat. Yes, even Marcus!'

'Talking about that damned Siamese of yours again, Oliver?' Henry enquired, hoving to beside them. 'What a waste when you've got a lady with you whose eyes are just as blue and who can actually talk instead of yowl! Eat your food, and enjoy — tell me, did you think the horseradish was a fraction sharp? I'm not sure that damned supplier of mine isn't sending me imported roots instead of what I ordered!'

The conversation turned in a different direction. Henry asked Oliver, humorously, whether he still went in for 'that damned meditation, the arm-waving stuff!' It turned out that he meant Tai Chi, the slowmotion martial art which was more of a movement form than a matter of fighting, and that Oliver was a devotee of it. 'It's extremely restful, and healthy at the same time,' he informed Henry. 'According to the Chinese, you can cure almost anything by concentrating on your energy flow. You can certainly reduce your blood pressure — '

'I'm not Chinese, and I'd rather eat, drink and be merry, and bugger my blood pressure! It's a fad, that's all. I could understand it if you were still doing that Aikido thing you used to go in for.'

'Much too aggressive. And Tai Chi is a very beautiful form. Jane, have you ever tried it? My dear, you should,' Oliver said as she shook her head, 'it would suit you! It's almost like a dance.'

'Stop making yourself sound like a fairy, when we both know you aren't one,' was Henry's caustic retort. He winked at Jane, then wandered off. Oliver gave a laugh and a shrug, spreading his hands wide to indicate that their host was a hopeless case. But he had nevertheless looked as if the teasing made him just a fraction uncomfortable, and turned the conversation smoothly on to a discussion of Chinese and Japanese customs altogether, and thence to oriental artefacts. Apparently the small ivory figures called netsuke were a particular interest of his.

It was not until they had reached the stage of coffee — and Henry had withdrawn, saying cheerfully that he was going to absent himself and put his feet up, but when they wanted to go they could strike the Lutine bell above the bar — that Jane decided she would try to elicit Oliver's opinion on antiques smuggling. Whether he was a relation by marriage of Chris Hollings or not. He was telling her the difference in trade terms between 'ephemera' and 'objets', and then gave her a direct lead by himself raising the subject of her previous enquiries to him.

'So, you see, almost everything has a category, and a specialist in that category. That reminds me, did you ever get any further with your investigation into that lady's list of marks? Miss Troughton, was that her name?'

'Troughton-Beck. No, I haven't, really. Though I did find out she specialised in jewellery.' She would not raise the subject of Laurence Beck's murder, a sure damper on a pleasant evening. 'As a matter of fact that made me wonder whether there could possibly be a connection with another investigation we've been doing. We were told there might be a smuggling ring, stealing small but valuable items from country houses here and probably passing them across to the continent. If somebody wanted to do that, how do you think they'd set about it?'

'Goodness, that's quite a question. Let me see . . . I suppose you might pass goods hidden inside other goods. There was a case last year where Customs found several stolen paintings rolled up inside vases. And I believe there was a case with desk drawers with false backs to them. Then there are freight-lorries going across all the time on the ferries, and don't those sometimes have false compartments? I'm only talking about the things I read in the papers.'

'Yes, there've been all of those. And I'm not trying to suggest you'd be an expert on smuggling!' Jane smiled at him. 'What about moving things by plane? Small aircraft, the sort amateur pilots fly? With the right connections, that might be possible, don't you think? Look, I'm sorry to spoil the evening by bringing my work into it, and this is confidential. I'd be grateful if you didn't mention it to anyone else. I'm only asking your opinion as a friend.'

'My dear, you couldn't possibly spoil this evening, and I'm most interested! And flattered that you should ask me. Did this Miss — Miss whatever-her-name-was — leave some kind of clue which led you to think about planes?'

'Possibly.' Jane refrained from saying that Old Mary had died at an airfield. Asking about smuggling during a social evening might be one thing, talking about death was another. And the map was no clue on its own. 'She did leave another document besides that list I showed you, but it's rather left me grasping at straws. If it means anything at all, it must be in code. It certainly isn't clear!'

'Perhaps you'd like to show me that, too, and we could both see if we can find out what it means. I'd be delighted to help, if I can.'

'I might just do that sometime. The case is more or less closed, so if I can't find anything to reopen it, I'm going to have to leave it. But look — this isn't really the time and place at all, and Henry's coming back so let's forget it for now. You were absolutely right, this is a most unusual place and

I have thoroughly enjoyed it!'

Henry seemed to have come back to say he had found an exceptionally good port, and would anyone like to try it? Jane gave him a smiling refusal, and so, she saw, did Oliver. They had both of them drunk quite enough. Jane suspected that Henry had also returned because he was bored with his own company and fancied some more conversation. He ran this place with splendid eccentricity — though also highly successfully, she imagined. He might only ever cater for three tables, but he probably charged the earth for them. And had managed to build the kind of reputation which made people want to afford them, too.

He joined Jane and Oliver for a while, then moved over to pull up a chair and start a long argument with the people at the other table, who were obviously well known to him. A surreptitious glance at her watch showed Jane it was almost midnight. She had a sense that Oliver was growing a trifle restive, too. When he smiled at her and pulled back his chair in a deliberate fashion, she hoped it was not with a particular intent. Though the way his eyes lingered on her, and his sudden decision to be gone, suggested it might be. She liked him a great deal, but a suggestion that they spend the rest of the night together would not be welcome. She decided she could count on the fact that his manners were too good for him to become insistent. Henry detached himself from his argument long enough to get her coat, and put it round her with a friendly bear-hug, and they were given a casual salute and a command to show themselves out. Informality was obviously the order of the day here.

'It's not the sort of place where you even get a bill?' Jane murmured with amused curiosity as they moved into the passageway and out of Henry's earshot. He had gone back to his cheerful discussion, anyway.

'He'll send me an account. He actually is a very capable businessman, as well as being a near genius as a chef!'

'And is this where you send your American customers? I'd imagine they'd love it. Particularly knowing that it's off the general tourist-track beat.'

'My goodness, no, I wouldn't send Henry most of my Americans. One or two very select customers, occasionally. But he'd be entirely capable of addressing some extremely rich Midwesterner rudely and telling him to go away and dress properly!'

Jane giggled as they went out into the dark. The small car park was a place of heavily pooled shadows, a cold wind rustling the tops of the trees. She felt Oliver take her arm as they crossed to her car. A clinch was probable. She wasn't sure if she would mind that, and she certainly owed him that much . . . He requested her car keys, with an offer to open the car door for her, and she took them out and handed them to him. Perhaps it had been a way to ensure that she didn't immediately escape, because his other arm came round her to pull her close against him. When he bent his head to kiss her, it was surprisingly hard, though not at all unpleasant, and he was wearing some kind of lemongrass aftershave which had a nice, faint, tangy odour. He lifted his head as soon as she began to pull away.

And then she felt him stiffen, in every muscle. And begin to shake.

His eyes had gone past her and were wide and fixed. Turning, Jane saw why.

Three feet away, there were two dark figures. Both in black ski-masks, black clothes, black gloves . . . They were standing there in silence, but their import was absolutely clear.

One of them was pointing a sawn-off shotgun straight at Jane's chest.

# 18

It had happened before. Not to her, but to a couple of wealthy Spanish tourists arriving late at night in a hotel car park. About three months ago. And they had never caught the perpetrators.

This had to be the same duo. And this time they had decided to try Henry's. With its rich clientele, and its nicely secluded car park.

She prayed the dining foursome would not suddenly emerge from the door and set something off. She moved her hands very slowly and carefully away from her sides, to raise them in a gesture of complete obedience. At the same time she said very clearly to Oliver, out of the side of her mouth, 'We ought to do exactly what they say. Don't try anything!'

She thought he would not; in fact, rather surprisingly, he was simply standing there shaking like a leaf. But her warning had been automatic with that gun-barrel pointing straight at them.

The second man gestured to his pockets, a sign to turn them out, then pointed at the ground. Yes, the Spanish couple had said their hold-up had been wordless. Out of a dry mouth, but with her mind working steadily, Jane said to Oliver, 'He wants you to empty your pockets and throw everything on the ground. Money's what they want mainly — yes, all right, I'll empty my handbag too!' She tipped its contents out rapidly and felt deeply relieved that she had not brought her warrant card. Better if they were ignorant of the fact that she was police. That gun was extraordinarily steady, not a movement from it, and she knew only too well what a shotgun blast could do . . . Oliver's wallet went down on the ground and was scooped up, its contents removed, the wallet thrown back down. The few pounds Jane had with her had already been flipped out of her purse, though she noticed her credit cards had been glanced at and rejected. Perhaps they thought she was unlikely to be worth much. Oliver's watch, his signet ring, her ring — her great-grandmother's ring which had been missed last time, damn! If they were working to form, it would be the car keys next. There was a sudden whisper from the man with the gun, clear but unidentifiably husky, and sure enough he said, 'Car keys.'

Oliver had already dropped hers to the ground in his desperate scrabble through his pockets, but he was signed to pick them up and throw them over. They wouldn't find much worth stealing in her Renault. Apparently they intended to look, though. Jane and Oliver were signalled to move out of the way, the gun following them. Oliver was still shaking and Jane began to worry that he would panic. She slid her hand through his arm and tried to press it reassuringly. A very quick look in the interior of her car, the glove compartment pulled open, nothing seen worth taking. A move round to the boot. She saw her briefcase lifted and removed. Oh hell, *hell*! He wasn't even looking in it to see there was nothing worth having, just taking it!

'There's no money in there,' she began. And stopped after a sharp warning gesture with the gun.

'Your car,' the whisper said briefly, the eyes within the ski-mask turning steadily to Oliver.

'It's — it's that one. You've already got the keys, they're in that pile.'

His car was a gleaming saloon with the most recent registration. A gesture of the head between the two men. No, they were not going to search it, simply take it. Why did Jane think the second man was nervous? It was the one with the gun who was plainly in charge, anyway. The whisper came again, as brief as ever, and to the point.

'Over there. Lie down.'

The gesture had been into the corner. Jane pulled Oliver with her — his legs seemed to be moving with difficulty, he really was a broken reed! But in some ways she had to be thankful for that. And he was not trained, as she was, to face danger. She pushed him down on to the ground, lying flat face-down beside him herself, an arm across him. As long as this pair had not changed from their previous MO they should be safe if they remained totally obedient — she hoped. She was horribly aware that the gunman had moved nearer, the barrel pointing down at them. Nowhere near enough to grab, though, and anyway, she knew too well not to try conclusions with a gun held as professionally as that. She heard a car door open, an engine start.

'Stay,' the whisper said threateningly. And then there was movement, steps softly retreating, a pause. The car backing out fast. The sharp clunk of its second door. The engine revving up smoothly and going off into the distance.

'Oh God, oh God, oh God . . . '

'It's all right, they've both gone,' Jane soothed him. She had lifted her head very, very cautiously. 'It's all right, Oliver. Oliver?'

'Oh God. Oh God. He could have shot us both. He was going to — '

'It was theft they were after. Your car, I'm afraid. I hope you didn't have anything too valuable in it?' The car itself would be well worth their time. Last time they had got all the luggage as well, travellers cheques, the Spanish woman's jewellery. 'Oliver? Come on, you can get up. Oh, hell, they've slashed my tyres. And the ones on the other car, I expect. Come on, Oliver, get up!'

'I'm sorry. I just can't — I can't stand violence and blood and — '

There had been no blood, thank goodness. Helping him to his feet, Jane was aware of a deep thankfulness that the other party of diners had not come out into the middle of things. A car, money, credit cards, and Oliver's extremely expensive watch were nothing compared to their lives lost after interruption and panic. The thieves had not bothered with her watch, which was a very ordinary one. They knew precisely what they wanted. Very professional.

And a briefcase might have held valuables, so they had taken it without even bothering to look inside. It was no use thinking about that now, though it was a bitter irony.

'What — what do we do now?'

'We go straight back inside and get Henry to ring the police,' Jane said to the shaking man beside her. He was at least trying to pull himself together now, she saw: he had begun to smooth his hair and straighten his clothes, though still with shaking fingers. 'Come on, the quicker we are, the more likely we can get the slags — I mean, the criminals — caught. And we might tell Henry to put some very bright lights out here, too,' she added grimly as she pushed the door open.

The next few minutes were full of startled faces, a rush of horrified sympathy, offers of brandy. The next hour was full of police business. And the hour after that. Jane was aware that Oliver had been taken home, but she was giving a clear description of events, raking her mind for every detail she could summon up. 'Yes, I'd say it was the same two. We thought last time that they must have gone straight out of the country with the stolen car, didn't we? If that's true, they obviously decided to come back. No, no identifying marks, and they were both wearing those soft lace-up boots which can be bought anywhere. They knew exactly what they were doing . . . Yes, a sawn-off. Just like last time. And he held it as if he knew how to use it, too.'

She had to go through it all again for Chris Hollings the next morning. The same morning. She had only had a couple of hours' sleep before she was back on duty. And had to put up with Kenny saying, 'You do seem to be jinxed at the moment, Sarge, don't you? Maybe we should follow you about, in the interests of catching a few blaggers in the act!'

Jinxed . . . The Old Mary investigations were certainly that. Thanks to a piece of random ill-luck — or one solitary foray to where the very rich went, and were known to go — she had lost everything. Before she had got round to making those copies, anything which might possibly have been evidence was gone, kaput, vanished with her briefcase. Jane managed to give Kenny a weak smile, along with a rueful shrug.

'It sure as hell wasn't my lucky evening. And I've got two slashed tyres now, just to add insult to injury! They weren't taking any chances, those two.'

Chris Hollings wanted a detailed run-through of the whole event, his case to solve since it was a hold-up, along with Peter Pettigrew because it was car-crime. A rapid APB last night had given no result on a sighting of Oliver Devereux's car, but pros like these two would have been ready to do a switch of plates. Jane was aware that the DI raised an eyebrow on hearing with whom she had been spending the evening, but he let it pass without comment.

'They couldn't have known you were police, you say? That's just as well, or you might have had more trouble from them.'

'I wasn't carrying my warrant card, since it was only a social evening. They may have wondered why I kept calm — though they could just have thought I'd been through something like that before.'

'Yes. I'm sorry about your personal losses. Oh, just as a point of procedure, I presume you didn't have any papers from here in your briefcase? After what I said last week about tightening up on people taking confidential papers home with them, I assume you didn't?'

'No, sir. Only some personal things. Oh, and the rota I'd started to make out, but that's scarcely going to be important enough for anyone to want to keep!'

'No. Good. Right, I think we've got as much as we can on it, and this time we do at least have the advantage of a trained eye. You definitely thought the second man seemed nervous?'

'A little. He knew what he was doing, but I certainly had that impression. He was looking to the gunman for instructions a couple of times, that's for sure. That one was the boss. I'm sorry I can't give you more on the voice, but it was a whisper, and not enough of it to catch if there was an accent. We thought, last time, that they might be foreigners because they didn't speak. This time one spoke, but . . . '

'You did as well as you could. And kept your companion from doing anything stupid, too. You're right, it was lucky the other diners didn't come out. Our perps must simply have decided to take whoever was first. Well, I must go and talk to Mr Henry Myerscough, and see if he's remembered yet whether he's seen anyone hanging about lately. They must have cased the place, to know how conveniently secluded its car park is, so we might be lucky!'

Even if they were, and managed to pick up a trail, Jane knew she was unlikely to get her briefcase back. Certainly not intact. The contents would be well gone, emptied out somewhere as random rubbish. All she had to go on now was memory . . . and what use would that be? She had had little enough. Now even the most tenuous proofs were gone, to show that there had been something important behind Marianna's death. She had not even got her photocopy of the list: foolishly, and with a false idea of security, she had put it in with the map, the newspaper, and the diary. Any hope of proving that she had been acting on something more than imagination was blown away.

Now she had no way of finding the owl, the rat and the scavenger — if they existed at all. If they did, she particularly wanted the scavenger. But it seemed she had lost him.

★ ★ ★

She would have expected to have had to face Kieron with the news that she had come to a dead stop over Old Mary's death; that it was going to be impossible now to convince anyone to reopen the case. Kieron, however, seemed to have decided to be conspicuous by his absence. An uneasy thought struck her, and she hoped that did not mean he had asked one too many questions of the wrong people. If that had been the case, however, surely another 'accidental death' would have shown itself . . .

Before she could worry unduly, she caught sight of him, briefly, in the street, simply walking along. She was driving by in her now mended car, and pulled up, giving a hoot to draw his attention. She could have sworn he saw her but instead of responding he ducked down a pedestrianised sidestreet and rapidly vanished. Odd. Unless it was against his principles to be seen talking to her in public. He would probably turn up, not least to have another fiddle at her sounds system. However, several days went by and he did not.

She had tried looking further into the death of the vagrant Sofia, but that was a dead file, and there was nothing in it which could offer any help. Just the information Jane had already seen: that the girl was found dead from an overdose of badly cut heroin, the syringe still beside her.

She heard nothing from Oliver Devereux. Her connection with the police — let alone her demonstrable ability to keep cool, and her witnessing the fact that he had not — must have turned him right off.

She had a message from Andrew Beck to say he

intended to bury his aunt next week, and would Detective-Sergeant Perry be present please? He had made the arrangements for ten am next Tuesday at Barham Crematorium. She could only presume that he had got all the details as to where Marianna Troughton-Beck's body could be found from someone else at the station while she herself had been out.

She ran into Adrian.

Ironically, it was at the newsagent's again, where they had first spoken to each other. Another Sunday morning meeting. They found themselves walking back together too. After all, it was the same direction. He asked her politely how work was going and she asked him equally politely the same question. Then, when they reached the stairway up to his flat, he hesitated and asked, 'Come in for coffee?'

'Yes, if you like.'

Why not? The grapevine had told her the drugs scene was quiet. If someone had been doing runs by light plane they had been thoroughly frightened off. Quentin might never have been involved anyway. And Quentin wasn't Adrian. Added to that, there was a voice in Jane's head which said she had lost out on promotion anyway, so why the hell should she not let her private life take precedence for once? Besides, she had missed him.

She told him, when they were up in the flat, what had happened about the DI job, making it rueful but casual, so that he could take it as he pleased. His reaction was to look at her gravely and say, 'It doesn't make any difference to me, does it to you?'

Gradually, however, they seemed to reach a point where she told him she was sorry she had been a pain, and he said he had been just as bad a one. And it seemed to be on again — tentatively, and with care, and a great need to be polite to each other.

That was at least something. More than something — against her dispirited feeling that she was being completely unsuccessful in all directions, just at the moment.

Not at work, really, or not that anyone else would have noticed. She was carrying her weight in the usual rush and scurry of villain-chasing, providing her usual efficient reports, doing a sergeant's job to DI Hollings' satisfaction. She had DCI Morland a great deal less on her back now, too, since apart from casting her the odd look of smugly satisfied disapproval, he seemed to have let up on his trench warfare. He had even forgotten to imply that it must be all her fault she had been involved in a hold-up; nor, remarkably, to lay it at her door that the case was showing no signs of solution. And he greeted the news that she needed to go and attend Old Mary's funeral on Tuesday with no more than an acid, 'It's about time that case was closed, so I'm glad to see we can put it to rest at last. Very well, Sergeant, if Mr Beck has requested your presence, you had better go. As long as Inspector Hollings agrees!'

The DI had already agreed. Jane wondered why Andrew Beck had particularly asked for her to be there as she drove in through the crematorium's arched entrance, off the road which led down to

293

Folkestone and the coast. If she had seen Kieron, she might have told him Old Mary was to be cremated today in case he wanted to be there. A dearth of cars in the gravelled car park suggested a distinct lack of mourners. She picked up the small bunch of flowers she had brought as a suitable gesture, and followed a sign which indicated the chapel. As she did so, a hearse turned in at the gates behind her, with one car behind it.

There were four men in undertaker's black to slide the bleakly bare coffin out on to their shoulders then pace solemnly the few yards to the chapel entrance. And Andrew Beck, alone, with a wreath in his hand, falling into step behind.

He looked as bad-tempered as ever, and those very dark eyes really were like his aunt's.

He gave Jane a brief nod as he came past her, indicating that she was meant to follow. There was no one else. The chapel's pale pine pews were empty, and the one vase of flowers on display looked dusty, as if they had been resuscitated as a token. The coffin was placed with due ceremony on the rollers which would carry it discreetly through the red curtains beyond. Then the four bearers withdrew after a glance at Andrew Beck, the door closing behind them. At the same moment soft organ music, obviously taped, started up from somewhere, a conventionally soothing, characterless sound.

It seemed as if this was all. There was no minister, and apparently there was going to be no service. Just one tall man, Marianna's sole surviving nephew, and Jane, in a bleakly impersonal chapel.

She felt an involuntary shiver at the memory of the other nephew, and the way she had last seen him. Laurence — the only person Old Mary would admit in the diary to ever having been fond of. Well, he was gone too. And violently. There was a DCI in London who thought that violence had been down to Andrew Beck, but he had turned out to be wrong. Or else to have had no way of proving himself right.

Andrew Beck stepped forward and placed his wreath on top of the coffin. He had at least chosen something opulently showy — white lilies and dark red roses. Without turning his head, he said carelessly, 'Perhaps you'd like to add your flowers, Detective-Sergeant Perry, before I press the button. Yes, you're quite right, this is all there is to be. My aunt Marianna was never religious, so I can't feel any show of piety is really necessary.'

An undeviatingly unpleasant man, Mr Andrew Beck. Jane moved forward and put her small bunch of flowers on top of the bare wood, next to his. He glanced at her — with mockery, she thought — and then pressed the red button beside his hand. There was a deep rumbling sound, and the coffin began its stately progress.

Into the fire, to be finally and totally burned. Jane was not more than conventionally religious either, but she felt a sudden outrage that there should be no more than this. No ceremony, no farewell prayer, just two people, one of them a man who had disliked Marianna, the other a virtual stranger. Mad the old woman might have been, and a drunk, and a nuisance, but a life was worth more than that.

As the coffin ground its slow way on, Andrew Beck reached into the inside of his overcoat, then leaned forward and placed something else next to Jane's small bunch of flowers.

If there was one thing Jane would recognise after her hours of poring over it, it was one of the two items he had placed so deliberately. There was no chance that she could be mistaken. The scruffy plastic cover with its Mickey Mouse decoration. The grubby edges of the pages.

Marianna's diary . . .

The other item was the map on which she had marked the crosses.

'Don't try to snatch them back, I'd only stop you. I think it's entirely suitable to burn her possessions with her, don't you? I thought it worthwhile to let you see them go. Considering you'd been so troublesomely inclined to guard the book, and not let it out of your sight!'

The very dark eyes, steady on Jane's face, showed no particular change of expression. Just that same bad-tempered carelessness. She knew her jaw had dropped, and that she was staring at him with an idiotic look of disbelief. She closed her mouth rapidly. He was telling her . . . They were alone in an empty chapel, so it would matter little what he told her!

It was almost as if he could read her thoughts. 'Nobody's going to believe you, without any documentation,' he said coolly. 'It wasn't much proof, as it turned out, but if you had a sharp mind I suppose you might have seen something there. However, I can always complain that you seem to have become hysterical if you try to claim we ever had this conversation at all. I hope you're clear about that? Now that you have no diary and no map — oh, and not the photocopy you showed me either, it was foolish of you to keep everything together — you really will have to let things rest, won't you? It was inadvisable of Marianna to turn suddenly sane after all these years and start being a great deal too observant. And to write things down, in whatever form. But now, of course, everything has gone.'

The disappearance of the coffin between the curtains echoed his words. So did the clearly audible roar, the sound of the furnace beyond starting up. Gone beyond recall. Jane stared at the man in front of her — at his casual arrogance, his bad-tempered, dark-eyed face.

'She found out it was you, so you killed her?'

'Oh, I wouldn't do a thing like that myself. Other people have better skills for that. Once we found her, and she had seen me, however — and I'm glad to say that surprised her — she couldn't be allowed to . . . . continue her clever games. She had obviously discovered far too much.'

The last words were waspish. That annoyed him, Jane realised. That Marianna, whom he had discounted, had got so close. 'She saw you at the airfield when you were having the jewellery smuggled out?' she enquired, and saw that annoyed him too. Perhaps she should be careful. This man was dangerous. And why was he choosing to tell her? Still, after what he had already said, she might as well go on. 'I suppose you had your cousin

Laurence killed too? It actually was you?'

'I think we should go with the theory that Laurence's death was a gay-bashing, don't you? Unless you want to accept responsibility for it. You realise he would still be alive if it hadn't been for your persistence? He had nothing to do with the carefully arranged thefts, of course — but he was just a little bit too expert. You really couldn't be allowed to consult him. Once you had made the connection . . . You see, poor dear Laurence's death really is your responsibility. Unless it was done by a bit of rough trade. Let's go along with that, shall we?

She felt a loathing for Andrew Beck which made her swallow hard, as if downing some extremely poisonous bile. 'What made you decide to bring me here and tell me the truth?' she challenged. 'You can hardly believe I'm just going to let it go!'

'But you'll have to. You have not a shred, not a hope, of proof. Even — as I said — of this conversation. Besides, what I have been . . . occupying myself with, is over. So there'll be nothing in the future for you to latch on to, either. I'm afraid you've lost. I merely thought you might like to know that. While paying your suitable last respects to my aunt, of course.' He gave her a smile, or what could be supposed to pass as one; a mere rictus on that sour-tempered face. 'Now, with our little ceremony over, I shall go. I don't think I'll bother to reclaim the ashes. Goodbye, Detective-Sergeant Perry. Better luck next time!'

He turned and strolled away. A cold, arrogant man. If only she could nail him! If only there was a way. He thought he could simply say, 'It's over,' and it would be, did he? She knew damned well why he had chosen to tell her the truth: to prove how clever he was. He had been unable to resist it. He had apparently seen Jane as the one person who had tried to oppose him, the one person who might believe Marianna, someone whose persistence had acted like a goad. He did not consider her dangerous, just someone who had to be shown how easily he could dismiss her.

He was a thief. He had money, and could arrange an armed hold-up just to get Marianna's diary back. He was responsible for at least two murders. And she had to let him walk away.

But he thought it was over, did he? Oh no. No, it most definitely was not.

# 19

If Dan Crowe had still been DI Jane would have gone to him with all of it. He might growl, but he would believe her. Chris Hollings . . . No, she was too conscious of not knowing him well enough to count on anything. They might have been on the Special Course together, but that was a long time ago and he knew little about her nowadays, with only their very recent reacquaintance to go on. She would need to be a lot more sure of his trust before she could approach him. When he was new here himself, she had an exasperated vision of his consulting the DCI — and Morland's opinion would be a foregone conclusion!

Andrew Beck was unbearably sure of himself It was clear that he was the one who had been running the antiques ring, arranging the thefts organising the smuggled exports. Mr Big. How the hell had he known about the diary? And for that matter, how had he known that she was going to be so conveniently at Henry's, with its nicely out-of-the-way and thoroughly unlit car park? He must have had her followed. Unless he had her phone bugged? That seemed unlikely and the other theory far more probable. It would have given the chance for someone to have seen her put the briefcase in the boot of her car, too . . . though if she had been followed over a period of time it could have been seen that she had been doing that recently as a habit. But why did they not just jemmy the boot while she was indoors dining? I could have looked like a perfectly ordinary theft.

Not such an effective way to scare her, though A masked man with a shotgun made a good frightener.

A small shiver took her with the knowledge tha Andrew Beck must only have decided she was no danger to him after he had seen the paucity o the evidence she had. He might easily have had her shot anyway, and Oliver along with her, in an apparent killing in pursuit of theft.

Instead he had let it stand as a warning. A display of power for her to take in along with his careless admission of the truth. He had decided his operation was over, but he still wanted her to know how easily he could have blown her away.

A very conceited man, Mr Andrew Beck. That, along with his coldness, his arrogance, and his cruel carelessness with other people's lives, was plain.

A coldness touched Jane's thoughts. Maybe she had just been face to face with the evil Marianna had described.

She knew almost immediately that could not be so. Andrew Beck could not be Old Mary's scavenger. She had not known about him until the last moment. 'Once we found her.' At the airfield, presumably, where she had gone in search of proof. She must have died very shortly after that . . .

Andrew Beck was the commander in the background, but the ones Marianna had been watching were local. People she had observed in and around the city.

And one of those had 'better skills' for killing than Andrew Beck.

A discreet cough just behind her made Jane jump and swing round, but it was only some official, hovering with the obvious intention of not disturbing a mourner's grief, but needing to enquire how much longer she would be. No, thank you, she did not wish to walk in the gardens, or select a rose tree to be tagged in memory of the departed. As she left, she saw that both the hearse and Andrew Beck's car were gone. The hearse to its next appointment, presumably, and he by now on his return to London. To the profits he must have been amassing, and to further wealth now as Laurence and Marianna's sole heir. So he had no need to continue the series of thefts. Perhaps he would have had to discontinue them anyway, if the Dutch police had started to get too interested in flying operations.

And perhaps the realisation of Marianna's discoveries, her death and the need to dispose of her body, the need for Laurence's death to follow that, had all put him off. Jane fervently hoped it was that — that Marianna *had* been the one to put a spoke in his wheel. That would at least offer a small measure of justice for the old woman's death.

She returned to work, difficult as it was to keep her attention totally on it. One part of her mind was seeking continually for some way round, some means to find proof of what she now knew. She had a date to go to the theatre with Adrian that evening, and went, trying to seem cheerful and lighthearted, though they both agreed the play was somewhat turgid. They ran into Chris Hollings and his wife there, and Jane made a point of taking Adrian over to introduce him. Her life was her own. There was no reason why she should not spend it with whom she chose. Even with this new knowledge that Marianna really had been on to something. And if Marianna had marked a photograph of Quentin . . . Jane was not prepared to let her life be ruled by that. The future must take care of itself.

'So that's your new boss?' Adrian enquired as they went back to their seats. He realised, Jane thought, that she had deliberately introduced him, and was taking it in thoughtfully. 'He seemed reasonably likeable.'

'Yes, he is, I think. His wife was too, wasn't

she?' The tall dark girl had made a laughing point out of teasing her husband with, 'If Chris keeps on introducing me as, 'This is Elizabeth, she's a microbiologist,' one of these days I'm going to introduce him as, 'This is Chris, he cuts his toenails!' ' Her reception of Jane had been friendly, curious, and very amiable, and she had been delighted to hear Adrian was a vet since it meant she could quiz him on whether her pet labrador really had to spend so long in quarantine.

Back at work next day, Jane's mind went on with its restless quest. She thought of, and rejected, contacting the Chelsea police again. Small use: Andrew Beck had obviously covered his back too thoroughly. There would be no connection to find between him and the masked gunmen outside Henry's, either. That MO, though fitting with one already on their files, had very likely been a coincidence. Jane could bet grimly that Chris Hollings and Peter Pettigrew were going to get nowhere in finding the men concerned. She might try Oliver again. Little as he would want to see her, she could attempt to pick his brains more thoroughly on who, or what, Old Mary could have seen. Surely there had to be a clue somewhere!

There was one thing Andrew Beck had not considered when he destroyed the diary. Jane had studied it so thoroughly that its contents were still vividly present in her head. There were parts of it she knew almost by heart. The rat, the owl, and the scavenger. Even if the operation had been closed down, those three were still here on her patch. And if she could get them, she could get, through them, to Andrew Beck. She thought — hoped — that he had not even opened the newspaper, taking it for one she had simply with her. Yes, if he had known there was a reason for its presence he would surely have made a demonstration of burning that too. So he would know nothing about any photographs. That might offer a weak link, something Jane could catch and hold.

But the one readily identifiable connection was Quentin Hurst, and she was still reluctant to think about that. Even if it seemed she would have to . . .

Her phone rang, and she reached for it. As the only one in the CID room at the moment, if it was an urgent summons, she would have to take it.

'There's a call from Amsterdam, asking for you by name, Sergeant Perry. An Inspector Dirk Kuypers of the Netherlands Police.'

'Put him through.'

'Detective-Sergeant Perry? Oh good, I'm glad to catch you,' a male voice greeted her in the usual good English of their European counterparts. That would save Jane practising her not totally fluent Dutch. 'Inspector Kuypers here, NDP. I believe you sent a list to your Customs, and they faxed us a copy. It turned out to be extremely interesting, so could you tell me where you got it?'

'A list of hieroglyphics?' Her attention instantly focused, Jane blessed the fact that there had been that second photocopy and that she had sent it off. It had seemed such a slight chance, and she had completely forgotten it. 'Is that the one you mean?'

304

'Yes, jewellery marks. Not all jewellery, one or two other small artifacts too, but they come under that general heading. Some of the pieces which match the list have turned up here, after a lucky raid on a particular fence. We've been looking out for various stolen items for your Metropolitan police — you too, presumably? But the list isn't theirs, I think?'

'No, I found it among some papers belonging to an exdealer who was murdered.' Since she was alone in the room, Jane could say that without raising anyone's curiosity. And without fear of contradiction. 'I didn't know what it was and I couldn't find anybody who could translate it, so I sent it to Customs on the offchance. You say it definitely is stolen goods?'

'Yes. I'm not surprised you can't translate it, it's a different code from any I've seen before too, but the same marks appeared on a list we found with the fence. And he was eventually forced to agree that they matched up with the goods. There are only some of them there, and unfortunately we have nothing else from him so far and he's turned close-mouthed. But your copy, you say, was among the papers of a murdered dealer? One who was part of this operation?'

'One who was trying to make her own investigations into it, I think. And died because of that. I don't have any other documentation, no proof at all in fact, but it's a theory I'm following. Do you have anything else from your fence on where he got the stuff?'

'No. As I say, he's clammed up. I hoped you

might have something else we could use, to open him up!'

'You could try a name. Andrew Beck.' Jane spelled it out quickly. 'That's on the word of a snout — an informant — and I don't have any proof of that, either. Although I know for a fact that Andrew Beck's involved. He's a clever bastard, but I haven't any way of nailing him. Perhaps you'll be luckier. The word is that he's closed down the operation now, but he was definitely part of it. Probably running it. He may have been working partly through intermediaries, but some of the time he's certainly been personally involved so you may be able to catch someone with the name.'

'I'm very glad I've spoken to you — thanks! Anything else you can offer me?'

'Try your drugs people. I think — though again I've got no proof — that small planes were being used to smuggle the jewellery out. It seems the same route may have been used to send drugs in, because your people sent us a tip about that, though unfortunately we didn't get a result on it.'

'I wish I'd got on to you sooner! Or did you not have any of this then?'

'No, I didn't, or I'd have been on to you,' Jane told him, knowing there had been a reproachful question in his voice. She hesitated then added, 'As it is I'm sticking my neck out. I don't have anything my superiors think is — is more than theory. The fact that some of the jewellery has turned up with you is the first hard fact I've had. I'm more than glad Customs passed that list over to you!'

'An advantage to both of us. And if I come up with anything else, I'll ask for you personally again.' A very sharp Dutch Inspector, and an understanding one too. 'Thank you for what you've given me, and I'll follow it up!'

'And if I get anything else which might be relevant to you, I'll give you a ring — Inspector Kuypers, wasn't it?'

'That's me. I'll give you my number and extension.' He did, clearly and pleasantly. 'Oh, by the way — the bottom part of the list. That's not jewellery marks. I wasn't sure if it could be something else — map co-ordinates, maybe?'

Map co-ordinates. Yes, oh yes, indeed. If he was right, that could be where Marianna got her markings from! Why had Jane not thought of that? She wondered rapidly whether to ask Inspector Kuypers to fax her back a copy of the list — but there was no point, really, if the operation had been discontinued. Or no point from here. 'Try that one on your drugs people too, against a map of Kent,' she suggested, 'it might match up with what they heard. Though I think chummy's been scared off from this end. Still, it would be worth seeing if it fits!'

'And making the tie-up,' the pleasant voice from the other end agreed. 'Good, we've got quite a long way, I think. Thanks again, and from your side, good hunting!'

Jane wished him goodbye in Dutch, which brought an appreciative laugh and a civil farewell in that language, and then the line was disconnected.

A break — it might just be a break! A way to

get Andrew Beck after all . . .

And the rat, the owl, and the scavenger.

There was one thing she seemed to have inherited from Old Mary. A grim desire to catch the scavenger.

Andrew Beck first and foremost, but the scavenger was somewhere right here on her patch. A killer. And more than Andrew Beck's other creatures, she wanted him.

She was still at a loss to know what to do from this end. Quentin . . . There was no excuse she could find to question him on his flying habits. And she certainly was not going to pump Adrian. It might be her job to get information any way she could, but — no, not that.

She should let everything lie fallow, perhaps, and see if the Dutch police came up with anything concrete.

Oliver? He had offered to help her translate the diary, she remembered. And even without it, she could still appeal to him for any ideas he could offer. Even though he had made no attempt to contact her, she could perhaps smooth things over by pretending that she had totally forgotten his terror or had never even noticed it . . . He was the only private contact she had with the antiques trade, anyway.

After her conversation with the Dutch police, she probably ought to talk to DI Hollings. He was suddenly caught up in a round of meetings, however, giving her little chance to catch him at a good moment. So maybe she should try Oliver first . . .

She was still contemplating that as she drove back from an examination of a warehouse break-in when she caught sight of Kieron again. This time he was walking along the road out of the city — on his way to Lymans Oak, presumably, though he must have lost his wheels since he was plodding along on foot. There was no one to observe them, so he could hardly complain about being seen with her in public, Jane thought drily, as she pulled up right beside him. Winding her window down, she called to him amiably.

'I'd offer you a lift if I wasn't going in the opposite direction. The sounds system is great, by the way, and — Kieron? Kieron!'

He had simply turned his shoulder on her and gone trudging on. Jane revved her engine and backed until she was a yard or two in front of him, then watched him levelly as he came up beside her.

'You may like to now that your friend Old Mary has been cremated. I attended the ceremony. What the hell's the matter with you, Kieron — not even interested in that?'

'Not interested in *you*. Since you turn out to be as bent as all the pigs!'

'You'll explain that!'

She had used her most arctic voice, the one guaranteed to make strong men blench. Kieron was scarcely a strong man, and she saw it give him pause. It also made him stop to answer her.

'Well, you are, aren't you? I thought you were different but you're not! I can tell by the company you keep!'

For one cold moment she thought he meant Adrian. Adrian was the only person he had seen her with . . . and he had given Adrian that very hostile look. 'I'll have a fuller explanation than that!' she told him, fixing him with a cold gaze. 'What company? And if you mean the man who was at my house, you'll need a bloody good reason to . . . '

'Not him. He's just one of your lot, isn't he? I imagined so, from the short hair,' Kieron said with scornful dismissiveness. 'I meant your other company. The one you go choosing Chinese meals with. I thought,' he said in a sudden rush, and blinking hard, 'that I could trust you about Mary. I really thought so! But you've been in cahoots with him all along, I suppose? The one she didn't trust, the one she was watching! You've been having a good laugh together about it, have you? And I suppose you didn't imagine I might walk past and see you, framed together in the window, as happy as two peas in a pod.'

'Kieron! You've got to give me more on this! I *don't* know what you're talking about, I swear I don't but if it's the man I think you mean . . . You said you didn't know who Old Mary was watching!'

'I didn't know his name. I still don't. I know what he looks like, though.'

'Describe him!'

'Tall. Fair. Fancy clothes, very establishment. Owns a shop. Oh, I'm going, I can't trust you any more!'

'Get in the car. Get in, I said! And you can trust

me. In fact, if you *had* trusted me . . . ' She was cold all over, with a creeping feeling down the back of her neck. Oliver . . . and she had been about to ask him for help! Had already asked him, in the past. Oliver Devereux?

But who would be more likely to have a piece of antique jewellery in his pocket, to offer as a cruel tease to an unstable girl?

And who had known from quite early on that she had the diary? Oliver — because she had shown him the list. And she had told him Old Mary's real name; had even said to him that she would have to go and ask Marianna's nephews!

'Get in, Kieron,' she told him commandingly as he still hesitated. He was shivering in the cold wind, and a spatter of rain was beginning too. 'For God's sake, get in instead of standing there. We can either stop here or go wherever you like, but we need to talk! And this time I want the whole truth, since you obviously know more than you've ever told me!'

'And then you can arrest me, like you're always threatening to do?' he retorted — but climbing in beside her, bringing a cold blast of air with him. 'Can we have the heater on? We've run out of paraffin at the farm, and the kitchen's been the only warm place for days. All right, I do know more than I've told you, but I gave you the diary, didn't I? And look where that's got me!'

'It's got me further than you'd think. And you were right that someone wanted to steal it, by the way. They have now, and it's been destroyed. Now, tell me about Old Mary and Oliver Devereux!'

'Is that his name? If he's a friend of yours . . . '

'He's an acquaintance of mine. No more than that, I swear. Tell me! What was that about Oliver Devereux being the one Marianna was watching?'

'I don't know much,' he said sulkily. 'She didn't tell me, and I wouldn't know at all if she hadn't needed me. It was just — well — she certainly didn't trust him. And there was one night when she needed to get into the shop. So I got her in.'

'You what? You broke into Oliver Devereux's shop — with Old Mary?'

'That's right. She said there was something she wanted to see. We didn't take anything.' He gave Jane one of his sidelong defiant glances. 'She just said she needed to look. I can't tell you what she found, either, because she left me on watch. She just wanted to find something, see if something was there. And I suppose it must have been. She seemed to be satisfied when we come out. But she certainly didn't trust him. She called him a 'bad bastard'. Or 'a greedy bastard', I can't remember which!'

May be both. But probably the word had been bad.

Behind the charm, and the aristocratic face, and the smooth good looks, something dark and corrupt and cruel. Was it possible? It could be . . . Sofia? Probably Old Mary? Yes, if he was a student of martial arts, the blow which had broken Old Mary's neck would be simple for him. Even Jacko. A brick cracked against a drunken and befuddled head, and a swift push into the river . . .

No wonder Andrew Beck had known Jane was

spending the evening at Henry's. He had not needed to have her followed, he knew in advance. He had prearranged it with Oliver. And Oliver had made sure she would take her car, too, by suggesting that they meet there.

And she had been playing right into his hands — trusting him, asking his advice. She had been about to do it again.

She felt anger and revulsion, but also a sharp triumph. Another break — and this time, thanks to Kieron, she had found the one of the three she most wanted. The worst one — the scavenger.

# 20

No . . .

It had seemed so clear when she was talking to Kieron. Now, later, she could add in other facts which made the picture look different.

She could not be mistaken about Oliver's terror in the car park at Henry's. True, a bully could also be a coward. True, if he knew Andrew Beck at all well he might have thought they were both going to be shot, that the trap he had laid for her might also be for him. The operation over, he himself no longer any use. But he had been abject with terror, babbling with it, that gasped remark about not being able to stand violence or the sight of blood clearly genuine. He could not possibly be that good an actor!

Oliver was mixed up in this all right, but he was far more likely to be the rat. The golden rat, Marianna had written. A very good description. Jane had seen his long aristocratic face as being like his Siamese cat's, but you could visualise the same configuration in a rat. Long nose. Elegant hands which you could see as a rat's narrow paws. The slightly finicky manner. It would really only take the addition of whiskers and a long leathery tail, and the picture would be near perfect.

Had all Marianna's pseudonyms been as simple as that, an actual physical description?

Damn Kieron! If he had only told her all the truth sooner! Apparently it was her stern warning after she had found him in her house which had made him go on keeping quiet about that other illicit entry. She had meant to frighten him off, but not to make him too wary to tell her something important!

He was obviously horrifyingly good at burglary. He had bypassed Oliver's shop alarms. 'It's perfectly easy if you know how,' he had said defensively, 'and I used to know someone who worked in security systems, any way!' He had let them both in through a locked side door, easy again, and had then opened Oliver's safe. Which had not been much of a challenge, Kieron pointed out witheringly, since it had not even been an up-to-date computerised one. Then he had gone to keep watch until Old Mary had finished looking at what she wanted to look at. He had closed everything again, and made sure there was no sign to show they had been there. He had simply done what she asked him to do, without further enquiry.

She had apparently told him gruffly that he was better ignorant, safer out of it.

It was afterwards that he had borrowed the maps for her. Maybe to check map co-ordinates she had found on a list in Oliver's safe; the list she had found along with whatever else was in there, and had copied and put back. Yes, that would make sense.

But Oliver as the rat made more sense the more Jane looked at it. In the diary the rat was described as the one who stored things. And then passed them on. Sometimes to one of the other two, sometimes the other. If Jane was remembering it right, that was all the rat did — take things in, store them, pass them on.

Oliver knew Quentin. He had every reason to — since he had a high pedigreed, delicately bred cat.

And, dear God, what could be an easier way of passing over something small and valuable than having it concealed in the bottom of a wicker-sided cat basket? With a highly temperamental animal on top which nobody would wish to disturb?

Oliver, the rat. Quentin, the owl. Yes, it wasn't only that an owl had wings, though that one was a clear enough indication already! Quentin had broad shoulders, a rather round head, big eyes. And a habit Jane had noticed of standing with his shoulders hunched. It was another obvious picture, one you knew what you were looking for.

Two out of three. She still had to find the third one. The most dangerous one of all.

'You're restless,' Adrian's voice said quietly out of the dark beside her. 'I can tell when you're not asleep.'

'Sorry, was I keeping you awake? It's all right. I'm — I'm just having a white night or something. I'll probably settle in a bit.'

'Talk about it?' She felt his hand stroke the back of her neck gently. 'If I promise not to be quarrelsome?'

'I can't.' She heard the bleak sound in her voice. 'I wish I could, truly. But I can't. It's — a rather nasty case I'm on. With complications. And yes, I do know, I'm being hopeless again and bringing work home with me. Look, this is me trying not to.' With that she turned over to lie close against him, her head against his shoulder. 'That's better, now I'm going to sleep.'

'You can talk if you want to. I'm a listening ear that doesn't go any further — if that's not too mixed a metaphor!'

'But I've taken a vow not to wear out your patience,' Jane said with deliberate lightness. And trying not to think bitterly, what could she say? 'Excuse me, but I think your friend and partner is a villain, and I'm going to prove it if I can. And I think he knows who at least two other villains are, so I ought to grill him — if I could think of a reason which would allow me to. They've finished running their scam now, but I'm still going to catch them.'

'Goodnight,' she said, making a yawn out of it, and snuggling her head against him.

'Goodnight. But wake me up if you get restless

again and do want to talk.'

He was being so damned sweet-natured. Why the hell did her two worlds have to collide? It had to be sod's law. She waited until she heard his breathing deepen and become even. Then her mind began to turn again. Turning and turning.

She really ought to go to Chris Hollings now, after Kieron this afternoon. There were enough pieces of the puzzle.

No, godamnit, she couldn't! Quite apart from shopping Kieron, who trusted her . . . now . . . it was still all hearsay. Only that one piece of hard evidence from the Dutch police, and she had no proof that Marianna had copied her list from Oliver Devereux's safe. And, oh hell! Oliver Devereux was an old school chum of the DI's *and* related to him by marriage. She had forgotten that. So she was going to do to him and say, 'I've got no proof but the word of an amateur burglar, but I believe your ex-brother-in-law has been right in the middle of the Met's antiques thefts? And I've got no proof of this either, because he's going to deny it, but the Mr Big of the whole scam confessed to me? And apart from the people I already know about, and about whom I've got no proof, I think there's also a very nasty killer on our patch.'

Oh, great. You'd better take some leave, Detective-Sergeant Perry — unless you'd just like to step into this nice comfortable strait-jacket! Oh, and by the way, in case you haven't heard, there is such a thing as slander.

And also by the way, if you genuinely suspect your lover's partner of being a criminal, why is he still your lover? If it's with the object of finding out more about this Quentin Hurst, why haven't you done that?

To hell with that one. Yes, she could pump Adrian about Quentin's flying habits. Dates and times and where he said he went. She could, but she was damned if she would. It was bad enough already — but he wasn't going to be able to say she had used him.

She did already know one time Quentin had been flying. That weekend. The one when Marianna had risked trying to get eyewitness proof, and had died for it. Quentin had been flying that weekend, and that was why he had not been on call when he should have been.

And if he had flown the jewellery out on the Friday, picked up a return consignment of drugs, but then could not come back to the same airfield because they had left a body there — or because a rave had arrived and the place was crawling with police? — that might explain why he had got stuck somewhere, to Marilyn's annoyance and his partner's inconvenience. Jane had a clear memory of Quentin's unease at having the subject of his flying exploits raised. And his suddenly disconcerted look on hearing exactly where Adrian's cottage was, too, together with the knowledge that Jane had been staying there that weekend.

A few more pieces of proof. Or non-proof.

Now if she could only find hard evidence that Andrew Beck had been in Kent on that Friday . . . If the Dutch police could come up with an arrival time for the stolen valuables they had ound . . . If they could also make a tie-up with a consignment of drugs coming the other way . . .

If, if, if. She would still have nothing. Just a set of unsubstantiated connections.

It would not even be any use to get Kieron to burgle Oliver Devereux's shop again — and she almost desperate enough to consider that — because the scam was over. If Andrew Beck said it was, then it certainly was. He had shown plenty of care not to allow the least risk before, and she knew, bitterly, that he would be taking none now.

★ ★ ★

Going back to work in the morning, Jane knew she ought at least to go and inform John Clay that she had given the Dutch police a speculative tie-up between drugs and stolen jewellery. If it came back to him at second hand, he would not be best pleased to hear she had been offering theories in his field without telling him. She went into the Ladies to shake the raindrops off her mac before hanging it up, and with the idea of checking her sleep-starved pallor to see if it could be improved; but found Ellen Rushman there, wiping what appeared to be tears from her cheeks in sharp angry gestures. She looked too fraught to allow a polite pretence not to have seen the situation. Jane hesitated, the spoke.

'Hi — what's the trouble?'

'Nothing! Nothing at all! I could just do without *some people* taking it out on me,' Ellen said in a burst, swiftly contradicting herself. 'I can't be

expected to know any more than anyone else i
things go on without our being told about it! Car
I? It's not my fault if Customs decide to do thei
own observation and don't inform the local force
And all I said was, maybe they decided to do i
on their own because there was a tip-off last time
I didn't say it was anyone's fault! And of cours
they should have let us in on it if they thought a
consignment was coming in, but I can hardly be
held responsible for the fact that they didn't!'

'Someone flew some drugs in? And Custom
caught them?'

'It wasn't by plane, it was by fishing boat coming
in to Whitstable harbour. Customs had a tip-of
but they didn't share it. They usually do, goodnes
knows, it's only courtesy to include the local force
But this time they didn't, and Tom — of cours
it's not fair, and it's a shame, they ought to have
shared the kudos. Our unit do all the work the
rest of the time, and it's right in the middle o
our patch! But why anyone thinks I should have
known . . . I mean, how could I?'

'Ah. Well. People always blame the neares
person, don't you find?' Jane offered to that appeal
She added drily, 'He's not worth your time, Ellen
No, sorry, I know that sounds interfering, bu
honestly, do you *really* like Tom Cooper's type?'

'He can be very nice. But after seeing his tempe
this morning, you're probably right,' Ellen said with
a flounce.

'Mm. Did you say Customs managed to ge
somebody, in their snatch?'

'Yes, with a whole lot of 'E'. You'd think Tom

320

would be glad about that. At least it won't be circulating! Apparently the boat hung around after coming in and it looked as if they were waiting for someone to take delivery. But nobody showed up, so when it seemed as if the skipper had decided to take off again, they stopped and boarded. And caught the guy red-handed with his consignment. He's not talking, I've heard.' Ellen seemed to have garnered a lot, but then she always managed to be a centre of information. 'Sergeant Clay's furious that our Drugs Unit wasn't included, and you can see his point. After all, it may have been somebody they stopped and questioned who was on the way to take delivery, and got frightened off. I gather he's gone up to the Super to complain. So that they won't be blamed even though they hadn't been informed, I expect!'

'Did you hear where the drugs consignment came from?' Jane asked.

'Holland, I think. It was a Dutch skipper, anyway. Well, I must go. And I hope nobody else loses their temper with me this morning,' Ellen added sniffily. 'I'm only supposed to be the collator, not God!'

A consignment of 'E' coming in by boat? Maybe the plane route had got too dodgy altogether, now the authorities were on the watch for it. And maybe Andrew Beck had been paying off the pilots, too, so that now his particular end of things was over . . . Jane went off thoughtfully to the CID room, to her own work.

This would definitely be a bad moment to go and have an apologetic chat with John Clay. Not when

321

he was stamping about with fury because Customs had decided to play things too close to their chest, and had moved in on his territory without the courtesy of a by-your-leave. And that could even be Jane's fault, because of the last leak.

Sergeant Clay was certainly looking unapproachable when she passed him in the corridor later, not at all his usual amiable self. Jane went on to the canteen in search of a cup of coffee more drinkable than that offered by the machine in the corner of the CID room. She saw Tom Cooper across the room, and watched absently as he walked away from her in his black leather jacket with its decorated back. Typical of him to have turned round and berated Ellen just because she was overfond of him; he was just the type to offer a slap to anyone who had become too easily available, and save his charm for the next one to be chased and eyed up.

Not that he looked in the mood to eye anyone up today, too busy scowling as he went to sit down beside Neil Bettley — and snapping his head off too, from the look of it. Jane looked away before he could glance up and find her eyes on him. Bad temper or not, he might have taken it for an invitation, conceited little sod that he was.

She returned to her own thoughts, frowning, until someone stopped by to ask her cheerfully whether she had heard if Dan Crowe was well enough to come in for a few leaving parties yet. It was known that he had been discharged from hospital at last, though he was still in plaster.

If he had still been the CID guv'nor — well, it

was no use thinking like that. The DCs had started to slip into calling Chris Guv, though Jane had not quite got her tongue round it yet.

She decided she would take her full lunch-hour today — crime permitting — and go and do a half hour work-out in the gym at the sports centre. She had not been there for a while and it was time she put her muscles through their paces again. It might liven up her brain, too. Unfortunately, as she pumped away at the spring-weighted bar in the big room full of gleaming machinery, the place only brought her mind back to Quentin.

Quentin the owl. The man who played squash here. Maybe Jane should come and do some exercising in the evening, which was probably when he played his squash. Then she could meet up with him casually and start a conversation and do some carefully casual probing. She felt a strong distaste for that, but he had to be guilty! And she had to find a way in somehow.

Quentin would know who the scavenger was. If only she could get all three of them, and get them linked to Andrew Beck. She had already found an easy link between Quentin and Oliver Devereux; may be she could find how he connected up with the scavenger too. He might even play squash with him. This place stayed open until ten o'clock at night, and if Jane started making a regular thing out of doing evening exercise sessions . . .

As she packed up, she felt the soreness in her shoulders, and knew she ought to resume exercising regularly for her own sake. Maybe she would come just for that; maybe she should give up the rest of it.

Letting herself get obsessed with one case — and an impossible case at that — was, basically, both stupid and counterproductive. Finding the third of Andrew Beck's minions would probably get her no further than the other two had. No way of nailing any of them. Perhaps she should, in fact, give up.

She called goodbye to Keith, the owner, who was doing some body-building on one of his own machines, with a concentrated effort which made his flat-top haircut stand up in a crest. She knew him quite will, since she had given him amiable advice on security, and what the best locks would be for his doors and windows to satisfy his insurance. Since then, he had made a habit of chatting to her whenever she was in. He was an ex-army fitness instructor which gave them some common ground since Jane had grown up on army bases following her father's postings.

Trailing her way back to the station, she felt the comfortable glow of exercise, which did at least make her feel she had done something constructive. Nothing else was proving constructive, and maybe she really would do better to let everything lie fallow and hope Inspector Kuypers came up with something. She had enough else she ought to be concentrating on, goodness knows.

It was late in the afternoon when something came to her and made her stop dead in the middle of what she was doing.

Since she was in fact conducting an interview, that was awkward, and she had to try to cover the abrupt lapse in her attention. The suspect in front of her was showing no inclination at all to put up his hand to burgling the small factory where he used to work, and she was in the process of winding up, despite a clear suspicion that he was as guilty as hell. If he really had spent the afternoon in bed with a girl whose name he had omitted to ask, Jane was a monkey's uncle. Her sudden halt in the middle of a sentence made Gary Peters, beside her, glance at her queryingly, and she pulled herself together and leaned forward to speak into the tape recorder.

'Interview terminated at . . . five-fifteen. DS Perry and DC Peters present; Mr John Michael Snow had stated that he did not wish to have a solicitor attending.' She switched off the machine and turned to their suspect. 'All right, Mr Snow, you can go. And if you should happen to remember the name of your girlfriend, do let us know, won't you? It might save us having to go through this again. If, of course, you can find her, and if she remembers you!'

She could scarcely wait for him to leave. Or for Gary to take the tape away for transcription and filing. The idea which had come to her — the picture which had appeared in her mind — was beating in her brain.

Surely she had to be wrong!

No, it would fit. And all too well. Go back to square one and think about Old Mary. Who in particular she could have seen. Almost anyone in her daytime plodding round the streets, so you could only guess this was someone she had seen at night. And at times when he did not pretend to be anyone other than he was, either. Which meant that the rest of the time, he had a more acceptable appearance . . . Then consider this: it was someone who had been there ever since the beginning. Think of someone who had always been able to keep one jump ahead of her, because he was so well informed — oh yes, very! An expert in keeping his ear to the ground. And quick-thinking enough to be able to turn a situation to his advantage. He could even put in a drip of disinformation if he had to . . . But someone who was central, and had been using Quentin Hurst, and Oliver Devereux, and even Andrew Beck, while still keeping control of the situation. Playing his own game as an equal partner.

Not as a minion but a major operator, joining up with the others because they had come usefully to his hand.

And very profitably, too — if you cared little where your profits came from. But he had been clever enough to keep his profits hidden as well, so as not to look too flush or too flash.

She knew who the scavenger had to be.

Because Marianna had described him. And the description had dawned on Jane out of the middle of nowhere. She should have seen it. She simply had not made the link.

Or had not wanted to.

She found she was ice-cold. And very, very angry.

Yes, she knew who the scavenger had to be, because there was only one person who fitted the description.

Now she was going to have to prove it.

# 21

Jane had only one choice. To set a trap.

And she would have to do it on her own. There was no one she could go to, she thought grimly. Not on the grounds of suspicion, however certain she felt inside herself. She was still exactly where she had been before. Oh, the clever, clever bastard, with his innocent front for his operations — and his vicious stalking of the people of the night when they got in his way. He had had it so easy. Now she had seen it, she could, bitterly, understand that.

She could still be wrong . . .

If she was, a trap would tell her. Because somebody else would fall into it. She could even hope to be wrong, with a bitter distaste for the conclusion she had reached. But if she was right, if she put out a certain message, the scavenger would come in answer to it. He would not trust anyone else to deal with it. He might think she was easy meat, but he would need to be sure.

Her mind worked steadily but swiftly over the possibilities. The place had already occurred to her. It would be ideal, in more ways than one, and might offer an extra worry to her quarry, too. But she had to see if she had the means . . . She went in search of Kieron. That meant by passing a hostile Rocky to get to him — a more thoroughly hostile Rocky than last time, and even Mel was no more than stiffly polite to her now — but Kieron came out to talk to her. And he accepted her proposition at once.

'Oh yes, easy,' he said, 'I'd only have to — '

'You don't need to tell me how, only that you can do it. You're sure? Good. I'm going out on a limb enough asking you, you do understand that? Let alone taking you with me. But I need you, and I also need you to act as my whistle-blower. You're the only person I can ask!'

'You're lucky I've got the skills I have, then, aren't you?' he said with a touch of smugness which made her deliver a sharp warning.

'You're going to have to do as you're told. Once I'm in and ready, *all* you're going to do is the following. You'll go outside, keep hidden, watch whoever goes in through the door we've left unlocked, wait not more than five minutes, then go and dial 999. Report that you've just seen an intruder breaking into the sports club. Say he's still in there, give them the address, and then get the hell out! Go as far away as possible. Go home!'

'Are you sure you don't want me to — '

'No, I don't. I'm taking enough risk using a civilian as it is, don't you understand? But this happens to be something I've got to do on my own — because it's the only way I'm going to be able to prove who killed Old Mary. I don't want to involve you, I'm only doing so because I have to!'

It had taken a lot of thought to come up with the details of her plan. The sports club. It was an ideal position for what she wanted because it had been made out of an old factory building at the end of a cul-de-sac, and no one would be around there at night. That made it a good place for a meet. The telephone box she had told Kieron to use was down on the road, but he should be able to slip down there easily and quickly through the shadows. After seeing who came to let themselves in through the small side staff door which was the one Jane planned to use. There was an easy place of concealment near it, behind some bushes . . . She hoped she had covered everything.

She had better have covered everything, she thought grimly.

The sooner, the better. Apart from anything else, there was always the danger that her body language would be out of true, however hard she tried not to let it be, and would give her knowledge away. She made her other arrangements, which included checking that Oliver Devereux was there opening and closing his shop as usual. The message she was going to send had to go through Oliver, and only him. That way, she would know for sure that the person who came had got his information on where she would be, and when, from a co-conspirator.

She was counting on the fact that Oliver would panic. But she calculated that he would not come himself.

She wrote him a note, praying that it looked a lot less clumsy and deliberate than it did to her own eyes.

I'm sorry I haven't seen you since the evening we had dinner. It was rather shattering, wasn't it?

But I thought you might like to know, I think I'm going to solve the case we talked about! I've got a meet with an informant tonight at 2 am at the sports club in St Stephens — some mystery man who won't talk to me openly, but claims he can tell me exactly how Marianna Troughton-Beck died, and what the whole thing has been about. Please don't pass that on because it's highly confidential and he'll only talk to me and no one else. I'm only telling you because you were so helpful and took such an interest, so I know you'll wish me luck! We did have a nice time at Henry's for the rest of the evening, didn't we? I'm still glad to have been there, and with you!
Love Jane.

It sounded horribly gushing and girlish, and she would never, *never* in her right mind pass on that kind of information to an outsider. She could only hope that Oliver would fail to guess that. Would assume, rather, that she had fallen for his charm and was hoping to impress him; hoping too for another invitation. It was the best she could do. She had managed to make her handwriting look as if she had dashed the letter off in a fit of excitement, anyway.

If it didn't work . . .

She was still wondering whether it would as she gave Kieron his final instructions hours later.

She spoke in a whisper which seemed necessary in the empty darkened building, but was not, since at the moment they were locked in and could be sure of being alone. They were in the gym, starlight

iltering in through its upstairs windows and making
he exercise equipment gleam eerily, looking like
large alien insects frozen into stillness.

'You go down in a minute and let yourself out.
You leave the door on the latch and hide where
we agreed. I'm betting that whoever comes will try
he main door first and then come round to the
side to find that one unlocked. Keep thoroughly
out of sight until well after he's come in, Kieron.
I'm relying on you, all right?'

At least there was no moon, and the cul-de-sac
was shadowy. And they had been here well in
advance. A long time in advance, in fact.

'Yes, I do know what I'm supposed to do. You're
pretty sure someone will come, aren't you?'

She gave him no answer to that. She had already
told him that if nobody showed up he was to wait,
still concealed, until she came down and fetched
him. If it was a wasted night . . . If it was, she
had probably blown it. Her note to Oliver had been
too specific. Then, she thought grimly, she would
really have to watch her back — in case someone
believed she knew too much. She banished that
thought and looked at Kieron, skinny beside her
in the dimness.

'As soon as you're out I'm going to draw the
blinds and put a light on in here. With my car
outside, the — person — will know I'm here, and
the light will show him where. For Christ's sake, I
wish you'd got a coat. You'll be standing out there
with your teeth chattering if you're not careful, and
that's not going to keep you hidden!'

'I'll bite my tongue. And these were the darkest

clothes I had,' he answered her in injured tones. He had been showing troubling signs of looking on this as a game. She would just have to pray he was going to be sensible.

If this worked, it was no game.

If it worked. Once she had sent him downstairs she had nothing to do, after she had drawn the blinds and switched on a light, but think about that. She knew the risk she was taking. Anything might go wrong. She had had no business to involve civilians. She was so far out on a limb now, doing it on her own like this, that she was asking for trouble. Yet it seemed the only way: to set a trap, and see who fell into it.

If she was right . . .

If she was right, one person would come.

A dangerous person with a lot to lose. One who had shown an innocent face to the world, and would intend to go on doing so; not letting anyone — even her — stand in his way.

She leaned against the wall in the corner she had chosen. The big room looked bleak with just one of its strip-lights shining. At the far end there were doors through to an aerobics studio, but no separate way in from that end. Anyone who was coming would have to arrive through the door on her left. The rows of gleaming machines cast striped shadows across the polished wooden floor. It was very quiet. Kieron must be outside now, behind his bush — well behind it, she prayed, and thoroughly invisible. Jane glanced up at the silent speaker just above her head, trying not to imagine she could hear a crackle from it. Was she wasting her time?

Was all this going to be for nothing?

No muzak to fill the air anyway, she thought drily.

She had not needed to make an excuse not to see Adrian tonight. He had left her a note to say he was on call-out to one of the farms, and didn't expect to be back until very late.

It might be Oliver after all who came. Part of her almost hoped it would be, and that he was a far better actor than she had credited. Not at all afraid of violence, deeply corrupt inside to counter the elegance outside. In that case her message had gone straight to the mark without needing to be passed on.

But no, she still thought Oliver was the golden rat. And he would not come, but would leave that to someone else: he would be too fastidious, too unwilling to know what really went on. And he would be equally unwilling to be seen. He would leave this to the scavenger.

Jane hunched her shoulders inside the padded anorak she was wearing, glad that there was at least a minimal warmth in this room — the heating in here was left on low all night, Keith had told her, because of the hydraulics in some of the machines. It was chillier than was comfortable to stand still in, even so, on a winter's night. She kept her hands in her pockets, fingering what lay in one of them. In spite of all her training and all her experience, it was nerve-stretching standing here waiting.

For a man she knew to be violent, and dangerous, and sharply clever.

To come face to face with him, and have her proof.

She heard a faint sound from downstairs, something which was almost a scuffle. She stiffened and it came again. Followed by very light footsteps on the stairs. Early ... But then she had calculated he would be, if he thought she was going to meet an informant.

As someone appeared in the open doorway, she turned her head and met an amused, mocking glance.

'Hallo, love. I heard you were on a meet, and since I was out and about, I looked in to see if you needed some help.'

Tom Cooper came stepping across the room towards her, his usual dapper, muscular self in jeans and leather jacket. Jane watched him without shifting her position. Oh, yes, she had been right. Her voice came out as sharp as a whiplash.

'That really won't wash, DC Cooper. The only person who knows I'm here is almost as dirty as you are. Christ, if there's one thing I hate it's a bent copper! How long have you been dealing drugs instead of catching dealers?'

'I don't know what you mean, love.' He came right up to her. Then before Jane had caught more than a blur of movement he had her arms in a vice-like grip, twisting her round to do a rapid body-search. What he pulled out of her pocket made him grin, both scornfully and wolfishly, and he pressed the stop button on the small tape recorder.

'Yeah, I'd have heard about it if you were wired,

wouldn't I? But you thought you were going to catch me with this? So it's a set-up all on your own, isn't it? Well, well, what a clever little sergeant. But not quite clever enough!'

'What about any evidence I may have left in a safe place? You can't think I'd . . . '

'You haven't got any, or you wouldn't have needed to do this. You know too much but you can't prove it, eh? Rash, girlie, far too rash — you can hardly think I'm going to leave you to prove it!'

He was still standing close to her, though he had let her go — but he was a lot stronger than she was, and just as highly trained. He was probably faster than she was, too.

'You're going to kill me like you killed the others?' Jane challenged. 'To cover your back again? Surely that will be one too many? And you can't break *my* neck without questions being asked, or tip me in the river like you did poor old Jacko!'

'Sussed them all, did you? Even the old man? You really have been a bit too busy, haven't you? You keep on poking your nose into things which don't concern you! And refuse to let well alone when you're given every chance to.' There was an ugly look in his eyes though he was still smiling. But there was satisfaction too . . . and his smile widened.

'You're relying on your amateur back-up? Tough luck, darlin'.' He stepped suddenly and swiftly towards the doorway through which he had entered, and called, 'Neil, bring him up!'

335

Jane felt cold run down her spine. Neil Bettley too? That she had not known. Or guessed. And she was horribly aware of how wrong things had gone even before Tom Cooper turned back to her with that wolfish grin of his.

'We caught him coming out. I didn't think he could be your meet, but if it had happened very early . . . Luckily we were early too, just in case it was the fly-boy who needed to be stopped from coming to spill his guts to you. And trying to get himself a deal in exchange for information, now that he's getting queasy in case he's asked to go on taking risks. But it wasn't, was it? It was just you and that hippy boy from the farm to go and phone for a patrol, so you could hand your tape over and have me bang to rights. Not a good choice, the boy, though I suppose I'll have to deal with him as well, now!'

Kieron, looking pale and with a gag in his mouth, was being propelled into the room by Neil Bettley. DC Bettley seemed deeply uncomfortable, Jane saw with sudden hope, and was doing everything he could to avoid looking at her. She might be able to use that . . . Kieron had his hands tied behind him as well as the gag and as he was pushed towards her she saw that he was trying to shake his head desperately. No, of course he would not have reached the telephone — if Tom Cooper had jumped him on the way out. She spoke very quickly.

'He doesn't know anything, I just used him to pick the lock and get me in. Let him go, he won't talk! Particularly not if you pay him off.' She saw

336

Kieron give her an outraged look, and cursed his stupidity. 'And there's another thing, Tom. Why do you think I did all this on my own? Because I want in, that's why. Now I know about your tidy little scam, I want my cut. Savvy? Give me that, and you won't get a murmur of trouble out of me. I can even give you the odd tip-off, too, if any of our snouts say anything which might lead to you!'

'Whose leg do you think you're pulling?' Tom Cooper asked her pityingly.

'No one's. Promise me my cut, and I'll — '

'No, I'm afraid you've had it, girl. You gave yourself away earlier, didn't you? Besides, if you weren't straight, you wouldn't have been giving us so much trouble.' She saw the inflexible look in his eyes, and knew there was no hope of catching him with that one. She rushed into speech again rapidly, all the same.

'If I sussed as much as I did, don't you think someone else will? You can't get away with killing off the opposition indefinitely. I suppose it was Andrew Beck who told you to kill Old Mary, after she'd recognised him? But I bet you never told him that the reason she was there was because *you* were her lead!'

She saw his swift frown, and that the sting in her voice as well as the words had got him. 'Stop giving me bull!'

'I'm not, I'm just pointing out your mistake. Oh, yes, you do make mistakes, Tom Cooper. Old Mary got on to you because you killed Sofia. And Sofia had shown her that piece of jewellery she took out of your pocket, and Mary had recognised it! Making off with someone else's profits as well as your own, were you?'

'You can mind your own bloody business!' For a moment she thought his balled fist was going to lash out at her. Instead, he got himself in hand, though his eyes were ugly. 'No, no bruises for you. We'll set this one up more carefully than that. So it was Sofia who set the old bint off, was it? Not that it matters, since she took the needle without a murmur, silly little cow, and nobody asked any questions! As for the old woman . . . ' He made a scornful gesture with his hand, a grinning demonstration of a chop. 'She'd had it from the minute we caught her. I'd hardly let her wander around after that, would I?'

'But it was you she was following. She'd really got you sussed. And if you're thinking that Andrew Beck doesn't know that, I rather think he does. He'll have read the diary before he destroyed it in front of me. Maybe that's even why he pulled out. Because he knows now that you're a bit more careless than you think you are. And I should watch out, because you might find that one a dangerous enemy!'

She had hoped to taunt him into an answer, but he gave her none, just a narrow-eyed look, calculating. And then turned to his partner who had simply been standing there with an increasingly uncomfortable air. Nervous too. Neil Bettley liked this not at all.

'Neil, tie her hands and both of their feet, and watch them. No, she's only bluffing about Beck. He's too deep in with what we know about his own little game! But I think we'll get someone else involved in our latest bit of disposal, just to make sure that one remembers to keep his own mouth shut. Get her tied, and watch them while I make a quick phone call.'

'To Oliver Devereux?' Jane asked quickly. 'I shouldn't bother, you can't think he'll come!'

'Ollie? No, he's already packing up to leave.' The words were scornful. Tom Cooper was making for the door with his light tread. 'You threw him into a loop and he was babbling that it was the last straw. Don't let them try anything, Neil. I'll be back in a minute!'

Jane saw Kieron look at her in mute panic, but he could only pray. And calculate. They were left with Neil Bettley, but though he might dislike what he was doing, he was clearly enough under his partner's thumb not to be an easy mark if she tried to fight him off physically. There would still be Tom Cooper to contend with anyway, and she doubted if he would be away long enough for her to untie Kieron. The second Drugs Unit DC had already tied Kieron's ankles and was coming towards her with nervous care. She held out her hands in front of her to show that she was going to offer him her wrists with no resistance, but spoke to him quick and low, putting all her persuasion into her voice.

'You don't have to do as he says, Neil. Do you realise what you're getting into? Murder of a fellow officer, on top of corruption? You know nobody will let that rest! Because that's what he's leading you into now, isn't it? And I'll lay a bet that it's only

Tom who's had a hand in any killing before. You're not the type. And not the type to go bent, either. How the hell did you let him drag you into this? Get yourself out of it now, before it's too late!'

'I can't.' It was the first time he had spoken and that was husky. 'I'm too far in, Sarge.'

That he gave her rank was a cause for hope, so was the agonised look on his face. 'Help us now and I'll speak up for you. It's not too late. You know how these things work! You'd be out of the service, of course, but they'll give you a deal which will keep you out of jail. Come on, Neil, cut free, and give yourself a chance! He's a bad one through and through, but you're not. He's just pulled you — '

'It's not going to work,' Tom Cooper's voice said from the door. He was back sooner than Jane had expected. She looked round at him sharply, but he was speaking again, smoothly, coming in on the conversation whose end he must have overheard. And he had a mobile phone in his hand, she saw, and was folding it away as if he had just used it. He had not used the club phone for his call then, but must have fetched one of his own out of his car. He must have decided to be careful to make sure there would be no sign of him here. 'Neil needs the money to give to his dear old mum, don't you?' he went on. 'And wouldn't want dear old mum going to jail along with him for receiving the profits, either. Would you, sunshine?' There was a world of gentle menace behind the apparently cheerful words. 'No, you're not going to budge him, so you might as well give up trying

Besides, he's my partner — and we look out for each other.'

Menace in that, too, however softly delivered. Jane saw how it hit home with the other constable as he bent to bind her ankles. And there was something in the way he moved which struck a chord in her memory, and made her look across at Tom Cooper as he came watchfully back to join them.

'It was you two who were the hold-up men in the restaurant car park, wasn't it? Yes, you're the right size and shape! I should have guessed. Another favour for Andrew Beck? And using a handy copy of an MO out of the files!'

'Handy enough. Want to know about the burglary at your house, too? Now that was another case where records have their uses!' There was a look of knowing satisfaction in Tom Cooper's eyes which made Jane think of his hands pawing through her clothing. Sure enough, he brought the subject up. 'That's some fancy black lace underwear you've got, love . . . I've enjoyed imagining that underneath your prim suits!'

'You're a shit!'

The words came from Kieron. He must have been working away to get his gag free. 'A shit and a piece of pigswill!' he pronounced with angry and staunch defiance, ignoring the urgent look of warning Jane was trying to give him with her eyes. 'And you won't get away with it, you don't have a hope of — '

'Shut up, Kieron, he's not worth your time. How *do* you think you're going to get away with it?' Jane

341

asked Tom Cooper quickly, making it a scornful question to keep his attention on her. 'Both of us with rope-marks? Signs that he's had a gag in his mouth as well? You're hardly going to make that look like an accident, are you? Even with Old Mary you made a bad mistake in breaking her neck, and thinking the fire was enough to hide it. Pathology's a lot more sophisticated than you give it credit for.'

She had deflected him from Kieron, and, it appeared, had silenced her accomplice as well — since she saw him swallow hard and close his eyes. Trying not to think she meant Tom Cooper was planning to put them to death by fire, she guessed . . . If he had thought of firing this building with them in it, he wouldn't know how thoroughly Keith had gone into fire-proofing for safety. She did. Before she could acknowledge that there would probably be enough smoke to do a final job on human lungs anyway, she returned to the attack. She might as well get one more thing about the Old Mary case out of Tom Cooper — even if it looked as if she was going to get no personal use out of it.

'Did you start the hangar fire? I'm assuming you did. But just for my interest, when?'

'Can't stop being curious? Still playing the clever detective? All right, then, since we've got a wait. We were on our way over there to get the body and dump it in a ditch when we heard the call come in about the rave. That made things a bit urgent, you might say. But we were nearest so we were well first at the scene. All it took was a fast nip round the back to set the fire. It looked like a nice little arson by the time I'd finished. All I had to do was throw a lighted candle in through the door, and whoosh! And everyone much too busy raving to see anything. Passed muster nicely, too!'

His careless satisfaction was hard to stand, and his vanity — when he had fired a building with hundreds of people in it. But keep him talking, pray his smugly confessional mood would last. And that it was giving Neil Bettley doubts. That seemed to be the only hope they had. She was opening her mouth to tell Tom Cooper pointedly that the cause of the fire had not passed muster, since she personally had spotted the whole thing was dodgy so there was a good chance somebody else would eventually. However, he must have caught her intention to influence his partner because he turned his head and issued a swift command.

'Time you went downstairs, Neil, to watch for our next arrival. I told him to make it quick, so he should be here soon. When he comes, let him in and send him up here, but stay down there on watch, okay? Though we're nicely enough tucked away down this alley not to get any casual snoopers at this time of night!'

The last was delivered with a wolfishly satisfied look at Jane as his partner obeyed him silently. Once Neil Battley had gone, Tom Cooper squatted down in front of Jane where she had been pushed to sit against the wall. Ignoring Kieron, who was still sitting with his eyes shut as if trying to absent himself in spirit, he spoke directly into her face with clear enjoyment.

'Well, the place was your choice, darlin', wasn't it? And you want to know what I'm planning for you, to explain the rope marks? It's a nice one, and came to me while I was thinking about your fancy undies. A nice little sado-masochistic orgy with your hippy boyfriend. Him still tied up, you with signs that you've been playing the game too, both of you half naked and with welt-marks, and a black leather whip lying about. Luckily I happen to have one in my car. Picked it up the other day during a raid and forgot to hand it in . . . Oh, and there'll be lots of drugs scattered around you, too. Unfortunately, you'll both have overdosed on some smack. Careless, or you were just too high to realise. I think that'll answer, don't you?' He glanced round. 'We might do it here, with the machines to add something extra to your play . . . or we might take you home and set it up there. It's a possible one. I know how quiet your street is at night. I'm still thinking about that. No comment?'

'You scarcely need one,' she said clearly and icily.

'It'll make a nice headline when it's leaked to the press, won't it? 'Woman police officer dies in sex-play with hippy lover.' Yes, I think we will do it here — more public, no chance of a hush-up! And I wonder if we can get the bearded wonder to perform? By the time he's had the uppers I'm going to thrust down both your throats — before we get to the final dose of smack, that is — he just might. It'd be a pity not to add that, to make it 'as well as' rather than 'instead of'.' He thrust his

344

face closer to Jane's, watching her eyes. 'It's a pity about DNA testing, or I'd have you myself. You may not have much in the way of tits, but you're still quite a fancy bird. And it'd be amusing to see what's behind the snooty looks. Still, I'll just have to be satisfied with egging the lad on, won't I?'

She might have spat in his face if ignoring him had not been better. And if there had not been the rapid sound of footsteps on the stairs, to make him rise to his feet and turn away from her. She couldn't see who arrived, with Tom Cooper in the way, only a pair of legs — but she heard Quentin Hurst's blustering voice.

'I've brought you what you asked for, but I've got to make it clear, I'm not going on with any of this. I did what I was paid to do, but now that part's over you'll have to make other arrangements. From now on I don't want any part — '

He broke off with an audible gasp as Tom Cooper moved and left him with a clear sight of Jane.

For a moment, with a leap of her heart, she thought it was going to be worth calling out to him with an urgent heartfelt appeal. The aghast expression on his face as he looked from her to Kieron, taking in their bonds, suggested she might have found a defender.

Then his eyes slid away from her, and she saw only his profile as he cleared his throat and addressed Tom Cooper stiffly.

'Here you are, this is what you wanted. And I don't want to know what it's for. I'll — simply leave you to get on with whatever you're doing.'

# 22

What happened next left Jane dazed. There had been no time. Even if her words had got through to Neil, there had not been enough time for him to bring in help! But the room was suddenly invaded by several very efficient-looking figures, none of whom she recognised, but all of whom had that air which could be nothing but plain-clothes and on official business. One of them was even wearing a side-arm.

None of whom she recognised aside from one. Chris Hollings.

She heard Tom Cooper trying the beginning of some rapidly invented lie, but it was cut short by a barked order and the click of handcuffs being applied. Quentin Hurst had simply collapsed to his knees and was offering no one any resistance at all as the packet he had been holding was taken away from him, inspected, then handcuffs were put on him as well. She saw all that before Chris Hollings, grim-faced, arrived to stand over her.

His first words, delivered with a bite, were a long way from sympathetic. In fact, they would have chilled a polar bear.

'What the hell do you think you've been doing, Sergeant Perry?'

'Catching a very bent copper, sir. How did you — '

346

'DC Cooper has been under covert observation
for several days. And you could have wrecked the
entire operation!'

At least he had reached down to untie her. Before
Jane could speak again, he cast a look at Kieron and
added icily, 'Who is this?'

'My sound engineer, sir. And you won't have any
difficulty knowing what's been going on. Everything
that's been said in this room tonight should be on
tape. There are microphones in those two speakers,
and the PA system's been reversed to feed into a
recording machine hidden on a shelf below the
telephone in the club office.' Jane gave it to him
with a cool efficiency to match his own — though
not without a prayer of thankfulness that Tom
Cooper had not chosen to make his telephone call
from the unlocked office. He might so easily have
heard the soft whir of the machine, and looked
for the source of the sound. She was aware that
she had to spoil things by adding with a sudden
doubt, 'If it's worked . . . '

'Of course it worked,' Kieron said with outrage.
He seemed to have revived remarkably quickly, and
sounded much like his normal self. 'I told you it
would!'

'And you did all this without a — ' The look
she was getting from her DI was no less grim than
before, as he bit off the rest of his sentence. In fact
if anything he looked even more icily furious. 'You
set up an unofficial wire, on private premises, to
follow up some crack-brained scheme of your own,
without coming to me, or anyone else?'

'Yes sir, I did. I thought it was the only way to

get proof. I did have permission from the owner to use the premises, although I have to admit he thought it was official. And he didn't know what we were doing to his PA system.' She had known she could trust Keith to be both helpful and completely discreet, and it had seemed better to get a key from him than to let Kieron actually pick the locks. She was caught by a brief shiver as she realised that, if Tom Cooper had succeeded in what he planned to do, Keith would definitely have thought what she had wanted his premises for was unofficial when he arrived in the morning . . . She quelled that memory, but knew it was the light-headedness of relief which made her look up at DI Hollings with a lift of her eyebrows and offer him a cool question. 'Hadn't we better go and see if we're still being recorded?'

'You'll have to take me too. I'm the only one who knows how it's rigged up, and your lot will probably make a mess of it or something. Besides, I do think somebody might untie me!'

The injured note in Kieron's voice made Jane move swiftly to him. DI Hollings had turned to do the same. Kieron was looking downright smug as they untied his hands and feet. Jane had the suspicion that he had gone back to thinking of the whole thing as a game, and had already banished any realisation that there had so nearly been lethally disastrous consequences. For which she was responsible. She had had no business to be that careless, and let Kieron get caught . . . She left that for later (and that was one more thing DI Hollings would scathe her for in due time, she was quite sure) and turned round as someone else approached.

There were only three of the plainclothes officers besides Chris Hollings, though her first dazed impression had been of half a dozen. Two of them were waiting with Tom Cooper and Quentin Hurst, in grimly deadpan attendance on the two prisoners. The third had come over to this side of the room, and was looking at DI Hollings with a query in his eyes.

'We'll take these two out to join the other one — your station? Do you want us to radio for someone to search here?'

'There isn't anything else here,' Jane said quickly. 'I fixed up the meet to see if he'd come. I wasn't expecting his partner as well, I didn't think he was in it.' They had obviously got Neil . . . voluntarily? Seeing the watchers and letting them in? She hoped so. She saw the curious look the unknown plainclothes officer gave her, but something else needed to be said and she turned to Chris Hollings quickly. She said steadily, 'There is someone else involved whom you may not know about . . . DC Cooper said he's about to skip the country so you'd better send someone to pick him up. Oliver Devereux.'

The shocked flicker in Chris Hollings' eyes told her he had not known. Only about Tom Cooper, perhaps, under covert observation because they had not yet been sure . . . They would be now. He took her word without a murmur, however, and issued a quick request for his colleagues to radio out from the car and ask for Oliver Devereux to be brought in. At once.

When they had heard Tom Cooper's comment on the tape, they would have something to hold him on. The passing on of Jane's message was proof of his involvement, too. It was likely that Quentin would talk as well. He looked a broken man.

Poor Marianna, who felt the type of people the police dealt with 'couldn't be very nice'.

Quentin was being taken out. Jane looked across at Tom Cooper, who had his back to her, waiting to be hustled out of the door in his turn. There would be her word, Kieron's to back her up, and — she hoped and prayed — everything she had deliberately asked and taunted and drawn out of Tom Cooper, clearly recorded from the microphones Kieron had placed.

The now far less menacing figure, held as it was in firm custody, disappeared from her view. And with it the emblazoning on the back of his leather jacket. An animal's face, sharp-toothed and snarling, probably meant to represent a wolf — but far more like one of nature's scavengers, a hyena or a jackal.

Jane had seen it any number of times. But it was only when you got inside Marianna's mind that you could understand the literalness of her chosen descriptions.

With the prisoners gone, it was time to show Chris Hollings Kieron's handiwork. The tape was still whirring away in its place. A rapid playback from somewhere near the end of it gave the DI's voice saying very clearly, 'You set up an unofficial wire, on private premises, to follow up some crack-brained scheme of your own . . . ?'

Relief made it possible to bear with equanimity the further grim look DI Hollings gave her. No approval, oh no, she had gone out on a limb and chopped herself off, however effective the result. The tape machine was carefully detached to be borne away. Kieron's offer to set about rewiring everything into its proper place met with a blank refusal.

'That will have to be done later. Along with an official apology. You — What's your name?'

'Kieron Stafford. If you don't need me, then, I'll go home.'

'You'll come with me. We need a full statement from you. Sergeant Perry, I presume I can trust you to follow in your own car?'

'Yes, sir,' Jane said meekly.

Beneath the meekness, she was deeply inclined to wish rot on his icebound soul. She had got him more on Tom Cooper than he could ever have achieved any other way. And given him the jewellery scam as well, including Andrew Beck. But he had no means of knowing that yet.

And he would not be aware either, until he played the tape back, how near she and Kieron had come to a nasty death.

His icily grim demeanour was understandable anyway. She had walked all over a secret operation of which he was part, probably because he was too new to have any possible connection with Tom Cooper. And she had demonstrated besides a lack of both trust and proper behaviour in not going to him. He would not like the way that reflected on his department.

And, above all, nobody in the force liked to find out there was a rotten apple in the barrel. To have a face the fact of a bent copper.

★ ★ ★

Nobody told her how Tom Cooper had come under suspicion enough to be covertly observed, though since at least one of the people who were around the station for the rest of the night was a Customs Investigating Officer, she made a guess that the Dutch skipper caught in Whitstable harbour might have talked. Or DC Cooper had been seen in the wrong place at the wrong time — maybe too near where that delivery was to be made, only warned off by instinct at the last minute — and somebody had added things up enough to feel a doubt.

It almost certainly was Tom Cooper who had given the warning about the earlier airfield stake-out. Right in the middle of things as he was, nothing could have been easier. That gave Jane a sense of relief, since she had no need to imagine it was her own careless words which had caused the leak.

No, Adrian had not passed on anything innocently to Quentin.

Maybe it was even that first leak which had added enough suspicion to cause the covert watch on DC Cooper. And this time, he had not had his ear to the ground as much as he thought. Had had no idea that a net was beginning to close round him. He had thought the only person to deal with was Jane.

And had supposed — as she hoped he might — that the choice of the sports club by someone as a venue meant the danger came from Quentin, who knew the place as a member.

He was sharp but not really intelligent, Tom Cooper. Conceit made him undervalue the opposition. That was how she had caught him with the distraction of the hand-held tape recorder in her pocket. Andrew Beck would never have been taken in by that one: although he, too, was a conceited man, he would have looked for a trick.

DCI Carter in Chelsea would be pleased with her for giving him the chance to pull Andrew Beck back in. A tape which showed his involvement in crime by hearsay would not be evidence, but the Chelsea DCI would now have another approach to follow. Yes, Andrew Beck was likely to get his comeuppance.

If DCI Carter would be pleased with her, DI Hollings still plainly was not. After a long night of going through and through everything — before a variety of audiences — Jane was instructed coldly by the DI to go home, and come back at four o'clock in the afternoon, when he would talk to her again. She was to communicate with no one in the meantime and report directly to him when she arrived. That figured as normal procedure anyway, Jane knew, as she took herself home to crawl into bed and sleep. In a corruption case, any officer involved, either as a suspected contact or as someone concerned in the fingering of a corrupt member of the police, went immediately into limbo.

As she drove wearily home, and made the turn into her own street, she passed the veterinary practice and saw a police presence outside, and uniformed officers going in and out with a serious air. A premises search would be called for: Quentin had been bringing in drugs . . . She did not see Adrian. It was eight o'clock in the morning and probably soon, if it was a clinic day, people with cats in baskets and dogs on leads would find themselves being turned away.

Jane left the scene behind her, went to let herself into her house, unplugged the telephone, set her clock alarm to wake her at the right time, and went to bed. Sleep was a good way to escape her numb feelings.

When she drove back to the station in the afternoon there was still a police car outside the practice, though no other sign of activity. She parked in her usual place in the police station yard and went to sign in, aware that there was an air of subdued grimness about the place. The duty-sergeant opened his mouth as if to ask her something, then shut it again. As she went to report to DI Hollings, she reminded herself drily that at least she was alive to do all this. And but for the watchers on the covert operation, she might not have been. The tape would still have been there to finger the killer, but that would have been small comfort to her and Kieron personally . . .

The DI was seeing her in a borrowed office upstairs; more private than his glassed-in corner of the CID room, she guessed. He was alone and gave her a level unsmiling look as she presented herself

354

with brisk efficiency, and sat down on his nod.

'I've listened to the whole tape now. I presume you realised that an unofficial recording wouldn't be allowable in court, but decided it could at least be used later to get a confession out of him?'

'Yes, sir.'

'Luckily both the others are giving us everything like singing birds. Neil Bettley, too.'

'DC Bettley didn't seem to me to be in it willingly, sir. For what it's worth, I think he . . . '

'Yes, that's being taken into account. And you're damned lucky he broke!' Hollings said explosively. 'We might not have gone straight in after Hurst arrived if Bettley hadn't come out, seen us, and babbled at us that you were going to be killed! You do realise, Sergeant, how close you came to causing your own death, and a civilian's along with you?'

'Yes, sir.'

'Why the hell didn't you come to see me? If it was because of Oliver Devereux, and the fact I presume you knew that he's related to my wife by marriage, then you should have gone higher! To Superintendent Annerley,' he added unsmilingly, a clear indication that he knew the impossibility of her going to DCI Morland. 'Though I assume — and trust — that it wasn't because you thought the relationship would actually make a difference to my behaviour.'

'No, sir. I just didn't have any proof. Of anything. I nearly did come to you after Andrew Beck's confession, but he hadn't left me with any proof of that either. And I admit I should have reported my conversation with Inspector Kuypers, but I still had no means of proving there was a genuine connection, so I decided to wait.' There was no need to say that it was just as well she had not passed that on to Sergeant Clay. And she so nearly had. That one might have alerted Tom Cooper enough to make him extra careful and render a surveillance on him useless. 'As I said last night, I didn't conclude that DC Cooper must be the other person involved until very late on,' she went on, keeping her voice briskly official, continuing to take care not to let her words sound like special pleading. 'And I decided I couldn't . . .'

'Point the finger at a fellow officer without any evidence to offer? Yes, I'll accept that. On the other hand your superiors are the people you go to if you have the least doubt. And *if* you had behaved in the proper manner, and passed on what you knew — or even thought you knew — you wouldn't have landed in last night's near fiasco!'

No, but she would not have got the case so tightly wrapped up, either. Jane kept her mouth shut. Otherwise she might have been tempted to point out that she had solved a case he had dismissed, given him the jewellery scam, given Chelsea the true answer to Laurence Beck's murder and provided enough material to get Tom Cooper sent down for a very long time. An unofficial tape might not be admissible, but she had broken his ring to pieces, and provided so much which could be followed up that, in the end, one could hope for a complete result. Even without anything else, it was incontrovertible that Tom Cooper had planned to murder her, and there were several witnesses to prove it.

However, she was equally aware that she was in no position not to sit here and take the hard time Chris Hollings was giving her. She had not exactly gone by the book.

'I've been left to deal with this myself because you're my officer, but it's still an open question as to whether I'll recommend an official reprimand. The problems caused by the internal connection will be taken into account, and so will the reasons you gave last night for your behaviour. However, the fact still remains that you went out on your own and involved a civilian in police business — two civilians, if I include Mr March, the owner of the sports club. And nearly got one of them killed at that! Even from a raw rookie that kind of behaviour would be unacceptable, and at your rank, you have no excuse at all.'

'Yes, sir. Can I ask a question?'

'Yes?'

'Kieron Stafford . . . ' She had an undeniable responsibility for him. 'There won't be any charge against him for the break-in at Devereux's shop, will there?'

'He's been given a warning, but in the circumstances it will be let go at that.'

'Thank you, sir.'

'Don't thank me. Thank the fact that he's behaved helpfully, in spite of what you landed him in.'

Kieron had, in fact, become extremely chirpy last night, considering his experiences. And also seemed to decide that for once he could bear helping the police rather than treating them with his usual distrustful scorn.

'There's another point I have to raise,' DI Hollings added, his voice still level, no change of expression visible. 'Hurst's partner. You may wish to know that he was in no way involved with the stock of illicit drugs at the veterinary practice. In fact, he knew nothing at all about it. Hurst has admitted as much — that he was solely responsible for the hidden storage space, and that no one else in the practice had ever known anything about it. There's certainly nothing to show anything to the contrary, and everything indicates that Mr Reston is completely clear of any kind of involvement.'

'I already know he wasn't involved.' Jane found she was sitting up even straighter, keeping her eyes on his face a little more firmly. 'As you're aware, I — '

'Yes, I am aware he's a friend of yours, since you introduced him to me. A close one?'

Jane looked at him levelly, and decided to give him this to think about. 'He's the man I've more or less been living with — sir. But he wasn't aware of my investigations, either. Naturally, I couldn't talk to him about it.'

'No. I imagine that placed you in an awkward situation.' He paused for a second, then asked, 'And is this a relationship you see continuing?'

It was merely an official question. Jane looked at him drily, then answered it.

'I'd say that depends on him. In the circumstances Sir.'

'Yes. I see. Now, Sergeant Perry, your situation at the moment. There'll be a senior investigating officer coming in from another force over the Cooper affair, and you'll be on leave until you're called in for interview. That will happen in a few days' time, I should imagine. You must know the drill, and that there should be no talk with any of your colleagues here in the meantime. I think we've covered everything else. I have to make it clear again that I'm thoroughly displeased with the way you handled this.' He tapped the pencil in his hand on the desk, looking down at it, then raised his eyes to look to her face, regarding her dispassionately. 'I'm going to make another point too, just between us, for your own good. I've had a look at your file, and I can see why you failed to make the short-list for the DI job. You're far too inclined to do things on your own. You may have achieved some lucky results, but you're not going to be considered as promotion material until you've learned to work within the proper guidelines, and delegate more thoroughly, rather than following your own private path!'

And where would that have put the Old Mary file? Delegated into the bin, since nobody else had believed it was a case of murder besides her. And without that, none of the links would have been made; most, at least, of the villains would still have been running around free.

Jane resisted the urge to cast him the sort of look which would remind him of that fact. She got to her feet instead, since he had plainly

359

finished. There was only one answer she wa
allowed to make, so she might as well make
it.

'Yes, sir,' she said.

# Epilogue

She could seek Adrian out and offer an apology
For what it was worth. She had nothing to do fo
the next few days but sit at home, after all.

She could go to him and watch him receive he
with awkwardness, and probably dislike. Or wait
and see if there was silence to speak for him.

There was nothing but silence that evening
which Jane spent listening to music and trying to
read a novel, until she went to bed. She reminded
herself — when her thoughts refused to be battened
down, so that she needed reminding — that she had
chosen a police career. Detection was what she was
paid to do.

Whatever else.

She could at least let him know she was sorry fo
what must now be happening to him. But maybe
she had walked all over his life enough?

In the end the decision was taken from her. She
went out in the middle of the following morning
into a grey but dry and blowy winter day, to get
a newspaper. The Christmassy decorations which
were beginning to show in the shops were totally
at odds with her mood, making her feel sour as

she turned back for home, her eyes determinedly on the paper in her hand. It was only when she reached the corner of the street and nearly bumped into someone that she looked up. And found it was Adrian.

She had known they would inevitably run into each other sometime: the neighbourhood was too small for it not to happen. He had obviously been as deep in absent thought as she was, and moving in a hurry. When they found themselves face to face, he stopped dead.

'Hi . . .'

There was a questioning look in his eyes, and he seemed to be waiting, after that one word, to see what she would say.

Jane drew a breath.

'I'm sorry.'

'You were only doing your job, Guv.' He made the attempt at a joke with a shrug and no apparent sarcasm. There was a hesitation, then he asked carefully, 'That was the 'nasty case' you were working on? How long did you know, for certain?'

'Not very long at all. I certainly didn't know anything when we went to dinner there. I really am sorry, you know. You do realise I couldn't have told you?'

'No, of course you couldn't.' He hesitated again, his face grave but his eyes still questioning. Then he asked, 'So what happens now?'

'You tell me to go to hell?' She made that as light as possible, and went on quickly before he could answer. 'It was just one of those situations

nobody could help. I got landed in it . . . What's
going to happen to the practice?'

'I'm going to work all the hours God sends to
keep it going. I spent most of last night and some
of this morning ringing round urgently to find a
locum. I think I've got one, too, though he can't
start for a week. Luckily he could be someone
who might want to come in permanently as junior
partner. Quentin's hardly going to demand to be
bought out,' he added, very grimly, 'and he's in
no position to, either. Considering we've got a
partnership clause about dismissal for bringing the
practice into disrepute!'

'Oh, good. I was afraid you'd . . . Anyway, I'm
glad you're going to be able to keep it going. And
I'm sorry that you must have been faced with a lot
of — with police all over the place — '

'They've stopped taking everything to pieces now,
so I've been able to open up again. In fact, I've
got an appointment with an Irish wolfhound in a
minute.' He glanced briefly at his watch.

Jane had not missed that he had said he was
going to be very busy. And was now, so that he
only had a moment for their chance meeting. It
was an easy and polite excuse. She tried for a
pleasant smile, an equally polite acknowledgement
that he had made his choice and she could perfectly
understand it. But then found he was speaking
again, watching her face.

'You said, I might tell you to go to hell? Not
the other way round?'

'No. Look, if you've got to go, I understand.'

'Stay,' he said firmly — and just as if she had

362

been one of his animals. 'No? You said no?'

'I've got no reason to tell you to go to hell, have
? None of it's your fault. I just had a lousy job
o do, that's all. By the way, one of our lot was
nvolved too. If it helps. That's why I'm not at
vork. I have to — to keep out of things for a
:ouple of days, until I've gone through everything
vith the powers that be, in due process. It wasn't
ust Quentin.'

'Bugger Quentin,' Adrian said clearly, and
orcefully. 'He deserves anything he gets! And
ie certainly isn't going to snarl up both sides
>f my life. Look, darling, I really do have to go
ind see to this dog. You say you're not at work,
rou're going to be at home? I can't give you any
>articular time, and I'm going to be doing double
he work for at least this next week, but — '

'You know where I'll be. And if I'm not, by the
ime you can draw breath, I'll ring you, shall I?
\nd see how you're surviving?' Jane felt a smile
>eginning as she looked at his determined face.
\nd received a smile back, a vivid one, there all
it once to light his serious dark eyes. 'Go on, go
>ack to work, I'll be around. Oh, and don't let the
volfhound bite you!'

'I've told you before, they're the gentlest of beasts.
3ut he's probably arrived for the appointment by
iow, and I do have to go and do something about
he cyst in the poor creature's mouth.' He began
o move; turned back; leaned forward to give her
i deliberate kiss on the cheek. 'That's for now. See
rou later!'

As she watched him walk away, a man in a hurry

to get back to work, Jane reflected on the words he had used. 'See you later.' It was as much of a Kentish idiom as 'Ciao' was to the Italians, meaning anything or nothing.

This time, however, it clearly did mean something. Exactly what it said.

It was just as well she had nailed her colours to the mast with DI Hollings. As she moved on with a sudden lightness of heart, Jane knew how little she cared what he or anyone else around the station made of it. Top brass included.

For once, that was totally irrelevant.

*Other titles in the*
*Ulverscroft Large Print Series:*

## THE GREENWAY
### Jane Adams

When Cassie and her twelve-year-old cousin Suzie had taken a short cut through an ancient Norfolk pathway, Suzie had simply vanished . . . Twenty years on, Cassie is still tormented by nightmares. She returns to Norfolk, determined to solve the mystery.

## FORTY YEARS
## ON THE WILD FRONTIER
### Carl Breihan & W. Montgomery

Noted Western historian Carl Breihan has culled from the handwritten diaries of John Montgomery, grandfather of co-author Wayne Montgomery, new facts about Wyatt Earp, Doc Holliday, Bat Masterson and other famous and infamous men and women who gained notoriety when the Western Frontier was opened up.

## TAKE NOW, PAY LATER
### Joanna Dessau

This fiction based on fact is the love-turning-to-hate story of Robert Carr, Earl of Somerset, and his wife, Frances.

## McLEAN AT THE GOLDEN OWL
### George Goodchild

Inspector McLean has resigned from Scotland Yard's CID and has opened an office in Wimpole Street. With the help of his able assistant, Tiny, he solves many crimes, including those of kidnapping, murder and poisoning.

## KATE WEATHERBY
### Anne Goring

Derbyshire, 1849: The Hunter family are the arrogant, powerful masters of Clough Grange. Their feuds are sparked by a generation of guilt, despair and ill-fortune. But their passions are awakened by the arrival of nineteen-year-old Kate Weatherby.

## A VENETIAN RECKONING
### Donna Leon

When the body of a prominent international lawyer is found in the carriage of an intercity train, Commissario Guido Brunetti begins to dig deeper into the secret lives of the once great and good.